Also by James C. Glass

BRANEGATE

BRANEGATE

JAMES C. GLASS

FAIRWOOD PRESS
Bonney Lake, WA

BRANEGATE
A Fairwood Press Book
September 2012
Copyright © 2012 by James C. Glass

All Rights Reserved

Fairwood Press
21528 104th Street Court East
Bonney Lake, WA 98391
www.fairwoodpress.com

Front cover illustration by
Keith Boulger
Book & Cover Design by
Patrick Swenson

ISBN13: 978-1-933846-33-0
First Fairwood Press Edition: September 2012
Printed in the United States of America

*This one is for John Dalmas, for all the first reads,
teaching and friendship over the years.*

CHAPTER ONE

Trae Nowok was four years old when he saw the outside world for the first time, and discovered danger there.

It began as a game of hide and seek. Mother and Father had been working long hours all week, leaving him alone in Petyr's care. Ordinarily Petyr was fun when he wasn't tutoring Trae in letters and numbers. When teaching, his face would sometimes get long, scowling and serious, but Trae knew it was an act and he would laugh, and then Petyr would laugh, and so even the lessons could be fun.

Petyr Vlasok was more than a tutor to Trae. He was a constant companion, and took Trae everywhere with him. Trae saw more of him than he did his own parents, who seemed terribly busy all the time. Petyr took him on explorations of all four levels of the city, and sometimes they rode the broad escalators up and down just for the fun of it. On all levels they watched the dome of light above them brighten and dim, colors changing from red to orange to yellow, then back to red again as the day progressed.

Petyr held his hand when they walked in the street, and Trae often thought of him as a brother, a much older brother with chiseled features attracting admiring glances from other people, especially the ladies. He was tall and slender, but Trae had felt the muscles in his arms and they were very hard. Petyr's eyes were constantly moving when he was with Trae, and the boy learned to imitate him, always aware of his surroundings. Petyr was everything to Trae, and without knowing the meaning of the word, the boy loved him.

"It's important to be aware of what's around you," explained Petyr. "Not so much here in the city, where we share beliefs and simple lives, but in the outside world you'll live in someday. It's much more complex than here, and dangerous."

"I won't live here when I grow up?" asked Trae.

"No. The world will be much larger for you." Petyr patted his head. "I'll go with you when you're ready, Trae. I'll never leave you."

Trae felt good when he heard that, but wondered why Mother and Father hadn't said anything to him about moving to another place. They didn't talk to him much, probably because he was too young to understand a lot of things. Petyr tried to explain what they didn't.

Nobody lived on fourth level. It was a kind of park, with a few marked trails for strolling among the boulders and stones, and a little clearing with some tables for a picnic, a place to breathe strange scents and watch the birds fly. There were many tunnels and fumaroles, but entrance to all of them was forbidden. Iron gates blocked some, and signs warned of their danger, thus making them attractive to a four-year-old boy who had just learned to read.

So it was that on a day when the lessons were over and he and Petyr had played every cyber-game in the family collection, Trae was bored and wanted to do something exciting. "I want to feed the birds," he said.

"It's getting late for that. It'll be dark up there in a couple of hours. There are no lights," said Petyr.

"Just for an hour. I worked hard today," pouted Trae. "I want to play." He put on his best scowl to let Petyr know he meant business. It was a joke they shared.

"Okay, one hour," said Petyr.

They rode the escalators to third level, an elevator to fourth. When they got off there were patches of deep blue above them. A few people strolled the paths, most of them men dressed in the yellow robes of meditation. A delicious, mint scent was in the air. Petyr followed him around the paths, but it didn't take much time to walk all of them. They went to a table in the center of the cavern to eat their fruit bars. A few birds were flying, but when Trae tried to entice them down with a few pieces of his fruit bar they ignored him. He was quickly bored again. "Let's play a game," he said.

"What kind of game? We have less than an hour left here," said Petyr.

"I'll hide, and you have to find me. Close your eyes, and count to a hundred," Trae grinned excitedly.

Petyr smiled like a patient father. "One game, and then we go." He closed his eyes. "One—two—"

Trae sprinted away, jumping from one trail to another. He found a flat slab of rock jutting out from behind a bench. The space beneath the rock was large enough to accommodate him if he lay flat. He squeezed himself into it, his cheek on mossy rock, and he waited, breathing slow and shallow.

Time passed. A bug crawled out of the moss and walked across his nose. Trae flicked it off with a finger and sniffed just once.

"Where's Trae?" said a voice right above him. "Where can he be?"

It was Petyr. Trae held his breath to stifle a giggle, and pressed backwards in his wedge-shaped place. Suddenly a big hand reached in and began tickling his stomach.

"Theeere he is!"

Trae laughed, but was disappointed. "You looked. You found me too fast," he complained, and slithered sidewise out of his hiding place.

"We have to go," said Petyr, "and what counts is knowing where to look."

"I had to hide too fast, Petyr. One more game; we have time, since you found me so fast. One more and we go, and I won't argue about it. Please?"

Petyr relented again, so he was in a fun mood.

"Count to fifty this time," said Trae, and Petyr began to count with his eyes closed. Trae didn't hesitate; he had quickly decided exactly where he could go to win the game.

The iron grate over the tunnel entrance was not fastened to the rock, only leaned against it. A sign warned of falling rock and mud pits beyond the entrance. Trae pulled the grate out just enough to slip himself inside, and crawled a few feet back into darkness. The rock was cool and dry.

He saw Petyr's boots before the man had a chance to look into the tunnel, and crawled backwards out of sight around a corner. A light suddenly played on rock near his face. Petyr was using his flashlight to look for him.

Trae held his breath. "Trae?" said Petyr softly. "You'd better not be in there. It's dangerous, and there might be spiders. They'll bite you."

Trae had seen pictures of spiders, and he wasn't afraid of them. After a minute or two Petyr went away, and was calling his name as he searched elsewhere. His voice got louder and louder. Petyr couldn't find him, so it seemed Trae had won the game with his cleverness in hiding.

He started to turn around for his return to the grate, but saw a red light blinking in the darkness. His eyes had adjusted to the gloom, and the light faintly illuminated the tunnel when it was on. He crawled up to the light, found it was coming from a small metal box mounted on the rock. Beyond it was another blinking light. He crawled to it, found a sharp turn in the tunnel and another light blinking beyond it.

There was a shout from behind him. "Trae, you get out here right now! We have to go."

Petyr couldn't come after him, now. The tunnel was too small for him. Trae thought about answering, but didn't want to give up the secret of his hiding place. He might use it again someday.

From where he was he could be out of the tunnel in a minute, and he could see well with the red, blinking lights. Trae crawled on, around another curve. Another light blinked ahead of him, and a bright yellow glow showed a gradual curve in the tunnel beyond it. There was a sound like wind, and he felt a faint vibration in the rock. A two minute crawl back to the grate, now. He was having an adventure. *I'll see what the yellow light is, and then go back before Petyr gets too angry with me,* he thought, and curiosity overcame his fear of risking the man's disappointment in him.

The yellow light was steadily brighter as he advanced along the tunnel, and warm air with a sour scent suddenly caressed his face. He squinted at a blaze of yellow from a wall ahead, the tunnel curving past it. Up close he saw there was a break in the wall, and he was looking at a blazing orb of light. There was a rush of wind in his face. A wire mesh covered the opening in the rock, but when he touched it the thing fell aside. An opening to the outside world, and he couldn't resist it. His shoulders were narrow enough for him to squeeze through, and—

His heart hammered hard as he looked down at foam-crested waves of water hundreds of feet below him. The roar of surf breaking filled his head. For one instant he was dizzy, and felt like he was falling. He jerked back inside and scraped the back of his head on rough rock.

Far out on the shining surface of the sea something black floated, an oblong box. A thing left it like an insect flying, with wings and drooping legs. The thing grew larger, and there was a humming sound. At the same time Trae heard shouting from behind him in the tunnel, and his name was called. Now he was in big trouble. He pressed his back against the rock, eyes misting.

"Hey! Whoever you are, get out of there right now. The gate's open this end. Get away from the port and come out this way. It's only a few yards. Hurry up!"

The voice came from ahead of him, a man's voice, and the insect-thing outside was coming closer and closer, straight at him. Trae twisted left, got his feet pushing hard so that he fairly squirted out of the tunnel after a distance of only four body lengths. Rough hands caught him.

"Stars, it's Nowak's ward. Where the hell is Petyr? Rudi, get in there and close up the port. Should've been done long ago. Control, where's that Scorpion now?"

The man gripped Trae's arm tightly. Black uniform, headset mounted on a gray helmet, the grip of his sidearm was at the boy's eye-level. Trae had never seen a weapon so close up.

"Okay. Rudi's in there now, and should have the port blocked up before the thing swings back this way. Keep watching it. We don't know if it picked up an infra-red flash from the kid or not."

A small, wiry man in brown coveralls had scrambled into the tunnel, dragging a string of many-colored polymer blocks behind him. In seconds, the yellow glow from the tunnel disappeared.

The big man let go of Trae's arm and knelt down, face close to his. His swarthy face was stubbled with black hair, and his friendly smile didn't make Trae fear him any less. "Exploring, huh? Well that's okay, but not on this level. Too close to the outside. Petyr will have to explain some things to you."

Trae's heart was still hammering hard, and a single tear ran down one cheek. "I almost fell," he said solemnly. "I saw water way below me, and I almost fell."

The man brushed Trae's tear away with a thick finger. "Can't let that happen, boy. You're too important to be lost in such a—"

"Trae! I knew it. You *were* in there."

It was Petyr, looking afraid, then stern, and Trae burst into tears.

"Easy, lad," said the policeman. "Everything is fine now."

Petyr knelt down on one knee and put an arm around him. "Don't be afraid. You're safe, and no damage was done, but you shouldn't run away from me like that."

"I *didn't*," sobbed Trae. "We were playing a game, and you couldn't find me."

"You hid very well," said Petyr, and smoothed Trae's hair.

"Clever boy," said the policeman. He looked at Petyr and put a hand to the headset on his helmet. "Coincidence, it seems. The Scorpion was probably coming out for its usual surveillance; it's miles down the coast now. We were lucky."

"I didn't mean to do anything wrong," said Trae.

"Nothing you could know," said Petyr, then took Trae's hand gently in his. "Come on. We'll eat some sweetbread and talk about it. You just got a glimpse of the big world outside these caverns, and you're old enough to hear why we don't live out there."

They went down the escalator to second level, hand in hand, and straight to a brightly lit bakery filled with wonderful odors of yeasty dough. Petyr bought pastries for them, and they ate at a table in the corner of the shop. Petyr talked softly, as if everything he was saying was a secret. The fact it seemed a secret held Trae's attention raptly.

"There are seven kingdoms," said Petyr, "each a world like the one you saw outside today, and many millions of people."

"I didn't see any people, but something was flying in the air," said Trae.

"The world is huge, Trae. It goes on and on, but the people who rule it don't like us. We don't follow their rules, and they think we're a danger to them. If they catch us outside we could be put away in a prison, or even killed. We don't live in these caverns because we want to; we're hiding here. Someday we'll leave and go to another world where we can be safe and live by our own laws, but until then we have to hide. That black, bird-like thing you saw today is always looking for us or any other people who aren't where they're supposed to be. It can see heat coming from people's bodies, and when you looked out that port it could have seen you."

"It didn't see me. The man said so," said Trae.

"I know, but it was close. Promise me you'll never run away from me again, Trae. Please. I'm not just your teacher; I'm here to protect you. You're important to us. You're important to a man who left us just before you were born. He went away to find a new world for us. He will live for a very long time, Trae, and so will you. We have to keep you safe so you can learn and grow the way you're supposed to, but you have to let us do that."

Trae's young mind whirled with confusion. "I was only playing a game. Are you mad at me?"

Petyr smiled. "No. We just want you safe. Lyraens take care of each other. We're like a single family."

Petyr squeezed his hand warmly, and Trae looked up at him. "I wish you were my daddy," he said, and Petyr quickly looked away.

They returned to the family cell on second level, a series of connecting rooms laser-hewn out of granite seams in black rock. Petyr worked with Trae on his reader until Tina and Karl Nowak returned home. Immediately there was a stern lecture to Trae about running away, but Mother hugged him so hard he could scarcely breathe. At one point she looked at Petyr and said, "You know his father would be furious about this."

Trae didn't understand that. Father was standing right there, and he didn't seem angry at all.

CHAPTER TWO

They were eating lunch in the kitchen, a cheerless place with gray stone walls and ceiling, a sink, counter and tabletop made from slabs of black slate.

"What got you into such a pensive mood?" asked Petyr. He sat down at the table, across from Trae, took a bite from his sandwich. When Trae didn't answer he reached over and lifted up the boy's chin with a finger.

"Hey, say something to me."

"Say what? Talk doesn't help anything," said Trae.

"Sure it does. What's bothering you? You've been like this for days."

Trae slapped meat and a slab of cheese on one slice of bread. "You can't do anything about it, anyway. I get enough smart cracks about you hanging around me all the time. I'm the rich kid with the hired bodyguard, and special classes out of school. I don't ask for any of it."

"The other kids are giving you a hard time. Is that it? Well, that's what fifteen-year-olds do to each other."

Trae looked up at him with misty eyes. "I don't fit in. They think I'm weird."

"Have they said that?"

"No, but that's what they think, and they're right. I mean, the teachers think it's great. I'm their perfect student. They even say so in class. So what if I have a photographic memory, and can solve any math problem. That doesn't make me a freak."

"Of course it doesn't, Trae. But you have gifts they don't have. They're envious, or jealous, or both. Ignore the smart cracks, and be nice to them. It'll get better if you do that."

"Maybe, but I *am* different, Petyr. There are other things, too, like the dreams."

"Are they getting worse?" asked Petyr, and looked darkly at him. At times, that look made Trae shiver.

"Not worse, but more varied, and it's not just the fire anymore. People are talking to me. The language is strange or garbled up. Two nights ago I was face to face with Leonid Zylak himself, but when I woke up I couldn't remember anything he'd said."

"But you're studying his work in school, aren't you? The dream is transference of some kind."

"No. When we began studying his early ministry I knew it all, even before I opened the file. What's happening to me, Petyr? Why did I know all that? And why is it that when I get a scrape, cut, or bruise, the thing is totally healed and faded away within a day? The other kids have noticed it. It's no wonder they think I'm weird."

Petyr sighed. "Oh Trae, I'm sorry."

"For what? It's those medical tests I'm always having, isn't it? They never let me stay awake to see what's going on. What's wrong with me?" Trae's voice rose in pitch.

Petyr reached over and patted his shoulder, tried to smile. "Nothing at all. A little spoiled, maybe, but a good person a parent can be proud of, and easy to care about."

"I never see my parents. I spend more time with you in a day than I spend with them in a week. It's like they've signed me over to you."

"They work very hard to give you the best."

"The best isn't good enough. I want *them!*" Trae's vision was blurred by tears. When Petyr touched his shoulder again Trae was embarrassed when a single tear rolled down his cheek. "I'm not looking for sympathy," he said.

There was a long pause, Petyr's hand still on his shoulder, then, "We have to have a meeting. It's overdue. We'll do it this evening, but let me talk to your parents first. You get out of the house, spend the afternoon in the parks, wherever you can find a quiet place to think about what's bothering you. We'll talk this evening, and get it settled. Okay?"

"Get *what* settled?" said Trae.

"What's troubling you. Eat your sandwich, now, before you mutilate it."

Trae's nervous hands had twisted his uneaten sandwich into a doughy ball. He looked at it balefully. "I'll eat later," he said.

Petyr smiled. "I don't blame you; it's a mess. Now get out of here. Come back at dinnertime. I promise we'll get some things settled this evening." Petyr grabbed a tear off Trae's cheekbone with a finger, and Trae felt something coming from the man that made him feel suddenly safe.

"Okay," said Trae.

"I'll clean up here. Feed the birds, pet a butterfly, and try to feel good for a while." Petyr dumped Trae's mangled sandwich into the trash, the dishes in the sink, and left the kitchen. Trae remained behind for only a moment to think.

It was Petyr who made him feel special with his stories about normals and Immortals, and his unexplained connection to a man who'd fled from the caverns to find a Lyraen paradise somewhere else. A myth, of course, but one believed by many. For some reason, Trae was important to The Church: the special treatment, tutor, the mysterious treatments he had to take. Every three months he would present himself to a Church appointed doctor who would give him an injection, and then he would lose an hour of consciousness while something was done to him.

Trae put on a jacket and left his quarters when he ordinarily would have been studying. He took the broad escalator up to the shops on level two and had a sweet drink there, then went on up to Three and bought fruit from a vendor by the hydroponics farm. Strawberries, a rare treat, and he ate all of them, one at a time, dipping them out of a paper cone with his fingers.

Trae could remember when the park on level four was new, but now the trunks of slender trees reached nearly to the grow lights on the ceiling, and vines covered the walls. The escalator ended at a small foyer and he entered the park through a screen door. Butterflies of every color fluttered in the air, and birds called to each other from high in the trees. Creatures scurried in the tangle of plants beneath the trees. One of them, a green Chameleon, regarded him with yellow eyes from a tree branch at eye level. The air was humid with mist from vents in the walls above, and there was a perfumy odor from the scattering of purple flowers in the undergrowth.

A narrow trail of white pebbles wound its way through thick foliage for a hundred steps and came out on a green, artificial plane of rough carpet with picnic tables and benches in front of what looked like a window with a grand view of the outside world. A vast sea stretched to the horizon, whitecaps glistening, and gnarled fingers of brown rock rose from the surface.

It was not a real window, but a screen on which was projected an image taken by a remote camera camouflaged carefully from an outside view. Usually there was a crowd there to watch it, everyone dreaming of someday living under open skies when the Emperor was gone. Trae had never been here so late in the day. Now only one person sat on a bench, a slender, dark-haired boy near Trae's age. He recognized the boy from school, but didn't know him. The boy's head jerked around when Trae scuffed a pebble with his shoe.

"Hi," said Trae.

The boy nodded, then turned his head back towards the viewing screen. Trae sat down beside him.

"Sun is real bright today. I bet it's warm out there. It must be nice to be warm all the time."

"So put on a jacket," said the boy, staring straight ahead. "It's The Church that keeps us in here. They're afraid if we go outside we'll pick up new ideas and turn against them. We're prisoners in here, except for people like you."

"Like me?" asked Trae.

Now the boy looked at him, eyes glistening dark and brooding. "I've seen your bodyguard at school, the big priest. You belong to The Church."

"Petyr? Well yes, he sort of guards me, but mainly he's my tutor. I get extra lessons at home."

"Rich kid." The boy smirked at him.

"No, we're not. The Church pays for it."

"Why? You something special to them? We don't even go to church anymore. We never will again, either."

"My folks still go. I finished my Catechism last year. Mostly boring, but I don't see anything wrong with it. We're all Lyraens."

"Not me," said the boy. "I don't believe in Universal Energy or Heaven, and I don't believe in some savior who will come to take me there."

"Prime Zylak," said Trae. "He has gone to prepare the way for us."

The boy snorted rudely. "More Church mythology. Leonid Zylak was a man who fled this planet fifty years ago when his little cultural revolution against Emperor Osman failed, and he had to save his own ass. He didn't leave to find ancient gates to paradise. He went underground on another planet and died there unless the League of

Emperors found and executed him first. And we're *still* waiting for him inside this rock."

Trae's face flushed. He'd never heard such heresy. "Wow, you *do* hate The Church. I get mad at them too, sometimes, when they try to control what I do, but I can always do something about it. Tonight I'm—"

The boy stood up and leaned over to glare at him, his face twisted in fury. "*Do* something about it? For two years we've tried to leave here and live on the outside with the rest of the world. My folks have petitioned The Church over and over again. They won't let us leave. They've called us subversives, and threatened us with prison, and this morning they did it. Three thugs like the guy who guards you came when we were eating breakfast, and they took my father away. My mother has been crying all day. She says he either won't come back or will return without emotions and half a memory. I came here to get away from the crying, and now I've got *you!*"

"I'm sorry," said Trae, and meant it. "I didn't know that could happen to anyone."

"It has happened to a *lot* of people. Don't follow me, now, and don't ever come near me at school. If you do, I'll lay you out." The boy turned, and began walking away.

"What's your name? We can talk. Maybe I can help."

"You've *got* to be kidding," said the boy, and disappeared into the heavy foliage.

A moment later Trae heard the screen door to the park bang shut. He sat in stunned silence. The boy's emotions had been so raw and real; if what he'd said had happened to his father was true, surely there was more to it. The man must be a criminal. The Church would not arrest a man just because he wanted to leave the safety of the caverns and risk his life in the Emperor's realm. Would they?

Now he sat alone in front of the viewing screen, and for the first time in his life watched the red orb of the sun sink beneath the horizon, painting the sky in crimson and purple streaks.

Trae had learned enough from his Catechism to know the Lyraen Code was that of an anarchist. It was not surprising they had been outlawed, and driven literally underground to escape imprisonment or worse. It was also not surprising that Lyraens were beginning to doubt the sense of their living conditions. Why not quietly infiltrate back into outside society? Who would know them there now, after three generations? Leonid Zylak had gone to find them a world where they could live with personal freedom, but he'd been gone a very long time. Trae had seen the man's photographs so many times in his classes and elsewhere that Leonid's face even appeared to him in his dreams of fire, like a savior.

The lights in the ceiling flickered. The park was closing, and now Trae had to meet Petyr again.

A light was burning above the sliding carbonyl door to his residence. The light was left on when visitors were expected, but perhaps it had been left on for his return. The rest of the passageway that was his neighborhood was now deep in gloom, with only maintenance lights glowing high up in the ceiling.

Trae used his cardkey and let himself in. His father was sitting in a chair, his book of meditation closed in his lap. "Ah, right on time," said Karl Nowok. "Dinner is nearly ready." He smiled.

"I went to the park, I've been gone all afternoon," said Trae.

"So I hear. Tina! Trae is home."

Mother was in the kitchen. "I hear, dear. Why don't you both sit down at the table now. I'll bring things right out."

Trae and his father sat down at the wooden dining table beneath a glowing crystal globe. Mother brought out a tourine filled with a vegan stew of vegetables and soy. Father served.

They held hands. "Source of all energy," intoned Father, "bless this food for our nourishment so we may serve all your creation. Amen."

They ate silently for a few minutes, then Father spoke. "Petyr called to tell us where you were, but we were getting worried when you finally came home."

"Sorry," said Trae. "Where's Petyr?"

"He'll be here soon," said Mother.

Trae felt anxiety welling. "We have some things to talk about."

Father still didn't look at him. "I know, Trae. Try to finish your meal."

Trae ground his teeth together, put down his utensils and waited nervously for his parents to finish eating. Mother only glanced at him once. Finally they were finished. Trae hadn't eaten a bite. Mother gathered up the plates and took them into the kitchen. Father rubbed his face with his hand, and looked saddened. He looked at the clock on the wall as Mother came back to the table. "Any minute," he said.

There were tears in Mother's eyes as she took away Trae's plate filled with food.

A single chime announced a visitor at the front door.

Father went to the door. Mother came back from the kitchen, wiping her hands vigorously on a towel. A single tear rolled down her cheek.

Petyr Vlasok came into the room, and with him was an older man in the orange flowing robe of a Lyraen priest in meditation. He held up a hand in benediction. "Blessings of The Source are on this house," he said, and looked at Trae with cold blue eyes.

Trae experienced an involuntary shiver. The priest held out his arms, and Mother rushed to him. He embraced her, and she sobbed into his shoulder. "I'm sorry. I'm so sorry."

"There is no evil in a good heart filled with love," said the priest, and stroked her head in comfort. "Now, let's see this young man." He looked at Trae again.

What was going on? This was supposed to be a meeting with Petyr. Trae bit his lip and glared at the man.

Petyr smiled back at him. "This visit's all about you, Trae. We can sit at the table, or you can come in here and get comfortable."

"This isn't what I was expecting," said Trae.

"I know," said Petyr, He gestured at the priest standing beside him. "This is Proctor Riven, Trae. He's a member of the Lyraen Council of Elders, and also an historian for The Church. He has some things to tell you about yourself."

The old priest smiled, and motioned for Trae to sit by him on a cushion.

"Please, Trae," said Mother. The sadness in her voice prompted him to move. He sat down by the priest, Petyr and his parents sitting close on cushioned chairs. His hands were sweaty, and there was a tightness in his throat that wouldn't go away.

"Well, here we are," said Proctor Riven kindly. "The Council felt it best to keep this as private as possible. The specialized treatment we've been giving to Trae has already drawn unwanted attention to him." He turned to Trae. "I hope you realize you've been receiving much education and watchful guidance that other young people never get."

"Extra classes and a bodyguard, if that's what you mean," Trae said. "Why am I so special?"

Riven smiled. "Some are blessed more than others, but your blessings are truly unique, Trae. There is no one else like you here."

"You mean the Immortality thing," asked Trae. "From the time I was little I've been told I'm supposed to live a lot longer than other people. Well, I don't see it yet. I'm growing up as fast as anyone else I know."

The old priest laughed. "By all appearances you'll grow old like anyone else, Trae. The difference is that while others die, you will not. We really don't know your lifespan. Our experience is limited because there have only been a few like you on planet Gan, and as far as we know you're the only one left here. And very soon, it will be time for you to leave us."

Mother let out a little sob. Trae was totally confused, and the statement about his leaving hit him like a hammer.

"I don't understand. What do you mean, I'm leaving?" He looked at his parents, but their heads were bowed. Even Petyr looked away from him.

"Not right away, but within a year or two, depending on how fast your studies progress," said Proctor Riven, and leaned over to pat Trae reassuringly on the shoulder. "We thought you'd be reclaimed when you were born, and fifteen years later it still hasn't happened. We can't remain in these caverns much longer. Spies and informers have infiltrated our ranks, and we know who only a few of them are. We have to leave this planet soon, but we have no defined place to go to, and nobody to lead us there." The old priest's tone of voice was rising with emotion.

Trae shook his head slowly in confusion, and the man sighed. "I don't know how to tell this without hurting someone," he said.

"Then I'll say it," said Mother suddenly, and startled everyone. She stood up, came over to Trae and kneeled in front of him, taking his hands in hers. Tears ran down her cheeks, and her hands were like ice. "Trae, I know we haven't been the best parents. We haven't been home as much as we should be for you, but your father and I love you with all our hearts. Do you believe that?"

Trae looked around, embarrassed. "Yeah, I suppose," he mumbled, and Mother squeezed his hands hard.

"There's something we should have told you a long time ago, but we couldn't because you might have told someone and then you wouldn't be safe. I wanted to, I really did, but sometimes I didn't want to admit it to myself—when I first held you—knowing how brief it could be—"

"Tina," said Father softly.

Mother swallowed hard, head bowed. Trae's fingers were beginning to go numb.

"You're not our son, Trae," said Mother. "We weren't able to have children of our own, and when you were born the Lyraen Council honored us with an appointment as your guardians and foster parents. I've been selfish. Maybe I've spoiled you—maybe I don't want him to come back and claim you again—but it looks like I'm losing you anyway—oh, Trae!"

Mother pressed her forehead against Trae's numbed hands, her shoulders heaving as she sobbed. Trae shuddered. It was as if a hot flame had passed near his face.

"You used to tell me about your dreams," said Petyr. "You still have them. The dreams of fire."

"Not as often," said Trae.

"And in your dreams you see the face of Leonid Zylak."

"Not when I was little, but more recently. Sometimes a woman is with him when the fire is gone and I'm close to awakening. It isn't Mother, but the woman is beautiful. She has red hair and skin like porcelain. She smiles at me and talks, but I know it's a dream."

"The woman is Tatjana Zylak, Trae. She's your true mother, and Leonid is your father. You were taken from them by an act of terrible treachery and deceit, and now you've returned," said Petyr.

It was getting silly. "You're the one who taught me the history of the Zylaks, Petyr. Leonid Zylak left here over fifty years ago, and he had no children."

"Leonid disappeared shortly after the Emperor's secret police set his house on fire. His wife and child were trapped in the house and were presumed dead; their bones were found the morning after the fire. The child was only four. His name was Anton. The dreams you have are dreams from a childhood, Trae. You were murdered by the secret police of Emperor Osman over fifty years ago. You are the reincarnation of Anton Zylak, and sole heir to a fortune that is likely spread over several planets."

Mother looked up at him pleadingly, and finally released his hands. Trae's fingers tingled.

"Reincarnation? I don't believe any of this," he said.

"You'll have to, young man, or all of us are doomed, not just on this planet, but in all the systems scattered light years from here," said Proctor Riven. "There's more to this than reclaiming a vast fortune. You might be the last remnant of a line of Immortals brought to us by the Zylaks, but we believe there are others, scattered—well, elsewhere. We don't know where the Immortal ones have come from, but it's far beyond our systems. Zylak is quoted as saying their technology is vast, and beyond our limited imagination. Even so, his race believes in peace, freedom and self-determination. They have spread their ideas wherever they go. They were attracted to our planet by the tyranny of the Emperors' League. Your father was left here to achieve a democratic revolution. He failed, and fled, leaving loyal followers in great danger. We thought he would return soon with the power to save us, or lead us to a better place. He hasn't come back, and we don't know why."

"The boy you met today," said Petyr, "only fifteen, but his father was an officer in the secret police. We didn't know it until recently, yet that family has been with us for ten years. Any day we'll wake up to find the Emperor's troops in these caverns, and there will be no prison for us, but death. They know we're here. They're only waiting patiently to get a lead to the identity and location of all The Immortals that are their real enemy. We have to get you out of here, and into the outside world. Other planets. We need to find your father, or other Immortals, and fulfill their promise to take us to freedom. If we can't do it, Trae, then it'll be up to you. Only you, as an Immortal, can bring together the wealth and connections externally to give us release from two centuries of tyranny."

Mother squeezed his hands again. "We've done what we can, Trae. You are Leonid Zylak's son, and only you can fulfill his promise to us."

"Petyr will go with you," said Proctor Riven. "He is a soldier of The Church, and will guard you with his life."

"And you will be the savior of the Lyraen people, wherever they are," said Father softly.

Trae swiveled his head, staring at each of them with an expression of total disbelief. His mind was telling him it was all a lie, but his heart was saying it was true. He looked at their faces, and saw expressions of priests in prayer, awaiting a benediction.

It made him angry.

CHAPTER THREE

The day before Trae was scheduled to leave his home of sixteen years, Petyr took him to the clinic for another examination.

In the year since Trae had first learned his origin, Petyr had become his only teacher and constant companion. Trae had been taken out of school and away from the few friends he'd had. His classes, excursions, even exercise were private, and scheduled by the Lyraen Council. He had become invisible to the Lyraen community, outside of it, and lonely.

It was late evening. The clinic was closed, but Petyr had a keycard and got them inside. Doctor Gella, assigned to the care of Trae's health, was a devout Lyraen, but not obnoxious about it. Trae liked him.

Gella met them in the clinic's day surgery. He was short and plump, with black hair and dark eyes that always had a hint of amusement in them. He smiled when he saw Trae, and motioned for Petyr to sit down away from them a few paces. Petyr obeyed, which was not usual for him.

All was prepared: a large flat table with a thin slab of foam, a pillow resting between the poles of what looked like a huge magnet, racks of instruments on either side of the table. Gella patted the table with his hand. "Time flies. Here you are, ready to leave us and take on the universe."

Trae hopped up to sit on the table, then swung his legs around and laid himself down, nestling his head into the pillow. "You have some new superpowers for me this time?"

Gella wiggled an eyebrow at him. "Anything special? Something for the ladies?"

Trae laughed, relaxing.

"I think we'll stick to the standard stuff, and let nature do the rest," said Gella. "Lift your head a bit, please."

Trae lifted his head, and Gella slipped the sensor-laden cap on it. As usual, the thing made his head feel warm.

Gella patted his hand. "Let's chat a bit before I shoot you full of new mysteries. Are you still having the dreams as often as before?"

"Pretty much the same. Not so intense, maybe."

"Any other change in the dreams? Anything new happening?"

"No. I don't think so—well, maybe. The faces are there more often now. Their lips are moving, but I still can't remember what they're saying."

"You can't hear *anything*? No names of planets, no talk about gates or portals?"

"I can't understand anything they say, I said. What do you mean by gates or portals?"

Gella flipped a switch near Trae's head, and a low humming sound filled the room. "Lyraen mythology, maybe. Immortals like your father gave birth to our species; they've been around a lot longer than us. Some of the old Lyraen writings say they originated far across our galaxy, or even another galaxy. They have a network of gates, or portals, places where space-time is folded so they can travel huge distances in no time at all.

"My hope was that in your dreams of past life your father might have told you where he was going. Part of the injection I'm giving you today should help you listen better, filter out parts of the dreams you've seen before."

"How will we do this after tomorrow?" asked Trae. "Will I come back here?"

"No," said Gella. "We can't risk letting you return here. You'll find Lyraens wherever you go, or they'll find you."

Gella turned to Petyr. "Every three months. I'll leave it to you, and give you a list of healers on Gan. Off-planet I can't help you."

Petyr nodded. "The identity codes are likely the same everywhere. If not, I'll still find them."

The humming sound intensified, and Trae felt drowsy. "Seems like a lot of trouble. Can't I just take a pill?" He closed his eyes, heard the doctor chuckle.

"One magic shot, coming up," said Gella.

Trae felt the insect-like bite on his arm, but was already drifting away. The humming filled his head, and he let himself go, entering a place between consciousness and sleep, a place where his body might react to the slightest stimulus by jerking, and he would feel like he was falling.

He fell.

And awoke, waiting for the fire to come. He felt warm. He was lying on his back, hands at his sides. Something soft covered him up to his neck. He smelled wood-smoke, and knew he was not in the clinic, so he was back in the dream and the fire would come any moment.

He waited. The fire did not come, and he dared to open his eyes. The first thing he saw was an ornate ceiling with heavy beams of dark wood separated by frescos of tangled vines with roses in reds and white. He turned his head slowly to look around. The entire room was ornate, with wallpaper decorated in vines and rolling hills covered in green. There was a fireplace against one wall, and a small fire was flickering there, giving off a sweet smoke from flames in blue and green. He was lying in a huge, plush bed, his head enveloped in a pillow smelling of flowers, his body covered with a comforter inches thick in quilted fabric.

To his left was a door, now closed. He remembered the door, its vines and strange runes, but he'd never seen the entire room so clearly, only as a vague vision of something there. The fire always came so quickly, and burned it all away.

Suddenly there was a soft knocking on the door in his room. He was startled, drawing the covers up to his chin. His arms were small and devoid of any hair. He was a little child again.

The door opened slightly. A woman peeked in at him, and smiled. "Ah, you're awake. I want to talk to you before you go to sleep again."

The woman came in and sat down on the edge of his bed. She wore the orange robe of a priest, but her blonde hair had been done grandly in great swirls to frame her face, and her slender fingers were adorned with silver rings. When she leaned close she smelled like cinnamon and musk.

"Do you know me?"

"I've seen your face before," said Trae. The sound of his voice surprised him with its high pitch. She was so beautiful.

The woman stroked his cheek with a cool palm. "Oh, Anton, you're awake, but still asleep. This must be confusing for you. Maybe you'll remember my touch."

"Are you my mother?" he said, a sudden compulsion driving him.

She smiled wonderfully, and her eyes brimmed with tears. "I'm a memory, dear, but I wanted to be here. When there's a need for us to talk it's your father who'll usually be here. We miss you terribly. One day we'll be together again. When we meet in the mind, like now, it's to give you knowledge you'll need to accomplish the many tasks ahead."

"But you're dead, and Anton is dead, and his father has run away. I don't understand who or what I am. They tell me I'm an Immortal; I have to go out into the Emperor's world and find my father, and I don't even know him. If Anton was his son, then who am I? Did Anton come back to life in me? This isn't me; I'm not a little child. My name is Trae, and I'm sixteen."

The woman stroked his forehead and smiled lovingly down at him. A tear ran down her cheek. "I'm not good at this. I just want to hold you in my arms. I promise your questions will be answered. You might not be aware of it, because much of what we tell you must remain buried deep in your mind. It must not fall into the Emperor's hands. Your father will be here any minute, so it's time for you to sleep again, but I want you to know I love you very much, and I don't want you to forget me."

Trae opened his mouth to speak, but then there were footsteps from beyond the door. "Ssshh, he's here," said the woman. She reached out with both hands and tapped his temples simultaneously. Everything went black.

And he awoke.

Gella's face was close, and he was frowning. "Back so soon? You haven't been out for more'n a minute."

"It didn't seem much longer than that," said Trae. He rubbed both temples with his fingers, and sighed deeply.

"Head hurt?" asked Gella. Petyr came up behind him, arms crossed, and he looked worried.

"No, not really. Usually I wake up and feel like I've had a full night's sleep, but now I feel blurry, like I've been concentrating for a long time."

Trae told them what he'd just experienced. "It was so real. I swear I can still smell her, but then she tapped me on the side of my head and I was gone."

"No other sensations: a tone, music, voices, nothing?" asked Petyr, and Trae shook his head.

"Subliminal, maybe," said Gella.

"But we have no idea what he got, and we leave tomorrow. We'll be flying blind." Petyr looked angry, now. He picked up the syringe Gella had used to give Trae his injection. "Don't any of you people know what he's getting in these things?"

"Something to activate certain areas in his brain," said Gella, "but all that's written down anywhere is the order of the injections, and when they're to be given. Anyone in the underground will have that information wherever you go on Gan. Off-planet I have no idea how you can continue. I presume Trae will know that when the time comes."

"Know what?" asked Trae.

"Contacts, mostly. There are healers, cell leaders, off-worlders who've been trusted to get you off Gan and onto your father's trail. He had no formal holdings here, except for the house. Everything is off world, scattered across Source-knows how many planets, maybe across the galaxy."

Gella looked over his shoulder at Petyr. "Yes, you're flying blind. There's no choice here; we have to assume Trae is being given the necessary information about contacts, passwords, codes, anything he needs to stay out of the Emperor's grasp. It's vital he get all his injections on time, and that's your biggest concern. His physical safety comes after that."

Trae started to say something, but Petyr shook his head and glared at the boy, silencing him. What Gella had just said made no sense at all to Trae.

Gella looked at Trae again. "Nothing new coming yet?" he asked, and smiled. He reached over and tapped him on the forehead. "I'll bet there's a lot more going on in there besides dreams of fire and beautiful women. Just be aware, Trae, aware of anything that comes into your head. Any or all of it could be important."

"Okay," said Trae. Then, "Can I get up, now?"

"Sure, we're finished, for today, maybe for good. I might not see you again, young man, but I'll be thinking about you. Good luck out there. You, too, Petyr. If you can't bring the power of The Immortals back to help us it's only a matter of time before our beloved Emperor has us all for lunch. So if you don't succeed don't bother to come back, because there won't be anything to come back to. These caverns will be empty."

Gella accompanied them to the door, shook hands, and waved goodbye to them from the doorway. Trae had a strong feeling he would never see the man again.

Petyr said not a single word to him all the way back to Trae's apartment, where his parents were anxiously awaiting him on the eve of his departure from their world.

CHAPTER 4

Petyr took him to a place he'd never heard of before. It was deep in the bowels of the caverns, and there was no heat or light. Petyr had come for him at midnight, and Trae had been waiting for him in the street outside the only home he'd known for sixteen years. He was dressed warmly in layers of rough, woolen clothing Petyr had given him the night before.

Petyr arrived, and led him silently down the street into an area of closed, dimly lit shops. They went to a door marked "Service." Petyr had a key to unlock it. The door appeared to be a side entrance to a shop, but instead there was only a dark staircase descending steeply into darkness. They stepped inside, Petyr closed and locked the door behind them, and then a hand-lamp flared brightly. Petyr handed it to him, and a second lamp flared. "Keep the light at your feet," said Petyr. It's steep all the way down, and there's no hand railing, so lean towards the wall."

They descended stone stairs in a helical staircase for a minute or so. There was a cavern at the bottom and they followed shallow stairs to the left into the black maw of what seemed to be another cavern. The stairs went down steeply again, and were irregular in height and spacing, cut out of the natural rock. Warm air rose from below, and there was a low, moaning sound. Trae leaned instinctively to his left until his shoulder felt rock. He stayed a step behind Petyr all the way down, focusing on each move, for he knew that one step to his right there was only a great abyss.

Perhaps it was not as deep as he thought. In only a few minutes they reached level ground. The air was wetly chilled, and Trae smelled salt. Petyr motioned him ahead; they had come all the way down without a word. They walked across a cavern floor strewn with rubble and into a tunnel. Almost immediately Trae saw a light ahead, and heard voices. The light flashed once—twice, and Petyr answered by swinging his torch back and forth.

They came out of the tunnel, and four men surrounded them. A rain slicker was thrust into Trae's hands. "Pouring outside. Couldn't be better weather for us," said a man. All the men wore ponchos, cowlings pulled up, their faces hidden in the gloom.

"Is it sunny where we're going?" asked Petyr. His face was tense, his shoulders hunched, and Trae thought of a cat ready to spring.

"The sun never shines in Lycos," said a man, and Petyr visibly relaxed.

They followed the men across a sandy area, winding between boulders as tall as Petyr, to a rock shelf hanging over a narrow channel of black water. A large rowboat was there, nearly as wide as the channel. The four men took up the oars after seating Petyr and Trae in bow and stern. Even as they pushed off, Trae could hear the pounding of surf some distance down the channel.

The men pulled hard on the oars, the channel water first smooth, then rougher until Trae grabbed the gunwales for support. They came out into a half-submerged cavern with a wide entrance to the sea, and the boiling water beyond it was foaming white. The rowing men never changed the beat, but charged the foaming turbulence and went up over it with a shudder. Trae squinted against sudden rain and hung on for his life as the boat lifted and twisted beneath him, but then there was only a rocking motion and the mess of surf breaking was behind them. In the darkness ahead Trae saw the dark outlines of a boat with three tall masts, sails down. The wind was gentle, but as Trae watched, the boat's crew was already raising sail. The rowers never slowed, but suddenly raised oars and the hull of the boat appeared, rope netting deployed for boarding. Two men remained in the boat, the other two scrambled up the netting, then Petyr, Trae following his example. It was fortunately a short climb; the rope was hard to grip and kept moving. Trae almost fell near the top, but Petyr grabbed his arm and steadied him.

Trae stood by Petyr, puffing hard. Winches squeaked and timbers groaned. The air was salt and seaweed. Sails rose above him, and he swayed with the rocking of the deck.

"Don't get much exercise, does he," said a man.

"He'll come along fast enough," said Petyr. "You just get us to Lycos before sunrise."

"Well before. Get below, and I'll send down some tea. Soon as the landing boat is berthed, we pull anchor."

The man turned away. Trae got one glimpse of a bearded, grizzled face, but he never heard a name or saw a face long enough to recognize it again.

They went below-decks, a single chamber the length of the hull and nearly as wide, loaded with packing crates, rolls of twisted steel cable and flat sheets of what looked like copper. Petyr went to one packing crate marked "Fabrik" and pressed an edge of it with a finger. There was a click, and the front panel opened outwards like a door. Inside were the ends of fabric rolls, top to bottom. Another click, and a second panel opened inward, fabric roll ends only going back a few inches in length. A table and two chairs were inside the crate, a fluorescent lamp and slowly turning vent fan in the ceiling. They went inside and shut the two panels behind them. A few minutes later there was a soft knock outside, and a man brought them hot tea and sugar.

The little room was soon stuffy, and the rocking of the floor gave Trae a queasy feeling in his stomach. Petyr looked at him with narrowed eyes. "We'll be in here at least three hours, and your eyes are already large. Take this." He handed him a white capsule, and Trae swallowed it dry without question.

"The first days will be hard," said Petyr. "You'll have to build strength and endurance."

"And we're supposed to be finding a way out?"

"You are. I'm along to get you started in the underground here. Beyond that I have no useful knowledge. I know the workings of the Emperor's police; I should be able to keep them away from you. Once we're off planet it'll be easier, but even then I expect they'll send pursuit squads after us. They'll search for you, Trae, but mostly they want your father."

"He ran off and abandoned me and everyone else a long time ago; how can he hurt the Emperor?"

"We don't know a lot of things, Trae. We don't know why he left. We don't know for sure that he *has* left. He could use his financial empire to shut down all interplanetary commerce with Gan, or at least force sanctions against it. What powers he could bring to bear from The Immortals is unknown. There could be entire leagues of planets under their influence, huge armies your father could bring against the Emperor, but it hasn't happened and we don't know why. It's even possible the Lyraen commune has lost his favor, and he's left us to our fate, but your presence speaks against that."

Trae took another sip of tea and rubbed his stomach. "The pill worked. I'm feeling better."

"Talking helps, too. Makes you forget about it."

Trae hesitated, then, "Gella slipped up once, and told me there were little machines working in my head. Is that where the dreams come from?"

"Probably. The wiring in your brain is constantly being redone. We couldn't wait any longer, Trae. There were too many spies. We had to get you moving, and we don't really know where we're supposed to take you or what you're supposed to do. First thing is to get you off planet, and the underground can help get us to that point. After that it'll be up to you to show the way. I'm working by instinct here."

"So am I," said Trae. He paused, sipped tea, studied the cup in his hands, then said softly, "Have you ever been outside? You know— outside the caverns, and in the city with people walking around in sunlight."

"Yes," said Petyr. "Quite a bit, since you were small, mostly with the underground, mostly in Lycos. I'm a familiar face in the streets there. It's different, Trae. Lots of people, busy going somewhere, and the Emperor's troops are on every corner, always watching. Our papers are the best, and we'll be moving fast. A little luck, and we'll be off planet within a week."

"It's like I'm off planet right now, Petyr."

"I understand. That's one reason I'm here."

"My teacher, older brother, always scolding me, *and* a priest."

"I'm a Soldier of The Church, Trae."

"Still a priest. Don't you have a family somewhere?"

"All gone, a long time ago."

"I'm sorry," said Trae, then smiled. "I guess I'll have to be your family, for now."

Petyr actually chuckled, a rare thing. "I can accept that."

"You're a complicated man, Petyr. What else are you that I don't know about yet?"

Petyr reached out and squeezed his shoulder. His eyes seemed very dark in the dim light. "I hope you don't have to discover that for a while," he said, and Trae felt a tingling at the base of his neck.

*

The men came to get them when it was still dark. They went up on deck and the sails were down. They were surrounded by fishing boats a hundred yards from rock cliffs rising above a narrow beach. A crew of two men rowed them to shore without a word and they jumped into cold surf up to their knees. The little boat was already beyond gentle breakers when they reached the shore. Men were loading rowboats along the beach: duffels, boxes, nets, the daily supplies for a long workday of fishing. A man came up to them, looked only at Petyr, handed each of them a roll of rope netting and pointed towards the cliffs. Men were going up and down a path cut into the rock. Trae followed a step behind Petyr as they went up the path, staying to the inside and jostled by men descending with their loads. There were no greetings, not a word, and nobody even looked at them.

They reached the top and Trae looked back just once at a terrifying drop to the beach. Beyond the cliff was not so much a village as it was a preparation area, with drying racks for nets, wooden shacks filled with boxes and barrels and what looked like an open kitchen shed with large, metal tables, all of it stinking with the odor of fish. Men milled around the area in a seemingly random fashion.

Beyond the kitchen shed was a smooth, dirt area where several trucks were parked, some with flat beds, others bearing long, cylindrical tanks. A cab door opened, a man stepped down and came over to meet them. His angular face was clean-shaven, his eyes darting to Trae, then Petyr. "Well, here we are at last," he said. "Everyone is waiting for you."

"Good to see you again," said Petyr, but he did not introduce the man to Trae.

"The smell is bad, but the ride is short," said the man. He led them to his truck, a thick, silver cylinder behind the cab, took the rolls of netting from them and put it all in the cab. They followed him up a curving ladder to the top of the cylinder where he opened a port the width of three men. Trae jerked backwards as a rush of fish smell came out of the port. The man whispered something to Petyr, who beckoned to Trae to follow him down a ladder into darkness. The port clanged shut above Trae before he'd even reached the metal floor. He breathed shallow, the odor of fish suffocating. Darkness was total.

Petyr grabbed his hand and they headed in the direction of the cab. There was a soft click, and a door opened in front of them, a chamber there with two comfortable seats and illuminated in deep red. Petyr closed the door and they buckled themselves into the seats. "All set," said Petyr, and the truck began to move.

They drove for several minutes before stopping. There were voices from outside, a metallic bang that rattled the walls, then more voices and the truck began to move again. The ride was longer this time, perhaps ten minutes before they stopped and a voice came out of the ceiling, saying, "We're here." A click, and the door to their little chamber popped open. They unbuckled themselves and were assailed again by the stink of fish. Light appeared as the top port opened. Petyr climbed the ladder with Trae right behind him, the driver helping them out.

They were in a large garage. A sliding metal door was closed behind them. Several men were working on four trucks, and several others watched from a high catwalk along one wall. Four of those men carried rifles, and two others wore the orange robes of priests. The air smelled of solvents and burned metal, and a torch flared beneath one of the trucks as they descended to the floor. The driver pointed to stairs leading up to the catwalk. "You're expected," he said, then turned to look straight at Trae. "Good luck."

Trae didn't know what to say, but smiled at the man, and Petyr smiled at him doing that, so apparently it was okay. Petyr held his elbow; they went to the stairs and climbed them together. The two priests met them at the top, other men pushing in around them, rifles at the ready.

"Petyr," said one man, and extended a hand, but his eyes were on Trae.

Petyr shook the man's hand. "I appreciate the risk you're taking, Joseph."

"It's no risk at all, not for this young man." The man called Joseph extended his hand to Trae. "So, at last you're ready to be sent into the world, and we're to be a part of your journey." He smiled.

"Thank you, sir," said Trae.

"You favor your mother, I think," said Joseph, then turned to his orange-robed colleague and pulled him closer. "This is Abelius, the rector for this cell. He handles the day to day business here, and will arrange your travel out of Lycos."

Abelius shook his hand, but said nothing, giving Trae a disturbing look that seemed almost reverent. The guards surrounding them seemed to be pressing closer to also look at him. Trae looked around at the heavily armed men.

"Are you expecting trouble?"

Joseph laughed. "It's routine. Our workers come and go, and security checks are not perfect. The Emperor has his spies and assassins in places you wouldn't imagine. We've survived all these years by being cautious, but perhaps the time will come when our lives can be open and free."

"If it be the will of The Source," said Abelius softly.

"Of course," said Joseph, "as long as we remember there are no miracles without our own efforts to achieve change. Let's see to our guests."

Surrounded closely by their guards, Joseph and Abelius led them along the catwalk to a door, then down a long hallway to another door opening to a room with tables and chairs and the odor of bread baking. Two guards entered with them, the others remaining in the hall. The door was closed and locked from inside. A man came out a side door leading to a shining metal galley and served them hot chocolate drinks and pastries. The priests excused themselves and exited the room, but the guards remained. Petyr seemed particularly alert, cocking his head to one side as if listening for something, and then Joseph returned a few minutes later.

"Your room is ready. You'll have a couple of hours to sleep, and then a car will come to take you elsewhere. Your final destination on Gan will be achieved in several steps, and each cell has knowledge of only one of them. It's for your safety."

"I understand," said Petyr.

Joseph waited silently until they'd finished eating, but kept looking at Trae and smiling at him. Trae was bothered by it, but said nothing, and soon the priest led them to a simple room with two cots, and hooks on the walls for their clothing. He locked them inside, and went away. Petyr got under his thin blanket with all his clothes on, and advised Trae to do the same.

"We might have to move quickly. Plans can change fast. At least we're both light sleepers."

"Right now I'm feeling trapped." Trae pulled a thin coverlet up to his chin. "I don't think I'll sleep at all."

"You'll sleep when you're ready to. Don't worry about it."

"You know these people, but they're all strangers to me," said Trae.

"I know them well, but I don't trust them completely, and I always have my own plan, Trae. We have to leave Gan by any port we can use. That's our immediate goal. It's *your* goal if something happens to me."

Trae looked at him with concern. "And how am I supposed to know what to do?"

"Oh, you'll know," said Petyr. He rolled over, reached out a hand to the lamp by his cot, and the room was plunged into darkness.

Trae didn't sleep a wink, but Petyr even snored some until Joseph came to tell them their car was waiting outside.

Two men were in the car with them. The vehicle was white, hydrogen-powered, and small; Trae was in the back seat and his knees were drawn up close to his chin. Hot sunlight beat down through the transparent bubble canopy, and the air rushing through a half-opened window felt hot on his face. Cars raced past them on a busy Lycos street. Interference films covered windows of buildings rising a hundred floors on either side of them. The sidewalks were packed with people, and on every corner there was a gray military vehicle with seated troops, their rifles slung. Each vehicle sported a trailer-generator powering the fifty-millimeter rail canon on top of its cab.

They followed side streets at a leisurely pace to avoid the heaviest traffic, and encountered no checkpoints operating during the rush of morning business. The man in the front passenger seat had a small device plugged into his left ear; he listened intently and occasionally mumbled instructions to the driver. Both men were short and swarthy, and wore rough, woolen clothes. Neither man had introduced himself to Petyr or Trae, and said not one word to them the entire trip. Petyr watched them carefully the whole time.

On a side street near the edge of the city a little white car identical to theirs pulled out of a garage ahead of them and sped away. The driver swerved sharply to the right and pulled into the garage even as the motorized door was descending to clang against a concrete floor. A black van sporting the Emperor's flag was waiting there with two men dressed in black livery and wearing peaked caps. They opened the doors to let Trae and Petyr get out, and led them to an office where another man was laying out two expensive-looking suits of clothing in raw silk dyed black. "Change into these," said the man. "You have ten minutes, and then we're taking you to Anwar Shuttle Port."

"Aren't we going to—" began Trae.

"Get dressed," said Petyr. "Talk later." He picked up the suits, handed one to Trae. "They even have our sizes. I'm impressed."

Even the shoes fit, but the man who'd put out the clothes watched with obvious amusement while they dressed. Buttons were everywhere, and a tie required a complex bow that the man had to do for both of them.

"There. You're now members of our diplomatic service, and here are your papers." He handed each of them passports and wallets tied shut with gold cord. The passport folders were in the gold of governmental servants.

"You'll go through regular check-in at Anwar. Tickets are first class to Saleen Space Terminal. You'll be met by car on the tarmac and taken directly to the launch area. Your luggage has been sent ahead, and won't be inspected. Once you're in space the responsibilities of all cells on Gan are ended. I presume you'll be met at the other end."

"What planet?" asked Petyr.

"I don't know. The people who meet you at Saleen have arranged it. You ask a man named Evan."

Something stirred in Trae's mind.

"We have to move quickly. You were being followed out there. Our decoy won't fool them for long."

They went to the black van and buckled into back seats. Their uniformed escorts awaited them, the van lurching forward as the door closed and they were in the street again, driving some minutes in an erratic pattern before hitting the main highway out of the city and into the countryside. They drove fast this time, speeding past traffic, the driver flashing his lights to move people out of the way. Very soon the traffic was behind them, and fields of grain were rushing past, a sight Trae had only seen before in pictures.

The driver kept checking his rear-view mirror and glancing at his companion. After a few minutes of this his companion was watching something steadily in his side-view mirror. Trae felt Petyr tense beside him.

"Are we being followed?"

"Perhaps," said the driver. "Do you have a weapon?"

"No."

"Give him one," said the driver. His companion turned and held out a dull black pistol over his shoulder. Petyr took it, worked the action and put the weapon on the seat between himself and Trae. The men in front of them were watching the mirrors again.

"Two of them."

"I see it. Four guys in the lead car, and I'm pretty sure the blue one is following them. Looks like two people in that one."

"They won't move until the white van turns off."

"I'm watching. Get ready to hit it. Damn, but they found us fast. There has to be a leak. I'd better call in."

"No," said Petyr, and with authority.

"What? This is our operation, and we have our orders."

"Yes you do, and calling in isn't part of them. Even if we're attacked. Let them have to guess at everything."

"He's right," said the driver. "Too late, anyway; the van just turned off, and the blue car is coming up fast." There was urgency and anxiety in the man's voice.

Even through closed windows Trae could hear the scream of a high-performance engine as a blue, two-door car with a hard top sped by them on the left and pulled back into their lane fifty yards ahead of them, slowing to match their speed. Two men were in the car, staring straight ahead as they passed.

"Blue is mine. Take the other."

"He's passing, coming up fast."

Petyr hit a button, lowering the back window as the driver lowered his, and three guns were drawn. Wind rushed into the cab. Petyr grabbed Trae's head and pushed it down towards his knees. Trae twisted to look at him and then there was the roar of a big engine from outside. Petyr fired first, then the driver. Windows shattered, and there was the thud of bullets striking metal and flesh. The car swerved left and crashed into something, and Petyr was still firing. There was a scream, and the squealing of tires sliding on pavement, then a horrible crash. The car swerved back and forth, and the man in front of Trae opened fire. The driver cried out in pain, the car swerved right. A second later, something hit them from behind, and a fusillade of bullets came in through the rear window. Trae pushed his head down between his knees as the car slowed, leaned, and slowly toppled over upside down, coming to rest in brush pushing through open windows on the driver's side.

Silence, the engine stalled. Not a sound from the front seats. Blood was rushing to Trae's head, his vision blurred. Petyr hung in his seat belts beside him, his eyes closed, still clutching his weapon. Trae nudged him, but the man didn't move. Trae opened his mouth to speak, but then a car door slammed outside and there were footsteps on gravel, then the crackling of crushed brush. And Trae held his breath.

A man thrust his head, then upper body through an open window in front of Trae, and looked up at him. There was a machine-pistol in his right hand, and he had the darkest eyes Trae had ever seen.

"Well, well," said the man, and smiled malevolently.

There was a series of horrible explosions right next to Trae's ear, and the man's face disappeared in gore.

Trae screamed.

CHAPTER 5

A hand slapped the harness buckle on his chest, and Trae dropped head-first onto the roof of the cab. Petyr tumbled down beside him, the gun still in one hand as he clapped the other over Trae's mouth. "Sshhh," he whispered, then turned and jammed his legs into brush blocking the open window on his side of the car. He motioned for Trae to follow, and kicked a hollow into the brush. Trae crawled out behind him. The brush thinned a yard from the over-turned car; Petyr slithered through it like a snake until they were several yards away and up near the edge of the roadway. The car was overturned in a deep ditch, and the legs of the man Petyr had killed were sticking out of the car window away from the road.

A car door slammed. Pressed up against Petyr, Trae peered over the edge of the ditch. A blue car was parked across the road, a man crossing over with a machine pistol in one hand. He went to the edge of the ditch, and looked down.

"Hey, what's taking so long? What'd you find?"

Silence. The legs of his companion were visible to him, and didn't move.

"Gerson?" The man took something out of his coat pocket and did a shuffling slide down the side of the ditch, leaned over and looked closely from the rear of the car.

"Awww," he growled, then flipped the thumb of one hand with a sound liked a plucked string and tossed something round and black into the car.

"Outlive *that*, you bastards," he screamed, and sprinted away along the ditch. At that instant, Petyr grabbed Trae's hand, jerked him up onto his feet and onto pavement. When they were halfway across the road there was a horrible explosion, and a ball of fire erupted from the ground behind them. The pavement shuddered, and they dove into heavy brush in the shade of large trees on the other side of the road.

The ball of fire was gone, and now there was a column of thick, black smoke. In crossing the road Trae had seen another column of black smoke far back from where they'd come. There was a sudden, sustained chatter of machine pistol fire, and then the man came up out of the ditch. He went straight to his car and got in. Before the door was even closed, Petyr was moving like a hunting cat, hunched over and covering several yards to the back of the car without a sound. He waited there. Trae heard a faint voice; the man in the car was talking to someone. The conversation ended. The car's engine coughed into life.

Petyr leapt for the driver's door, reaching inside with both hands. He slammed the driver's head against the door three times, then dragged him out sprawling on the ground and shot him twice in the head at point-blank range. Trae's face flushed in horror at what he saw.

Petyr gestured at him. "In the car. We can still make it if we're quick about it!"

Trae got into the front seat with him, the car moving before his door was closed. Petyr twisted the wheel hard, turning them a hundred eighty degrees and accelerating hard in the direction they'd been traveling before the attack. "Whoever he reported to he said he thought we were dead, but he wouldn't know for sure until the fire cooled down. We killed the rest of his people, but there might be more at the shuttleport," said Petyr. "Anyway, the Emperor's goons all have the same look. What are *you* looking at?"

"Nothing. I've never seen anyone killed before. It's horrible."

"Yes, it is," said Petyr, "even when necessary. I'm taking a big risk here, Trae, instead of hiding out on our own. I'm assuming people are waiting to intercept us at the shuttle-port. If I can identify them, I should be able to—"

A beeping interrupted him, coming from a radiophone hooked onto the dash of the car. "Uh, oh," said Petyr, then put a finger to his lips and peered closely at the device. Picked it up. When he spoke his voice was rough, even gutteral. His forefinger tapped lightly in random beat on the receive button.

"Jesse? Yeah, got 'em, but I'm hurt. Car's a mess. I'm comin' in." Petyr tapped the receive button rapidly, then held it down and whacked the phone hard several times on the dash until it fell apart in pieces.

"Maybe—just maybe," said Petyr, and pressed the accelerator to the floor. The little car leapt beneath them.

It was only fifteen minutes to the shuttle-port. They parked in the public garage and Petyr studied the terminal entrances for several minutes before making a move. There were four of them. Petyr sent Trae to the one nearest the garage while he entered two doors down. Trae was terrified, and fought not to show it, but his heart was pounding. The dark suit he wore was common enough, and he didn't seem to attract any attention. Petyr strolled over to meet him inside by a small fountain around which tables were arranged, and there was a cubicle with vending machines for people to purchase snacks. Petyr bought a sandwich and shared it with Trae at a table. His eyes never stopped moving as he scanned the area, then suddenly—

"There, by the entrance, three men, in coveralls. One's talking. I bet he has a throat mike."

Trae saw them. Working men, but not working, and hard looking. One man talked, the other two looked bored. When the one finished talking he said something to the others, and they all left the building without looking back.

"Now!" said Petyr. Trae followed him to the check-in counter. It was still three hours before their scheduled flight. Petyr smiled wonderfully at the woman who greeted them. "Do you have any seats on an earlier flight? If possible, we'd like to squeeze in a meeting before our connection time."

The woman looked. There were several seats open on a shuttle boarding in fifteen minutes. "You'll have to hurry," she said.

They walked leisurely to the hub leading to individual shuttle births, then ran the rest of the way. In minutes they were on board, and the door was closed. They were not sitting together, but were only four rows apart. Trae buried himself in a magazine, waiting for something nasty to happen, but it didn't. Still, after takeoff, and they were skimming the tops of high clouds, something was bothering him, something left undone. And suddenly, two things popped into his mind as if he'd just heard them.

Evan Reesus. 1793-1624-4. Trae remembered the first name, and then he knew what had to be done. He unbuckled himself, went to Petyr, leaned over to speak softly to him. Two businessmen, one quite young-looking, discussing something. The older woman seated next to Petyr looked up at Trae and smiled when he spoke.

"We're going to be early. We have to call Evan and tell him when to meet us."

Petyr's eyes glazed over for just an instant, then cleared. "Do you have his number handy?"

"It's 1793-1624-4. Better call now. Tell him Trae says hi."

Trae went back to his seat, watched Petyr make the call from the phone mounted on the seat in front of him. He spoke for only seconds, hung up the phone, turned and smiled coyly at Trae.

"Hearing things?" he mouthed.

Not really, but where had it come from? Out of the blue, and yet Petyr had acted immediately on what he'd been told. And now there was the vision of a man's face in Trae's mind. It was a cruel-looking face, hawkish, with a beak of a nose, small dark eyes set closely together, and topped with a mound of snow-white hair. A shiver ran along Trae's spine; he felt fear of the man, but at the same time knew him as an ally. He was a man like Petyr. He was a soldier of The Church. And Trae's life would soon be in his hands.

Half an hour later they were descending to the spaceport on a high plateau dotted with scrub brush, a hundred miles from the nearest city. The plateau rose in shear sandstone cliffs a thousand feet above a valley of rolling red sand dunes. There were no roads leading to it. The spaceport gleamed in bright sunlight, a series of four concentric circles with a hub at the center and four radial spokes. V-shaped lifting bodies were parked just beyond the outer circle and near the ten-mile-long runways forming a concrete square around the entire complex.

They slowed to a horizontal stop and made a five hundred foot vertical descent to the third terminal out from the hub, coming down on a concrete pad surrounded by buses and a single, black limousine. Petyr and Trae were last off the shuttle. The other passengers headed straight to the buses for transportation to the hub and ticketing for connecting flights both on and off planet.

The back door of the limousine opened, and a man got out. His hair was brilliant white in the sunlight. Petyr dropped back and followed Trae by half a step. The man left the car door open and stood by it. The windows were black, so Trae couldn't see the car's interior, but he walked right up to the man and smiled. "Sorry about the short notice, Evan," he said. "We had a problem."

"So I understand. We also had a similar problem, but solved it," said Evan. He put his hand on the door. "Please. It's a short drive, and there's a lounge we can use until your flight is ready."

They got into the back of the car. There was plush, black leather, and a bar. Another man was sitting there. He extended his hand to Petyr as Evan climbed in and shut the door behind him.

"I'm Darian. We met a long time ago. I was a novice precept when you were in third year."

Petyr shook the man's hand. "Sorry, I don't recall you."

"You probably don't remember me either," said Evan. "I was a year ahead of you, but my hair was red, then. I managed to change the color by spending two years as a special guest of the Emperor."

"I'm sorry," said Petyr, as the car began to move.

"Don't be. It gave me a clear vision of what we're fighting against."

Evan turned to Trae, examining him. "You're quite young for one who's supposed to give us hope. You knew how to contact me. That's known to only a few."

"Someone gave us your name, said you'd meet us. After we were attacked your radio number came to me, and a vision of your face. I won't try to explain it."

"Do you know where you're going from here?"

"No."

"You're going to Ariel II. Your flight leaves this evening."

"That's not a planet," said Petyr.

Again something clouded Trae's mind for just an instant, a brief lapse of consciousness that made him startle awake. "It's—it's a station, an orbiting satellite. Someone will meet us there, a man in white."

Evan frowned. "I only know the destination from here. What else do you see?"

"I don't see anything. I just know it."

"It's not for me to ask questions. You have Petyr to protect you and I'm only a brief guide, but I'm naturally curious, and I've never been in the presence of an Immortal before. You look normal to me."

"I am normal; at least I feel normal," said Trae.

"Then you have no idea how you can free us from the rule of a psychotic Emperor, you, a boy of what—sixteen?"

"I don't know." Trae leaned against Petyr as the car turned a corner.

"Think about it, Trae," said Petyr. "Be aware of anything that comes into your head."

It suddenly occurred to Trae that both men were pressing him, and then the other man, Darian, said, "I think what he senses is keyed by certain words spoken to him. It could also be sights and other sounds."

"His last treatment was only two days ago," said Petyr.

"It seems an unreliable way to program a mind, and we're not told what's being done, even those of us who put our lives at risk." Evan's voice rose in pitch as he spoke. "All this subtrafuge, after waiting for years. Why don't The Immortals just come down and drive the Emperor out?"

Darian put a hand on his arm. "It's not our place to question anything, but you must understand our frustration. So many people in our cell have spent time with the rats in the bowels of the Emperor's palace. Their parents and grandparents served with The Source himself, and then He abandoned them. Now we're presented with the reincarnation of His son, said to be our savior, and it's difficult to believe, especially for those of us who are young. Our duties end when you leave the planet, and we wonder if you'll abandon us like your father did."

Trae didn't know what to say, and pressed against Petyr, who remained mute but seemed to be listening seriously to the two men.

Evan's face flushed. "We've been loyal for over a generation, but our waiting will end soon. The Lyraen underground, even in the caverns, is riddled with spies. Our own people are defecting every week. In a few years we'll be helpless, but our cell and many others will not wait for that. We'll bring terror to the streets, and to the Emperor's palace, even his family, knowing full well that without the help your father promised us we'll all die, and the Lyraen way will be gone forever."

"What do you want him to say?" asked Petyr. "The boy is as ignorant of what will happen beyond today as I am."

"Then how can he help us? By finding his father? I don't think we're being unreasonable when we ask for some assurance our fight can succeed and that The Immortals will keep an old promise to us."

"I will *not* forget you," said Trae. "I just can't tell you if I'll find my father again, or have any contact with The Immortals. The treatments I've been getting are supposed to help me do whatever it is I'm supposed to do. Finding you might have been the first thing. We were nearly killed, and suddenly I knew your face and how to contact you, and here we are. I wish I could tell you more." Trae looked at Petyr for assurance, but the man was glaring stonily at Evan, and the man glared back at him.

"It has been nearly two generations," said Evan.

"And I can tell you nothing will happen until we've escaped from Gan," returned Petyr.

Evan nodded curtly, but then Darian leaned forward and said, "You'll be in space by this evening. We don't know your final destination, or how to contact you. How will you tell us what you've found, and if we can count on off-world support to fight the Emperor?"

"I don't know," said Petyr, and Trae shook his head.

Now Evan leaned forward, his face an angry mask. "Two years is what you have, and likely less than that. We've tolerated the Emperor's spies and our own defectors beyond reason. Expulsions from our ranks will cease. The killings will begin within the month, and our enemy is sure to retaliate in kind. There will be war in the streets, with or without your help. Tell this to your father, or any other Immortals you meet. The Lyraens on Gan will live free, or they will all die."

Darian, the man with the gentle eyes, nodded somberly in agreement with Evan.

"We understand," said Petyr, and his body became rigid as stone.

They were taken to a small lounge apparently reserved for them in the outer ring of the complex and only a few steps from their departure tunnel. There were plush, leather chairs and lounges, and a bar with bottled water and juices. "Your luggage has been checked in for you," said Evan, and handed them their pass cards.

"We have no luggage. It was destroyed in the car," said Petyr.

Evan only blinked. "There are four suitcases, black, two for each of you. Each has a short strip of yellow tape on one end. Be sure to pick them up on Ariel right away. Use your diplomatic papers to by-pass any search. This is important."

"We presume someone will contact you there about your final destination," said Darian. "You have our number. We don't expect you to tell us where you're going, but you should contact us when you have information we need to know."

"Yes," said Petyr. "Thanks for getting us this far."

"Your thanks will come when you bring an army to fight with us. All our hopes go with you. Please don't desert us."

"We won't," said Trae.

"I'm sure you mean that. We're leaving two men by the door to see you to your departure lounge. Diplomatic servants such as you are accorded such a service. Have a safe trip."

They shook hands. Darian's eyes made him look sad, while Evan's were hard, like his grip. Evan leaned forward at the last second, and whispered into Trae's ear.

"Two years, maximum. We'll be waiting." The men left the room, and shut the door behind them.

There was a long silence. Petyr went to the bar, poured juice into two glasses and handed one to Trae. "Evan is an impatient man, but he's a good soldier for The Church, and he's right about one thing. Time is getting short for the Lyraens on Gan. I wish I could give them some hope."

"They seem to think the hope should be coming from *me*, and I don't even know where I'm going."

"You'll know how to do it. The method just isn't conscious yet."

"We know little about what's going on inside you, and your father isn't here to tell us about it."

"Because he ran away to save himself. That's what they think," said Trae bitterly.

"Maybe," said Petyr, and put a hand on Trae's shoulder. "Maybe not. I think your father has gone away to prepare for the freedom of all his people, not just the Lyraens on Gan, but other planets as well. Our Emperor Osman is certainly not the only tyrant in the universe, and I think we're being sent to discover that. Your father has left you a mission to accomplish before our release can come, and you'll know in time what it is. I can't tell you, and neither can anyone else."

"We've never talked about other planets," said Trae. "I thought all Lyraens were here on Gan."

"It's our newest world, the one your father came to build. There could be many others, dozens, even thousands."

"You're speculating. you don't know that for sure."

"It's logical. The Immortals have come from far away, and the Lyraen philosophy goes back before our history. My whole life has been on Gan, Trae. I'm speculating, but if I'm right the problem is much larger than that of a single planet."

"In hours we head to Ariel II, Petyr. It goes around Bode, a ball of cold gases, no civilization, so we can eliminate that one."

"Nobody told you that," said Petyr, and raised an eyebrow at him.

It was the first time he'd experienced space flight, and Trae was thrilled by it: the explosive acceleration, ground dropping away, then the lesser yet steady acceleration at high angle until the sky outside was black and the great sea on Gan was shining blue far below him. In two hours they made rendezvous with Han, the interplanetary vessel with open framework and cylindrical living pods pushed by eight mammoth thermonuclear engines. There was a slight bump at docking; a young woman gave them their compartment assignment and showed them to a tunnel leading to it. Their luggage was being transferred as they spoke.

The accommodations were small, but luxurious: two beds, gimbaled to accommodate directional acceleration, pneumatic bath, a bar stocked with snacks and drinks, a television with a grand library of entertainment programs and books in core, and two chairs. Meals were taken in the central dining room at the hub of the living module array twice a day. There was a gym, and two courts for a game called Carrom, played with a hard rubber ball in a small, cubic space. Petyr played well with his cat-like reflexes, but Trae had several bruises to show for his efforts before the trip was over.

They were in transit at one gee acceleration for six Gan days and nights. Trae slept soundly each cycle, controlled by the light spectrum in his compartment, but the cycle before his first glimpse of the great pinwheel of Ariel II he was troubled by a strange dream. He was not a little child, but himself, and he was sitting at a table on a stone balcony overlooking green fields lined with trees flowering red, and there were two moons in a sky so blue as to be nearly purple. A glass of juice sat on the table in front of him. He tasted it; the drink was bubbly, and had a sharp tang he didn't recognize. Petyr suddenly appeared, as if condensed out of vapor in the air, and sat across from him.

"Do you like it?" asked Petyr. "Has a bit of a bite."

"What are you doing in my dream?" asked Trae, and Petyr smiled.

"Well, it's not exactly a dream, and I'm not Petyr. You seem so relaxed around him, so I thought his presence would be good for this. You and I are going to be having some serious conversations from now on. Your mother won't be here for them, but she sends her love, and she'll come to you at other times. You're going to be busy, Trae."

Trae felt drowsy, even in his dream, and he felt amused by Petyr being there. "Are you going to tell me something I need to know?"

"Oh, yes," said Petyr. "Yes, indeed."

And he told him.

Trae awoke with a start. Light was dim in the compartment, all of it coming from the video screen that showed the page of a book. Petyr was lying in the bed next to his, reading, turning pages with a remote in his hand. He glanced at Trae. "Did I wake you? I couldn't sleep."

Trae shook his head, and Petyr looked closer at him. "You had a dream."

"Yes."

"Anything?"

"When we get to Ariel II we go to Port Four, Station Six. Our passes are waiting for us there. We're going to Galena, and someone will be taking us to the court of Emperor Rasim Siddique."

"Ah," said Petyr, and smiled.

CHAPTER 6

It was not the first time Fedor Quraiwan had been the bearer of bad news for his master, but this news was worse than bad and he feared for his safety. Emperor Khalid Osman was not a merciful man, and was subject to outbursts of temper in lesser circumstances than this. Bad news could be dangerous for the bearer, for Osman's rage was often manifested by the act of throwing any object at hand, be it knife, cup, or small furnishings. Good news, on the other hand, could generate a hearty laugh, a hug for an old servant, a trinket or gold coin kept for minor rewards in a small, oaken chest on his desk. Alas, today's was not good, and Fedor Quraiwan could only hope his master was in a peaceful state.

He'd been waiting for more than an hour, sitting on a bench by the great double doors of the judgment room, now closed. Osman was inside with an emissary from Nevice who had traveled four weeks to meet with him on a trade matter. Another step in the expansion of Gan's trading influence, and it would undoubtedly create new wealth for the intimate circle of supporters of the planet's monarchy. Osman made business simple for them, with few restrictions and generous tax benefits for those who created jobs, and higher taxes for those who were employed by them. It all seemed to work well, despite the unrest of the masses, despite threats in the past. But today there was a new threat. Fedor was about to announce it to The Leader of All The World, and he was afraid.

The doors opened and Osman came out with his arm around the shoulders of a small, dark man with amazing amber eyes. They were laughing at some private joke. The small man bowed and pumped Osman's hand vigorously, whispered something and walked away with a smile on his face. Osman was smiling, too, rubbed his hands together, then turned and saw Fedor sitting there. Beckoned to him.

"Come in, come in. Took longer than I expected, but was worth it. Those Neviceaens do love to bargain."

Osman seemed pleased with himself. That was good. He closed the tall doors behind them, a golden robe spilling over the curves of his bulk. There was no one else with them in the room: domed ceiling held up by eight, marble columns, a rosette window of stained glass covering a wall, a floor of polished, black marble with the huge, oaken desk at its center. There were two chairs and a roll-in bar with carafes of coffee and tea. They went to the chairs. Osman glanced twice at Fedor, then poured tea for both of them without asking for a preference.

"I presume you have news for me, but I'm not encouraged by the expression on your face, my friend," said Osman.

They sat. Osman handed him a cup of tea with pudgy, ringed fingers, and took a sip from his own cup. "The news isn't good, but is also inconclusive," said Fedor.

"They haven't been found? We had five different sources of intelligence on this."

"Oh, they were found, Excellency. We could have taken them on the beach, but you wanted as much information as we could get on their supporting network. We've identified two cells in the operation, and arrests are being made as we speak."

"So why are you frowning at me?" asked the Emperor of Gan.

"Our principle targets have suddenly disappeared. The boy and his bodyguard got away when we attacked their car on the highway to the shuttle-port. The car was burning so furiously it took hours to discover the remains inside weren't theirs. They killed six of our people and escaped to the shuttle-port in one of our cars. It was found at the shuttle-port. Our men didn't see them. They might have flown out, or been taken somewhere else. We're going over passenger lists there and at spaceport. We've found unused tickets that might have been theirs. It's possible they're still on Gan."

Osman sipped his tea, and though he spoke softly there was a dangerous glint in his closely spaced eyes. "I think that would be a poor bet. If they have any intelligence at all they know we've penetrated their cells. Their structure is crumbling; a year or two, and we'll have all of them. This so-called Church of Lyra will disappear forever.

"Meanwhile it's important we get the boy in our hands. He's a figurehead, a symbol to them." Osman shook his head, and sniffed. "They think he's an Immortal."

"We've put agents on every flight since we discovered their bodies were missing from the car," said Fedor, "and our listeners in the cells have been alerted."

"The longer he's free the more hope these fanatics have, and the more people we'll lose when we bring them down. Eventually we can dig them out if they remain on Gan; the difficulty lies off planet, especially on Grenolda and Galena. The League is fragile, Fedor. You've been with me long enough to know that. There are some who at least sympathize with the democratic and anarchy preaching of the people who came here out of nowhere to stir up trouble. My father fought it for twenty years, but I don't have his patience, Fedor. Any remaining Immortals must be arrested and killed, their followers arrested, their caverns emptied out. I want their church destroyed, and their philosophy erased from our history. I want *order* on Gan, and I will have it. That boy is to be found, and killed, and his body brought to me."

"I understand, Excellency. It will be done."

"Of course it will, old friend. I trust you. We've been together too long for you to fail me. Who was in charge of the attack on the car?"

"Del Onsager, Excellency."

"I want him arrested and shot without delay."

"He's dead, Excellency. He was in a pursuit car, and it crashed into a tree, killing four operatives."

"And who was his overseer?"

"Captain Kirman planned the operation."

"Then have him arrested and shot instead."

"But Excellency, the Captain—"

"Symbolism, Fedor. Every action is a symbol of leadership. My leadership. And failure is not tolerated. Now carry out the order."

"Yes, Excellency."

Osman made an effeminate gesture of dismissal. "Don't report on this matter again until you have something positive, but that must be within a month. You have one month to show progress, Fedor. The responsibility is now yours. You're an old friend, and it would grieve me to make a symbol out of you."

Fedor stood. "I will not fail you, Excellency."

"A positive attitude is a good attitude," said the Emperor of all Gan, and he turned towards his desk.

Fedor hurried from the room and closed the doors softly behind him.

His armpits were soaking wet.

CHAPTER 7

Everything happened the way his father, in the guise of Petyr, told him in the dreams, or whatever fugue state Trae was now experiencing with increasing frequency. Mostly it was like daydreaming, a lapse of consciousness of only seconds, but something would happen. He would become aware of a face, a scene, a sequence of numbers flashing past his consciousness so quickly he could only recognize their presence before they were gone.

Trae slept soundly each cycle on the way to Ariel II. If there were dreams, he didn't remember them, but each time he awoke to find Petyr watching him, and each time the man would ask if he'd learned anything new. Trae answered patiently, realizing once they'd left Gan his teacher and guardian had no plan to follow, and was relying solely on his ward for direction.

Two days out he told Petyr about how it was his presence in the dreams, now, his Immortal father using a soldier of The Church as a kind of familiar disguise. Petyr seemed pleased. "I'm flattered, but I wonder why he doesn't use his own face. It's not like you haven't seen it before."

"Everyone knows his face," said Trae. "It was in every cubicle in the caverns. But some mistakenly worship him as The Source."

"He's a part of it, and so are you," Petyr said reverently.

"And you?"

"No. A soldier of The Church is not an Immortal. The Immortals come from The Source, and bring us a new way of life if we'll accept it. We don't know what The Source is, or where It is. It could be beyond the stars."

"I don't have time to get there," said Trae, and his vision blurred for an instant. "It will have to come to me. I have the feeling right now it's not important. It's not even important I find my father right away. What I need to do first is find other Immortals and convince them I'm who you say I am."

"Who *I* say you are?"

"You say I'm the reincarnated son of Leonid Zylak, an Immortal man who left us seventy five years ago. That makes me an Immortal, and now I'm supposed to save the Lyraen people from an Emperor who'd like to kill them. I know I'm different, but I don't believe in reincarnation, Petyr. I really don't believe what people are telling me, but here I am, following directions from visions I get in my head. I'm feeling The Immortals are waiting for me. I have to find them, and that's why we're going to Galena. It's not about raising an army, either. It's about money. Economic power. Not one Emperor, but several, a League of Emperors."

Trae put his hands on the sides of his head. "It's a babbling. It comes and goes."

"Confusing," said Petyr, and smiled.

"Bursts," said Trae, "like just now, and it's already fading. It's getting worse."

"Relax, and listen. All comes from The Source in various ways. You're being given what you need as you need it, but we still have to do our part."

Trae still didn't know what that was when they docked at Ariel II. Nobody was there to greet them. Petyr got off first to scan the people near the port, then came back for Trae. They walked the long tunnel to the lobby to stretch their legs. The cylindrical tunnel walls glowed a fluorescent light blue, and there was a breeze with a scent of pine in it. The lobby had four levels, and they came in at level one. They took an elevator up to level four for ticketing. There was no line at Station Six, and Trae walked right up to the young man checking in passengers there. The man smiled.

"You must be Lan," said Trae. "I'm Trae, and you're holding two tickets to Galena for me."

"All ready for you," said the man, and handed Trae an envelope. "Your departure was scheduled for tomorrow, but there have been inquiries about you so you'll be boarding in an hour. Please remain here in the lounge until twenty minutes before boarding, and we'll arrange a diversion to send you on your way. Your luggage is already on board."

"Thanks for your attention to this," said Trae.

"Wherever or whatever," said the man. "The Source is with all of us."

Trae told Petyr what had happened. "More spies," mumbled Petyr. "How far do we have to go to be rid of them?"

They sat in a corner of the lounge, their backs to the Station counters, and watched the stars go by on a giant observing screen on one wall. The time of their departure approached rapidly, and Petyr was checking his watch to begin their sprint to the port when there was a loud commotion behind them. Two policemen came out of the tunnel leading to Port Four, and they were dragging a red-faced, struggling man between them. A woman followed them, waving her arms and screaming for everyone to hear.

"Right in front of the counter he took it from me! Tore it right off my wrist and tried to run! Criminal!"

"Let me go, or you'll regret it," snarled the man. "My identity card is in my inside pocket. This is a sham; she shoved her hand into my pants pocket to put the bracelet there, and *you're* interfering with official business!"

The police dragged him away, and as soon as he was out of sight Trae and Petyr walked rapidly down the tunnel to Port Four and boarded the city-sized vessel that would ferry them to Galena over the following four days.

It was like boarding an asteroid with engines, the rocky exterior of the great ship pitted and scarred by high speed collisions with interplanetary dust and debris. Only a tenth of ship's volume was living and working space, the rest of it filled with frozen water for reaction mass, and eight thermonuclear reactors for power. Inside the living space one could imagine being in a fine hotel, with restaurants, entertainment lounges, a casino and shops featuring the wares of several planets.

There were nine levels. Petyr and Trae had a room with two beds on the third. After disconnect from Ariel II it was awkward at first, moving about like drunken monkeys swinging from strap to strap on walls and ceiling, then buckling into recliners for acceleration, low at first, rising to one gee within an hour and lasting for most of the trip.

They watched films in their apartment, but ate in the restaurants, even gambled a bit. Petyr's eyes never stopped moving; Trae found himself looking for a furtive glance, a face appearing often near them, the close-spaced eyes of one of the Emperor's thugs. The whole trip he saw nothing to disturb him, and there were no dreams to break up his sleep. The time passed peacefully for four days, and then they arrived at Galena.

There were few comparisons with the world of Gan. No soldiers were visible at the spaceport, and there were no checkpoints in or out of the arrival area. People dressed casually in light, loose fitting clothing so that Trae and Petyr stood out in their formal, dark suits. They walked the long tunnel leading to the baggage claim area. Soothing music with no defined rhythm came from speakers in the ceiling. A man dressed in the orange flowing robe of a Lyraen priest went by them in the opposite direction without so much as a glance at them.

Trae was amazed. "That can't be a Lyraen priest in public, can it?" he asked Petyr. "Nobody even looked at him, except me."

Petyr turned to answer, but looked sharply over his shoulder in surprise.

"Yes, it's a Lyraen priest," said a voice from behind them. "There's no religious persecution here."

Trae slowed, and twisted to look behind him. A small man in baggy pants and a loose, white sweater was right behind them, following their stride. "Welcome to Galena. I'll guide you to our car. Your luggage has already been picked up, and we'll be taking you directly to the palace."

There was good reason for suspicion; the man had appeared out of nowhere. So why did Trae feel safe with him?

"I didn't notice you when we came in," said Petyr.

"That's because I was on the flight with you from Ariel II. I was to clean up any residue of some problems we had there. As a soldier of The Church I'm sure you know what that means. You may call me Pavel, but it's not my real name."

The man moved in between them and looked up at Trae. "You're younger than we expected, but I'm sure it won't matter. Our hope is you'll be open with us about the purpose of your coming here."

"Will we be meeting with Emperor Siddique?" asked Trae.

"His representative will conduct your interview. Our Emperor cannot be directly involved at this moment. The politics of The League are delicate, and have considerable influence on our economic development. You come to us from the most conservative of planets, while we are quite liberal. The other five worlds are somewhere in between us in their policies, but lean towards the conservative side.

So far Galena is tolerated as a wealthy and successful rebel, and we want to keep it that way. This way, please."

They turned into a branching tunnel and after a few paces Pavel went to a door marked 'Flight Personnel Only' and unlocked it. They went down a level on concrete stairs to a lounge overlooking shuttles parked on the tarmac. A shuttle crew was sitting at tables there, eating light meals from vending machines lining one wall. Pavel nodded politely to them, went to another door. Trae and Petyr followed him down a long, empty tunnel leading directly to the street outside the terminal. One look, and Trae was reminded of a dream he'd had of two moons in an azure blue sky.

A limousine awaited them, a large, black thing with heavily tinted windows. A plate mounted on the front grill of the car showed a flag striped in green, red and yellow. A uniformed driver opened the back door for them, and they got inside to a plush interior, Trae and Petyr facing Pavel.

"We're naturally concerned about you being seen here," said Pavel, and the car began moving, "but private accommodations will be provided for you in the palace until you wish to move on."

And when would that be? There were no new fugue states to tell him anything. "Thank you," said Trae.

Pavel smiled at him. "I've never seen an Immortal before. Excuse me, but there doesn't seem to be anything special to distinguish you from other people."

"For the present, that's to our advantage," said Petyr.

"Are you aware of any Lyraen churches here?" asked Trae.

"Oh, yes. There's one near the palace. The state, of course, doesn't officially sanction religion. There are no subsidies or tax benefits, but several religions exist, some going back to ancient times. Emperor Siddique isn't a religious person, but he insists on tolerance for all beliefs. It is a matter of respect, and our people feel secure with his policy. I think it's why we've had no unrest on this planet, while the rest of The League has experienced instabilities, especially on Gan. Your Emperor Osman is not a friend of ours, and has publicly called our Emperor weak."

"Osman is nobody's friend on Gan," said Petyr.

Pavel nodded, his hands folded neatly in his lap. "Yes, well, these things will be discussed. You'll meet soon with a representative of The Throne. I don't know who it will be, or what agenda he'll bring to you from our Emperor. I can only assure you your beliefs are respected, your needs fairly considered, and you have the protection of The State while you're here."

The drive was short, at high speed. The palace was a complex of white stuccoed buildings surrounded by a ten-foot-high wall. They drove inside to a courtyard with beds of flowers and a gushing fountain. Pavel led them inside to an empty, vast foyer with columns and floor in brown marble. Trae wondered briefly where everyone was in such a state building. The air was still, and there was a sweet scent about them. They crossed the entire foyer to an ornately carved door. Pavel put his hand on a lever to open it, and stood aside. "I'll wait for you here," he said softly, and gave them a slight bow.

They went inside, and the door closed quickly behind them. The light was dim, and it took seconds for their eyes to adjust. It was a large room without windows. Lamps glowed from stonewalls, spaced between gleaming portraits of richly dressed men in regal poses, and there was a faint odor of the oil paints they'd been done with. A long, broad table with many chairs occupied the center of the room. A single lamp glowed from one end of the table, bright enough to reveal someone sitting there.

"Please sit," said a man's voice, deep and rich.

They sat down to the right of him, Petyr sitting closest. The man's face was barely visible in the dim light. It was a long face, with deep-set eyes. His lips were thin, and curved into a faint smile. "You may call me Assan, and I will speak for our Emperor Rasim Siddique, who is your host. May His Wisdom continue in all matters."

"We greatly appreciate your hospitality," said Petyr, "as well as your willingness to listen to us. We're here to seek counsel and possible aid regarding the plight of the Lyraen people and others being oppressed on Gan."

"Directly put," said Assan, and leaned forward to put his forearms on the table. He was wearing the rough, brown robe ordinarily used by Lyraens during their meditations at home. "I intend to be equally direct with you so there will be no misunderstandings. I speak for our Emperor and his policies, but I also have my personal opinions. I will try to distinguish those for you."

Trae could hold back no longer. "Your robe is familiar, sir. I'm wondering if you're a believer in the Lyraen faith. I'm Trae, and this is Petyr. He's my teacher, and a soldier of The Church."

"I know," said Assan, "and yes, I'm a believer. It's the primary reason I was chosen for this interview. I know who you are said to be, and who your father was. His missionaries were quite active on Galena until he went away, but that was in the time of Selah Siddique. Your youthful look is amazing. You must be nearing eighty."

Trae's mind blurred for a heartbeat. "I'm sixteen, sir. I've been reincarnated into this body after being murdered by the Emperor of Gan shortly before my father fled. I still have memories of it in my dreams. The Lyraen people have been hunted down and slaughtered for nearly a century on Gan. Only a few have managed to avoid capture, but it's a matter of time before they'll also be gone, and the Lyraen faith with them."

"On Gan, perhaps, but the faith will survive elsewhere. Khalid Osman is a hard man; this is well known. His policies have incurred the anger of his subjects. He's insecure. The Lyraens pose a direct threat because they stand for freedom of the individual, and Osman will have none of that. His rule must be absolute."

Assan leaned back and steepled his fingers in front of his face. "The same is not true here. Rasim Siddique as Emperor could also be a total dictator, but is not. Our senate has representatives from all classes, and judges all policies. In the rare cases when a judgment is overruled, satisfactory compromises are made. The system has worked for hundreds of years, well enough that even the Lyraen Mission founded by The Immortals has not sought to change it. Individuals enjoy freedom here, but we are not a democracy. Is that your purpose in coming here? To change what we have? Or is it to solicit our military support in overthrowing the government of Gan?"

"I wish I could tell you exactly why we're here, sir," said Trae, "but my primary purpose is to save the lives of innocent people on Gan."

"Ah, but from the point of view of Gan's Emperor the Lyraen people are not innocents. They advocate his overthrow. They'll accept only a pure democracy, a utopian concept brought to them by a foreign people who have come from far away, and who say they're Immortal. Even that concept is difficult to believe, and I say that as a member of the Lyraen faith. The Church here questions things; it doesn't blindly accept them. We question the idea of a pure democracy when personal freedom and high quality of life can be accomplished in other ways. The Lyraens on Gan do not question the teachings of The Immortals. Their thinking is narrow and rigid."

"Would you allow them to be killed, then?" Trae felt heat in his face, and anger stirred in him.

"I haven't said that," said Assan quickly. "The point I'm trying to make is that even among Lyraens on planets of our local system the reputation of The Church on Gan has always been poor. It is rigid and uncompromising, and the problem has now coupled with the existence of a cruel Emperor who's threatened by it. To topple an Emperor means war, *or*, the threat may be removed by a mass migration of the Lyraens on Gan. But who will take them? Should we open our doors to them on Galena, allow them to come in and then make trouble because we don't meet their ideals? There are seven planets, and seven Emperors in The League. None are purely democratic, and most are dictatorships to some degree. Good relationships between us are of mutual benefit. So what are we to do with the rebellious Lyraens of Gan? Do you see the dilemma?"

Trae stared at Assan for just an instant, and then his eyes focused again. "I see that unless my people can compromise their beliefs the only way I can save them is to take them far away from here. Their neighbors won't take them in, and there's no way they can overthrow Emperor Osman without outside help."

"We cannot give you that kind of help," said Assan. "Our military is purely for defense, and we will not intervene in the business of other League members unless it threatens our safety. Emperor Siddique wanted this made clear to you. On the other hand, if The Church on Gan could adopt more liberal views of what a free society is, we would consider taking them in as citizens, provided they make no plans to return to Gan or plot against the government there."

"I can't speak for The Church, but it might be possible," said Trae, but then Petyr touched his arm.

"I don't think it's likely. The conservative element of The Church has dominated since your father left us. We don't have time to persuade them to soften their views."

"Then we can't take them in," said Assan. "That leaves arrest, imprisonment or death, exile at the best. I'm sorry, but extremists are often the source of their own problems. One thing my Emperor has mentioned to me; Khalid Osman has spoken of the Lyraen problem in League Council, but it's common knowledge his reign is considered oppressive by all his people, not just one group. If he brings it up again, an Emperor known for compassion might suggest exile of antagonists to another colony world and give Osman an opportunity to allow it. He has good reason to be concerned about his image on the Council these days."

Trae looked at Petyr, who shrugged his shoulders in resignation. Assan smiled. "It's the best we can do for you right now, but the two of you can remain here as long as you wish. You might visit with officials of The Church and get their views. I think it will give you a new perspective."

"Thank you," said Trae. "It's not what we'd hoped for, but I'm sure it's all you can do for us. There's so much for me to learn, and I don't have much time. I really think Osman will begin arresting Lyraens soon. He obviously knows they've sent an emissary off-planet. We were followed and attacked on our way here."

"That alone might delay any arrests he'd like to make. Any outward signs of oppression are signs of instability. The League of Emperors is working for free trade between all their worlds, and wants permanent agreements. They'll shy away from worlds showing unrest. It's a lever Emperor Siddique can use, and he has suggested it in my presence. Please believe me when I say he's sympathetic to the plight of any oppressed people, but all he can do for you now is subtle and political. He certainly wishes you well, and I need to get back to him. Your escort by the door will show you to your rooms and see to your needs."

Assan stood up, and extended a hand to them. They shook it. "You will not see me again, but I pray The Source will give you a safe journey."

"And for you and your Emperor a good life," said Trae with a nod.

Assan smiled broadly. "Amazing, such a youthful look. One would never know. Perhaps one day your own people will return to show us better ways." He turned and left the room, and Pavel, their escort, was instantly standing in the doorway.

"My own people?" said Trae.

"The Immortals," said Petyr. "That's what you are."

Pavel led them to their rooms.

Assan's face flushed as he quickly crossed the foyer and down a long hallway to the adjoining office building. He was feeling a strange mixture of awe and shame, awe at having met an actual Immortal and shame at not providing what the man had come for. Khalid Osman was a despicable despot, and sooner or later The League would have to deal harshly with him before the cancer of his policies could spread. Now was not the time.

An Immortal, so old, but a strip of a boy, and at one point it seemed his eyes had glowed. An Immortal on a mission, but there was more to it than just a fight against a harsh Emperor, of this Assan was certain. Perhaps The Immortals would return in force to create new systems of government in The League. Perhaps this boy he'd just met, this reincarnation of the son of an Immortal missionary, was being sent to fetch them. And if The Immortals returned, what would happen to the Emperors, good or bad? What would happen to their devoted servants?

Assan mused on this as he reached the preparation room, and went inside. He changed out of his robe of humility, and put on the white robe of wisdom and purity of thought, then went through the door to the judgment chamber.

It was empty. Good. He had a few minutes to think. His hard-soled sandels clicked hollowly on the marble floor, the sound echoing from the high vaulted ceiling above him. He went to the throne on a dais rising three feet above the floor, and sat on it, bowing, and placing his face in his hands.

"Source of all things, give me the courage and wisdom to do that which you would have me do," he prayed, then straightened, and enjoyed a few moments of quiet meditation.

There was a knock on the great door.

"Come!"

The door opened, and a secretary stood there. "The delegation has arrived, Excellency."

"Send them in," said Emperor Rasim Siddique, the ruler of all Galena, and a clandestine Servant of The Source.

CHAPTER 8

After his visit to the palace of Rasim Siddique, the dreams were suddenly more frequent and intense. The first night Trae was startled awake, face hot and sweaty. His feet hit the floor with a thud that awoke Petyr. Trae had never felt such a sense of urgency before. He tried to grasp the reason for it, but it was gone, fading with the dream. He'd been talking to Petyr, or rather his father, and there'd been drawings, technical things, on a table in front of them, and long lists of numbers. He awoke remembering nothing except a visual flash of the scene, but his head hurt, and somehow he knew all the details were still in his mind, and it was urgent he find the key to release them. But why?

Petyr questioned him, and seemed concerned. "The Church is supposed to provide for you wherever we go, but I have no new contacts. We'll have to ask them whenever they decide to meet us. I'm sure Siddique will expect us to move along quickly. The treatments are initiating these dreams, Trae, and I don't know how or why."

They had to wait three days before being contacted by the Lyraen church on Galena, and then it was only a note delivered by an unknown messenger. It told them where and when to go, but Petyr was suspicious enough to ask Pavel for a military escort. There was another delay of a day before the meeting, and in the meantime the dreams came every night, a jumble that confused Trae and frightened him.

It was no longer conversations with a familiar face in a familiar room. There were visions of other places: forests, and two moons in a deep blue sky, a huge room in polished brown marble with frescos on a high, vaulted ceiling, then domed huts made of bricks and surrounded by sticky mud he struggled to walk through. The fire came again, and he was beating at the flames with crisping hands, the same dream he'd had since childhood. All of this happened in one night, and repeated after that. Each morning he awoke exhausted and shaking to find Petyr there, sitting on the edge of his bed, looking down at him.

Pavel took their request seriously and showed up with a heavily armed escort of a dozen soldiers and three armored vehicles. They were driven to the central Lyraen church in the capital city, an unadorned building that could have been offices or a bank. They were met by three, young priests, and an elderly proctor named Nicolus Shue, all dressed in business suits. The entire time they were in the church the young priests were never introduced to them, were apparently present only to listen and learn. They bowed in deference to Trae, watched his eyes constantly, and hung on his every word.

"They've never seen an Immortal before now," explained Nicolus. "I was a small lad when your father passed through here, and we've not seen him since. It has been a disappointment to us."

They went to a large room with white undecorated stucco walls. Rows of tables went back from a stage and podium. One table was prepared with two pitchers of water, glasses, and notepads in front of six straight back chairs. They sat.

"I'm trying to find my father, or any other Immortal who can lead me to him. The Church is in serious trouble on Gan, and lives are at stake," said Trae.

"So I hear," said Nicolus, "but that has nothing to do with us. They've made their own nest, and broken contact with churches all across The League."

"They've been driven underground by threat of imprisonment or death. There can be no communication because of the risk of discovery."

"Yet here you are." Nicolus smiled.

"The leaving was planned for many years," said Petyr, "but our destination was kept secret from us until the last moment."

"Not a very well kept secret. You were attacked, and apparently killed."

"How do you know that?" asked Petyr, and glanced over his shoulder. Pavel was there at the doorway with four of his soldiers.

"We have our sources," said Nicolus.

"Are you questioning our identity?" Petyr's eyes narrowed.

"I am. There have been recent attempts to infiltrate our ranks, and the bodies have been returned to their masters on Gan. Like all planets, we also have soldiers of The Church."

"And I am one of them."

"He's been my teacher and guard since I was a child," said Trae. "If you question his identity you question mine."

"Yes, I do. There's a simple test, if you'll permit it."

"Of course."

"Not so fast, Trae," said Petyr, and motioned to Pavel. The man came running, the soldiers right behind him. Nicolus recoiled in surprise, and the young priests pushed back their chairs, ready to flee. Four rifles were now leveled at them.

"You question who we are, but how do I know you represent The Church?"

"What's the test?" asked Trae quickly.

"We need a small drop of your blood, that's all," said Nicolus, and looked straight at him with fear in his eyes. The muzzle of a rifle was only a foot from the man's head.

"Then do it," said Trae, with authority. "I need no proof of your identity. I've seen your face before, and the faces of these young men. You've stored things my father left behind for me. They're in a black, wooden box, and I need to have them before we can move on. Take the blood and make your test. We can't waste time with this."

"Trae, I—"

"Please, Petyr. They're only questioning me. Their agents have seen you before at a concave on Gan when I was small. They believe who you are. The test will tell them I'm an Immortal, and also that I'm the son of Leonid Zylak. Put the guns down. You're frightening them."

Petyr hesitated, then raised a hand. Pavel mumbled something, and the rifles were lowered. Petyr glared at Nicolus. "At best, you're arrogant. Make your test, but one sign of threat and I promise you won't survive it."

Nicolus' hand shook as he withdrew a leather wallet from an inner pocket, and opened it flat on the table. The implements in it were familiar: analytical syringe with a display for blood sugar and hemoglobin count and a built-in chamber for sample prep. Trae held out his hand, felt a jab of pain. Numbers appeared on the screen of the instrument. Nicolus pressed a button, and a small glass square was ejected from a slot under the screen. He handed it to one of the priests, who walked quickly away with it.

"It'll take a few minutes. The readings here are normal. When did you last see a physician?"

"He had a treatment just before we left Gan," said Petyr, still looking and sounding angry.

"He won't have one here, but we'll want to scan him."

Now Petyr seemed to soften. "I understand."

"I don't," said Trae.

"Just a check. You'll be having a lot of these to see how you're reacting to the treatments, and we don't know when the opportunities will arise."

Everyone seemed to relax just a bit, and Nicolus said, "While we're waiting, perhaps you could tell us what happened on your journey here. We all had our individual assignments, and it seems to me security was penetrated on Gan even before you left."

Petyr told him what had happened, but wasn't finished when the young priest came back with the results of the blood test, handing a sheet of paper and two photographs to Nicolus. The man studied them, looked up at Trae and smiled.

"You are the Immortal son of Leonid Zylak, and his heir. We'll do as he's ordered us to do."

Trae pointed at the photographs. "Can I see those?"

"Of course," said Nicolus, and handed them to him. "They're the signiature of your heritage."

Trae studied them. They were pictures of his blood, taken in the deep cold of a proton microscope. Red blood cells: round, fat and healthy, each surrounded by a dilute cloud of specks, like tiny insects. The one picture was at high magnification, and the specks were not insects but huge molecules frozen in an instant of their functioning. There was one looking like a partially closed fist, with two extended fingers caught in the act of unraveling a bacterium. Another shaped like a tripod and a telescoping shaft with a bulb on the end had been probing the surface of a red blood cell. Others had floated freely, tangled knots of small molecules with cavities, bumps, and bizarre protuberances. "They look like little machines," said Trae. "This is what I get in the treatments?"

"They do what modern medicine cannot," said Nicolus, "but they're activated and sustained by a messenger molecule that occurs naturally in only the blood of Immortals. The molecule is too small to be seen at this magnification, but without it the machines can't survive. Those of us who are normal humans are not helped by the kind of treatments you receive. We wish it were otherwise, of course. Perhaps one day we'll find the answer. But these pictures identify you as an Immortal, and you must somehow be the blood son of Leonid Zylak. Two of the machines here are his specific design. He and his wife Tatjana are the only two Immortals I'm aware of who have ever remained in our system for any length of time, and your coming here fits with instructions Leonid left behind when my father held the position I now hold. Leonid told us his son had died, but would be reborn, and follow him to where he was going. He left a package for you in our care; it has been secreted in our historical archives for nearly a century. I will take you to it."

"What's in the package?" asked Trae. Nicolus shook his head and didn't answer. The priests stood up and looked anxious to leave. Petyr still looked uncertain about what was going on, and Pavel hovered only a step away with his soldiers.

"Our escort comes with us," said Petyr, and Nicolus only nodded at him in reply.

They walked across a foyer, sunlight beating down through a glass ceiling with yellow rays radiating from a red center, a symbol of The Source. There was a long hallway. Robed priests passed them, looking curiously at their military entourage. Winding stairs in polished stone took them down three levels in increasing gloom to a set of double doors where an armed guard opened a panel in the wall. Nicolus placed one thumb on a small screen, and there was a dull thump. Trae felt a small shock wave beneath his feet. The door opened, and they went inside. It looked like a warehouse, illuminated by incandescent lamps in a high ceiling, row upon row of shelves stacked on top of each other to three times the height of a man. All were crammed solid with like-sized boxes labeled only with large numbers in black.

Nicolus led them down a long row of shelves and went straight to a box labeled 997 at shoulder height. He slid it off the shelf without effort and led them farther to an array of cubicles, each with chair and table. He beckoned Trae inside one of them, and put the box on the table. "We'll wait out here. The contents are only for you to see."

It was clear Petyr didn't like what was happening; his eyes narrowed and he looked around rapidly. Now he was suspicious of what was inside the box. Poor Petyr. Trae had no suspicions, except it was vital he know what had been left behind for him. He was to go where his father had gone, a father seen only in a dream. Nicolus had actually seen Leonid Zylak when he was young. The man was real. And Leonid Zylak had left something for his murdered son who was supposed to be reborn and eventually follow his father to wherever he'd gone.

The top flaps of the cardboard box were loosely sealed by something sticky, and Trae easily loosened them. Inside was a second box, ornately carved in black wood and packed in crumpled paper. Trae immediately remembered the box. It had been on a table near his bed, in the room where the fire had come. He pulled it out, held it gently in his hands, a thing from a dream, perhaps a thing from another life.

The box was not locked. He lifted a small latch, and opened it.

There were three plas-disks stamped with the ringed-world logo of League Bank, a box of holocubes, unlabeled, a velvet bag containing a handful of gold sovereigns and an envelope marked "Anton" in an elaborate hand-script. The envelope flap pulled loose easily. A faint scent, musky, wafted from inside it. Trae felt a momentary lapse in his attention, as if in a daydream. Conscious again, he pulled a folded piece of paper from the envelope and opened it. This time he was flooded with a musky, sweet odor that reached up behind his eyes, and he blinked.

A letter in beautiful script, and he read it. In his mind flickered the vision of a sharp-featured man with black hair and trimmed beard, but it dissolved into Petyr's face again, mouth moving with the words Trae read, and a voice that was not Petyr's.

"My Dear Anton:

"If you're reading this, then you've reached Galena and are prepared to take your rightful place in The Family. I don't know your age at this instant, but will know it before you finish reading this letter. We're connected, you see, connected in a way that will soon become clear to you. All Immortals are connected, my son. We can be apart physically, yet remain connected through mind and spirit, if only we listen. And as of this moment, you will begin to listen.

"It was necessary for me to go away when treachery first took you from me, but I never really left you. That treachery has been answered in part, and final steps in our vengeance will be taken today. But now you are reborn, as is your mother, and we wait for you. We love you very much, but you must find us. It is part of life's journey for you. You will learn from it, and gain the maturity and wisdom you need for leadership in a world of mortal men.

"You should give the holo-cubes to whatever guardian The Church has assigned to you; he will know what to do with them. The disks are for you; they give you access to two accounts and a safe-deposit vault in League Bank of Lycrus, only blocks from where you are now. Further instructions will be there. Put all other concerns aside. Finding us is the task you must accomplish. All else is a journey.

"We await you with hope, and love.

"Your Father, and Mother

"Faithful of The Source Within Us."

Trae's head swirled with musky scent, and when he looked up from the letter his eyes wouldn't focus. The vision of Petyr was still there, and the man's eyes were moist. Suddenly there was a sound in his head, not of one voice, but two, a calling that was a murmur.

"Trae. Trae. Trae . . ."

His eyes suddenly focused and he was startled to consciousness. Sweat covered his brow, and there was a tingling in his hands. The musky odor was gone. He left the letter in the box and removed the other contents, then placed the box in its storage container. The entourage was waiting when he stepped outside the cubicle. "I know what I have to do," he said solemnly. Nicolus smiled, but not Petyr.

"In private," said the soldier of The Church.

"We're at your service." Nicolus bowed.

"We need transportation to League Bank of Lycrus right away." Trae looked at Petyr. "Pavel and his people should come with us."

"See to it," said Nicolus; a small, commanding gesture with his hand and the two young priests quickly left them.

Trae blinked his eyes hard. Musk seemed to penetrate his brain, and his vision was still fuzzy. "There's a letter for the Emperor of Galena, and I have to get it for him."

"What?" asked Petyr, and then Trae's vision suddenly cleared.

"Now," he said. "Our work isn't here, Petyr. We have to move on."

Now Nicolus looked concerned. "What about the Lyraens on Gan?" He replaced the storage box on its shelf, and led them towards the exit.

"The problem will be solved, but not by me. There is another. We're all connected, mortals and Immortals alike."

He was only confusing them. Petyr looked blank, and Nicolus had an embarrassed smile on his face. "It'll all be clear soon," said Trae, and followed the two men up the stairs again, Pavel and his soldiers right behind him.

The car they'd arrived in awaited them, Pavel and his men going to a gray military vehicle right behind it. They were in and out of the car in minutes after a drive of only a few blocks.

League Bank of Lycrus was housed in a seven-story building without windows or adornment, the interior softly lit by ceiling panels in full spectrum light and polished marble ceiling and floors in light green. Pavel and his men remained outside, but Pavel watched as Trae marched up boldly to one of ten clerks and handed two disks to him. "I'd like to update the balance in these accounts, please, and get a printout of it."

The clerk smiled at Trae's formal tone in his attempt to seem older than he was. But his smile faded when the accounts came up on his screen. "I'll need proof of access. Thumbprint, please." The clerk pushed a identity pad across the counter, and Trae pressed his right thumb onto a small transparent square of plastic there.

"It'll be a moment. Is there anything else?" The clerk looked very serious, now.

"Yes. I need access to this box." Trae handed him the third disk. The clerk seemed distracted. He was looking at his screen, and his eyes seemed quite large. "Of—of course. Ah, the printout is ready." He handed Trae a small sheet of paper. Trae only glanced at it, and put it in his pocket. The clerk gaped at him.

"The box. More proof of identity? My name?" His heart was pounding.

"We use no names here, sir, and the box is listed under your accounts. Any business you do here is safe with us, sir. Here is your access card, box twelve-sixty-nine." He pointed to his left. "The vault clerk will let you in. And thank you for your business with League Bank of Lycrus."

I should think so, thought Trae, still considering the numbers he'd seen in a glance at the accounts printout.

A young woman scanned his access card and opened the vault for him. Petyr waited outside. Inside was like an entire floor of another building, box drawers floor to ceiling, and cubicles with closed doors and partitions the height of a tall man, all of it in silver metal. The woman used her card and his to open box twelve-sixty-nine. Trae slid the box out. It was light. The woman showed him to a cubicle and closed the door behind him as he put the box on a table and opened it.

It was nearly empty. There was a sealed envelope addressed to "Ruler of All Galena, May The Source Sustain Him," and signed "Leonid Zylak" in elaborate script. A single sheet of paper, folded in half. A vial of yellowish liquid with a pressurized enhaler attached.

Trae unfolded the paper and read: "My son. A bit more mystery, and you're on your way. The letter is for the Emperor of Galena. I assume it's Rasim Siddique; I knew his father and he was a good man, his family among the faithful. It's vital the letter reaches him unopened after you leave the planet. You will go to Elderon. Everything you need to know is in the vial of liquid I've left here. Take all of it, both nostrils, before you sleep tonight, and destroy the vial. Destroy this note. I promise you'll be full of answers to your questions in the morning. We love you. Father."

Trae put the vial in a breast pocket, the crumpled up note in his pants' pocket, and closed the box. *Trae. Trae.* He shivered. *We're waiting. Soon, now.*

He returned the box to its place in the wall and the clerk let him out of the vault when he rang for her. Petyr looked anxious.

"Well?"

"There's this, and a note. We're going to Elderon."

"When?"

"I don't know. Ask me in the morning. I have to see Nicolus again right away. He has the contacts in the palace, and this letter has to be delivered privately to Emperor Siddique."

"What's in it?"

"I don't know, but it's vital he receives it after we've left."

"Why?"

"I don't know."

"Trae!"

"Tomorrow, Petyr, please be patient with me. I don't understand what's happening either." He patted his breast pocket. "There's something I have to take tonight. A drug of some kind. Maybe all this will make sense in the morning."

"A liquid?" asked Petyr.

"Yes. I inhale it."

"Ah, hah. Well, let's get to Nicolus again, and put you to bed. I expect to be enlightened in the morning. I'm not just along for the ride, you know."

Something was left unsaid, something Petyr understood, but not Trae. Petyr seemed anxious to get moving again. They went back to the car and drove to The Church. Pavel and his soldiers finally left them. They met with Nicolus, and Trae gave him the note to read. The priest refolded the note, and it was like a moment of prayer or meditation when they burned it to ashes in a porcelain dish. He took the letter, said he'd immediately contact Assan and make sure it was personally delivered to Emperor Rasim Siddique in privacy.

It was time to leave. The priest gave Petyr a small, metal suitcase to take with him. While Trae wondered what was in it, he didn't ask. And while Nicolus had seemed somewhat hostile at first meeting, now he was reverent. He bowed to Trae, and wished for him the wisdom of The Source in his journey, and as he did this it seemed to Trae there was a chorus in his head, saying, *"Listen, now, and The Source of All will be with you in each step you take."*

A car came for them from the palace; it was small, plain and unmarked. The driver was unfamiliar to them, and had the bearing of a military man. He drove with wild abandon and they were at the palace in two minutes. He opened the car door for them. "Follow me, please. Your luggage is in your rooms."

They went past the room where they'd met with Assan and up a flight of stairs to a long hallway with closed doors. The end suite was theirs, and Trae was impressed by the opulence: five rooms, plush carpets, deep-cushioned furniture, and huge bay windows looking out on the gardens behind the palace. Their driver pointed to a telephone in its cradle on a glass table. "Just lift the receiver and wait. Someone will bring you whatever you wish, and your meals will be served in here. Please remain in your rooms; there will be guards outside your door. Feel free to use the balcony; the gardens are in full bloom now."

He left them, and closed the door behind him.

"Very nice," said Petyr, looking around.

"I feel like a prince," said Trae.

"Maybe you are. Why don't you pick up that phone, and order some food for us. I'm hungry, and you should eat something before I scan you."

"What?"

"Brain status check, whatever you want to call it. I wondered how we'd find someone to do it, and here it is." Petyr raised the little suitcase Nicolus had given him. "A portable unit, even has a battery, and it takes those holocubes you found. Now show me that drug you're supposed to take."

Trae showed him the vial with its compressed-gas atomizer. Petyr peered at it. "That's an awful lot of liquid."

"You know what it is?"

"Probably like the stuff you've been getting in your treatments, only a lot more of it." Petyr smiled. "Maybe you'll be a genius in the morning."

"I'll settle for knowing how we get to Elderon. I don't even know where that is."

"I've heard the name," said Petyr, and flipped up the latches on the suitcase. "One of the first colonies, closer to the galactic core. For now we need to do a scan, and I want your blood sugar up for it. I need an updated neural map of your brain before you take that drug. The telephone. Use it."

Trae called, said who he was, was informed their dinner was already on the way. It arrived a minute later, served by two men in white livery, and they ate at the glass table outside on the balcony. It was dusk, and the air was sweet. The meal was plentiful: green vegetables, yellow yams, a shank of lamb that fell from the bone at the touch of a fork, and a sticky pastry rich with dark honey.

"Oh, I'm stuffed," said Trae, and pushed away from the table. "Now I'll be sleepy." He poured a cup of tea; maybe that would help.

"Take a nap, then, I can do the scan early. You only need to be drowsy."

They went back inside. Petyr pulled a tangle of wires from the metal suitcase, and Trae lay down on a couch so deep it seemed to envelope him. He was immediately drowsy, and closed his eyes. Petyr swabbed his temples and forehead with something cold, pressed sticky patches several places there. There was a dull whine from the suitcase, then nothing. Trae was relaxed, his mind blank, but very much awake. A minute later Petyr pulled the sticky patches from his skin, and Trae heard the lid of the suitcase snap shut.

"That's it, you're done," said Petyr.

"That's all?" Trae opened his eyes. Petyr was sitting beside him, holding up a vial of yellow liquid.

"It's all in a holocube. Now you take this, and I'll do another scan in the morning." He handed the vial to Trae.

"We haven't even unpacked yet," said Trae.

Petyr smiled. "You scared?"

"Nervous, maybe," Trae lied. "I don't know what's in this stuff."

"Your father left it and says to take it now. That's enough for me, but I can understand the nervousness. That's five times what I've seen used in ordinary treatments on you, even the last one. I'll watch you close. You've never had any reactions to treatments before, and I doubt there'll be any this time. Let's get it over with." He held out the vial to Trae.

Nervous, yes, but the fear was of the unknown, and Trae somehow knew he must do this. It would be an act of faith: believing the note was really from his father, the drug not tampered with. The bank accounts were certainly real enough, his access to more wealth than he'd ever imagined. And would Petyr ever tempt him to harm himself? No, he'd give up his life first.

Trae took the vial from Petyr's hand, and as his fingers touched the glass his forehead suddenly cooled and a voice he could only be imagining in his mind said, *"Trae. This is the only way. Take it now. You can't wait much longer to find us.*

He listened, and lifted the vial to his face. The nozzle of the atomizer had a hair trigger, and the first blast up his left nostril made his eyes water. The second blurred his vision, and he felt like he was falling backwards when he knew he was lying down.

And in one instant, life changed dramatically for the reincarnated being of Anton Zylak.

CHAPTER 9

As Assan, and wearing the brown robe of humility, he hurried down the hall towards the preparation room. He clutched the envelope tightly to him, and though pressed against his body, his hand was shaking. The meeting with the priest had only taken a minute, but his heart was still pounding from the shock of it. A letter from a missionary of The Immortals, it was, and addressed to The Ruler of All Galena. Delivered privately, for Nicholus knew his real identity and often confided in him regarding problems of The Church.

He reached the preparation room with time to spare. There was to be a hearing for two merchants convicted of secretly exporting military-grade weapons off-planet without payment of either taxes or tariffs. If proven to his satisfaction, his judgment would be severe, for crimes of this sort reflected badly on his government. They could destabilize friendly planets, or aid and abet planets not so friendly with Galena.

Assan removed the robe of humility, and was Rasim Siddique once more. He donned the red robe of judgment, and sat down to read a letter addressed to him before he'd even been born, and from a man who was legend to most people in the streets. The envelope was sealed tight and he used a knife to tear it open. There was a popping sound when the seal first broke, and a wonderful scent of pine flooded his senses. The letter inside even smelled of pine, as if it had been rubbed with pitch. He breathed in deeply, opened the folded sheet of paper and read the instructions written there in a few lines. What he read frightened and appalled him, for it told him to do a thing he would never have considered doing in a dozen lifetimes. But this was an unusual time. The son of an Immortal was on a mission, not just for The Church, but for all people, even the ones who ruled them, and as a communicant member of the faithful a humble emperor was being called to take part in it.

Rasim breathed pine scent, felt the debate within him rise, then decline. A part of him felt the orders on the page both foolish and dangerous. Another part of him, growing with each breath, knew it had to be done. And so he obeyed.

He went to the Chamber of Judgment and sat on the throne in silence for a moment before people began arriving. He half-heard the proven case against the merchants, but enough to learn that some of their secret shipments had gone to the military government on Gan. The merchants had appealed to him to reverse their five year sentence at hard labor, and he denied it. He ignored the mumbled curses of the merchants as they left the room with their attorneys to be embraced by the military police. The air smelled like pine, and a plan was forming in his mind. He gestured to his secretary, and the man came forward, bowing.

"I want to have supper with my Security and Defense Ministers tonight. Tell them it will be in my chambers at seven."

The secretary bowed again, and hurried away.

"I don't like it," said Evan. "What does Galena have to do with our problems on Gan? They don't even agree with our interpretations of the Elements of The Faith; they think we're zealots."

"It came direct from the head of The Church, and used the current code. We cabled direct for verification, and got it. It's real," said Darian. "You just don't want to believe Zylak's kid could work so fast."

"What it could be is a huge trap. If we assemble all our people in front of the palace like that, they could bag the lot of us in one move."

"There's no demonstration until the flag comes down, and there's supposed to be an announcement of some kind. We're just citizens in the street, and no weapons. If it looks right, then we protest. You'll be in touch with every cell, Evan. You'll have complete control."

"We still have moles in The Church. This could get leaked. I won't announce anything until the last minute, and I mean last."

"Okay, but at least let me select protest captains and go over a 'hypothetical' plan with them."

"We only have two weeks."

"It'll be enough. Not too long to wait for freedom."

"We'll see about that," said Evan.

"Every cell received the message independently. Whoever sent it knew the entire network, and Galena is definitely the origin. Zylak has gone directly to the Emperor. It's his operation, and all the rectors are cooperating." Joseph handed the message back to Abelius a second time; the man had read it once, but seemed shocked by it.

"We're acting on the word of a boy."

"His instructions come from his father. They were in a letter. All we're supposed to do is get a demonstration ready. I think it's a diversion. Our signal is the flag coming down. My bet is they've organized some kind of coup. We know there are friends inside the palace."

"We'll be exposed," said Abelius. "Some of us have never been seen on the streets. If there's trouble we need something to distinguish our people. A leather thong around the wrist would work, with a silver bead on it. We need a dispersal plan if this is a trap."

"I'll get to work on it."

"The cell rectors meet in two days. We'll discuss our options, and I'll get back to you. This is exciting, but frightening, Joseph. We've been living as oppressed people for over a generation. Perhaps our day is coming at last, and The Source hasn't abandoned us."

"Our faith has indeed been tested," said Joseph. He pointed at the note in Abelius' hand. "Destroy that paper. Our secrecy must be absolute. I have to check the garage, now, and see how many vehicles are operational. I should have a dispersal plan for you by tonight."

"I'll be here," said Abelius. He lit a candle and held the paper out towards the flame as Joseph left the room. The door closed, and he was alone. He pulled the paper away from the flame, folded it twice and put it into his pocket. The telephone was in an adjoining room, half-buried with paper on his desk. He lifted the receiver and punched in six numbers.

"Cero's," said a man, and it was Fedor Quraiwan.

"Abelius Zorn here. I left a set of linens there last week, and it's most important I get them back today for a special dinner I'm having. Can I pick them up now?"

"Of course," said Quraiwan. "I'll be here until six."

"I'll be there within the hour," said Abelius, and hung up. He breathed a sigh of relief, for Fedor was not often in his street office this late in the afternoon. The meeting would be face-to-face, and he could report with precision the terrible plot being hatched against the Emperor. He went to the door, and opened it.

Joseph was standing there with a pistol leveled, and two men were with him.

"What is this?" said Abelius.

"Take him," said Joseph. The two men grabbed his arms, and marched him along the hall, Joseph behind him.

Abelius struggled, and glared at his captors. "What has he said to you? The man is taking power for himself."

"I suppose you're the one who nearly got Zylak killed, and Petyr, too. We'd elliminated all other possible people; that left only you. Your telephone was rigged for voiceprint, and as far as I know the Emperor's Security Chief doesn't run a cleaning establishment."

"You're mistaken!" shouted Abelius. "Why are you really doing this?"

"In here," said Joseph. The two men hauled Abelius into a room filled with cleaning supplies and turned him to face a concrete wall as Joseph kicked the door shut.

"What are you doing?" screamed Abelius Zorn.

"Solving a problem," said Joseph.

The shock wave reached Abelius' ears just as the heavy bullet blew away the back of his head and sprayed his blood on the wall in front of him.

CHAPTER 10

Trae was startled awake by a gust of wind and a strong scent of jasmine. He was sitting on a bench connected to a plank table, and had apparently fallen asleep with one cheek resting on his forearms. His cheek felt numb, and he wiped a patch of drool from his chin. Two trees were close on the other side of the table, the trunks like giant cables woven from brown velvet and topped with purple fronds of a fern-palm mix he'd never seen before or even imagined. Immediately, he was suspicious.

The table was covered with a red cloth fuzzy to the touch and there were porcelain plates stacked neatly at the end of it. Trae's head turned at a sound behind him. A few steps away a man stood by some kind of cooker, back to him. The cooker spewed smoke, but the wind blew it away and Trae smelled only Jasmine from the field of flowers coming up to their location on the brow of a hill. Rolling hills covered in violet hues spread out before him, broken occasionally by clusters of strange trees with swaying trunks and purple tops. The sky was a clear, powder blue and the crescents of two yellow moons were just above the horizon. It was a beautiful place, magical, not real. Trae knew instantly it wasn't real.

Even from the back the man looked familiar, but when he turned slightly to one side a neatly trimmed black beard was visible and before he turned away his face seemed to blur, shimmering, dissolving into something else.

"Ah, you're awake," said the man, and it was Petyr's voice. He turned around, a spatula in one hand, and indeed it was Petyr. He smiled. "Hungry, yet? We're about ready here."

"I saw you changing," said Trae. "You were someone else a few seconds ago."

"We're all different people wrapped into one," said Petyr. "Even you, Trae. You aren't who you seem to be, even here."

Trae was suddenly conscious his appearance was normal in this strange place. He was not a small child here.

"So this is another dream. The setting is new; I've never seen such strange plants."

"Not a dream, Trae, a sharing of minds. We're connected now, son. This is Tabor Reserve. Your mother and I used to bring you here when you were a baby. It was one of our favorite places. Dear Anton, in fact, was conceived out there in that field of flowers. I don't think even you can remember that."

"You're Petyr, not my father."

"Images, images. You have a fixation about that."

"I've seen pictures of my father. I saw his face just before you turned around."

"A face isn't a person. I can be anything I want to be. So can you. Most of life is an illusion we create in our own minds. It helps us hide from reality, which can be far better for us than the illusion if we acknowledge it. I've had many faces, Trae. It's one of the reasons I'm still alive."

"Alive where?" asked Trae. "You ran away, and I only see you in dreams. Is that the reality you mean?"

"I didn't run away. I've always been with you, son; you just didn't know it."

"Not when I'm conscious, no," said Trae sarcastically.

"I don't think that'll be a problem from now on. Here, try one of these." Petyr stacked pieces of something on a plate and brought it over to the table. He put it in front of Trae along with an empty plate, knife and fork. Gobs of burned flesh, it looked like. Petyr served himself, motioned to Trae. "Dig in."

"What is it?" Trae found the faint odor of the food somewhat nauseating.

"Cowry. It's a flightless bird native to Tabor."

"It smells awful. It isn't real, anyway."

Petyr cut off a piece, shoved it into his own mouth, and chewed vigorously. "You're missing something, son, and you need your protein. What kind of meat will you eat?"

"We had fish in the caverns," said Trae.

Petyr waved his fork over the serving plate like it was a magic wand. "Then let it be fish."

The plate blurred, shimmered, cleared again. Where there had been two lumps of blackened flesh were now two slices of golden brown fish, flaky at the touch of a fork.

"Like you said, it isn't real, but eat it anyway," said Petyr.

Trae tried one slice, then the other. It was delicious.

"Of course this is all illusion, manufactured in my own mind and shared only with you this time. No watchers here, except your mother, bless her. She was willing to be a tree just so she could watch over you while we talked, but there are things I cannot allow her to know in the event she's stolen from me by people who'd like to see me dead. There are many such people, Trae, and they'll try to get to me through you if they have the chance. Your life isn't safe."

"The Emperor's police have already tried to kill me," said Trae. "It'll go on until the Emperor is thrown out, but so far I'm getting little help from other worlds, only words of sympathy. The Church of Gan isn't respected; the believers elsewhere consider them extremists."

"Indeed they are," said Petyr, "but they're no longer your problem. There are far greater dangers than the Emperor's police. You've now reached a stage where Immortals scattered across the galaxy might become aware of you. You might have experienced signs of that."

"I've heard voices calling my name. I thought my mission was to find you and save our people on Gan."

"The voices were your mother and I when you came of age. The mental ties are within the family; it's part of our genetics. And you've accomplished your immediate mission well enough."

Petyr swallowed the last of his meat. "Oh, that was good. How was the fish?"

Trae ignored the question and pushed his empty plate away from him. "I've accomplished nothing," he grumbled, "except to nearly get myself killed."

"You've pulled a trigger that will rid Gan of its Emperor. The Church has its own problems to solve if it expects to reintegrate into society there. The Church was not my doing, Trae. All I brought to Gan, all I bring to any planet, is a philosophy. It's not a religion. What the priests call The Source is in all of us; it's a part of us that gives us wisdom and creativity. Our people, yours and mine, learned how to tap its energies fully a long time ago in a place far from here."

"The Immortals," said Trae.

"Not really," said Petyr, speaking for another. "We live a very long time with perfect health, but even so our bodies don't last forever. There is a reincarnation process, but it's artificial. Your mother and I have lived several lifetimes, half of them spent in ships making the transit across this galaxy. You're already in your second life, Trae. You were Anton, our first-born, and your mother died with you in a fire started by the Emperor's troops. I wasn't there, but I experienced it with you. Your death agonies were probably experienced by every Immortal within light years of Gan. Those last moments were lost to you, but not to me, and I've returned them to you. They've been in your dreams since you've been reborn. And our technology has given you and your mother back to me."

"In new bodies."

"Yes."

"My earliest memories of the caverns are from when I was only two years old."

"Physically you were a year old at reincarnation, but only a few memories were introduced then. The process was accelerated after you were six."

Petyr paused, and a frown creased his forehead. "There were not a lot of memories to reintroduce. You were so little when they murdered you."

"What about my mother?"

Now Petyr smiled. "We chose the age of twenty-five. It was a very good year."

"We all have spare bodies lying around, just waiting to be used for reincarnation?"

"Not exactly," said Petyr, and he chuckled. "I'll tell you more later. Total reintegration is complex, and more than a bit traumatic. It's not to be taken lightly. Have you finished eating?"

Trae laughed. "If you say so."

Petyr smiled again. "Doesn't have to be real to be tasty. I want to show you something, and we have to fly there to see it."

"So now you'll conjure up an aircraft for us," said Trae, getting into the spirit of the moment.

Petyr stood up, and Trae with him. "No, just hold out your arms, and follow me."

Petyr held his arms out from his sides at shoulder height, and

Trae did the same. There was an awkward pause, Trae feeling silly, then Petyr rose slowly from the ground, straight up, and Trae, without thinking, was following, and the ground was rushing away beneath him. The rolling hills and fields of flowers extended to each horizon and became a patch of purple as the sky turned to dark, dark blue, then black. The purple patch shrank to a dot, then vanished on the surface of a ball colored in swirls of blue, green and tan and then the ball was a point in a field of black as they rushed higher and higher. Points of blue light appeared in the blackness and then fuzzy wisps in red and green, rushing past them. Trae was exhilarated yet frightened at the same time. All an illusion, he thought. A dream-state, and none of it is really happening.

Petyr seemed to sense his mood. "Relax!" he shouted clearly in the blackness of space. "You've had flying dreams before. Anyone with imagination has had them. Come on, faster. We have a long way to go!"

Stars and nebulae raced by, and ahead the density of stars was increasing, a great ovoid cloud of stars. Lanes of dark dust were like spider web and there was an intensely bright spot in the center of the cloud. They were no longer rising, but descending, and the bright spot grew quickly. Stars and luminous gas flowed past them like mist, and suddenly they were in a clear space and ahead not one, but four points of bright light, close together, and positioned as if on the corners of a square.

Getting closer, Trae saw swirls of stars and dusty gas in tight spirals around each bright point, and in the center of the square another light appeared, glowing green. Petyr pointed at it, looking back at Trae. "The local gate; you can just barely see it now."

The thing was indeed green, an oval shape, pulsing in intensity at a regular rate. Wisps of dust and gas laced its edges, feelers extended to the array of bright points surrounding it.

They slowed and came to a stop in front of the thing. Petyr moved up alongside Trae, put an arm around his shoulders. Trae felt nothing, and Petyr made a grand gesture towards the object in front of them.

"This is where we came from," he said dramatically.

Trae looked at shimmering green, then Petyr. "What?"

"It's a gate, a portal to our universe, son, the universe our people came here from. What the priests call The Immortals didn't originate in this universe, but came through this gate from another one. Your great grandfather came through here, and never had a life outside the ship he was traveling on, even though he lived nearly a dozen normal lifetimes before he chose to end it."

"I don't understand," said Trae. "We're not human?"

"Must be. We can breed with the normal lifetime folks. Nobody knows when the first gates were formed, but the one you're looking at came from your great grandfather's generation once they'd learned to tap vacuum energy.

Trae frowned at him.

"Sorry. It's all part of your education, and it comes soon. The family fortune depends on our knowledge of vacuum-state energy and how to manipulate it. The power is unlimited. Any energy, any mass you want, you can have it. You know what black holes are?"

"Yes."

"There's a really big one on the other side of the gate, in our home universe. It has a mass of a billion stars. Spacetime is highly stressed and we've engineered worm-holes into it, spacetime tunnels so small they penetrate through what's called a brane. It's a boundary between the two universes. Once on this side, four more black holes are arranged to stabilize the exit." Petyr pointed to the four bright points of light nearby. "Black holes evaporate slowly, but the system is dynamic; we have to continually funnel vacuum energy in to keep things stable. Even the spatial arrangement has to be changed, and it's no small chore to move black holes around."

Trae was staring at him, a slight grin on his face.

"What is it?"

Trae smiled. "I think my own imagination is running wild. I'm somehow making it all up in this dream I'm having."

Petyr nodded. "I can understand that. Not a dream, son. You're in my mind right now, seeing what I remember, and we're talking as sure as if we're standing next to each other. Our connection is outside of spacetime. Here's something else for you to disbelieve, but I was there to see it when it happened, and it happens every day we're alive."

Their motion was instantaneous, and away from the yawning, green chasm Petyr called a portal. They rushed in towards one of the bright points of light surrounding it. Details were suddenly there. It was not a single point of light, but a tight vortex of stars, dust and gas, an intense glow at its center. They moved in even closer, and chaos surrounded them, and ahead was a dark spot, then a speck of black near it that seemed to be their target. The speck resolved itself into a sphere, not black but dark brown, connected to a monstrous funnel-shaped thing spewing forth something that blurred the space before it far into the distance.

They drew close. The thing was not small; it was easily the size of a planet, and Petyr sensed Trae's wonderment.

"It's the size of a typical gas giant, around twenty standard-terra masses. It's a ship, Trae. Has a crew of fifty people, and it's only one of ten ships that police the gate and make the necessary adjustments to keep it stable. When I saw it I was a small boy, and it was pushing on that black hole ahead of us, a minor correction, by the looks of it. With a major push the space around us would be so blurred you wouldn't be able to see the ship. It doesn't actually push on the black hole; it produces a localized distortion in spacetime with bursts of vacuum state energy, and the mass sort of rolls along with the distortion. The required power, of course, is incredible. Ninety-eight percent of the ship is field generator to suck up vacuum state energy and redirect it. Impressed?"

"Still hard to believe," said Trae, "but I'm seeing it."

"The technology came from our universe, not this one, son. Your world is even larger than you see here. And there are four gates in this galaxy, not one, all of them near the core center. Even with a vacuum field drive it's typically a fifty-year trip to any of the planetary systems we've occupied here. We're working on that. You'll be working on it, too. The travel time has to be shortened for reasons I'll explain to you. The family fortune is also involved, but mainly we need to be able to respond quickly to whatever comes through the gate, and right now we can't do that."

"Are we in some kind of danger?" asked Trae.

"We could be. Our people have enemies other than the Emperor of Gan, people more powerful than him. I left Gan for a reason. My mission is yet to be accomplished. As we speak I'm on a ship nearing the gate you see before you. Within a year I'll pass through that gate and return to our home universe. There's a political crisis, a bad one, and I'm considered to be the leader of our people in this universe we've migrated to. Some would have it otherwise. They might already have sent agents through the gate to terminate me. That means you could also be in danger. Your mother is with me, and you're the only family member left in this universe. I'll tell you where to go and what to do, and the knowledge you have to have will be fed to you in an unconscious state. The problem you left Gan for is about to be solved. You'll be leaving the local system, and beyond it only a few of our own people will know you're my son. You'll be in charge of the empire I've built there, Trae, even though you're so young. You'll know what to do, and I'll be in constant touch. Other Immortals might contact you from a distance. Be wary of such contacts. Do not let such people know where you are or what you're doing, and right now you're wide open to them. You'll have to learn to mask yourself, and I'll show you how. Oh, this is enough for now. You're stunned; you're not getting all of this."

"I hear you," said Trae, but his mind was whirling.

"Another time. I have less than a year to do all of this. I'm going to let you sleep a deeper sleep so I can start feeding you data on our companies. The tech stuff can come later. Time to go back, and—oh, oh, your mother is here."

The universe was suddenly black, gate, black holes, the great ship and swirling gases all disappearing, and then Trae was back again on a bench looking out on rolling hills and fields of flowers beneath an azure sky. Petyr was sitting across from him, looking sheepish. "I thought she'd be content to just watch this time. Sorry, dear, I wasn't thinking of you."

Petyr disappeared in a blink, and a cool wind brushed Trae's face. The light seemed to dim, and when Trae looked up he saw the sky was darker than before, a hint of purple mixed in with the blue. The fields of flowers were still there, but more mixed now, not just lavender, but splotches of deep red, white, and there were more trees with purple tops.

Out in the fields of flowers someone was standing. She wore a long, white dress, sleeveless, and was waving to him. Even at this distance he could see her hair was blond. He waved back, stood up and went to her through the flowers, feeling his feet pushing aside their stalks, their scent enveloping him. And when he drew near he saw her face, and recognized it.

"Anton," she said, and held out her arms to him.

He felt a compulsion to embrace her, but held back and saw tears well up in her eyes. "My name is Trae," he said.

She came up to him, sliding her arms around his neck and pressing her cheek to his. He felt pressure, but no warmth. "I know it is, but you'll always be Anton to me. And now you're becoming a man."

She took a step back and grasped his arms. "I think you favor your father a bit, but that nose is mine." She smiled. "I've missed you so much. I hope someday you'll understand why we had to leave you. I feel so badly about it, but I have to be with your father, especially now, and you have to carry on for us in the place we really want to be."

"Petyr—Father—he said something about a crisis in your home universe," said Trae. "Right now I'm trying to digest and believe what I've heard. I might be making this all up in my own head."

"You'll accept it all in time, dear," she said, then reached down and took his hand in hers. "Walk with me, now, and tell me all about your life on Gan."

There was no real sense of time. They strolled together, shoulders touching, and Trae's story was a steady stream without conscious voice, a detailed data dump of the experiences of sixteen years in the caverns. When he was finished, the woman he supposed was his true mother pursed her lips in a sad smile.

"No girlfriends? No romantic attachments yet?"

"My friends were few, and there were no girls. The Church doesn't encourage it for people my age."

"Ah, The Church," she said, and sighed. "That was becoming a problem even before we left Gan."

"It advocates belief in The Source, brought to us by The Immortals," said Trae reverently.

She squeezed his hand. "We had nothing to do with the founding of The Church. Your father preached democracy and equal opportunity for everyone during his mission. He wanted all people to recognize and use the natural powers within themselves to make their lives better, and to stop depending on the grace of rulers who only stole from them. The concept of 'The Source' was invented by a few ambitious men who obtained power by making up a new religion, and sad to say they were successful."

The sky suddenly darkened. Trae looked up and saw that a dense cloud had covered up the sun, but even as he watched, the cloud slid away and the sky was bright again.

"Sorry," she said, "but the subject of The Church makes me angry. We objected to it from the start, but the instigators only tried to pacify us by making us out as some kind of superbeings. What non-sense. If there *is* a God, we're certainly not it. It's our technology that allows us to do what we do, and that's a product of our own brains and hard work. Nothing has ever been given to us through worship or prayer to the so-called 'Source.'"

Trae was struck mute, and looked down at the ground. They walked in silence a few steps, and then she squeezed his hand again.

"I know I've offended you, but it had to be said. There will be more to your education than technical matters. Try not to hate me for it."

Still stunned, Trae said nothing. A few more steps and she stopped, grasped his arms and turned him around to face her.

"Trae, look at me."

He did so, his eyes moving slowly upwards to meet hers.

"I'm your mother, and I love you with all my heart, but I have very little time before I leave my only child in another universe, at least for a while. Your father and I are going back to a bad situation, and the only reason I'm even with him is because of the political influence of my family. I have to be there. You have to be here. You have to take charge of our affairs here, and be ready to react to any negative consequences in our political maneuverings. Billions of lives could be at stake, and I don't want your judgement being clouded by religious teachings you've learned as a child. Your father can stuff you full of technical and business information, but your use of it must be realistic and practical and free of religious dogma that doesn't apply to the vast majority of people in all universes. Do you understand what I'm saying?"

She shook him for emphasis, and tears welled in her eyes.

"I don't see how my belief in 'The Source' can hurt anything I do in everyday life. How can faith, trust and love hurt anything?" said Trae.

The woman who called herself his mother released him. For a long moment they just stood there looking at each other. She wiped her eyes with a hand, finally, and said, "I guess you'll have to learn as you go along, and that's the hard way. I can only hope we all survive it. We'll talk another time, because your father is aching to get back to you with all his technical data. But before I go, I need to know one thing: do you remember me at all, from when you were little—before your rebirth, I mean?"

"I remember your face—in—dreams." He told her about the dreams, the big bed, the ornately carved door in his room. The fire.

"They locked us in, and the house burned down around us," she said. "I don't remember the end of it; they told me they found us together on your bed, all charred. I'd covered you with my own body, trying to protect you. At least I was spared a direct memory of it. It doesn't haunt me so much that way."

Now tears were streaming down her face. She hugged him and buried her face in his shoulder. Trae stood there stiffly, not knowing what to do.

"We're reborn and hardly know each other, but you're still my Anton and I love you," she sobbed.

"I know," said Trae, and immediately felt stupid. There was more he should say, more he should feel, but couldn't. The woman was a vague memory from a dream. He didn't know her.

A voice came out of the clear sky, saving him. "Tatjana darling—give him time. This is all a huge revelation. The poor lad is paralyzed by all of it, so let him rest a bit. Besides, there are other things he has to assimilate before he wakes."

She kissed his cheek, stepped back and sniffed once, then wiped her eyes again with her hand. She looked a bit angry as her eyes moved away from Trae's. "Very well, but next time I'll not give up so easily. Next time I'll have him know his own mother, even if it means you have less time with him."

The woman nodded curtly to Trae, and her image faded to nothingness, as if she'd been a projection on a screen of air.

"She's going to be very angry with me," said a voice behind Trae, "but it won't be the first time."

Trae jerked around in surprise. Petyr was standing there, now dressed in a dark business suit, strange looking and out of place in a field of flowers. "A mother's love for her only son extends across an eternity, Trae. Be good to her, as good as you can, until you get to know her again. The two of you are all the family I really have in this universe. Now, however, it's time to get down to business. I'm going to let you go into rem sleep for half an hour or so, then bring you up a bit and begin feeding you data. At the same time I'll do a bit of downloading to update my records of your memories and experiences. Make sure your guardian, whose image I'm using without permission, does the same as soon as you wake up. Updates will be necessary every night from now on until I tell you otherwise. This is important, Trae. Don't miss a single update. I can already hear your question about memory updates. Ask your guardian. His instructions are being supplemented as we speak. No more talk; time for you to sleep. I'll return soon."

Trae opened his mouth to speak—and went away somewhere.

If there were more dreams, and likely there were, he didn't remember them. He awoke on his bed, staring up at a white ceiling. There was a faint buzzing sound. He turned his head, realized the buzzing was coming from an open briefcase on a table in one corner of the room. The table lamp was lit. On the bed next to his lay Petyr, on his back, breathing deeply, and the man's eyes were moving beneath his eyelids. Trae watched him for several minutes, then lay back and tried to recall everything that had happened in his dream. It was all there, in detail, total clarity. Not like a dream at all.

A sudden, rattling intake of breath, and Petyr woke up. He sat up and rubbed his eyes, looked over at Trae. "Get up. I have to test you again," he commanded, and swung his legs off the bed. "Now."

Petyr went to the recording instruments in the briefcase and fiddled with them while Trae got up. "You said you were monitoring the effects of little machines in my body, but it's more than that, isn't it? You didn't tell me the truth, Petyr."

"It was truth as far as it went. Sit down here. We need to do this quickly. No drugs this time."

Trae sat down in a chair by the table, and Petyr hooked him up in the usual way. "You're scanning my memories up to this moment, even private things," he said. The thought made him feel a bit angry, even violated.

"Welcome to the world of The Immortals," said Petyr. His fingers moved over a small keyboard. The buzzing became a sing-songy pattern of sound, but otherwise Trae was not aware of anything unusual happening. The sound stopped. "Done. I'll make copies of this one. Four, I think."

The man was talking to himself. "How did you know that had to be done as soon as I woke up?"

"I had my instructions," said Petyr. "Anyway, I was sure we'd have to do it after you took that huge dose of whatever it is they gave you. I've just had some revelations myself, Trae."

"Baloney. You knew exactly what had to be done before I even said anything."

"Instinct. I have a lot of experience with this." Petyr bent over the briefcase, took out four data-cubes and put them into storage boxes on the table.

"You were told what to do. You know what just happened to me. I think you were there. I think you were still there when I woke up. Maybe you even know what just got stuffed into my head. I've never felt so alert in my life."

Petyr closed the briefcase after depositing two of the cubes into it. The other two he put into his pocket. "What you just experienced changes a lot of things, and yes, I was there. It's my privilege as a soldier of The Church."

"If you were there then you know what my father thinks of The Church. You're there for another reason, and I want to know what it is. Why are you so important to my father, other than just protecting his son? And why does my father use your image every time we meet in dreamland? You never give me an answer to this, and I'm tired of being lied to, Petyr. Don't you care?"

Trae stood up, glaring at his guardian of sixteen years. Petyr gave a big sigh as Trae turned and stepped back to his bed.

"Of course I care," said Petyr, and then there was a long pause.

"I'm your father, Trae."

Trae sat down hard on the bed.

CHAPTER 11

This is too sudden," said Khalid Osman, ruler of all Gan. "I've heard no rumors regarding overtures from Galena, and I've certainly not had their support on The Council."

"I agree, sire," said Fedor Quraiwan. "My inquires suggest the initiative has been sparked by several prominent businessmen on Gan who wish to have open access to Galena ports."

Breakfast had been served in the Emperor's private quarters: a meal of fruit, fish, eggs and a doughy flatbread laced with honey. Now they sipped a new tea with a flowery scent to begin their day.

"Ah, the name Azar Khalil comes to mind," said Khalid.

"He seems to be pushing the hardest, sire, but there are others."

"All of them in munitions industries, of course." The Emperor smiled. "This could be a subtle way to suggest I reduce port taxes. I might even consider it."

"It's more than that, sire. Our ports haven't been renovated for over a decade. They can't handle the new freighters being used for interplanetary transport. It's not just size; they're much too close to population centers. The renovation costs are prohibitive, sire. It would be to our advantage to entertain any commercial overtures from Galena, and could also reduce the tensions between us."

"I doubt that. We'll never agree on how to rule an ignorant people. If Azar and his colleagues want better relations with Galena I won't interfere with their efforts."

"Underway, sire. Meetings are being arranged at the Galenan embassy for microwave conversations with their Economic Minister. I've been promised an invitation, but that's weeks away."

"You were going to tell me about this, of course," said Khalil.

"I just have, sire. I've only had reason to consider matters seriously in recent days. They were only rumors, but then Azar himself called to brief me, and my people reported increased traffic at the embassy. Several new people have arrived."

"More spies, perhaps. That seems to be the major function of the foreign embassies on our world these days." Khalil took another sip of tea and wiped his mouth daintily with a napkin.

"Azar says they are staff members from the economic ministry."

"I'll expect you to verify that soon, my friend. So much seems to be happening without my knowledge. Azar and I used to communicate rather freely when I was more involved in everyday affairs, but that was before I turned things over to people like you."

"You know what I know, sire, but I try not to give you information that's false or misleading. Even this tea we're drinking has been thoroughly checked. Mountain tea from Galena, a gift from Azar Khalil; he wants to begin importing it. I've tasted nothing more flavorful, sire. Do you agree?"

"A heady aroma," said Khalid. "Three cups I've had before hearing the origin of the product. And just how was it tested for safety?"

"There was only a single box of it, and I've taken the liberty of drinking small samples over the past two days. You trust your tasters more than I do, sire."

Khalid smiled. "You have a suspicious nature, Fedor."

Fedor gave him a nodding bow. "I'm well rewarded for my suspicions. Tea is the least of them. The Lyraen cells have been unusually quiet lately, and then yesterday my people found the body of a priest floating in a canal. His lower legs were gone, and the front of his head had been blown away by a high caliber weapon. He'd likely been weighted down to submerge him, but it looks like scavenger fish chewed away the legs and set him free."

"Your assassins were careless, then," said Khalid.

"But it's not my doing. The priest was one of my moles in a cell headquartered near the palace. He called me a week ago to arrange a meeting, but didn't show up. He had something important to tell me, and was killed for it. The other moles have heard nothing. This worries me, sire. I'm investigating it further; terrorist activities by the Lyraens might be planned to disturb our talks with Galena. The Lyraens are everywhere, even in the embassies. They're replaced as fast as I can ferret them out."

"When I'm sure you've identified all the cells I'll make my move,

Fedor. Their heads will decorate our streets on posts for all to see, and I expect that will be soon."

Fedor shook his head. "It's difficult. There is a central intelligence that coordinates the cells, and not even the Lyraens have a clue to its identity. I fear it's not within the common people, but highly placed. We must find the head of the snake before striking at its tail. Please be patient with me."

"I'm a patient man, Fedor," said the ruler of all Gan.

"Of course, sire," said his servant, and swallowed the rest of his tea in one gulp.

The Embassy of Galena was three blocks from the palace, the most prominent among its neighbors, a three-storied structure with many windows and a collanaded portico at the front entrance. A ten-foot steel bar fence surrounded the grounds of green grass and manicured flowerbeds and there was a gate with a guardhouse and two armed guards. Two other guards continually patrolled the periphery of the fenced area, their rifles slung casually, but their eyes alert.

A black limousine pulled up in front of the guardhouse and three men got out of it. Two of the men were young, but wore expensive business suits. The third was older, tall, with snow-white hair. The men presented their papers at the guardhouse, A call was made, and the guard opened the gate for them. They walked directly to the front entrance of the embassy, where another guard met them at the door and again checked their papers before letting them go inside.

They deposited their coats on a table in a high-ceilinged foyer, a broad, black-marble staircase winding up to the higher floors. An elderly butler appeared on the first landing of the stairs and gestured for them to follow him. They climbed two flights to a long hallway and were ushered into a dimly lit meeting room with a long table in dark polished wood, and a dozen chairs around it. A bottle of spring water and a goblet were at each place.

They sat down and waited silently for only a moment before another door opened and three other men came in to sit opposite them at the table. Two wore officers' uniforms of the Galenan Marine Corps, and the third, middle-aged, wore a black suit. The older man spoke first.

"I hope you gentlemen had a pleasant trip."

The two young men opposite him nodded politely without a word.

"No names are necessary, Azar. I don't know these people. I've never seen them."

"I understand, Mister Ambassador," said Azar Khalil. "I provided their lodging last night, but assume you'll keep them here until the operation is complete. This is the last of the team members." He smiled, and ran the long fingers of one hand through his thick, white hair.

The ambassador made a phone call and a butler appeared. "This man will see you to your quarters, gentlemen." He waved his hand in dismissal and the two young men went away with the butler. "Military assassins are sometimes necessary, but always disturbing. I've seen such cold, cold eyes before." The ambassador sat down again and faced the man across from him.

Internally, the Galenan Ambassador to Gan shuddered. There was something predatory about Azar Khalil. Like the young ones who'd arrived with him it was mostly the eyes, so dark brown they were nearly black, and wide-spaced in a gaunt, bloodless face. "The team will be housed here. There will be no further contact between us until after the evacuation of the team. In the meantime, our people will quietly circulate stories verifying your importance in the economic initiatives being made. It should help to cement relations with your colleagues so they'll back you when the time comes."

"They support me now," said Azar. "They depend on me."

The ambassador's heart skipped a beat. "Dependence can change. An ally one minute can be an enemy the next. We're depending on you to restore friendship between Gan and Galena, and to run a democratic state here. Don't think for one minute that what's about to happen to an hereditary Emperor can't happen to you." His face flushed in embarrassment at his own directness, but it was a thing that needed to be said. "Even The Church won't lift a finger to help you if you fail us."

Azar blinked slowly. "Threats are not necessary, Mister Ambassador. I'll not fail The Church, but enhance it. A democracy cannot function without a spiritual core for its people. The Church could not have existed without my support during increased oppression by the present regime. That oppression was a crime against the human spirit." His voice raised in pitch with unusual passion for a man of his stature and influence.

"I agree," said the ambassador, "but we want stability here, and a stop to the proliferation of weapons of destruction. The Galenan market will give you more profits than you have now, and with only a fifth of your weapons production."

"I'll devote many of my facilities to the reconstruction of Gan. There will be a home for every person. That is my promise. I know you don't like me, Mister Ambassador. I'm not sure why. Perhaps it's the way I've made my fortune. I do not crave power or fortune; I already have those things. What I do crave is the opportunity to better the lives of people subjected to the long rule of a selfish ruler, and I will do that if I'm given the chance. That alone is my ambition."

The black eyes narrowed, an intense stare the ambassador felt to the core of his soul. There was power in the man, and a will of steel. He would accomplish whatever he set out to do. But could he be controlled?

"When it comes to the election we can do no more than support a candidate who will make you seem desirable to the common people. We can do nothing obvious to help."

"My organization is already in place, and a constitution is being written. We'll be ready. Is there anything else?"

"No. My staff has prepared a small lunch for us. The economic ministry has sent along a gift of flowers which grow from seed to maturity in days, and there's a list of Galenan industries you might consider for the new construction on Gan."

Azar smiled. "I appreciate your hospitality, Mister Ambassador. You're most kind."

A butler arrived without a command and led them to a small dining room with linen-covered tables where they had a meal of fish with mustard sauce and accompanied by white rice and delicious tea smelling like flowers. And then there was a gift of real flowers, large, orange blooms shaped like teacups on thick stalks covered with razor-edged thorns covered with thin plastic for safety. Their scent was delicate, with a hint of cinnamon. Azar accepted them graciously, but declined to discuss business, and took with him the documents sent by the Economic Ministry of Galena.

Parting was friendly, though Azar knew the ambassador still harbored suspicions about him, but his good mood was shaken by what happened as he was getting back into his limousine. He'd been holding his flowery gift carefully, feeling their sharp points through the plastic wrap. As he leaned into the car his hand hit the top of the door, jolting the flowers from his grip. Instinctively he reached to grab them as they fell. His driver also reached for them, and they caught the flowers simultaneously, the driver pulling back as Azar gripped the stalks hard. Pain made him cry out as a thorn penetrated the wrapping and tore a horrible gash in the palm of his hand. Blood went everywhere, his clothes, the door, and the back seat of the car. His driver was near panic, and wanted to seek help in the embassy.

Azar forbade it. "I'll not embarrass my host, and you'll say nothing about this accident. Just clean up the car when I'm home."

He wrapped his hand in a handkerchief and squeezed it hard. In a few minutes the handkerchief was soaked red in blood, but the pain was gone. The driver drove him home quickly, kept looking back, but Azar kept his hand down where he couldn't see it. He ordered the man away and went inside the main house where a servant brought him water, bandages and gauze for his wound. By the time he washed it out the bleeding had stopped, and Azar thought he could see strands of undamaged tendon deep in the cavity. He wrapped it carefully, and retired to his study for work before and after a light dinner.

Bedtime was early, since he habitually arose before sunrise. He unwrapped his hand, then, and inspected the wound. The cavity was completely filled with new tissue, and the edges of it were sealing before his eyes. There would soon be a scar, but that would be gone by morning.

As he expected.

The underground church of the faithful had survived for years by its own wits, and intelligence provided by the external community. Money also arrived regularly to fund their operations, delivered to cell headquarters in neatly packed cardboard boxes filled with used, unmarked currency. Best efforts had failed to locate the source of the funds, or to identify the callers from unlisted numbers who regularly fed them intelligence, particularly on movements and plans of the Emperor's secret police. They'd been saved by this intelligence on several occasions, and had learned to trust it. They'd also learned not to question the monies they received to keep The Church alive. It was clear their benefactors were wealthy, highly placed citizens who in a clandestine way were expressing their belief and faith in The Source. Pet names had been developed for them over the years, the most active caller a man they called Faith, a man who'd himself suggested the name as a token of his commitment to The Source of All Energies.

It was Faith who called near midnight only three weeks after Joseph had shot the traitor Abelius in the back of the head and become cell rector in his place. Joseph himself received the call.

"Ah, Joseph, I have something important for you. For your ears only, as a soldier of The Church."

"I'm listening. No one is here with me at the moment."

"Another traitor has been found in our midst. His capture offers us the opportunity to strike the first blow for our freedom."

"A priest?"

"No, a worker, a mechanic servicing trucks for another cell in your area. He somehow learned the locations of several garages for our transportation and was caught setting up an information drop with our old friend Fedor Quraiwan. He's only blocks from your location."

"So why call me? Kill the man, and be done with it."

"As you so efficiently did with your late colleague, a bit hastily perhaps. We missed an opportunity then to track down the location of Quraiwan's intelligence center outside the palace and eliminate the man. Now we have another opportunity. My suggestion is we allow the man to make the drop and follow him or his contact to Quraiwan's street headquarters. We know he routinely receives information before business hours in the morning. We thought he was using a cleaning establishment, but that has proven to be no longer true. This is a one-man operation, and requires a true Soldier of The Church."

"Me," said Joseph.

"That is correct. I'll give you an address. If you leave now you'll have time to interrogate the prisoner and go with him on the drop. If The Source is with you, Quraiwan will be dead before sunrise."

"He'll only be replaced."

"That will not be so simple. The police will be in disarray for weeks. A revolution is coming, Joseph, and soon. You will fire the first shots in the war for our freedom."

"A suggestion, or an order?"

There was a short pause, then, "If you wish, it is an order."

Joseph felt the short hairs stir on the back of his neck. "Then give me the address."

It was given, along with a signal for identity, and Joseph hung up without a reply. The coldness of the man's voice was somehow gratifying, the willingness to kill for The Church, something he shared. He went to his room and selected a heavy caliber handgun, bulky, but balanced and vented to minimize recoil of the four-fifty-five caliber projectile.

It was after midnight when he exited to an alley through a side door of the garage. He dressed in workman's clothes: heavy overalls, heavy coat and a cap with a bill down to his eyebrows. The garage of the other cell was only blocks away, and he was there in ten minutes, keeping to side streets and alleyways. Next to a baffle, pull-down door was an entrance marked "Office." He knocked softly on it, put his ear to the door and knocked again.

"What?" came a muffled voice.

"Joseph. Faith called me."

The door opened, and it was dark inside. Joseph stepped in with trust, for his weapon was not yet loaded and locked. "Keep going straight ahead," said a voice.

A door opened, and there was bright light. A burly man motioned him through the doorway. It was an office, a desk heaped with papers, three chairs. Two men stood over a young kid sitting in one of the chairs. The kid took one look at Joseph and blanched white as a ghost. "No! I said I'd cooperate. I won't give anything away. You promised!"

"Promised what?" said Joseph, and then the other men looked nervously at each other, eyes darting.

"He lives if he leads you to Quraiwan."

"He's a traitor," said Joseph.

"They threatened my family. They said they'd kill them all if I didn't cooperate," whined the kid.

Can't be more than fifteen, thought Joseph. "How'd they find out you're in the underground?"

"I don't *know*!" said the kid, and tears welled up in his eyes.

Joseph bit his lip. "You know where Quraiwan is?"

"No, but I make the drops and someone picks them up. I can tell you where it is and when and you can follow whoever makes the pick up."

"You ever see the guy?"

"No."

"So when's the next drop?"

The kid looked at a clock on the wall. "Three hours; it's at four. I have to be there exactly at four." His breathing seemed to ease, now, as he calmed down.

"Tell me where it is." Unlike the terrified kid, the other men only looked at him darkly, and he sensed their fear.

The kid told him what he needed. "I'm leaving now. You won't see me when you get there. You do anything that looks or sounds like a warning and I'll blow you to pieces. Understand?"

The kid nodded his head rapidly, eyes wide.

Joseph left the room in deathly silence. The door to outside was open for him; he walked to it through a darkened room. "Good hunting," said a voice in the darkness, and the door closed behind him.

Again he kept to side streets and darkened alleyways. It was a twenty minute walk and he was nearly delayed when two toughs came out of an alley and blocked the sidewalk in front of him. Joseph's steps did not miss a beat. His hand flashed to his waistband and came up clutching his weapon, loaded and locked, the hammer back. "I will kill you," he snarled, and the men jumped away from him and into the street, a knife clattering to the pavement. He passed them without looking back; if they even said anything he would come back and kill them, but they were mute.

He came to the site of the drop: a wire-mesh trash can at the head of an alley next to a neighborhood grocery. A light glowed dimly in the back of the store's interior. Above it and along either side were cheap apartments, lights glowing in a few windows even at this hour. Joseph melded into the shadows at an entrance to one building and waited. The watch for any movement along the street or above it kept him alert for nearly three hours. It was cold and damp, but he didn't feel it. There was nothing he could feel but anticipation.

The kid arrived exactly on time. He carried a white paper bag with him and casually dropped it into the trash-can as he passed by. Did a good job of keeping his head down and not looking around to see where Joseph might be. In minutes he was out of sight.

Joseph waited again, prepared for a long one, and was surprised when only a few minutes later a man appeared at the alley's entrance by the trashcan, took three steps from it and retrieved the bag left by the kid. Immediately he stepped back into the shadows of the alley and was gone.

Oh, oh, a bad situation. Joseph had to cross the street first, and his target could be watching from the darkness. He froze in place, his senses acute for any sound, scent, or motion. He was rewarded with a faint thud coming from the alley. The man was moving. Joseph sprinted across the street on cat's feet, body scraping stone as he flowed around a corner into darkness. Light came from a street at the other end of the alley and a shadow moved there, away from him. When it turned the corner, Joseph sprinted again.

His target had doubled back in the direction from which the kid had come. The street was dimly lit and Joseph darted from shadow to shadow, his target looking back several times. But the distance he had to follow him was mercifully short. The man went to a doorway, and next to it another man stepped out of the shadows and unlocked the door for him. They both went inside, and came out again moments later after Joseph had moved to an entryway only a dozen steps away. His target walked away, and the white bag was no longer in his hand. The other man stepped back into the shadows. Joseph waited a few minutes, then shuffled slowly down the street, his head swaying drunkenly from side to side. His gun was back in his waistband, safety on, hammer at half-cock. The man guarding the door did not move, but Joseph knew exactly where he was, and reaching his position, stumbled into him hard.

"Hey!" The man was heavy, his neck thick, but Joseph's arm was a steel snake around his throat, knuckles of his other hand digging into the carotid artery. The man thrashed for only seconds, then slumped, and Joseph snapped his neck with a single, violent twist.

It took him four tries to find the key that fit the door. Every little scratching sound made the hair on his arms rise, but the door itself opened quietly. It was gloomy inside, a set of stairs rising to a landing where a single bulb hung from the ceiling. Amazed, he heard music, a violin playing something classical.

Weapon in hand, he ascended the stairs sideways, back to the wall. There was only one door at the top of the stairs, the music coming from beyond it. *Too easy*, he thought. *It can't be this easy.*

He swallowed hard, gun leveled, boldly turned the doorknob and the door opened. Before he was inside, an angry voice said, "What's wrong now! I'm trying to—"

Fedor Quraiwan was sitting at a desk in an otherwise bare room. Music came from a recorder on his desk, sitting next to a white paper bag, and the man had been reading from a small sheet of paper. He took one look at Joseph, and his eyes got very large.

"Greetings from The Source," said Joseph, and shot him three times through his left chest, the explosions deafening in the small room.

Quraiwan tipped over backwards off his chair, slid on the floor and banged into the wall. In a minute he was lying in a pool of blood. Joseph waited until satisfied with the size of the pool, then picked up his empty cartridge cases and left the room.

The street was still silent, and no lights had come on in any windows. Joseph walked quickly and retraced his steps back to the garage where he'd interviewed the young traitor to The Church. He was let in as before. Two men and the kid waited for him, as before. "It's done," he said. "Quraiwan is dead. Do not go out on the street for any reason. There might be retaliations."

"The boy is the only one known to them," said a man. "We can have him out of the city before dawn."

"They don't even know my real name," said the kid. "My aunt has a farm fifty miles from here. They'll never find me there."

"I don't think so," said Joseph, and instantly the kid was panicked.

"What do you mean? I did what you said, and you got Quraiwan. You promised to get me out of here!"

"I promised nothing, and neither did The Church. The promises came from these ignorant men who should know better."

"Now wait a minute," said one man as Joseph drew his gun from his waistband. "You have no authority in this cell."

"You're not even a priest," said the other man. The kid made a squeak, and backed up against a wall.

"We make no promises to traitors in The Church," said Joseph, and he shot the kid through the heart with a single round. The body crashed to the floor and a great, red oval framed a single hole in the wall.

"Whoever you think you are, there's gonna be a reckoning for that when the right people know what you did."

Joseph put his weapon back in his waistband. "Better you worry about the reckoning for what you were about to do," he said.

He turned his back on the men, and the gore in the room, and left them without fear of his own safety, a true Soldier of The Church.

CHAPTER 12

I don't believe you," said Trae. "My father's somewhere near the galactic core, and you're right here."

"True," said Petyr, and smiled faintly. "Mysterious it is, but I'm still your father. Not complete, of course. I don't get the regular upgrades you get, but I just got a big one while you were strolling in the flowers. We're all copies, Trae. The originals have long since died one way or another."

The man was excited, gesturing with his hands as he spoke. Trae had never seen him so animated.

Petyr sat down on the edge of the bed next to him, leaned until their shoulders touched. "Here's the wonder. I'm only two days older than you. I was cloned to watch over you, two days before little Anton was reborn. Actually, you were six months old at birth."

"I'm a clone?" said Trae.

"Of Anton, yes, but modified. Anton would not have looked exactly like you, just like I don't look like the previous clone of your traveling father. Our identities are changed. They're constantly changing. We're partially loaded with genetics, memories and experiences of people we're similar to. We're new people, Trae; that's the secret of The Immortals, that and all the nanochemistry inside us. Our bodies last a long time, but even nanomachines can't repair random DNA damage. Our neural nets are scanned regularly to update our cortical files. When we die we're cloned at centers all over the known universe. Some of us are even placed in good families of normal people, but there's always a watcher."

A pause, then Trae was startled when Petyr put an arm around him. "I was your watcher, Trae. Your father never left you." He squeezed Trae's shoulder. "Well, I guess a piece of him did. I didn't really know who I was until a few minutes ago. I guess it's safe to know, now that we're off Gan.

"The memories I've had are from a priest Leonid Zylak knew on his homeworld when he was a young man. The priest was a militant who fought corruption in The Church. I had no context for the memories; for me, it all happened on Gan when The Church was young. Leonid just now gave me two lifetimes of his own memories, up to the time you were born. I'm two people: Leonid Zylak, and an unnamed priest."

Petyr shook his head slowly in wonderment. "I'm a father," he said softly.

"And an Immortal," said Trae.

"Not quite. I received nanochemistry at birth, but nothing since then. I don't have your enhanced neural network, but my health has been perfect. I might have suspected something, but didn't. Leonid seemed amused he fooled me so good, but he was serious about the fact I'm the part of him he left behind to take care of you."

"Two fathers?" mumbled Trae.

"Maybe more," said Petyr. "It's Leonid Zylak who has to go through that gate and solve whatever crisis exists in the home universe. He didn't tell me a thing about it. He *did* tell me what we're supposed to do next. How about you?"

The knowledge came to Trae without conscious effort. "We're going to Elderon and the Zylak corporate headquarters. That's over two years travel from here."

"Time to prepare for what you have to do. Pulling antimatter and other exotic stuff out of the vacuum of space does not sound like a simple task."

Trae shook his head, and felt a first twinge of the excitement that would continue with him until the end of his life. "Easier than you might think, but even with all the tech stuff I just got, I don't have the slightest idea about how I'm going to build a vacuum-state energy drive small enough to fit in a regular space vessel. And be able to generate enough energy to move a planet? Why would we even want to do that?"

"Ask him, Trae. Within a few months he'll be gone from this universe."

Suddenly Trae could accept all of it. He leaned against Petyr. "You'll still be here," he said, then smiled, and shook his head. "It

sort of comes together, now. I thought my father had run away, abandoned me. It made me angry, Petyr. When I was little, I wished that
you were my father. Guess I finally got my wish."

The soft squeeze of a hand on his shoulder was reassuring.

"You have a family, Trae, and maybe someday you'll meet all of
them," said Petyr.

CHAPTER 13

The great ship plowed through swirling dust and gas where pressure waves began to distinguish between the core and the great spiral arms of the galaxy. To the naked eye it was like a great comet, a small, rocky planet-sized nucleus with tails of dust and gas, a great halo and bow shock where the electromagnetic shield ionized and dispersed particles rushing past at near light speed.

Far beyond the vision of a human eye was the light-year-long, bright tail of a vacuum energy drive, exotic particles and their cousins giving themselves back to the false vacuum of their birth. Beyond the bow shock, at energies going back to the beginning of time, a stressed space-time glowed dully as particles once virtual were ripped forth to power the great ship.

The tiny fraction of the ship that served as living quarters for crew and passengers was larger than a major city, and built in seven radial layers, like an onion. Its occupants numbered in the thousands: crew members and their families, mostly, and only a few hundred passengers who had enough leisure time or interest to enjoy the views as they neared the portal to their home universe. Many had been gone for a short while. Others, like Leonid and Tatjana Zylak, had been gone several lifetimes, for they were missionaries to this universe, and it had taken a crisis to bring them back to their true home.

Leonid had worked late in the ship's environmental cycle, and the red lights of evening were already on when he left his office. Tatjana hadn't waited dinner for him, had left a list of places she might be when he got home to their suite of rooms near the shopping and arts quad on level five. The stores were closed, and nothing was playing at the theatres this evening. This left the exercise rooms and the many observation lounges on level seven. People were gathering there even now to witness their passage through the great portal to home. It was the end of a long journey, and a time for celebration, and everyone was in a festive mood. Everyone was going home.

He finally found Tatjana in the second lounge he visited. She was sitting by herself in a dark corner, nursing a tall drink made in layers that looked like a rainbow. Conversations were quiet in this lounge, everyone gazing up at the big video screen over the bar. He sat down beside her, put an arm warmly around her shoulders, felt pleasure when she leaned her head against him.

"Sorry I was so late," he said.

Tatjana sipped her drink through a blue crystal straw. "No matter. I wasn't hungry anyway. I'm not as excited as I should be about going home. I miss Anton."

Leonid kissed the top of her head and squeezed her shoulder gently. "It's Trae, dear. I don't want to leave either, but I couldn't let you go back alone. Besides, I have to defend the mission or the Council will simply abandon it and close the portal, or allow the Conglomerates to take the colonies over."

Tatjana pointed at the video screen over the bar. "It won't be long. I can remember when I would cry with joy to see that sight. Remember?"

"Yes," said Leonid. It had been over a hundred years and two clones ago, though his beloved had looked the same as she did now. Young missionaries on a quest in a strange universe with hard living conditions, and she had cried herself to sleep for several nights, wanting to go home.

The portal seemed alive on the screen, swirling green in vortices at the edges of the vertical ovoid, layers of yellow and red in bubbling depths. Still unstable, of course, as the planet-sized maintenance ships appearing as black specks focused a trickle of the very expansion energy of the universe to distort spacetime and move the portal's black holes into an optimal configuration. Leonid had a sudden, naughty thought, something he hoped might lighten her spirit.

"If I were in a festive mood, and maybe a bit drunk, I might describe that thing as the mother of all vaginas," he whispered.

Tatjana giggled, and her eyes flashed when she looked up at him. This made him happy. "I do see the resemblance, dear," she murmured.

They went back to their quarters and for the next two hours forgot all about what they were leaving behind or what they were facing in a universe that had once been their home but now might be hostile to them. And the few times Tatjana cried out, it was not in sadness.

They had experienced transition before, and unlike spacetime jumps in normal space it was not particularly disturbing to the senses. People were encouraged to be asleep during a spacetime jump, since the folding of space produced a discontinuity in time perceived as an event lapse by the brain. People in a conscious state suffered chaotic daydreams and hallucinations that seemed to go on for hours, but in fact only lasted seconds as the brain searched for a new reference point in time. Very disturbing. Transition, on the other hand, involved no trauma except to those subject to seizure in the presence of flickering lights. In transition, one only passed through the brane separating one universe from another, a single pore of the brane magnified hugely to accommodate passage. No discontinuities, since space and time for both universes melded together smoothly at each point on the surface of the brane.

Transition was nonetheless a spectacular event; the energies used to create a portal made memorable displays of ionized gases in the molecular clouds that often accompanied clusters of black holes. People bought and saved recordings of their transition adventures to show to their grandchildren, since each portal was different and any given portal changed from day to day.

People crowded to the bar as transition occurred, but Leonid and Tatjana sat in their corner, sharing a rainbow drink. One thump was felt through the floor as a tug-ship nudged them into an optimal position at the last moment, and then the flickering ovoid was swallowing them up. Gas flowed by, a myriad of bright colors, not rapid but steady, a vague impression of walls, like a tunnel. Ahead of them was flickering yellow, orange and red, and then a dark spot appeared, rushing towards them, then not a spot but an ovoid in black and then bright points of light and diaphanous clouds in red and green.

They were through. They were home. People applauded, and cheered, but Leonid and Tatjana sat quietly and finished their drink. They went back to their quarters for sleep before beginning to pack their things. It was only two days before their vessel would reach the border world of Cay Benz, where they would present their papers and be assigned a ship home. A delegation from Kratola was scheduled to meet them there, arranged for them by Tatjana's family.

They were excited about going home after such a long time, but wondered how terribly things could have changed there.

CHAPTER 14

Trae was nearing his twentieth birthday when they reached Elderon.

It was a blue world, with a single continent and a myriad of small islands dotting an azure sea. There was one season, the climate mild. This was due to the planet's circular orbit around a G3 star, and a rotational axis that was perpendicular to the plane of the ecliptic. No moon graced the sky, but the atmosphere was pristine and tight regulations kept light pollution to a minimum in the coastal cities. Young mountain ranges with sharp peaks separated the cities from the interior of the continent, a vast high plateau virtually unpopulated. One large river running north to south cut the continent nearly in half and was fed by a spider web of streams from glacial lakes high in the mountains. Along this river, slightly north of the continental center, a single sign of habitation could be seen: a scattering of buildings surrounded by a sprawl of family dwellings, acres of green fields stretching south along the river. Unseen from the sky were the millions of acres of underground steel and concrete that was the bulk of a substantial city.

It was the first city of The Immortals, had been the first permanent settlement of those adventurers and missionaries who'd penetrated the brane to discover new worlds, and who had found people biologically like themselves on the other side.

The debate on Kratola had raged for centuries, yet questions remained unanswered. The Immortals, as far as they knew, had constructed the first branegates to the neighboring universe, and people had been waiting for them, their DNA identical except for the number of random defects, especially seen in mitochrondrial studies. If one accepted these studies, then the ancestors of The Immortals had evolved more recently than those of the native people in this universe. The difference in the times of their origins was over a hundred thousand years, well before the first recordings of history in The Immortals' worlds. It seemed unlikely that random chemical reactions could produce identical species in any two universes; the currently favored theory was that another race, far older, had populated both universes, perhaps many others, leaving its seed to propagate at its own rate and fashion.

The hundred thousand year time difference might even explain why the settled worlds in this universe were so much farther away from the galactic core than were the worlds of The Immortals in their home universe. When Trae ran the numbers in his head they made sense, for without any spacetime jumps, unknown to the worlds of the Emperors' League, it had taken him over four years to travel only two light years.

The time had gone quickly, his life planned for him by his fathers. The technology of three hundred years had been squeezed into every dendritic link in his brain, but Petyr had also downloaded it all to cube in more organized pieces. The collection had grown to over a thousand of them: mathematics, physics, nanochemistry, economics, business, the history of two universes—these were only a few of the subjects. To recall and use material it was necessary to do it again and again, though his comprehension was built in. He understood everything, without conscious effort.

Synthesis was another matter. New knowledge generated from old was problem solving, and required constant practice. His older, absentee father had generated a workbook for him, filled with problems of increasing difficulty until reaching the unsolved problems intended as the tasks in his young life. At first glance, it all seemed impossible:

1. Resize the branegate from millions of miles to a size commensurable to the size of an interstellar craft.

2. Investigate the possibility of rapid intergalactic or intragalactic travel by using branegates to jump universes at one point and quickly re-enter at another distant point. Normal spacetime folding is inefficient in terms of travel distance shortened per terrajoule of energy consumed.

3. Compactify a vacuum energy generator from planet-size to shuttle-size. Spatial opening to access the false-vacuum state should be variable in both size and stability time in order to achieve a range of variable thrust.

Only three items, but it seemed to Trae it would take a thousand lifetimes, even with the technology available to him. And that technology was buried beneath a great plateau on a planet called Elderon.

They landed on the plateau at some distance from the visable part of the city. Two cars from the Zylak headquarters were there to meet them, without representatives, only drivers who said a few polite words and handled their luggage. Whether these men were normal or Immortal, Trae could not tell. Elderon was truly a planet of The Immortals, and Trae felt nervous anticipation at meeting them. So far he only knew his parents: mother, two fathers, one young and with him, one old and now in another universe. He remembered the strange voices he'd heard years before, when he'd first learned what he was. His parents? Perhaps not. The voices had not returned, yet his absent father had said that all Immortals, especially family members, were connected in some way. Trae still wondered who the voices belonged to and what they were to him. He wondered if they would come back to him, if he might even meet some of these people, now that he was on Elderon.

It was a two-hour drive back to the city they'd passed over seconds before landing. Trae didn't wonder why the shuttleport was so far away. Halfway back to the city they could hear and feel takeoff of the shuttle they'd come in on. The ground shook beneath them, and the car shuddered as if struck by strong gusts of wind.

The driver didn't say a word to them all the way in. They were on a speedway and traffic was heavy, little bullet-shaped cars with exhaust pipes flashing short jets of flame when they accelerated. Hydrogen powered, all of them, and a watery haze hovered over the speedway.

First there were houses arranged in neat blocks, looking like identical copies out of a mold. The downtown area was small, perhaps a mile square, the tallest building a few stories of glass and plas-steel reflecting bright sunlight. They entered what looked like a tunnel, a row of bright lights in a ceiling curving gradually, then tighter as they slowed, a descending spiral beneath the ground, but not for long. They came out of the tunnel and the true city was there: busy streets and windowless buildings several stories high, all illuminated by full spectrum light panels far up on a ceiling. In seconds their eyes adjusted; it was as if they were up on the surface, and the warm light of a sun was beating down on them.

They stopped in front of one of the largest buildings. When they got out of the car Trae noticed a breeze blowing, and there was a faint flowery scent in the air. The car carrying their luggage sped off again after the drivers spoke briefly to each other. The driver of their car motioned them to follow him, and led them inside the building. The first floor was a foyer with shining stone floors in black and walls of white marble. Two elevators in clear tubes and an escalator went up to higher floors. There was a reception desk, and standing before it were three people, a woman and two men, dressed in suits. The older of the two men smiled, and extended his hand as Trae approached them.

Trae shook the man's hand. "You must be Mister Meza," he said warmly. "My father has told me about you."

"Only good things, I hope," said Meza. He smiled, but looked Trae over carefully. "My associates Myra Dan and Wallace Hunley. Myra is in mathematics, and also runs my information office, and Wallace is our Director of Applied Research."

Trae shook their hands. They smiled and made nodding bows. The woman was quite pretty, he thought, and Wallace he knew had been a chief engineer long before moving into management. He'd been with father's corporation for over a lifetime. Wallace was an Immortal, and Trae wondered about the other two people. Were they all connected the way he'd been told?

Absolutely, came a thought, and Meza smiled broadly. *We're connected as much as you want us to be.*

Meza had heard his question, and Myra had heard everything. She was blushing.

"It will be useful when we talk about technical matters," said Wallace. "The brain is so much faster than the currents powering our motor reflexes. Your father has sent us a list of topics for our initial discussions. I must say the tasks he's asking us to do are formidable, even impossible, considering our present technology."

"I agree. New technology is necessary, but the old physics is enough. I've been working on some ideas for the past four years, and—"

"Time for that later," said Meza. "Right now we'll take you up-stairs for a light lunch, then Myra will give you a quick tour of the corporate offices. Tomorrow is my day, and the day after you'll be with Wallace."

"I look forward to it," said Wallace, his head cocked to one side. "Layered superconductors. What an interesting idea."

"What?" said Trae. The idea had surfaced only months before, and was to be part of his initial presentation.

"Sorry. I was prying; it's a rude habit of mine. Curiosity and impatience get the better of me sometimes."

Meza clucked his tongue. "Engineers can be so devious when it comes to new ideas. Don't worry, you two will have plenty of time together. Now let's eat."

Petyr had been standing there with them the whole time. *Careful,* came a thought. *The man is your bodyguard and companion, nothing more.* The thought seemed to freeze his brain. For the moment, it made sense.

Trae took Petyr affectionately by the arm. "This is Petyr. He's my constant companion, teacher, bodyguard, and many things. He does my scans, is there for my upgrades. I depend on him. I'd like to have him eat with us and attend all my meetings, please."

"Of course," said Meza. "Your father has told us all about your guardianship, sir. It seems you're his right hand."

"It's my honor," said Petyr, voice deep, and he shook the man's hand.

Meza winced. "Ah, a soldier of The Church. Religion is not prevalent on Elderon, but you'll be able to find a few of your kind here. There are believers on every planet, as far as I know."

I meant no offense to The Church, came a thought before Trae could even voice his opinion on what had sounded to him like an insulting remark.

"You're certainly welcome to join us," said Meza, and smiled. Petyr did not return it, but followed them dutifully up the escalator to a large meeting room with a round, linen-covered table where they had a salad with strips of marinated poultry and the edible petals of several flower varieties, a sweet biscuit, and tea.

Conversation was light, but it was clear father had told them a few things and not others. They knew about the caverns and the harrowing escape from Gan to Galena. They didn't seem to know about their royal visit on Galena, but knew of Trae's meeting with his parents and the vast information bank that had been loaded into him.

Trae followed his instincts; what Father did not want them to know they would not know. In only minutes with others like him

Trae could garble any thought he wished to with a mess of random information. It quickly became a game. Nearing the end of the meal, he was enjoying the game until another thought came to him.

Don't try so hard. It's distracting. Trae smiled faintly, looked around the table, but there was no reaction to be seen there.

Lunch ended, Meza and Wallace went back to their work and Myra guided them on a quick tour of two floors of offices and cubicles where the day to day business of Zylak Industries was conducted. There was really not much to see, except Myra, who also gave him a pile of literature and prospectus of the various holdings, and suggested strongly that he at least scan them. He didn't tell her that all the information was in his head; it seemed arrogant of him to do so.

Even with a quick tour it was late afternoon when they were finished. A new driver came for them and they went through the ritual of getting in and out of the limousine just so they could drive a hundred yards down the street to a hotel also owned by Zylak Industries. They were put up grandly in a penthouse suite of five rooms with large windows on three sides looking out over the subterranean city.

"Welcome to the world of extreme wealth," quipped Petyr when Trae grinned at him from the cushiony embrace of a long sofa.

"Does it bother you?" asked Trae, suddenly serious.

"No. It's part of the family fortune, so enjoy it. Just don't let luxurious amenities distract you from what you have to do."

"It's your fortune, too," said Trae.

"I don't need it, not in this way. Neither does Leonid Zylak. It's service that counts, service to an individual or an entire civilization. That's what we're about, Trae. Not the luxury, but while we have it I *will* enjoy it with you."

Now Petyr smiled, and Trae relaxed again.

Dinner was sent up to them, a roast with new potatoes and served with a fine red wine. Petyr drank most of it, but allowed Trae half a glass. It was Trae's first experience with an alcoholic beverage, and he didn't particularly care for it.

Their luggage had been unpacked for them and put away in two separate bedrooms. Trae thought it a courtesy, but Petyr was suspicious as usual. Even though his briefcase had been locked, he made several spot-checks of the memory cubes inside to see if they might have been recently opened. This took up half the evening, while

Trae watched a documentary on medically useful aquatic Elderonian plants on the giant screen in their living room.

They retired late to their separate bedrooms. Trae was over-stimulated by the events of the day, his mind still going over questions he wanted answered the following day. But as he finally drifted into the twilight of sleep, a pleasant thought came to him like a soft breeze, and it was not his own.

Good night, Trae. I hope you'll be happy here and want to stay a while.

He immediately fell asleep, feeling suddenly welcomed. And in the morning he remembered it.

He'd expected his day with Meza to be boring, but it was not. Trae gained new respect for the man. He demonstrated a solid grasp of the intricate networking required for the many units of the conglomerate while allowing the units to operate internally as independent businesses. His knowledge of interplanetary business and economics was profound and he was a "people" person, quick with a smile, a compliment, a warm handshake. If there was a flaw in the man it was arrogance, but Trae could tolerate that as long as the man's competence and performance justified it.

The conglomerate itself was incredibly diverse, with divisions in materials, electronics, energy, medicine, computer systems, manufacturing and astronautics. New sub-divisions came and went as the needs arose. And Meza was running all of it.

Myra appeared a couple of times to give Meza important messages that included cubes for his review. Meza seemed to sense Trae's interest in her. "She's much more than an administrator. Myra's an expert in both management information systems and economics. She does most of the geometric algorithm work for our modeling people. You can never tell, of course, but she's a third generation lady with well over two hundred years of experience. Not bad for a thirty-year-old, eh?"

Trae found it interesting, but disappointing. Myra looked twenty—tops.

The conglomerate that was Zylak Industries was not public, did not issue stock, but had a governing board. Meza was its chairman. He'd offered to provide a position for Trae on the board, but Father had refused it, saying that his son needed to be quietly hidden in the research division where all the new technology would be happening. This was fine with Trae. Business was interesting, but it was the practice of science and engineering he really wanted to do. That made the second day of his visit much more interesting.

The first day Petyr had seen him to the limousine, then stayed behind, saying only that he would find other things to do during the day. That evening he didn't say what he'd done, and Trae didn't ask. Trae suspected he'd spent the day with his collection of memory cubes. The second day was different. Petyr got in the car with them; they drove not to the corporate offices, but to a building near them. It was early, and the ceiling lights high above the city went from orange to light yellow before they reached their destination. Wallace Hunley himself was there to greet them.

Wallace ignored Petyr, who nonetheless followed them closely. "I was up half the night thinking about what your father has proposed. A lifetime or two might even put a dent in it." He laughed.

They entered the three-storied building of windowless concrete. The entrance was a short hallway with four elevator doors, and one was open. They entered the open elevator. Wallace inserted a key and turned it. They descended.

"The sub-basement isn't marked, and we'll give you a key for entry. This is where you'll be spending your time here," said Wallace.

The door opened. Soft music. Panel lights in the ceiling were a light green over a forest of cubicles. "Welcome to the think tank," said their host.

There was more to it than cubicles: meeting rooms, cafeteria, auditorium, several rooms with bunk beds, and an IC 1200 supercomputer with an entire wall filled with memory. Many of the cubicles were empty. "We're a bit early," explained Wallace. "A lot of folks work out and eat breakfast upstairs before coming down."

They walked around the periphery of the cubicles. "I have a small office down here. Your cubicle is right next door so I can pick your brain in person whenever I feel like it." In the far corner of the room was a small, glassed-in office. The cubicle next to it was twice normal size, and unlike the others had a door. Inside were blank walls, a curving table, book cases on either side of the door and not one, but two computer consoles. "The one is a PC, the other goes direct to the IC 1200," explained Wallace.

"We'll need another chair," said Petyr suddenly.

"Excuse me?" Wallace looked at him sharply.

"Another chair. I'll be working here with Trae."

"Our security here is more than adequate. I don't see why—"

"Petyr will be working with me on occasion," said Trae. "It's a requirement, not a request."

Wallace was momentarily stunned. "Well—of course—yes—I'll see to it. I just thought—"

"Petyr has his own projects, but is also my librarian for all the data Father has sent with me. It'll speed up our work."

"Yes—I see." Wallace was still confused, having thought Petyr was nothing more than a bodyguard. *If only you knew,* Trae thought evilly.

They went into Wallace's office and the man showed them the list of tasks he'd received. Trae scanned it quickly, tapped the page with a finger and said, "Number three is most important, and the rest will follow naturally. We know the physics of the vacuum state and how to access it. The problem is how to provide power systems, thrusters and field generators that will fit into a ship no larger than a current interstellar transport."

Wallace chuckled. "Any suggestions?" he asked with humorous intent.

"You already peeked at it. Layered superconductors at the nano-level, conductor pairs stacked anti-parallel to eliminate magnetic field effects. Infinite current in a nano-sized conductor. That's the beginning."

"You're proposing an entirely new technology. It'll take years at best."

"I'll show you how to do it sooner," said Trae.

"And the entire project has to be up to the testing stage within a few years," said Petyr.

Wallace practically snarled at him. "Impossible," he said.

But Trae knew he was wrong.

CHAPTER 15

Young Zylak has reached Elderon. It's obvious his enhancements are complete, or close to it. He's amazing everyone.

Hmm. Does anyone know what he's working on?

No. He's working with the research staff, and we don't have any people in there. They're keeping things hush, hush, even to board members. All we've been told is he's a bright young kid they discovered somewhere. What should we do now?

Azar Khalil sat in lotus position, a towel draped over his knees. Steam swirled around him, and his muscled body glistened with sweat. To the others who sat near him in the clouds of fragrant vapors he seemed to be in meditation, breathing deep and slowly, eyes closed.

Do nothing for the moment. The strikes should be coordinated and as simultaneous as possible. We're not ready here yet, but the team is assembled. I need to win a few more friends before we move.

What about the father and mother?

It's out of our hands. They went through the portal months ago. The deed is already done; it doesn't concern us. When I want the boy dead I'll tell you, and I'll expect it to be accomplished on the same day.

I have three good men here who can do it without being traced. Zylak and his bodyguard will cease existence.

Not the boy's scans. I'll want to know everything in him. We still have no idea what his father is up to, only that's he's certain to oppose us.

Perhaps we'll hear something new from home soon.

Azar hummed to himself, turned his palms upwards, knowing he was being watched. *We'll not wait for that. Be ready for my order; it could be soon.* He bowed his head, exhaled loudly, and opened his eyes.

"Back again," said a fat man sitting near him. "When I try that I just go to sleep and fall over."

Laughter.

"It only requires practice, my friend," said Azar, and stretched his arms languidly above his head. "Ten minutes of that is like three hours of deep sleep for me. Thirty minutes, no more. The rest of my time is for work."

"So that's how you do it. I'd just use the time for eating. I must say I admire your discipline, Azar. I've never seen a man expand his holdings as fast as you have."

"Ah, then we're all in good company. The most successful of us are in this room, and I like to feel I can call you my friends as well as colleagues."

"Indeed you can, Azar," said another man sweating in steamy gloom.

"Good. As friends I also hold you in my confidence. I feel I can talk to you about private matters, share my secrets, as you will. We're together in so many ways, not just in business, but in political matters."

The fat man edged closer to him. Faint shadows in clouds of steam, two men stood up on the other side of the brightly tiled room and came over to sit opposite him on a small, stone bench. "You said there was something serious for us to discuss, and here we are. What is it, Azar?" asked one of them.

Azar paused for dramatic effect, smiled nervously, shyly. "I hesitate. The subject itself could be dangerous to talk about. I wouldn't bring it up if I didn't trust all of you with my most intimate thoughts."

"What you say will not leave this room," said the fat man, and the others nodded in agreement.

"Very well, but it involves our Emperor in a difficult time. I don't want to make any hasty judgements about what's happening all around us."

"You're being polite," said the fat man. "He loses his police chief, and declares martial law. The man's in a panic; he sees assassins everywhere. He overreacts to everything. The offworlders see it as signs of instability. It's hard enough for me to get their business without Osman going on another one of his witch hunts."

"Quraiwan was a monster. He kept this city in a state of fear for years, and Osman never once tugged on his leash. I will personally not miss him," said another man.

"But now we have martial law, and more police on the streets," said Azar. "People are openly complaining. I've never seen such demonstrations before now. The people have lost all trust in their government."

"Have you had a chance to talk with Osman since Quraiwan was murdered?" asked the fat man.

"I've tried to, but he won't see me," lied Azar. "This is worrisome. I fear he's lost trust in those of us who've supported his policies over the years. And he's certainly lost touch with his people."

"He fears a coup, perhaps," said one of the men sitting opposite him.

There was a long silence in the room, and then the same man spoke again.

"Does he have reason to fear a coup, Azar?"

"Ah," said the fat man.

Azar leaned forward, and gave each man a long and sincere stare. "These are dangerous and unstable times, gentlemen. If something does happen, we want to be in a position to control it, for if the wrong people come to power we can lose everything we've worked for. I don't intend to let that happen. Religious zealots, or whoever the terrorists are, can not rule this planet, my friends, nor will a man who has lost his rationality and isolates himself in terror."

"Who, then?" asked the fat man.

"That's what we need to discuss," said Azar.

The fat man actually smiled at him. The others did not.

CHAPTER 16

Transition went smoothly, a spectacular light show that lasted several minutes as they passed through the boundary between two universes. Leonid and Tatjana had another drink as they watched it all on the view-screen, and held hands. Their mood was somber, wistful, leaving something behind but returning to something familiar.

Or so they thought.

The core of the home galaxy was crowded with great clouds of molecular hydrogen and new stars were still being born there at a prodigious rate. Illuminated by new stars the clouds seemed to boil, spewing forth tendril signatures of baby suns.

Picket ships were waiting for them, black insect shapes silhouetted against the glowing clouds. They made rendezvous with the great vessel that traveled between universes like a rogue planet. Passengers and their luggage were transferred to the pickets before the ship moved on towards Port Angel. There, it would be refitted in orbit before the return trip to the universe of the colonies. The pickets took all passengers to Cay Benz for processing and assignment to appropriate shuttles. Several worlds were still occupied near the core. One of these worlds was Kratola, the oldest stronghold of The Immortals, and its political capital.

For Leonid and Tatjana Zylak, it was home.

They packed their luggage, boarded a picket, and settled in for a one day sprint to immigration Cay. They amused themselves by reading, and watching a holo-play, and when the arrival at Cay Benz was announced they gathered their carry-on things and prepared to disembark with the others.

A cabin attendant asked them to sit down again, saying they were being met by a special delegation after the rest of the passengers had disembarked. Both assumed it was a delegation sent by Tatjana's family, for this had happened on occasion in the past. They waited, unconcerned. The rest of the passengers walked the connecting tunnel into the great orbital Cay, an artificial world the size of a large moon. Hollow inside, it was a city of twelve layers with a resident population of twenty million souls.

They waited in a departure lounge, the cabin attendant watched them from the exit, finally made a phone call. "They'll be here for you in a moment," she said nicely, and left.

Boots pounded the floor of the tunnel. Six men entered, military men with helmets and black armor. Five carried rifles, the sixth had a sidearm and saluted them.

"Are you Leonid and Tatjana Zylak?"

"We are," said Leonid.

"Your papers, please."

Leonid handed them over, wondering who he was talking to. He'd never seen men in such uniforms before. "Are you with immigration?" he asked. "As you can see, we're citizens of Kratola."

"Where are you coming from?" asked the man examining their papers. He seemed to be an officer.

Leonid told him, "We've been on a long mission for our government. It's all described in our documents."

The man smirked at them, closed the folder containing their papers and made no move to hand them back.

"My papers, please," said Leonid, and held out his hand.

"Your papers are invalid. You'll have to be detained. Come with us, please."

The soldiers with him stepped forward, rifles at port arms.

Tatjana gasped. "I don't understand," said Leonid. "We're representatives of the state."

"It will be explained to you, sir. Please." The officer gestured for them to follow him. His soldiers moved in close.

They walked the tunnel, their shoulders touching hard armor on either side. The reception lounge they came out into was empty. Two electric-powered carts awaited them. They got into one with the officer and a soldier. The others followed, and they went swiftly down a passage that had been cordoned off on both sides. People gawked at them from behind barriers as they passed by. A soldier was by each barrier, rifle slung. Leonid had only seen military in shuttleports on Gan, a product of a dictatorship. *What is going on here?*

They were taken directly to Immigration Control. The officer took them inside and gave their papers to a man in civilian clothes with a colorful sunburst pin on his lapel, a sun rising above a horizon.

They sat in chairs and waited while the man chatted with the officer and casually went through their papers. Leonid could hear nothing, felt nothing. There was no cerebral connection for him to these people. He wondered if they were even his own kind. He looked at Tatjana, but she was too afraid to even speak. *Don't worry, darling.* He took her hand, and held it.

The officer finally stepped away from the civilian and beckoned them to come forward. They stood before a desk, and the civilian smiled up at them. "You've been away for a long time, I see," he said.

"The better part of two lifetimes," said Leonid. "We're portal emissaries for the state, assigned to establish missions on the other side. We've worked on several worlds there."

"Your work is known, Mister Zylak. I'm sure The Church is grateful for what you've done. You've also established quite an empire for yourself."

"We worked for the state, the Council of Blue and Green. Both parties sent us. The Church followed later; we're not affiliated with it, though we have many friends who are. They've been the caretakers of our only son."

The man looked at their papers again. "It says nothing here about a child."

"He was born on Gan, on the other side. He was murdered when he was small by an Emperor who opposed our work." Leonid took a short breath to continue his story, but was stopped by a sudden, powerful thought.

Say no more! Let them think he's dead!

He gasped, and breathed again. "Sorry, it's difficult for me to think about it."

"It would help if you could tell me the child was baptized in The Church."

"What does that have to do with anything? We're returning emissaries for our government. Why are we even being questioned here?" asked Leonid.

"You said yourself that you're not members of The Church."

"That's irrelevant. We have total separation between Church and State."

"That is no longer true."

"What?"

The man sighed, and made a show of being patient. "I realize you've been gone a very long time and that communication between universes is slow. The fact remains the government that sent you on your mission no longer exists. It has not existed for the past twenty years, so you can see why your papers are invalid. By law, I could put you right back on the ship for return through the portal."

Tatjana's voice quavered as she struggled to control herself. "Kratola is our family home. Our families are still there," she hissed. "What kind of government do you have that will refuse family members to visit each other?"

"Now, now," said the man quickly. "I didn't say I was going to send you back, but that law would allow it if I chose to. Family is precious to The Church, and I'm of The Faithful." He pointed to the pin on his lapel. "But the government you represent became corrupt in its last days. Its extreme liberalism allowed policies despised by both The Church and general populace. The separation of Church and State you talk about was doomed to failure, leading only to anarchy. A healthy populace must be led spiritually as well as politically. A Grand Bishop and Council of Bishops have now accomplished that. They create and approve laws, working with a Congress of The People which is freely elected."

The Bishops rule. Democracy is gone. This is against everything I worked for on the other side.

Leonid blinked. "So what must we do now? We still want to go home."

The man smiled. "I can give you a transit visa to Kratola, but your stay will be limited to one year at most. You must present yourself to Immigration officials on planet. Your papers will be useful only for information purposes to them. I cannot predict how you'll be received."

"We'll take that chance," said Leonid. "We want to see our families again."

"Please sit," said the man. "It'll take a few minutes to prepare your visas and arrange spaces on the shuttle. It departs in three hours."

The man went away. They sat again, and waited. And waited. Nearly an hour had passed when the man came back with their shuttle tickets and visas in glossy, blue folders. He handed them over and pointed to the officer still standing at attention near them.

"This man will accompany you to the departure lounge. I've already arranged transport of your luggage. Have a nice trip, and I hope, once you've been here a while, you'll realize that our society is much better for the changes that have occurred since you were last here. Perhaps you'll choose to be one of The Faithful again."

I doubt it. "Thank you," said Leonid. "You've been quite understanding." He took Tatjana by the hand, and followed the officer out the door. A few steps and they were in terminal traffic again, and nobody seemed to notice they were following an armored military man with a sidearm. Guards were everywhere, at every departure lounge, even in front of the restrooms. *Are they keeping people out, or in?* wondered Leonid.

They reached their departure lounge. The officer sat down near them, but over the next hour refused their attempts at making polite conversation. After a while Leonid realized the man was trying to remain invisible, showing no connection to them.

He was still sitting there when their shuttle was called, did not move his head when they stood in line and were processed through to the departure tunnel. A hostess greeted them, and they were seated. There was the usual demonstration of the sedative masks for use during the two-spacetime jumps ahead. Takeoff was on time, a high angle burn for two minutes at two gee, then steady acceleration at one gee for several moments before reaching the first jump point.

They slept, and awoke for another seven hours of powered flight, then slept again. When they awoke the second time Kratola was a green disk the size of a sovereign coin held at arm's length on their view-screen. The next morning they touched down after a spiral, gliding descent through the atmosphere of the planet. Once again an attendant asked them to remain seated until the rest of the passengers had exited the craft. Again they walked the tunnel to the reception lounge alone.

An officer and four soldiers, all clad in black armor, met them at the door, and they were arrested on the spot for treason against The Church. They made no protest, did not respond in any way, were marched out a side entrance to a police van parked on the tarmac and put in the back like two common criminals.

At a nearby police station they were not fingerprinted or interviewed, but were placed, mercifully, together in a small cell. There was an open toilet, and two stone slabs for beds. A thin soup was their dinner. The man who served it said they would appear in court the following morning for arraignment on the charges. He picked up their empty bowls later and turned off the lights, leaving them in pitch-blackness.

Tatjana sobbed part of the night away before anger took over and she began attempts at contacting her family. But there were no friendly voices or thoughts to comfort them.

CHAPTER 17

Azar Khalil made a telephone call two hours before the strike. The assault team had already left for the palace and disturbances had begun in the streets.

Joseph himself answered the call. "Yes?"

"Joseph, it has begun. Today is the day we take back our freedom."

"I know. The others are in the streets. You said there would be special orders for me."

"Orders for my most dedicated Soldier of The Church. I'm asking much of you; your life will be at extreme risk."

"I will gladly give my life for The Church."

"Only if there is no other way to take the life of He Who Opposes The Church. The assault team is on its way. My hope is they'll accomplish the task. You'll be a backup, coming in from a different direction. You'll be on your own, without a support group. The Source will guide you. Your task is to search for and kill the Emperor of all Gan. You must first be equipped properly. I'll tell you where to go for that. The people there will give you your route into the palace and the best places to intercept your target once the attack begins."

"I'm ready. Where should I go?"

Azar told him, then, "You will enter the palace in two hours, my friend. Know that the blessings of The Source are upon you, and if you must die today you'll be taken into His loving arms for eternity. Blessed be The Source."

"Blessed be," said Joseph, and hung up.

I could use another dozen like him, thought Azar, and called his driver. "Get the car ready. I want to go to the club for lunch and a sauna. And I won't be taking any calls the rest of the morning."

*

The demonstration came as no surprise to the Emperor of all Gan. He'd been anticipating it for weeks, and his spies were well located, taking pictures of everyone in the crowd. It was orderly enough, no reason for a violent response, but his soldiers lined the fence around the palace, and the regional guard base a few miles away had been put on alert.

Khalid Osman watched the demonstration from his office window for only minutes before growing bored with it. "If they want martial law rescinded, all they have to do is turn over the assassins to me," he complained to an aid, then went back to work at his desk.

Outside, the crowd waved placards protesting travel restrictions, martial rule, brutal police, and isolation from other world-states. There was no chanting or singing; thousands of people marched shoulder to shoulder around the fenced periphery of the palace in a show of solidarity.

Near the rear of the palace grounds, away from the main street, a van pulled up, but was blocked by the moving crowd from reaching the entrance where deliveries were made. The driver remained patient for a few minutes, then began honking his horn. A few in the crowd gestured obscenely at him, but did not make way.

Finally a dozen troops came out of the gate and pushed the crowd back on two sides so the van could get through. It was a regular and familiar enough delivery from a catering service in the city. The van pulled slowly up to the gate, was just beginning to pass through when suddenly the side panels of the vehicle popped out as if struck from inside. Men dressed and hooded in black were in the van, and they opened fire on both troops and citizens. Brass scattered as bullets shredded cloth, flesh and bone. Troops standing nearby were the first to die. The crowd panicked and people trampled each other trying to get away. Other troops converged on the area and were cut down as their assailants poured out of the van and ran towards the delivery entrance of the palace. A single shot from a heavy shoulder weapon destroyed the door, and the terrorists were inside. Troops went in after them, but were cut down until their bodies piled up, blocking the doorway. Other troops retreated a few steps, but continued firing into the building as the crowd ran away, leaving behind both dead and wounded citizens.

Khalid was concentrating hard on a speech when he heard the screams of the crowd. His office was on the second floor overlooking the main entrance to the palace, and at first he didn't hear the gunfire. A strong shockwave passed beneath his feet, and then he heard the thrup of rapid-fire weapons coming from inside the building, not outside. His office door flew open and four troopers were there behind an officer who shouted at him, "We're under attack, sire! We have to get you out of here," then into a throat mike, "We're using the south tunnel. Get a car there immediately."

Khalid was on his feet and out the door without further encouragement. He sprinted down the hall to the stairwell, but they couldn't go down. Troops were downstairs and opened fire on something. One of them fell as bullets splattered a wall.

"Keep going!" yelled the officer, and Khalid sprinted again. They ran past two offices to a narrow staircase at the end of the hall and went down in single-file, troops front and back of him. Khalid knew where they were going, had practiced escape drills there with his guards several times, but never under fire.

They made it to ground level. A hundred yards to go, through two offices, then the bookcase and—

Bullets tore into the walls on either side of them. Two troopers went down, one howling, the other dead before he hit the floor. Men in black fired at them from the end of the hall. The officer pulled a sphere from his belt and flicked a switch on it before lobbing it far down the hall. Acrid smoke erupted there, and there was the sound of men coughing and gagging.

They ran again, through two offices and into a third. "Stay here," the officer ordered his two remaining troops at the doorway. "Cover us."

Inside the office a bookcase swung aside, behind it a door. The officer went first, gun in hand, Khalid following. A room used for storage, but a door there opened on a tunnel to the outside, where hopefully a car waited for them. Khalid turned to swing the bookcase closed behind them and started to close the door.

There was a sound behind him. He jerked his head around in time to see a man stand up from behind a packing crate and raise a weapon towards him. The man was slender, had a short beard on a chiseled face and wild eyes. He was dressed in the robe of an outlaw priest of the underground church. He raised his weapon to fire at the Emperor of all Gan.

The officer was faster. He fired three times in rapid succession.

The weapon spun from the priest's hand and he fell to his knees, his left hand grabbing his chest, his right hand scrabbling at his stomach. A beeping sound came from him.

"Who let you in here? Tell me and you'll die quickly," said the officer.

Blood oozed from the man's mouth. "All Power to The Source," he snarled, and struck his stomach hard with his fist.

The last thing Khalid Osman ever saw was the first flash of the explosion.

The steam was laced with Eucalyptus. Azar breathed deeply and paused to sip an icy drink through a straw. His colleagues had been with him until minutes ago, and were now showering. They'd talked about little things, including how to approach the Emperor in urging him into easing military restrictions on the general populace before demonstrations escalated to rioting. They'd all agreed that as long as Osman was supportive of the business empires they'd built it was best to keep him in place. They were not blind to the possibility of a coup, for Osman was long hated in many corners for his openly oppressive practices. A coup by the military might be tolerable, as long as the new leader was supportive of the powerful few who drove the economy of the planet. But a coup by the underground church could not be tolerated; their views were anti-materialistic at best and socialistic at the worst. A religious dictator would quickly bring the planet to ruin.

During many quiet conversations in clouds of fragrant steam, these few men who controlled the wealth of Gan had made plans for all political possibilities, and although the others did not yet know it, the day of their decision-making was at hand. While the others showered and dressed, Azar sat naked on hot stone, breathed soothing vapors and waited for news.

It came in the form of an attendant, who gave him a note in a sealed envelope. It had been delivered to the reception desk of the spa. Azar read it, replaced it in the envelope and closed his eyes. He sat that way for several minutes. Externally he was a man in quiet meditation. Internally he was roaming the great web of a common consciousness extending over many light years. He looked for a special signature, and found it.

Good news. The Emperor of Gan is dead. It'll be blamed on the underground church and agents from Galena. Everything's in place for my campaign, and I'll begin immediately. Are you ready to move?

Yes. Anytime you wish.

Then do it now. I want the boy dead before he receives news about Gan. No warning. Let me know when it's finished.

I will. All Power to The Source.

And to those who serve him.

Azar opened his eyes, then left the steam room to tell his colleagues the terrible news about their Emperor.

CHAPTER 18

I s it really necessary to do this every night? I'm tired," said Trae.
"It only takes a few minutes. Come on, get it over with."
Scanning disks dangled on cables hanging from Petyr's hands, and
he gestured at a chair.

Trae sat down in the chair, felt cold metal on his head, heard a
buzz and click, and it was done. "Another day, another cube," he
quipped.

"Oh, I periodically put a bunch of them on one cube."

"But you send something out nearly every day."

"Yep. Have to keep your work up-to-date. I admit it's a bit
redundant with all the records we have from your father, but you're
adding new ideas to it."

Trae smiled. "Which father are we talking about?"

"The old one," said Petyr, and smiled back.

"Don't you feel weird being treated like my bodyguard?"

"It's what I was, what I am. What's a father for?"

"You're supposed to give me sage advice about women and stuff.
Send me to my room when I'm bad."

"I can do that. Have you found a woman I need to worry about?"

"Not yet, but I wish I had. I'm attracted to Myra, but I'm a kid to
her. She's in her thirties."

"She looks pretty good to me," said Petyr, and you might be older
than she is if you count the years right. It's mental age that really
counts for us. We can change bodies whenever we want to."

"So make me thirty-seven," said Trae, "Maybe Myra will notice
me."

"Okay, I exaggerated. Arrangements have to be made. At least
we're not among the purists who insist on exact clones and want to
start all over again. We can use anyone's clone, and pick an age."

"All right, I want to be thirty-seven tomorrow. Let's do it." Trae was kidding, and his father knew it.

"Too fast. For that age you could be walking around in a few months. The younger the clone the longer it takes for reloads. When you died the first time it took around fifteen years to really get you back together again, and that was with structural modifications to your own clone. Your other father had a bank of them."

"Where?"

"Can't tell you that, Trae. Won't tell you that. I doubt we'll ever use those facilities again, anyway. And by the way, what makes you think Myra isn't attracted to you?"

"I've asked her out for coffee or lunch I don't know how many times. She's always busy."

"Maybe she is, but she's certainly spent enough time talking to you since the first night we were here."

"What?" Trae felt his face flush.

"You think I don't hear, every other night? I manage to tune it out quick, but it's tempting to eves-drop."

"She hasn't given me her name. All she does is say hi and ask me about my day, and how I like it here."

"It's Myra, all right, and she's not just amusing herself. She likes you, Trae. I saw it in her expression the first day we met her. You, of course, were oblivious to it. That's one of the dangers of being so focused, son. You don't notice what's going on around you."

Trae felt suddenly warm. "You haven't called me that for weeks. It's nice to hear it once in a while."

Petyr reached over and put a hand on his shoulder. "Nice to say it, but it's a slip of the tongue. Have to watch that, new feelings, and all. I like it. But as far as the world is concerned, your father is in another universe right now, straightening out who knows what. I'm just here minding the store. I'm still your bodyguard. Just because we're away from Gan doesn't mean we're safe. I wouldn't put it past Osman to send a hit team after us."

"I thought we were secure here."

"Not at all. It's an open society with a porous border, and the corporate police don't even know who you are. Don't dwell on it; let me do the watching. You do the research. How are things going?"

"Very fast. Everyone is so surprised about it. I told them father had passed on a lot of things to me, but they don't seem to believe it. We already have a design for energy storage, but it scares me to think of riding in that ship. It's a toroid with a billion wrappings of superconductor in structurally alternating layers to keep a zero field and net current. There's no limit to the current we can store, and we'll use beamed microwave power to initially charge it. One break in a single layer and the conductor can go normal. The whole ship will vaporize in a flash."

"Okay, but can you store enough energy?"

"Enough for a local folding of space-time and some short jumps. Going through the brane is another matter; we don't know if a small portal can be made in a stable configuration just using ship's energy. I'm doing the simulations now. Myra has helped some. I've never met anyone who can reduce things to geometry like she can."

"Beauty and brains is a deadly combination," said Petyr, and Trae blushed.

Petyr played with his memory cubes, condensing data into a few that he put into small boxes and labeled carefully. These would be gone somewhere the next morning; Trae never knew where. Trae watched another play from the video library in their suite, but it was an historical thing and quickly bored him. His eyelids grew heavy and he went to bed before Petyr had even finished playing with his cubes. More bored than sleepy, it seemed, for sleep did not want to come. He lay there awake, yet relaxed, for nearly an hour, and was suddenly aware of a presence keeping him that way, a presence sensed in some recess of his mind.

Hello? Maybe it was the girl again. It had been three nights since their last chat.

No answer, but the presence was still there. *Why don't you answer? I know you're there.*

The response, when it came, seemed a shy one. *I see you too. You're the missionary's son; we'd heard you were dead.*

Who's we? thought Trae, immediately on guard and masking his thoughts with random memories.

Friends, if you're who you seem to be. It's good for you to be cautious; your family has enemies.

I don't know what you're talking about. Who's the missionary's son? Now there was another presence in his mind, two people now, and both of them Immortals.

Another time. I'm not an enemy, but they exist. Be careful of your identity. I can help, but—later.

Gone, but still Trae felt like someone was watching him, peering into his mind. He tried to blank his mind completely, but failed. Images kept popping back into it, even images of the caverns on Gan.

You'll get better at it. I don't know the other guy. Might be a friend, maybe not. You can never be certain. Is that where you lived before you came here? Is that where they hid you?

It was so strong that Trae sat up and looked around the room to see if anyone was in there with him. But this time the presence seemed familiar.

The girl? He lay back on the bed, put his hands over his eyes. *I have no privacy. Who are these people jumping in and out of my head?*

I'm sorry. Maybe this isn't a good time.

It *was* her. *I can't have a private thought on this planet.*

Yes you can. You just haven't learned to mask yourself well enough yet. You forget, and leak things all the time, even about your work. Stop that.

You know all about it. You're Myra, aren't you? Why are you teasing me? Why should you care?

I'm not teasing you. And you seem lonely. I'm just trying to be a friend.

Someone else just said that, and I have no idea who.

I scared him away. You should thank me. He didn't identify himself. Don't talk to anyone without knowing who they are. I have the feeling you're in danger, and I don't like it.

A pause, then, *Well, are you in danger?*

I didn't think so until tonight.

So you must be dangerous to someone else.

Stop it, Myra, you know who I am.

A missionary's son, that's what he said. Why would anyone want to hurt the son of a missionary? And why would another Immortal warn him about it?

I don't have the slightest idea.

Well think about it. Maybe some other Immortal cares about you, an Immortal with a lot of life experience with the tricks that can be played. Don't be so quick to talk to people. And I'll come back when you're in a better mood.

And she was gone. *Now wait a minute!* thought Trae, but it was too late, and he'd made her angry.

He tried to sleep again, but couldn't and finally got up and went out to the living room where Petyr was just now closing up his briefcase. "What's the matter?" he asked.

Trae told him what had happened, and his bodyguard-father frowned. "It has to be Myra, but others might know who you are, and we've been careful to hide that. I didn't hear a thing, so whoever it is knows how to tune into you. That's part of your profile. Only a few people know it: your parents, and the doctors who've worked on your enhancements. Nobody else. We might have a leak. If someone strange comes back again don't give any indication of where you are or who you are. Deny everything, but try to get some clue to their identity. They don't have to be close by. They could even be on another planet. It's a field thing, Trae. We're all connected by a special field, and nobody has measured its extent.

"You'll have to do it alone, Trae. I don't dare listen in, even if I can. Nobody can be allowed to know who I am, not even Myra or the others you work with!"

Trae went to bed with that command ringing in his ears. Sleep came slowly, and there was no sweet voice to tell him good night.

He missed that voice.

CHAPTER 19

It was the longest night of their lives.

Tatjana whimpered and growled in her sleep until it was nearly dawn, and Leonid didn't sleep at all. By morning he felt groggy, for he'd not slept in forty-eight hours.

Shortly after dawn a guard suddenly opened their door after checking them through the peephole. He brought in their breakfast on a tray and put it on the stone bed they hadn't used the night before. "Eat it quickly," he commanded. "I'll come back for you in a few minutes." He closed the door behind him, and locked it.

The guard came back soon with two others. "On your feet; it's time for court. Behave yourselves if you don't want more trouble than you already have."

It was a hearing room, not a court. The room was paneled in dark wood. There was a raised dais with a heavy table, two other tables with chairs facing it, and a dozen benches for observers. The benches were empty, but a man stood by each of the two tables. One walked towards them as they entered and extended a hand not to Leonid, but Tatjana. She shook it. "Carl Osten, madam. Your family has hired me for your defense. I've considerable experience in matters related to immigration."

"We're not immigrants, we're citizens," said Leonid.

"I regret to say that's no longer true. Officially you're a member of a government that no longer exists. There's no precedent for this, so anything can happen. I urge you to cooperate with the court as much as possible."

Leonid started to speak, but Tatjana squeezed his arm. "We appreciate your help, Mister Osten. Thank you," she said.

They sat down at a table. The man standing by the other one gave them an unfriendly look, and examined some papers in front of him.

"Jan Herzel is our prosecutor. His skills aren't so good, but he's active in The Church. Please be civil to him," said Carl.

The judge entered the room, a man wearing the red robe and simple head covering of a priest. Leonid and Tatjana stood, following Carl's lead, then sat again. The judge glared down at them as if displeased by something. "This is very early for a hearing, but it seems someone has considerable influence with the court. It had better be worth my time."

He leafed through the brief on his desk, looked over his glasses at the prosecutor. "This is a show cause hearing. What are the charges you wish to file?"

Jan Herzel stood and pointed dramatically at Leonid and his wife. "We charge Leonid and Tatjana Zylak, two citizens of Elderon, with high treason to The Church by aiding and abetting a criminal state, your honor."

The judge looked at his briefing again. "By criminal state I presume you mean the Council of Red and Green."

"I do, your honor."

"That state has been dead for decades, counselor. How can these people have been at large for so long?"

"They were on missions beyond the great portal, and have just returned."

"They did not realize the government they represented had been overturned, your honor," said Carl Osten quickly.

The judge smiled nastily. "How unfortunate for them. You're their attorney?"

"I am, your honor."

"Look, I've read the brief. The only important issue here is loyalty to the State, and that means loyalty to The Church. I will ask a question of your clients, counselor, and if their answer is what I want to hear then charges will not be made and they will be considered good citizens of Elderon. Good families or not, there are certain requirements of all citizens, don't you agree?"

"Of course, your honor. May I confer with my clients?"

The judge only nodded. The prosecutor was sullen, had started to object, but then held himself back.

"He will ask you about your religious beliefs. Tell him what he wants to hear, and you'll be free," whispered Carl.

"We have no religious beliefs," said Leonid.

"That's the worst thing you can say to him. He's giving you a way out. Can't you see that? The Church pushes on one side, and a very powerful family, your wife's, pushes on the other. The whole family could be in danger if you throw away the opportunity he's giving you."

Leonid looked at Tatjana, saw her mouth pressed to a thin line, her eyes narrowed defiantly. "So let him ask his questions."

"My clients will answer your questions, your honor," said Carl, a bit relieved but nervous as his fingers tapped the point of an expensive stylus rapidly on the hard tabletop.

"Good," said the judge. "Here is the first. Do you believe that The Church of The Source is the one true church, and do you forsake all others?"

Leonid and Tatjana both stood, and Leonid answered for them. "We're not affiliated with any church, your honor, but we respect the beliefs of all people in this universe or others."

The judge scowled and paused, steepled his fingers in front of his face. "Choose your words carefully, sir. This is your second and last chance. Do you accept The Source as the one true power that rules the universe, and do you live your life according to His rules as set forth by The Church of His Faithful?"

Leonid paused, looked at his wife. Her gaze was fierce. She shook her head slightly.

"We believe in a spiritual power that brings order to the universe, your honor. We don't know its name; it's called by many different names by different people. Whatever the power is, we believe it's in all of us."

The judge leaned back in his chair, and sighed. "Very well. You've made your choice, not I." He turned to the prosecuting attorney for the state. "I've studied your brief, and witnessed the attitude of the defendants. The charge of High Treason to The Church is not sustainable, but evidence is sufficient to support charges of aiding and abetting a criminal government. You may file such charges, but be warned the court calendar is crowded over the coming year."

The prosecutor looked pleased. "I understand, your honor. The state is prepared to proceed at any time."

"We request a determination of bail, your honor," said Carl.

The judge glared at him. "I don't have to tell you there will be no bail, counselor. This is a capital crime against the state, and the defendants will be confined until trial."

"I will file a protest, your honor. This is not a capital crime by law."

"The Church will see otherwise. File your protest. This hearing is over. Guards, take charge of the prisoners."

The judge stood up, the rest of them with him. Leonid and Tatjana were both stunned. "I'll make calls. There will be more than protests. Even The Church can't get away with this," said Carl.

Guards came to get them. Their hands were shackled behind their backs, and they were led away. The guards marched them past the holding cell they'd spent the night in, and into another wing of the building. The cells there were even smaller, but windows to the outside were larger, the barred doors more open, and there were mattresses and blankets on the stone slab beds. The guards unshackled them, and pushed them into adjacent cells.

"Can't we be together?" protested Tatjana, as the doors clanged shut.

"Cells are for one person," said a guard. "Is better. You might be here for months, or years. The court can be slow. I think in your case it will be very slow." He locked their doors, and went away.

There was a long silence. Leonid sat down on the hard bed, and thought he heard a sob from Tatjana. "Well, I certainly didn't expect this. When we heard the government was in crisis, there was no mention of The Church being the problem."

"I've never been so humiliated," said Tatjana, and there was quiet fury in her voice. "Church or not, there will be repercussions for this."

"You really think your family can do something?"

"You have no idea what they can or might do. And there is nothing that money can't buy."

Leonid was heartened by his wife's fighting attitude, but quietly wondered why her family hadn't contacted them directly if they really had so much influence with the court.

CHAPTER 20

There are turning points in a life, beginnings and endings, and sudden.

Trae awoke refreshed after a good night of sleep laced with productive dreams about the day's work. The new simulations had needed tweaking, and designs had been coming out of the machines for weeks. Most had already gone to the manufacturing floor. An SRX-80 shuttle was being modified to accept the power torus amidships, and would now fly from orbit rather than ground. Once the prototype was static-tested its sister ships would be assembled in orbit about Elderon for full-burn runs and first attempts at short-pinch-spacetime folding. One year, perhaps two, was the current projection. Calculations for powering up a branegate were just beginning, using the SRX-80 and the much larger ST-40 freighter as models. Engineers estimated ten years to prototype development. Trae's estimate was three years, for there were things he'd held back from them, to release when he saw fit.

He awoke refreshed and eager for the day. Another visit last night; Myra was still playing her games, living out a kind of clandestine double life with an alter-ego that was sexy and fun and not so businesslike as when she was physically with him. She still wouldn't admit her double identity, but Trae was certain of it, or nearly certain. He hoped he wasn't misinterpreting the coy looks she gave him when they were working together.

The other voice that had warned him of danger hadn't returned. Perhaps it had been Myra in another disguise. For the past week, Petyr had seemed especially alert, following him to and from work, his eyes constantly roving the streets. It was still hard for Trae to think of Petyr as his father, but a part of him wanted desperately to do so. Only when they were alone in their suite, making small talk or when Petyr was kidding him about something did it seem real. The rest of the time he was still the bodyguard, the Soldier of The Church, and dangerous.

Though Trae was in good spirits, Petyr was sullen that morning. Few words passed between them at breakfast. The conversation was one-sided, Trae enthusiastic about the last step in his simulation, Petyr half-listening and distracted by something.

When the limousine came for Trae, Petyr was hovering over him. When they arrived at the lab Petyr was so close behind that Trae could feel his breath on his neck. The man followed him all the way upstairs to his cubicle, his hand darting inside his coat to his hip when Wallace suddenly came out of his office, startling them.

"Whoa," said Wallace, and held up his hands.

When Trae was settled in his cubicle, Petyr stayed right there. When he entered Wallace's office the man stood guard by the door, and watched them.

"What's going on?" asked Wallace. "For one second there this morning I thought he was going to shoot me."

"I don't know," said Trae. "He's been jumpy for a while. Any reason he should be?"

"Not that I know of," said Wallace, and they went back to work. Myra soon joined them, and frowned at Petyr as she entered the office.

"Is there a problem?" she asked, and looked right at Trae. *Are you in danger?*

Got you, thought Trae. *I don't know, but Petyr is worried about something.*

Myra blushed red, but Wallace didn't seem to notice and Trae said nothing more about it.

They worked on the simulation, changing one parameter, and three iterations later had the solution they wanted. The field generated by the torus made a wedge-shaped fold in the fabric of spacetime that was stable for twelve seconds before snapping back to flatness. Barely enough area for the ship to jump through, but a deep distortion nonetheless, and a ten light-year jump within the nominal power limit of the torus. Remaining power at twenty percent max, so recharge was necessary again, but at cruising speed the MHD generator was enough until they were within range of a microwave beaming station. Theory was finished; the only task left was to build the thing.

And that was out of Trae's hands. Even as he watched the simulation recycling on his screen, the dimple appearing, shaping, edges coming together, then fading slowly to blackness, his mind was already wandering to the problem of forming a branegate with a similar-sized ship. A much more difficult problem, since the geometry of the extra dimensions beyond spacetime was poorly understood, and also subject to local time dependent effects due to gravity.

He talked to Myra about it after Wallace went away to a meeting with people who pulled the purse strings for company research. "If all points in space are brane-connected to another universe and we have multiple gates on both sides of the brane there must be a connective geometry such that transits back and forth across the brane are equivalent to a huge spacetime jump in one universe," said Trae in one breath.

They tried to imagine it, Trae relying on Myra for geometrical support, and they spent the rest of the day drawing amoebic-shaped universes multiply connected by one brane or two. But by the end of the day they were totally befuddled by the problem, and Trae knew what directions his dreams would take that night.

He said goodbye to Myra, and she gave him a wonderful smile, and then Petyr took his elbow and propelled him out of the office. "What is wrong with you?" he said in an irritated whisper.

"Just move. Don't stop for anything," said Petyr. "Get right into the car."

They went down the escalator to the lobby. Others were already headed to the big, double doors leading to the street. Petyr's arm was hooked in his and he was being pushed along. They went out the door. It was bright. The car was waiting for them at the curb, and the driver in his black livery was holding the rear door open for them.

Things happened very fast at that instant, all of it lost to memory.

There was movement to Trae's right. He saw two men in dark business suits step away from the front entrance of the building and draw guns from inside their coats. They dropped into a crouch and brought the guns up, aiming directly at him.

Petyr pushed him hard towards the car, turned and opened fire on the men, a staccato of fire scattering brass cartridge cases on the sidewalk. Both of his targets crashed to the ground before firing a shot.

There was an explosion, high pitched, that echoed in the street as

Trae stumbled, looked back and saw the back of Petyr's head erupt in a shower of blood and white bone.

He didn't hear the second explosion, only felt the terrible concussion of the killing bullet that struck him in the chest.

And then he was gone.

CHAPTER 21

Away from the eyes of the common people, the election was decided before campaigning began.

In the days after the assassination of the Emperor of Gan things happened so quickly even news-people could not agree on what had happened or who was responsible. At first report the killing of Osman had been a terrorist act committed by the underground church, but new rumors quickly followed. Soldiers had been seen lowering the Emperor's colors fluttering beneath the flag of Gan, so they were also involved and it was a military coup. Strategic information was leaked. Agents of Galena in the uniforms of Gan secret police had participated in the assault of the palace, so it was an interplanetary conspiracy between Galena and the military establishment of Gan. It was also said that Osman had been blown up by a suicidal priest of an outlawed church, or had been shot by his own police. The news was flashed, and those who controlled the news waited for public reactions. There was only one: everyone could now openly agree that Khalid Osman had been a despised, self-seeking tyrant, and they were glad he was dead. The hope now was that he wouldn't be replaced by someone even worse.

They were pleasantly surprised.

The shakers and movers of Gan, those who built the industrial empires and created the jobs for the common people, the self-made men who drove the economy of the planet, all of them had come to a decision. The days of dictatorships inherited from one generation to the next had come to an end. There would be a new form of government on Gan, and it would be a government freely elected by the people.

In underground cells of The Church all over Gan there was cheering, and hope for religious freedom. The reaction of the general public was more subdued, but receptive. Any governmental system was fine with them as long as there were jobs, food on the table and a comfortable quality of life for everyone and not just a few. At least the industrialists had shared their wealth generously with their workers. The Emperor of Gan had only taken from them, and given nothing in return.

The ten wealthiest men on Gan formed a committee to suggest forms the new government might take. They elected a chairman whose wisdom they held in high esteem, and his name was Azar Khalil. The name was familiar to the everyday citizen. The companies within his conglomerate employed tens of thousands, and he'd funded a vast network of charities to help the poor. There was even a rumor he'd funded the underground church and was, in fact, a spiritual man who often meditated, and believed in a power greater than himself or any emperor. A humble man, yet wise and successful at anything he attempted to do.

The committee met regularly and held press conferences to inform the public about what models they were discussing. A pure democracy was ruled out immediately; without laws, checks and balances, anarchy would soon follow. But freedom of speech was a must, as was religious tolerance, two things that had been oppressed the most under the old regime.

Models poured forth from the committee, Azar Khalil acting as spokesman to the press: presidents with power, presidents as diplomats and prime ministers with power, presidents with appointed or elected cabinets of ministers, a plethora of congressional models all poured out in a span of three months.

In the meantime the everyday affairs of Gan were run by an interim cabinet of men who had enjoyed the trust of the people even under Osman's reign: a military general, former ministers of labor, economics and interplanetary affairs, men whose advice had often been publicly ridiculed by the Emperor while seeming reasonable to the people. One of these men was Sadam Halek, and it was said that without his wisdom and advice the emperor would have long ago driven Gan into economic despair. He was the most visible man of the interim government, having been selected by his peers to serve as president.

After a series of public opinion polls the committee chaired by Azar Khalil presented two models of government for a vote of the people: an elected president with elected congress of the people, or a figurehead president with elected prime minister and cabinet, and an advisory congress of the people. Polling places were established, and all citizens over eighteen were invited to register. Upon the public recommendation by Azar Khalil, amnesty was declared for members of the underground church, restoring them all to full citizenship and urging them to register and cast their vote.

The turnout of eligible voters was eighty-nine percent, and seventy percent of them voted to have an elected president and congress to share power in the new government.

Candidates appeared quickly; altogether there were twenty-five positions to be filled, and one of them was for president. Two candidates emerged for this powerful position; one was Sadam Halek, and the other was Azar Khalil. Since both men were respected public figures, a close race was predicted. Both were strong advocates of freedom of speech and religious preference. Both had records of fiscal conservatism and balanced budgets.

There were differences. Sadam Halek was a strong proponent of interplanetary commerce, particularly with Galena, his nearest neighbor. Azar Khalil believed in a focus on local industry to create more and better jobs to build a stronger tax base. He also had some misgivings about relations with Galena, reminding voters of the rumored but unproven involvement of that planet in the plot against the Emperor. "I believe in strong interplanetary relations, but I will not tolerate off-world interference in our affairs," he told them.

Halek believed in moral values, but advocated a complete separation of church and state in the making of laws.

Khalil's case for morality in government was even stronger, and he revealed for the first time his personal belief in The Source and the moral laws first established by missionary Leonid Zylak for The Church of The Faithful.

A prominent news reporter was contacted by an anonymous source giving him evidence that Azar Khalil had used his wealth to single-handedly keep alive an oppressed church driven underground. Voter registration centers were swollen with newly reinstated citizens for two weeks after the news appeared.

Another reporter questioned Sadam Halek about his regular trips to Galena, and a report he'd met recently with the Emperor there. Halek gave a complete accounting of his business meetings on that planet, but denied any meeting with its Emperor. The news was reported two days before the election with the headline, 'Candidate Halek denies recent political intrigue with Galena'.

The election was held, and ninety five percent of those registered cast their vote.

Azar Khalil received sixty four percent of the votes cast, and was sworn in as president of Gan and all its occupied territories. Following the ceremony, he attended the first public mass of The Church of The Faithful in twenty-four years, and was blessed by its Bishop.

CHAPTER 22

They were imprisoned for one month before visitors were allowed, and then it was only because Tatjana's family demanded it.

There was an apology from The Council of Bishops, but it was sent privately to Natasha Salizar, the eighty-year-old matriarch of the family. Her eight sons were the business minds behind a trillion sovereign a year empire, taking the place of their long dead father Carlos. One of those sons was Ernesto. And Tatjana Zylak was his daughter.

"Your apology will be accepted when my grand daughter is released on bail," said Natasha to the Archbishop when he called on her personally to apologize for the oversight. "I will not tolerate abuse of political power, even by The Church."

The presence of tiny Natasha Salizar was formidable, and the quilted chair she perched on was like a throne. Sky blue eyes blazed forth from a round face with pug nose and a small bow of a mouth rouged violet.

The Archbishop swallowed hard, and said, "I sincerely regret the necessity of arrest, Madam. If the Zylaks had not returned there wouldn't be a problem, but they represent a criminal government we fought hard to overcome, and we cannot allow them to remain free."

"Our previous government was inept, not criminal. Our economy is still a mess. Does that make The Church criminal? You spend your time flaunting power instead of tending to business."

"Madam, please be reasonable. Charges have been filed, but nothing has been proven in court. There will be a trial."

"Then why can't our lawyer see his client?"

"An oversight. It will be corrected immediately."

"Yes it will, and I'm giving you a list of other things to be corrected." She reached into a folio in her lap, withdrew a sheet of paper and handed to him.

"You should be pleased to note I'm not asking for bail if the rest of those things are done within a week," said Natasha. "If they're not, I'll go public with my demands and I'll release every piece of dirt my family has collected about The Church and its hierarchy."

"You're imagining things, Madam. I must caution you about commiting heresy."

Natasha laughed at him, a deep, earthy laugh. "Oh, my dear, we control all information on this planet. Nothing can be hidden from us: the lies, the assassinations of those you claim are imprisoned, the agents and saboteurs you send to the other side and the military fleet assembling near the Grand Portal. You cannot even stabilize the economy of a single planet, but are vain enough to think you can invade, conquer and control another universe on top of it."

"The public will not believe such lies, and The Church won't tolerate them," said the Archbishop, and now he was angry. "Don't think for a moment you're immune from prosecution, or worse."

Natasha's eyes narrowed. "Do not think you're immune from harsh treatment. The Source will not protect you from the consequences of stupidity. I can make one call, and the Council of Bishops will be dead within a day. It's already arranged if anything fatal happens to a single member of my family." Her gaze was steady, voice cold.

The Archbishop blinked, and cleared his throat. "I did not mean to threaten, Madam. Please, we're saying things we'll regret later. What you're asking for will be done, and I'll press for a trial in the near future. It's the best I can do."

"I can ask for no more than that," said Natasha sweetly, and lifted her ringed hand to be kissed. The Archbishop of Kratola kissed it grandly, and a servant arrived to escort him away from her.

Natasha remained perched on her throne, and closed her eyes. *The man is gone at last. Such impudence.*

The man has great power, Mother. Never underestimate it. Will he do what you say? The presence was strong, but came and went in her mind. Her son was doing something else at the same time.

I think so. We'll know within a day. Tell me when you hear something, Ernesto. They'll never release her, you know. We'll have to make other arrangements to get her back through the portal.

I know, Mother. We'll handle things, so don't tire yourself worrying about it.

A pause, and a tear crept into Natasha's eye. *Kratola is my home. I've always expected to be finally buried here, but now I think it might not happen.*

Leave it to The Source, Mother.

That's the problem. I think The Source will leave it up to me, just like your father did.

The guards were kind enough, could tell them nothing, but ventured an opinion it could be many months before a trial. But why hadn't their lawyer even visited them? And their family? Didn't they have a legal right to visitors?

This all changed thirty-two days after their imprisonment. Guards arrived in the morning, after they'd finished breakfast. Their cells were unlocked and they were allowed to embrace. The guards took them to another wing of the building. It was newer, cleaner, brighter.

They were still inspecting their new quarters when a guard came for them. "You have a visitor," he said, and motioned them down the hall. He took them to an interview room with tables and chairs and sat them down. Another guard armed with a high voltage prod was a permanent fixture in the room. They waited only a few minutes. The door opened, and their lawyer came in, a man they hadn't seen since their hearing. He smiled, and sat down opposite them at the table. "Please tell me that things have improved for you this morning," he said.

"They certainly have," said Leonid. "What happened?"

Carl Osten leaned forward, looked at Tatjana and spoke softly. "There was a subtle nudge from your grandmother."

"I doubt if it was subtle," said Tatjana. "That's not Grandma Nat."

"Indeed," said Carl. "The Archbishop himself has felt her wrath. At least your living conditions will improve, and you'll have visitors. This is important. I'm afraid the rest of my news is not good. The trial will not be soon, and it will mostly be a public show. You represent the old government, and the Bishops will make sure you're imprisoned for a long time."

"If things are so hopeless, then why are you here?" asked Tatjana, and her voice was sharp.

"I'll prepare the best defense I can and go through all the motions. I just don't want you to have any illusions about what the final outcome will be. Your grandmother doesn't believe this, but your father does. He's waiting outside to see you."

"Father!" said Tatjana.

"No matter," said Leonid, and his face was flushed. "We're not going anywhere, and we have a lawyer who's already given up. You go through the motions and collect your fee, and we're still here. What good are you?"

"Leonid!" said Tatjana.

"Well?" said Leonid, and glared at the man opposite him.

"I understand your feelings," said Carl. "Your family hired me; they can fire me if you wish. In the meantime I'll do the best I can do under the circumstances."

"I've had enough of your understanding. Please leave," said Leonid.

"Fair enough. I'll be back, if you'll see me. Perhaps you'll feel better when you talk to Ernesto." Carl stood up, leaned over close and nearly whispered, "One way or another, you will not be spending the rest of your lives in prison." He raised an eyebrow, then straightened up and walked to the door. The guard there let him out and instantly Ernesto Salizar was in the doorway.

Tatjana gasped, "Daddy!"

The man smiled, came over and sat down, reached across the table and took her hands in his. The guard rushed over and glared at them. "No touching. Let me see hands open."

They showed him. Satisfied, he went back to the door.

"Good to see you, Ernesto," said Leonid. "You're young again."

Black hair and trimmed beard, dark brown eyes, yet the skin on the man's finely chiseled face was like white porcelain. "Round two, just four years ago," said Ernesto. "I see you've done the same. Brings back old memories, when times were better."

"I'll say," said Leonid. "The news we just got is beyond bad. Your lawyer gives us no hope at all."

"I wish I could say otherwise, but he's probably right. The Church has the power to shut us down and take everything. I can't get Mother to believe this."

"Then it's hopeless," said Tatjana.

"The Church has to be brought down politically. We've started rumors. We have people everywhere, clear out to the Grand Portal. We're kept up to date on everything."

"Rumors about what?" asked Leonid.

"The spy network, here and elsewhere, the agents they've sent to the other side. It goes back to the time when the brane was first opened, and you went out on your missions. Church agents were right behind you, every world you visited. Two Bishops disappeared around that time. By the way, do you remember a document The Church issued to sanction your work?"

"I remember a letter," said Leonid. "All our old records are still on Gan."

"We need that letter," said Ernesto. "The Church formally sanctioned your mission; they cannot legally imprison you for it now. But the letter has been conveniently lost here. It might be irrelevant; we don't have the time."

Certain things must not be said aloud, and we may have said too much already.

Really?

Good, I thought you'd still hear me. Tatjana?

Yes, Father.

"Mother's her usual angry self, which means she's well. She'll try to visit you later."

"Oh, tell her I miss her," said Tatjana.

When we sent word about the crisis here we didn't expect The Church to take political control. Things have gone from bad to worse, and now the tentacles of the Bishops are reaching off planet.

"Grandma misses you, too. She's very angry about your arrest. If you're abused it'll go badly for The Church. We still have to abide by the laws, but maybe we can arrange an exile if things go badly at the trial. We're working on it."

Taxes are going up, and business is a shambles. All the money is going into the fleet they're assembling for an invasion through the Grand Portal. A crusade, they call it, spreading the word of The Source, but it's all about power. I don't see anyone stopping them, unless the Grand Portal is destroyed, and they even control that.

Only on this side, added Leonid.

"I wish now you'd remained here instead of going on those missions."

"There was no way to predict this happening to us, father."

Whatever. The family has discussed this; we don't see a future for us as long as The Church is in power. We have our own small fleet. We can be out of here and light years away in weeks. Only our heavy manufacturing facilities would be left behind, and we can do well without them.

"I still don't see how we can be responsible for acts our government committed long after we were gone. Maybe we should renounce our association with that government, and renew our pledge to The Church," said Leonid.

Oh, that's good. I hope they heard that. Anyway, the family is making plans. One way or another you're getting out of here. Try to be patient a while longer, and behave yourselves. We don't want visitation rights to be taken away.

But if we left, where could we go?

Our mineral surveys include several uncharted worlds within a hundred light years. And I'm sure you could find worlds on the other side that would take us in.

One in particular, but it's quite close to Gan.

"I'm sure it would make a big difference if you did that and really meant it. Do you mean it?"

"Of course. We don't have any basic quarrel with The Church except for what they're doing to us here."

Enough for now. We'll get back to you as our plans develop. It might take months.

"I'll tell our Bishop what you just said. He's sympathetic to your situation."

"When will Grandma Nat come?" asked Tatjana.

"Soon, hon. Very soon. Be patient."

Their fingers touched, then a short handshake with Leonid as the guard frowned at them. Ernesto left them then, and they were escorted back to their cell. Their hopes were now higher than before. They were together, their physical needs met, and they had visitors.

Nothing changed, and Grandma Nat never came to see them.

The Church denied sanctioning their missions on the other side, said any new pledge they might make to The Church would be under false pretenses and was thus unacceptable. The trial was postponed once, then again, then set for an undetermined date in the following year.

Four months after he'd first visited them, Ernesto came again and they made small talk about pressuring for a trial date. Their real conversation was short and private, and distinctly unpleasant.

It's no use. We have to leave. The Church now says there are irregularities in our tax payments, and has court permission to examine our books. It's a prelude to seizure. They also have no intention of releasing you. We can't break you out of here by force, but there's another way. When did you have you last scans?

Oh, no, thought Tatjana.

On the ship, just before transit, said Leonid.

Then we'll have to do another one. It'll complicate things, but we have inside help. Don't ask for details. It'll be soon.

He left them astonished and afraid. They returned to their cell depressed, and waited for something bad to happen. In the morning a guard came to serve them a breakfast of hot cereal and rolls.

By afternoon they were both seriously ill, and writhing in pain on their bed. The guards became excited and called a physician. He arrived and made a quick examination. "Looks like they've been poisoned!" he exclaimed, and ordered them sent to hospital.

A team of physicians worked on them behind closed doors, and they were pronounced dead shortly after midnight.

Word went out that Leonid and Tatjana Zylak had poisoned themselves to escape prosecution, but ugly rumors circulated immediately that The Church, in fact, had murdered them.

This was not a good thing for the reputation of The Church.

CHAPTER 23

Freedom was a heady experience for the citizens of Gan.

Within weeks after the election all underground caverns along the coast had emptied out; there was one continuous caravan of trucks, cars, and hand-drawn carts from the coast to the capital city. Most of the people, those bold enough to come out earlier for voter registration, had established friendships in town and had found a place to live. Many had no place to live, and so refugee camps appeared overnight in parks everywhere in town.

Established citizens grumbled about allowing refugees to use the parks, but were sympathetic about the plight of these people. The new president played on their sympathy and added to his exploding popularity by using his personal monies to provide food and medicine for those displaced. Four-square blocks of multistoried housing developments seemed to rise overnight. In just a year the parks were open again, and people who'd lived in caves for much of a lifetime enjoyed grand views of the city from the windows of their new apartments.

For nearly two years, life on Gan was good.

Industry grew rapidly, and jobs along with it. The government built special training centers for those who lacked necessary skills for the workforce, and it was free to those who were qualified. All graduates were employed. With nearly a hundred percent employment rate, taxes were nominal, a single fifteen percent tax on all goods purchased, and nothing else. The goods were available, the average salaries high. Spending was lavish, but still the banks swelled with what the people saved. The banks were now owned by the government, and there was no net profit in them. Paid interest rates were only a point below rates for a loan, except for special accounts for the purchase of a home, and for these the rates were the same.

The Church was free and open, after many decades of oppression.

President Khalil made a show of attending services, and encouraged his colleagues to do the same. He was quoted as saying, 'Those in government cannot lead properly unless they achieve spiritual growth and encourage it in others through their example. A good government must be ethical and honest for a state to be stable and strong.'

The people applauded his words, and flocked to masses in simple block buildings with humble furnishings, all over the city. Church coffers grew rapidly, and no taxes were paid. Such taxation would be a form of oppression, said Azar Khalil, and The Congress of The People agreed with him. Two years after the elections, nearly seventy percent of Gan's population was formal members of The Faithful. Of the remaining thirty percent, most lived in distant outlying areas where missions had not yet been established. The rest were dissidents and criminals, and considered to be useless elements of society.

The laws of Gan were fair and just, as approved by The People's Congress and their president, but there was no tolerance for crime. Those convicted of violent crimes, such as murder or rape, were summarily executed publicly by gunfire. Petty acts were punished by fines and also public service. Thieves, dealers of outlawed drugs, extortionists and the like were taken away and never seen again.

The people prospered. Nobody noticed that people rising in the hierarchy of The Church prospered even more. Nobody noticed that most of the taxes paid to the government came from the people's tax on goods. All the businesses, small to large, paid little or no tax because of deductions allowed by the government. And the conglomerates owned by Azar Khalil benefited the most.

Citizens didn't see the overflowing coffers of The Church, or the hoard of missionaries flowing to outlying areas and off planet. Few saw any significance when The Council of Bishops was established to oversee rapidly expanding church operations, and even fewer had concerns when The Council began supporting certain candidates for the first re-election of The People's Congress.

The Emperor of Galena *did* notice, for he was continually briefed on the developments on Gan through his embassy there. And he did not like what he saw happening.

His concern was heightened when he received a visit from his old friend Nicolus, who was now Bishop of The Church on Galena. They met privately in his chambers since, to this day, Emperor Rasim Siddique had never publicly professed his belief in The Source or a strict adherence to church teachings. The people only saw him as a good man.

They were served tea and cookies, and then the servant left them and closed the double doors behind him. Their table was small, their knees nearly touching, but the high, marble-ceiling room was so large they could hear their voices echoing from the walls. They spoke in near whispers, for the matter was most private, and not for public ears.

"I have a new concern," said Nicolus. "There has been a surge in immigration from Gan, and it seems most of them are priests."

Rasim bit into a cookie, and savored its sweetness. "Why would they come here, when their church is now free?"

"When some of our priests inquired, they said they came as missionies to the rural people, since it seemed we'd made no effort to do it. They made it sound like an admonishment."

"Is it true?"

"Not really. We've been to all the outlying districts, especially the farm towns. We attend town meetings, tell them about Our Faith and leave our literature. We only establish churches when the people request it. We don't work to convert people, or impose our will on them. It's their choice to make."

"And I agree with that policy," said Rasim. "I think religion is a very personal thing. I don't see what your problem is."

"It's their aggressiveness that disturbs me. They call themselves missionaries of The Church of Gan. They've established two churches in as many months, and the monies they collect are for the most part going back to Gan. Their tactic is fear. They tell people that if they don't convert to The Faith a vast armada will come from The Source and His Followers to destroy them. I don't like any of it, but how can I stop them?"

Rasim munched a cookie, and thought for a bit. "For the moment, I see nothing I can do. We have religious freedom, and these people are representing Gan in a way. Their new president has shown a great deal of enthusiastic support for The Church."

"Some say he's a zealot himself," said Nicolus.

"Perhaps. I've heard nothing from him since his election. He keeps a low profile with us for a reason, I think. His business empire, and those of his colleagues, have been extending friendly ties to us for months."

"You know there were rumors that Galena participated in the coup that eventually brought him to power," said Nicolus.

"Nonsense," lied Rasim. *Right now, I can't even understand why I participated in that operation when the man I indirectly helped now ignores me.* "Political rumors, used against Khalil's opponent, nothing more. I know he's expanding the horizon of The Church, and I certainly don't want Gan exporting zealots to stir up trouble here. Keep me informed. If they raise monies here and send them to Gan, give me proof of it and I can step in. The monies must be reinvested here, and the law is clear, even for The Church."

"I can get proof," said Nicolus.

"Fine, but otherwise you must compete with them for followers. That is also the law."

"I respect that," said Nicolus, then paused, averting his gaze from the eyes of his emperor.

"There's one thing I can say for Azar Khalil. He inspires attendance of services by example. He openly professes his faith."

Rasim put a hand on Nicolus' shoulder. "I don't have to prove my faith to you, old friend, or anyone else. I choose to show it in the way I live my life, and the way I treat those who depend on me for leadership. My ego does not require I appear holy, and to openly espouse one faith is to denigrate others. That's not a part of our teachings."

Nicolus smiled. "I must say I agree with you, but I suspect The Church on Gan does not share your views, or mine. I think they have a mission to convert everyone to their particular faith, and will not be tolerant of other beliefs."

"That is Gan's concern, but it will become my concern if it spreads beyond their borders. You must be my eyes and ears on this matter."

"I will," said Nicolus. "I was also wondering if you'd heard anything about Zylak's son. We've had no contact with him since he left here, and his task was to free his people on Gan. Now that it has happened I wonder if he's returned there."

"I've heard nothing," said Rasim. "He's likely with his own kind, now."

"Connected to us by faith, yet distant. The Immortal ones are strange; they are not of this world."

"Indeed," said Rasim, "but they are friends." He sipped the last of his tea. "It's good to talk to you, Nicolus. We don't do it often enough. Your presence warms me."

"As does yours for me," said Nicolus. "And as you said, I will be your eyes and ears."

They stood, and embraced. When Nicolus closed the door behind him, Rasim pressed a button beneath his table and in seconds a servant arrived. "Bring me a telephone," he said, and the man returned quickly with it. Rasim punched in four numbers linking him to his Defense Secretary, and the call was answered instantly.

"Sorry to disturb you, Nadir, but there's a matter that needs to be discussed. Right away. I've just heard something that makes me think we need to monitor closely the policies of the new government on Gan. No, it's not an emergency, but come as quickly as you can. I'll be in chambers."

He hung up, gave orders to a servant for more tea and cookies, and relaxed. It would only be a moment before his Defense Secretary arrived.

CHAPTER 24

Myra heard the gunshots from her second floor office, and rushed to the window to look down at the street. A company limousine was standing at the curb, its back door open. The driver was leaning over a prostrate form by the door, and shouting something. Three men ran from the building, two of them security officers, and they were looking down at something else she couldn't see because her view was obscured by a short hedge. The driver stood shaking, still shouting. A security officer knelt by the man at the driver's feet. The man's back was covered with blood. The officer rolled him onto his side, and Myra gasped when she saw his face. *TRAE!*

She bolted from the room, past the elevator, raced down the stairs and outside past an astonished guard who tried to stop her. Meza was already there, kneeling beside another body, and beyond it were three others. By the time she reached the limousine she was crying, and her head pounded behind her eyes. She knelt by Trae, her knees in his blood, and saw his glazed, dead eyes. Her chest was tight. For a moment, she couldn't breath. She reached out to touch him, but an officer grabbed her under her arms, stood her up and pushed her back.

"Pardon, ma'am, but the ambulance is coming in."

Her vision was blurred. She felt numb, stood helplessly by as ambulance attendants gently placed Trae in a body bag on a gurney and zipped it up. His body and three others were loaded in one ambulance, a fourth man still alive went into another. Meza talked to both drivers, and the ambulances sped off in different directions.

Meza spotted her, then. He came over and put an arm around her. She buried her face in his chest and sobbed for what seemed like a long time, but was not. Her heart had never ached so, crushed in the grip of some invisible hand.

"There, there, let it out. It's a shock for me, too. I never imagined this could happen. You can be sure we'll find out who's responsible. You'll see. There, there. Be patient, dear. You know he isn't gone forever, but it will be a while. Your secret is safe with me. I won't tell anyone how you felt about him. I'm sure Trae knew. And he'll know it again." Meza squeezed her gently, and she looked up at him.

"Where are they taking him?" Tears came again when she looked down at the pool of coagulating blood near her feet. Trae's blood.

Meza whispered like a fellow-conspirator. "Around the block to the other side of the complex, both of them. It might be difficult with the bodyguard; the back of his head was blown away. Trae was shot in the chest, so we should save something. Scans are being done in the ambulance. We have all their other records, Myra; you know we'll do the best we can for them."

"I know," she said, *but it won't be the same. He won't be Trae anymore.*

"The first medical report will come out later today. Do you want to be there for it?"

"Yes." *He won't remember me.*

"Let's get some tea and quiet, let our hearts calm a bit."

She nodded numbly. Meza led her to the basement cafeteria where they sat silently in a corner booth a while before he finally spoke. "It's a strange thing, this field of energy binding us together. The resonance we experience, even at vast distances without time lapse, and all of our science has not yet explained it. One is tempted to say we're a group mind, but we're not. We're individuals, attuned to one another by choice, even at short distances. Do you ever wonder why that is?"

"I've never wondered about it," said Myra, knowing he was only trying to distract her from her sadness, her grief. "I can speak to any of my own kind at short distance, and they to me. Thoughts can be masked, of course, but that's a learned process."

"Everyday interactions," said Meza. "That's not what I mean. I never felt a part of anyone except family until the day I met my wife, and it was a second lifetime for both of us. After that day she was constantly in my mind and I in hers, but as far as I know we didn't meet in our previous lives. It makes me wonder if we had lives we're not even aware of. There was an instant connection, a resonance, if you like."

Like I felt for Trae.

"It takes no effort to communicate, and distance isn't a factor. Perhaps it's an heriditary thing."

You mean like being related?"

"No, no, but it could be a specific coding in our DNA. I even asked Wallace to give it some thought as a project for our medical people, but he just sighed at me. Dear Wallace. He's going to be very upset by this. Trae was his most important information source. The delay will be agonizing for him; they were close to the field testing phase."

"How long?" asked Myra. *Not that it matters. He'll be a new person. Anything we had between us will be gone.*

Meza took a sip of tea, then, "Months, years, I don't know. It depends on the genetic material on hand, and how developed we want the clone to be. The stock for the Zylak family is quite complete. And we need Trae soon as possible to continue what he was doing. Do you want to pick an age?"

"No—well—adulthood, of course. He'll have to be changed. If the people who had him killed know who and what he was, they'll be looking for his reincarnation." Trae had not just died, but had been foully murdered. For the first, and not the last time she felt a surge of anger within her.

Apparently it showed in her face. Meza reached across the table to put a hand on hers. "Only a dozen people knew who Trae was: you, Wallace, myself and our Board of Directors. That narrows things down a bit, and hopefully the one assassin who survived will live long enough to answer some questions. I suspect whoever plotted this might well anticipate a reincarnation. Trae will have to be returned secretly, and will be known to only three of us. I have my suspicions about who might be involved with the assassins, and our medical people aren't among them. They'll also be sworn to secrecy."

He patted her hand. "You and Trae had unfinished work. Finnish it for him. Be ready. When he returns you must never acknowledge who he is, either verbally or mentally, at least not until we eliminate the criminals behind this assassination."

"I can do that," she said softly. *I will never open myself to anyone, ever again.* She pulled her hand away from his as she thought it.

Meza noticed the move, and smiled a thin smile. "I have to leave, now. Security is waiting for me; they've either questioned the surviving gunman by now, or know when it's possible. If you like, I can take you to the clinic tonight and we can get a prognosis on Trae's cloning possibilities."

"I'd like that," she said, tried bravely to smile, and failed.

Meza touched her under the chin. "Chin up. Meet you here at seven. We'll have a snack after."

He left her, and the booth closed in on her. The cafeteria was empty, the entrance barred closed while the staff prepared to put out the evening buffet. She smelled fish cooking.

Trae's face wouldn't leave her mind: his sparkling eyes, an eyebrow raised in a question, the way he chewed at his lower lip in thought. She'd been a part of him and he hadn't even noticed, had been too shy to say what he felt for her, but getting closer to doing it day by day. A body could be cloned, rejuvenated, but personalities so often did not survive the process. She was living proof of it, the iron maiden in her previous life, dedicated to work, no involvements, dying alone in a dark apartment after a century of personal isolation. So why had she been cursed by being born again as a person wanting to love, only to find it and then lose it again so quickly? Oh, Trae . . .

Myra came out of her reverie only an hour before she was supposed to meet Meza again. She went back to her office, sat down and stared at her monitor. Scattered fractals, a pattern emerging as she moved the mass sims around, looking for a symmetry that refused to come. She tried large masses, planetary size, still no good. Only with the masses of several suns could she achieve a stress topology remotely resembling the portal she was after.

Trae would have had it figured out in minutes.

Myra turned off her computer, and began to cry again in the darkness.

Meza took the elevator to third floor and walked the long hallway to the clinic. Security met him in east wing. One look at their faces, and he knew the surviving assassin was gone.

"Too late?" he asked.

Martin Emmerich was the chief security officer for the plant, a round man with coal black eyes and a beak of a nose. He cocked his head to one side. "Mmmm, maybe something. He was alert for a few minutes, cooperative, said they were hired for the hit. All of them were normals, all with records, mostly smuggling. Hired locally, all by telephone, but he did say they were being paid from off-planet. Had to wait weeks for their money, and the job was delayed because of it."

"Did he say who hired them?" Meza asked anxiously.

"Yeah—said they were paid by The Bishop. That's all he knew, We have the address for these guys; they lived together. We're searching their apartment now. Do you want us to bring in the police?"

"Absolutely not," said Meza. "Outside of our gates, nobody knows what happened today. Understand?"

"Got it," said Martin. "Figured you'd want it that way. Think it was someone in the family?"

"I do."

"Then we'll just have to ferret 'em out for you."

"Do that," said Meza, and shook the man's hand.

"I know who he was, you know. The kid, I mean. His bodyguard told me."

"Keep it quiet," said Meza, and Martin nodded in agreement. As he walked away, Meza thought, *and just how many other people knew about Trae's identity? Terrific news.*

He took the elevator back down and went to the cafeteria, Myra was waiting there in the same booth where he'd left her. Her eyes were red and puffy, her cheeks flushed. He wanted to hug her, but didn't. A few people were eating there, near the end of dinner hour, all of them scientists who marched to nobody's beat but their own. Some even slept in their labs on occasion.

"Hi," he said. "Want something to eat before we go up?"

"I'm not hungry," she said.

"Okay, let's get out of here."

He took her hand briefly, then let it go. Boss holding hands with the assistant could start rumors even among scientists who normally wouldn't notice such things. They took the elevator up to third floor again, but went left this time and over the enclosed bridge into west wing. Even being well known and wearing their badges they had to walk through the scanner at the security station there. The armed guards did not smile or show any signs of recognition of the man who paid their salaries.

A thumb-scan let them into 'Lab C', now empty but well lit. Another station opened the door to 'Special Projects'. A guard in an enclosed booth watched them come through, and gave them a nod.

Floor and ceiling were silver plas-steel polished to a mirror finnish. Ceiling panels glowed a restful, light green. At first glance the walls were red, until one noticed the tier after tier of chambers separated from the room by clear polymer, all filled with a viscous red fluid swirling slowly in vortical plumes accented by bubbles the size of a human fist. A man sat at a concave console in the center of the room, watching row after row of small video screens and monitoring the life-signals coming from each chamber in the walls. He only glanced at them, quickly focusing again on the screens in front of him to watch the first movements of new human beings now only inches long, humans who would grow at astonishing rates in the enzyme-laden, oxygenated nutrient they swam in.

They walked past him to an open doorway and down a hall past clear windows of other laboratories, some dark. Technicians hovered over what looked like a corpse on a gurney, attaching electrodes to its skull. The corpse was alive, and ready to be reborn. In another room two technicians chatted with a young woman in a hospital gown. Her body and head bristled with fine wires connected to a panel atop the throne-like chair she sat in. As she chattered away, the technicians were taking notes, and when she saw Myra looking at her she smiled beatifically. The joy in her expression was the joy of being alive again, and Myra wondered if Trae would feel the same way.

The hall came out into the morgue. Two bodies lay covered on steel tables there, and a man was waiting for them. When he saw them he picked up a clip board and held out his hand. "I'm Harold Piznik, Mister Meza. Welcome to my lair."

"My assistant Myra," said Meza.

Piznik shook her hand, too, limply. "I do the autopsies here, following a residual scan. There is good news, and bad." He consulted his clip board.

"In the case of the man named Petyr, brain damage was catastrophic, and we could get nothing. We have in our library a scan done six days ago, so that's the best we'll be able to do. That's the bad news." He smiled.

"The good news relates to the young scientist who I understand is very important to one of our projects. His last complete scan was also done six days ago, but when he arrived here there was still brain activity, though sporadic. I was able to get a residual scan before activity ceased. How much was there I can't say, but we got something.

With interviews and discussions post-manifestation it might be possible to fill in the gaps."

Myra stared at the two shrouded bodies on the tables, her eyes filled with tears. Piznik noticed it, touched her arm.

"The people you're here about are in another room. Did you want to see them?"

"Oh, no," said Myra quickly.

"Ah, well, we can begin cloning immediately. The deceased included instructions in the archives; a particular vial was specified for the young man, some written suggestions for his bodyguard.

"Timeline?" asked Meza.

"Instructions were to keep a continuous age. My guess is eighteen months. Six of that is neural net and implantation, and a couple for orientation. Let's say two years to get him back into the lab. Too long?"

"Not if it's the best you can do."

"So I'll try to do better," said Piznik.

"Will you clone the body he has now? Will he look the same?" asked Myra suddenly.

"I really don't know," said Piznik, flipping pages on his clip board. "One of our police died recently in an accident and he was in fourth lifetime. He'd lost his family, and did not desire rejuvenation. We're cloning him for your Mister—uh—Petyr. In the case of—let's see—Trae—hmmm, no last name listed—anyway, a vial was referred to that has been here for nearly a century. It was in an old section of the library reserved for the Zylak family itself. I thought there was an error, but then I found instructions in that same section reffering again to that particular vial and saying it should be used whenever requested by code number. The code numbers matched, and so the request will be honored. It appears that the new body for the young man named Trae will be that of a Zylak family member."

"Leonid Zylak?" asked Meza.

"No, the name on the vial is 'Anton'. He was the sole Zylak heir, and died in childhood. Quite an honor for this young scientist of yours, I think."

"It certainly is," said Meza.

Myra wiped her eyes dry. *And it's who he really is,* she thought. *But will he even know me?*

CHAPTER 25

A hundred yards away he could feel searing heat on his face. The entire house was involved. Two priests tried to pull him back, another lay dead by the open front door. He broke away and ran around one side of the house, desperate. The big window of the sun room had blown out, shards covering the grass. Inside, he saw a clear lane towards the back of the house, crawled over the windowsill and bloodied his knees on broken glass.

The fire was advancing fast. He knew where they would be, and opened the bedroom door. Flame spit at him from the ceiling; he covered his nose and mouth against a burst of hot gases from burning polymers. A figure lay on the bed, face down. Tatjana. He rolled her over, saw Anton unconscious beneath her. A priest shouted behind him, and he screamed back something, picked up Anton with one arm, his other arm looping around his wife. The priest helped—yes, the priest took Anton. They carried them to safety. They were all right. No, no, something else—the gases, hot, toxic—that was it. They'd breathed it in. It wasn't the fire, it was the gases. They'd breathed in the gases, then stopped breathing before he could get to them.

Everything was in slow motion. The priests were taking them away, but now the bodies had somehow become charred. We'll bring them back. You know we will. He didn't believe them. His feet were wet in the grass, the fire burned, but now he felt no heat, only his heart squeezing tightly inside him. His family was gone, all that he loved taken away. He felt a tear on his cheek, but when he touched it nothing was there. Nothing . . .

It was suddenly dark, and he was sitting on a hard floor wedged into a corner. His knees were drawn up and there was horrible pain in his stomach and bowels. He'd never had such pain, and he screamed. He couldn't see Tatjana, but heard her screaming too.

Others called to them in the darkness: Anton, a boy with another name he couldn't remember, but familiar, and then Grandma Nat shouting, "Stop it. None of this is real, so stop it and wake up. We don't have time for this!"

With Grandma Nat it was always a command. *Yes, ma'am.* He tried to open his eyes, but they were stuck. He moved his eyes back and forth beneath the lids, and something gave way. He opened his eyes, and immediately shut them again before a fierce, blue light could blind him.

"He's here," said a voice. "Go to deep red, now. We could use some suctioning, Dinae, ears and nose. I see residual nutrient in there."

Something tickled his ears deep inside, then went rudely up his nostrils, and he shook his head.

"Ah, welcome back. Now try to open your eyes again. This should be better."

Two masked faces looked down at him. A bank of deep red lights glowed softly above them. He heard a regular clicking sound, and felt a gentle, cool breeze on his face. He tried to speak, but only a strange growl came out of him, and he coughed.

"Can't you sit him up?" asked a commanding voice.

"In a few minutes, Madam. Not too quickly."

A new, masked face appeared above him. Even with the mask there was no mistaking the piercing stare of those blue eyes. She put a cool hand on his forehead.

"Get up, you lazy boy. Tatjana has been up and around for two days, now. And we can't leave until you're fit for travel."

Now he remembered: arrest, imprisonment, the family visits, then the horrible pain in his cell. "Did I die?" he asked in a whisper.

"Well, you were quite ill from what went into your food," said the masked physician attending him. "Your clones were ready by then, and once we had you both in the clinic we could do your residual scans and then give you something to put you away for good. We even leaked the name of the drug to the press. It seems the Council of Bishops had you murdered before your trial. I can't tell you how much fun we've had listening to the public reaction to that."

"Unfortunately we can't wait around to see where it goes," said the Matriarch of the Zylak family and empire. She gave Leonid a gentle pat on his cheek.

"We're packed, and ready to go. Seven ships are in our commercial orbit, and a shuttle is arranged with all the necessary papers. It cost me a small fortune, and I'll not allow you to slow us down. I'm sure the good doctor will get you up as soon as possible, won't you doctor?"

"Yes, Madam."

"Good. Let's do it, then. I've business to attend to."

"Where are we going?" asked Leonid, his voice raspy. The doctor fed him some water through a straw.

"We've decided to split up. Ignacio and Luiz will set up our new manufacturing facilities on Delano's Planet. We've been using it for years for new materials, but since the Bishops grabbed power we've turned smuggler to avoid their taxes. The planet isn't even on their charts. My sons have already left, and send best wishes to you and Tatjana. They'll also keep watch on The Bishops. I don't think the political system can last; the people will tire of such strict rule. The rest of us are going to the other side, but I know I'll want to return here someday, maybe in a lifetime or two. This has been my home, where my babies were first born. I'll miss it too much to stay away forever."

Leonid cleared his throat, took another sip of water. "It won't be so easy on the other side, either. So many of the worlds there are under dictatorships. Democracies are just starting, and the churches are more hindrance than help. The extremists always seem to get their way."

"But there are good worlds there," said Grandma Nat, for that was who she was to him. She'd treated him like a son, and he loved her for it.

"Yes. A few."

"Then you'll find one for us. We'll have over a lifetime to make a choice while our ships poke along at half light speed between jumps."

"And things can change in that time."

"Nothing will happen until we get to our ships." She pulled up her mask, leaned over and gave him a soft kiss on his cheek. The doctor made no move to stop her.

Her lips were soft and full, her nose tiny but finely arched. Even at an advanced age, the beauty of her youth still lurked there.

"I want to see you on your feet tomorrow. I'll be back." A faint smile, and she walked away.

"Better do it," said the doctor, eyes twinkling above his mask.

"Oh, I will," said Leonid.
And he did.

The reunion was emotional for two reasons: first, they were just happy to be alive again and in each other's arms, and secondly they'd both been restored in copies of their original bodies during mission work. Tatjana was as he remembered when she'd given birth to Anton, and she had first fallen in love with the high cheekbones and dark beard of a youthful Leonid.

The clones had been aged to thirty five, and performed magnificently during the first four nights they were together again. After that, all their time was spent escaping a despotic church rule and fleeing back to another universe.

The power and influence of Tatjana's family never ceased to amaze her husband. Grandma Nat was like a silent cancer: no obvious, detectable lump, but a spiderweb of tenticles reaching into every area at all levels in public life up to, but not including, the Council of Bishops. People she didn't own she rented or bribed. People who could not be rented or bribed were removed from their positions by firing or promotion to areas less threatening to family operations in far away locations.

The family came together just a month after Tatjana and Leonid had begun what was now their third lifetime together. Together with servants they totaled over a hundred people, even with two brothers and their families gone away.

A standard shuttle held sixty-five. A second vessel was needed. Commercial shuttles were watched carefully, not just cargo but also travel destinations and time schedules. Military versions came and went at the discretion of senior officers. One vessel went on a training mission and was reportedly destroyed by explosion. Fragments of radioactive debris returned by a salvage scow indicated fusion reactor overun as likely. Apparently some miracle occurred, because the morning the family was to leave for space, that same shuttle was docked next to theirs, freshly painted and numbered to fit records of the family fleet. The fact it had not been listed when the fleet first entered orbit was written off as a clerical error and signed for by the same man who'd approved inspection reports and cargo manifests for the fleet. Years later that man, a minor cog in the machinery of bureaucracy, retired handsomely to Delano's Planet, where he and his wife lived in great luxury in a mountaintop estate, and he kept himself busy with occasional consulting jobs from a manufacturing firm there.

A twelve-minute burn and an hour of coasting later the two shuttles made rendezvous with Atlantia, the flagship of a fleet of seven hauling plas-teel and carbon-36 wire to Cay Benz. Two orbits later all had disappeared from orbit after final clearance had been radioed from the ground and recorded in a log there.

Later, when the Council of Bishops filed charges against them, Orbital command denied issuing such a clearance.

The fleet headed directly towards Cay Benz, where it was expected in two days. It never arrived. No communication had been received or acknowledged since the fleet had left the thousand-mile limit above Kratola. An optical and infrared search was made, but nothing was ever found. And nobody ever thought to search the vast dust clouds above and below the plane of the ecliptic for Kratola's young star.

They passed Port Angel at a distance of three million miles above the ecliptic plane. The station was a faint star, twinkling off and on. Even with a bow shock of ionizing radiation, enough dust still got through the protective field to play a tune at half-light-speed on the ship's hull. *Sharp fingernails drawn across a sheet of slate,* thought Leonid, and tried to ignore the faint, dull shriek of it.

Tatjana came into the observation lounge from behind him, put an arm around his waist, and leaned her head against his shoulder. "Such a long way to go. So much can happen before we get back."

"Trae will be a hundred years old, a true sage," he said.

"Anton," she corrected. "He'll always be Anton to me."

"I know. Once through the Grand Portal we should be able to reach him. He might already be changed."

A beeping sound interrupted them. Both pressed a finger to one ear to get the call.

"Where are you two? I've been looking all over the ship for you."

It was Grandma Nat. "We're in the level four observation lounge."

"Oh, well, get down to the bridge. There's something here you need to see. It'll give you an idea of what your missionary universe is going to be up against soon."

"On our way," said Leonid, caught Tatjana by the hand until they found an elevator down to level two. The bridge was like a warehouse, now a mostly empty floor with a bank of instruments and a monstrous viewing screen at one end of it. Grandma Nat was there with three men, and they were studying something on a console screen.

"What is it?" asked Leonid, and Grandma pointed at the screen. At first it looked like a globular cluster that had been flattened out and compressed. Dozens of white dots on a green screen.

"The great crusade of The Church, and there it sits, just waiting for orders to make the transition. Must be a hundred ships there: freighters, cruisers, troop ships. Can't tell the difference from here. Know of any worlds that can stop a fleet of this size?"

"Military use of space hadn't really begun when we left," said Leonid, "but there was a lot of talk about it."

"You'd better hope it's more than talk, now. If those ships go through the Grand Portal your universe will belong to The Church, or should I say a handful of Bishops. Nothing will stop them."

"If they go through," said Leonid, and Grandma Nat looked at him sharply.

"You have an idea?"

"The Grand Portal depends critically on a specific mass distribution on both sides. Deviate even slightly from the equilibrium mass distribution, and the portal becomes unstable. I don't know about this side, but on the other side there are constant corrections to the positions of several black holes to even keep the portal open."

"I never understood any of it," said Nat. "You think it's possible to close the portal?"

"Yes, or at least make it unstable enough to prevent a safe transition. But even one ship working the masses is the size of a terran planet. We'd need an army to take just one of them."

"We don't have an army, Leonid, so think of something else." She dismissed the idea with a wave of her jeweled hand.

"Raise an army and fight them, then. If they wait long enough to invade, it might be possible. Once through the portal it'll take up to sixty years to reach the first manned outpost we know of on the other side. The first populated systems are a few light years beyond it. There isn't much interaction between systems, with a few exceptions, and those are based on commerce. Mostly dictatorships, a couple of democracies, military and police units large enough to control limited population centers on a planet.

"How large?" asked Nat, still watching the vast cluster of light points on the screen. Some were slowly moving.

"Up to tens of thousands, I suppose," said Leonid. "They've been pretty much isolated their entire history, Nat. There hasn't been any need for an interplanetary force, let along interstellar. Only older civilizations like ours have become that paranoid."

Grandma Nat laughed. "How true. But I think they'll become paranoid enough when their skies are filled with the warships of The Church."

"The Church is there, Nat, on every planet we worked on. We went there to preach freedom and democracy, and it seemed like The Church was right behind us every step of the way. Some of our aids must have spread the first literature. The only religions on any of those planets were humanistic to begin with. They worshipped no higher power. Whatever happened was quick, too. By the time we left each planet, small churches were already springing up. Some flowered, others were driven underground by dictators who tolerate no religions other than the worship of themselves. But The Church is there, Nat, everywhere. If the skies are filled with ships come in the name of The Source on a mighty crusade, the people might welcome them with open arms."

"And spend the rest of their days living under extremist dictates of Bishops in another universe," said Nat.

"Still possible," said Leonid. "I'm telling you, Grandma, we won't be able to fight them. The only way to stop the invasion is to destroy the Grand Portal, or make it very dangerous to use."

"We need an army to do that, too, you said."

"Maybe not. We had some good people with us, most of them in second or third lifetimes when we left. They were working on some things. By the time we get back to them it might be possible to control the Grand Portal with ships far smaller than planets. Our own son was working on it before we made transit and got ourselves arrested. I should be able to contact him as soon as we're on the other side."

"Why not now?"

"Something about the brane separating our universes. The field that connects us doesn't permeate it."

"Well, it won't be long. Try to contact him tomorrow."

"Tomorrow? We're days from the portal."

"Ordinarily, yes. Didn't you wonder why we didn't stop at Port Angel?"

"I wondered, yes. I assumed all the clearances had been arranged in your usual, efficient way."

"Well, it was a bit more complicated this time. Our clearance was radioed ahead to the portal three days ago. We have to catch up to it, so we're going to make a small jump in a few hours, just before Port Angel might pick us up on their scanners. You might want to take a nap then."

Leonid gave her a wry smile. "You are a devious person, Grandma Nat."

"So I've been told," she said, and patted his cheek with a heavily veined hand.

Asleep in their plas-steel cocoon, they didn't feel the jump. Both had taken a sleeping pill with a glass of wine and remained conscious long enough for some very pleasant moments in bed. Many years before, Leonid had been forced to experience a jump during a mechanical emergency that had trapped him in his cabin. Distracted, he'd forgotten to prepare himself and when the moment came it was as if the world was fluid and pliable. Everything was suddenly distorted, swimming rapidly about him, and flickering in and out of a strange darkness. His inner ear spun like a top, and he'd thrown up all over his cabin floor. Never again. He took the pill and the wine, enjoyed pleasures with Tatjana, and went soundly to sleep.

When they awoke, the walls of their tiny room were gently vibrating in short bursts. The vernier engines were on, maneuvering the attitude of their ship. It could only mean they were nearing the portal.

They dressed quickly and went back up to the bridge. Grandma Nat was there in her special chair, sipping a cool drink and watching the big viewing screen over the control console. At first there was only blackness, but then the great cats'-eye of the portal swung into view and centered itself on the screen. If this was normal magnification, Leonid guessed they were still hours away from transit.

Nat saw them then. "Finally you're up. You've seen this before, of course, but for me it's a first time experience in making a transit. It's rather exciting." She smiled, and sipped her drink.

"You must feel badly about leaving your universe," said Tatjana, and knelt by the throne of the matriarch.

"Actually I don't. Life is meant to be an adventure, my dear."

"Everything going smoothly?" asked Leonid.

"Oh, there have been inquiries. A picket ship challenged us earlier and gave us a bit of a scare, then apologized when they found our earlier clearance in their archives. It didn't come the usual way, so I think they'll look into that, and we're hurrying right along. A couple of picket ships are trailing us from a distance, so we've been noticed. I don't suppose it's possible to make a jump through the portal?"

"It's not the same kind of space, has a higher dimensionality. It could be suicide to try it," said Leonid. "Either that, or nothing would happen."

"Maybe on the other side," said Grandma, and then grinned at them. "You children might want to go back to bed."

"Grandma!" said Tatjana, and gave her a playful tap on the arm.

Leonid didn't laugh; he was thinking. "The brane has an extra dimension," he said, "but maybe the portal interior doesn't. The regular, four-dimensional spaces of the two universes might mix together in there. Folding one might fold the other. Interesting."

"All I know is, if those picket ships try to close with us we're not going to hang around to answer questions; we'll make a run for it, one way or another," said Nat.

Grandma turned away from them, then, gave instructions to her captain, and was on the earphones a while with the captains of the rest of her little fleet.

Leonid and Tatjana enjoyed the view. The portal itself was lovely, a glowing, flickering cloud in red, blue, yellow and green. The folds of its interior, where transition would occur, seemed solid from where they were. Deep red. An extra dimension there, theory said, the brane itself of unknown composition and invisible to the eye, yet connecting the two universes at every point in space. Only extreme stress caused by any of the four fundamental forces could open up a string-sized point to a portal large enough to accommodate a ship. The original discovery, three hundred years ago in their home universe, had been accidental, during the first experiments in recovering vacuum state energy.

There was somehow a link between the brane and the origin of vacuum state energy, for hadn't one universe originally come from another? And then there were all those exotic particles which hadn't yet been seen, but which must exist.

They knew how to stabilize a tunnel in the brane, knew how to open it up under the right conditions, and travel routinely through it, yet they did not understand one bit of the fundamental physics behind it. Even Leonid knew this was a dangerous thing. Nature might abhor a vacuum, and do something to fill it up, but it also had no tolerance for ignorance.

Grandma Nat sat next to her captain and murmured into her throat mike. There was a thump. The main engines had cut in and they were moving ahead more quickly now, the Grand Portal noticeably growing in size. They were getting close. Tatjana stood just in back of her grandmother, Leonid a pace behind her. Suddenly, Grandma grabbed Tatjana's arm, whispered something and released her.

Tatjana turned, said, "Find recliners. We're supposed to strap in. The picket ships started closing in as soon as we picked up speed. They're calling on us to stop for inspection. We're moving into an echelon formation and making transit together."

The floor lurched, and they stumbled. Leonid went to one knee. Rows of recliners were in the back of the bridge, could hold twenty passengers during normal shuttle operations, but this was definitely not normal.

They strapped themselves in. The top and bottom edges of the portal were now off the screen. The red of its interior was now flecked with vortices in green and blue, and there was a faint, dark patch at its center.

"Closing," called a man at the end of the curving control console. "They say they'll open fire or ram us."

Grandma suddenly shouted, "We have clearance to travel, and we're going through. If you inflict any damage on us I promise you'll answer for it personally to the Bishops. They have authorized our passage!"

She jabbed her hand rapidly in the air. There was another thump; they were picking up speed, and the portal was now rushing towards them. Again the beautiful display of swirling colors, the patch at the center black, then a kind of purple with threads of red, then—

The room swirled around them, images coming in bursts, and it seemed Leonid's head continued to turn, twirling on his shoulders. He was suddenly nauseous, and swallowed hard. He looked at Tatjana. Her eyes were closed, a strange pallor on her face.

As suddenly as it began, it was over.

"Where are they?" asked Grandma.

There was a long pause.

"Well? They were right behind us when we entered."

"They're not there," said the captain. "They're not anywhere. Nothing came out of the portal behind us."

"I don't hear anything, Ma'am," said another officer. "They're not there."

"Then we lost them," said Grandma. "Good. Now find out where we are."

"I don't think we lost them. They've disappeared. Their ships didn't make it through the portal. We made a space fold there, and something happened to them," said Leonid.

"We were just coming out of transition," said the captain. "It was a two minute jump, and that's where we ended up, see?" He pointed at the observation screen.

Indeed, the great portal barely filled the screen top to bottom. Two black spheres crawled across it, planet-sized ships doing their work to keep it stable and open, correcting some small perturbation.

"Something happened," mumbled Leonid again.

"We're here, and nobody is chasing us, that's the point," said Grandma Nat. "Now that we're here it would help if you could point us in the right direction, dear."

"I have the charts we brought with us. If you're willing to make a lot of jumps we can make the frontier in thirty years, even less."

"Another reincarnation," grumbled Grandma. "I should come back as an infant this time. Can't we do it faster than that?"

"With sub-light speed and power for jumps under five light-years it is. We're doing galactic travel, not interstellar between nearest neighbors. That's what Anton, our son, was working on when we left. I doubt a lot of progress has been made in such a short time."

"So call him and find out. We're in his universe, now. There are no time delays in the fields that bind us."

She was right, so Leonid tried. He tried hard to contact his son by calling him to the place where they'd met before on rolling hills covered with flowers. Tatjana went with him and also called, a loving invitation for Anton to meet them, but there was no answer, not even a whisper.

No one was there to answer them.

CHAPTER 26

The meeting of the Trustees' Board was somber. Ten men in expensive suits took notes on recorders while Meza sat at the head of the conference table and lied like he'd never lied before.

"I admit it's a huge setback for us, but our founder's instructions must be obeyed. Trae's body was picked up the morning after his death and went out by freighter yesterday. He's going home."

"Surely they'll clone him," said Thos Hyeran, the board president. Bald and slight, he was a fragile looking man. "Wasn't a residual scan done?"

"Yes, but not by our people. Trae's bodyguard had his own security team; they took charge right after the shootings. I approved it, according to the wishes of Leonid Zylak. This was an event he knew was possible. He said the entire family was to leave if it happened, and return to the home universe. I can show you his letter, if you like."

"Please," said Thos.

Meza called the letter up on his recorder, and shared it with them. There was a long silence as they read it.

"He seems to have become disenchanted with us," said Thos.

"Not at all. He's disenchanted with the futility of political solutions, and threatens a strong force to protect his interests. He's an angry man. Can you blame him? His only son has been assassinated twice, apparently on the orders of different people. The Emperor of Gan is dead. Who do we blame this time? We have no extremists here. The killers were hired by a man called The Bishop. Gan and Galena are the only two planets with a church structure formal enough to assign Bishops."

"It could be just a title used to confuse things," said Thos. "It could also be industrial sabotage by a competitor. Trae worked on important projects, and was clearly a prodigy."

"But who? We have no competitors, not in transportation or communications technology. Everyone sub-contracts from us."

"Maybe someone wishes it otherwise," said Thos, and a few heads nodded in agreement.

"We're exploring the possibility. The perpetrators will be found and punished, no matter who they are. In the meantime we salvage what we can. Trae's abilities are lost to us in the future, but we have his residual scan and it includes an important testing sim he'd just finished. For the present, at least, the project will move swiftly. We'll soon test a shuttle-sized ship in opening a gate large enough to retrieve vacuum state energy. Wallace has the details in a file he calls 'Anton R', but it's quite technical. And scaling up to produce a gate large enough for ship transition remains a project for the future."

The subject then changed to marketing matters. Meza bored them for half an hour, and the meeting broke for lunch. He went back to his office, passing Wallace's on the way, and knocked softly on the door.

"Come!" An anxious voice; Wallace was expecting him.

Meza closed the door, spoke softly. "Watch closely. I think it'll happen soon."

"I have markers on every machine in the building. Everything going out is being recorded, too."

"I won't tell you who I think it is. I don't want to bias your surveillance."

Wallace nodded, then, "Anything new on the cloning front? I really need Trae's help here, and Myra's efficiency has dropped to nothing. Just seeing him alive will pick her up. She's the best model maker I have."

"He could have a new persona," said Meza.

"She knows that. Just get him back here. Myra needs his presence, but I need his brain, and so does the project."

"He's in the tank. Better part of a year. Focus on the field tests for now."

Meza left Wallace there, and went to his office, past Trae's old cubicle. Myra was still there, working on Trae's machine. Her shoulders were hunched over, her chin resting in the palm of her hand. She stared at a geometrical simulation on the screen, the same picture she'd been looking at since early that morning. Nothing on the screen had changed.

A cold sandwich awaited him in his office. He ate it quickly while sending a pile of notes answering morning mail, then went back to the Board Room.

Everyone was there, and Thos Hyeran greeted him with a faint smile. "Perhaps we can hear some better news this afternoon," he quipped.

"Absolutely," said Meza with a big smile at Thos. *Make your move, you old bastard, and I will nail your body to the wall.*

He was wrong.

The man he was after did indeed make his move, only three hours after the Board meeting had ended and most of the staff was down in the cafeteria for dinner. But it wasn't Thos Hyeran.

Wallace called him to his office, and Meza joined him there for more whispers behind a closed door. Myra didn't even notice him, and hadn't gone down for dinner.

"Bugger didn't even examine the file, just went right to it and downloaded the thing. It was encrypted, you know, but he had the code. Wonder what other files he's stolen from me. The whole project's in here." He thumped his keyboard with one hand, pointed at the screen. "Marcellus Rosling? Who is this guy?"

"I'd call him a minor member of the Board," said Meza, clearly surprised. "Minerals and chemicals, some substantial holdings inherited from his family, a lot of interplanetary business, but no political leanings I've ever noticed. Rarely voices an opinion, attends regularly, has never missed a vote. Just sort of there, in an unobtrusive way. I'm amazed."

"Maybe someone knows the access codes to his system," said Wallace.

"Only if he gave it to them. The codes are changed weekly from his own list."

Wallace's fingers moved on the keyboard. "Well, he downloaded the file, then uploaded it again and sent it out to a relay. Here's the final address. Sent to a unit director. No name. Do you recognize it? It's on Gan."

"Thisken and Ost. It's an explosives and hypergolic fuel refinery. We've done some business with them in the past. Part of a big conglomerate there."

Meza's face suddenly flushed in sudden recognition. "Oh, my, that is interesting."

"What?" said Wallace.

"That conglomerate is owned and controlled by the recently elected president of Gan."

"Well, well," said Wallace, and grinned nastily. "Now what?"

Meza thought for a moment, then, "We begin feeding these gentlemen false information: theory, test results, new materials, that sort of thing. Send them on a lot of dead end tracks. Try to include something dangerous, if you can."

"I've been badly in need of a hobby," said Wallace. "Mind if I monitor his correspondence while I'm at it? Slip in a virus or two?"

"Don't go too far. I want him to feel safe. Be subtle about your misdirection. There are a lot of good scientists and engineers on Gan; they'll spot anything too obvious. Another thing, we need to find out who these messages are directed to. 'Unit Director, T Section' must be a routing code. It could be anyone in the plant, or a very important person on Gan. I need to know who it is specifically."

"I know a way to get a more personal response by controlling the server. Get him to try some other addresses," said Wallace.

"Keep me posted on everything. What I really want to know is who 'The Bishop' is. And if we can kill him."

Wallace's smile faded at that, and he nodded soberly.

"Right now, I need to take care of someone. See you in the morning."

Meza left the office, closed the door and took two steps to the cubicle where Myra was still huddled over her computer.

"Myra, get up," he commanded.

"What?" She turned to look at him. Her eyelids were droopy, as if she'd been dozing.

"I said get up. You're not eating or sleeping, and I've had enough of this moping around. Come with me -- now, please." He held out his hand, a bit surprised when she took it in hers.

He led her down the hall and into an elevator, pressed the button for third level.

"Where are we going?"

"Cloning. We're going to see Trae."

"No." She tried to pull her hand away.

"Stop it. You're torturing yourself, and it's affecting your work. I need you at a hundred percent. There's a lot of work to be done before Trae is back with us, things we can do without his help."

The door opened. He pulled her out of the elevator and down the hall to research wing. After a few steps she quit resisting, but was near tears. They went through the security station and two doors past the morgue to another station manned by a bored-looking male attendant who noticeably became alert as they approached.

"Good evening, Mister Meza," said the man. "What can I do for you?"

"We're here to see Zylak, C3. This is my assistant."

"There's really not much to see yet," said the man.

"We'll look at it anyway."

They followed the attendant to a heavy steel door, unlocked. The room inside was cool and looked like a bank vault, with rows of large drawers on every wall. Each drawer was labeled. They went to one at eye level at the back of the vault. Labeled Zylak, C3.

The attendant pulled at the front of the drawer. A flap opened down on hinges, but it wasn't a drawer inside. It was clear polymer, and behind it a soft, red light in a viscous liquid, and in that liquid was suspended a dark shape in a net of wires and polymer tubes woven in an ellipsoid a foot across.

"There he is," said Meza, and pulled Myra close up so she could look inside. "Already the first little bit of Trae is there, coming out of a chip in that mesh all around him. Memories of the womb, Myra. We all have them, we just don't consciously remember, but they're a part of us. Mothers sing to their unborn babies, talk to them, right up to birth, without thinking."

The shape was not an instrument, but a person: tiny hands and feet, a face with fine features. The eyes were tight shut, the fists clenched. One foot pressed against the surrounding mesh, and withdrew.

"You can talk to him if you like. Just put your hand on the window and speak to him. Growth is rapid in this medium. He'll be out of this tank in weeks. A few months to adulthood, and all the while those transcribed memory cubes will be fed into him. Every bit of it is Trae, in this life and the life he had before."

"But not his body," said Myra.

"Don't know. We used the Zylak library. This will be the body of Anton, Leonid's murdered son. He'll be Anton, now, but then that's who he always was."

Myra looked at him, but was silent, her lips pressed together. Meza squeezed her hand gently.

"You can come here anytime, at any stage of his development. Only you, and myself. Wallace is the only other person who knows about this outside of this lab. We'll harvest around age twenty-eight; it'll be a few months. The last cube we download will be the one involving you. We did get a good residual scan, you know. I'm willing to bet good money he'll remember everything about you, even things left unsaid."

But would he? The conversations without words, no words to convey the feelings. Had Trae ever known how she felt about him? Had he ever had deep feelings for her? Could any of that be transcribed to a memory cube packed with long-chain molecules?

"I know you're trying to make me feel better," she said. "I've been feeling sorry for myself, and I miss him, that's all."

"I know," said Meza, "but I need you, too. The lab needs you, even Wallace. I think he has a little crush on you."

That brought a little laugh from her, and a sparkle in her eyes. "That's not possible."

"Oh yes, I think so. He worries about you, and it's not just the work. We both want you to stop being sad."

Now she squeezed his hand. "I will," she said softly. "Maybe it would be good if I came here once in a while, just to be sure things are going as planned."

"Good idea. And now I'm taking you to dinner, and then you're going home to get a full night's sleep. But you must agree to be a company slave again in the morning."

"For you and Wallace," she said, and it was a beautiful smile that made his heart flutter.

CHAPTER 27

The grand temple of The Faithful went up in one year without a single sovereign of government money involved. Two spires towered over the city, a symbol of Gan as the religious capital of all the populated worlds known to man. Within two years of its construction, people from other worlds were arriving on pilgrimages to worship there.

Working with their president, the elected members of The People's Congress considered and decided on laws. They worked well together. The laws they passed seemed fair and just, following the will of the people. Nobody noticed the defeat of laws that might not favor the industrialists, or the close ties building between the military and giant business conglomerates on Gan. Nobody saw the flow of money and gifts either begin or increase as industry leaders bought their favors from men and women the common people had elected to represent them. And working above all of them, coordinating everything, was Azar Khalil, the President of Gan.

The honeymoon between Khalil and the populace went on for two years. By this time, The Church of The Faithful was a dominant force in the spiritual lives of the people, yet only forty percent of them regularly attended masses and tithed. The other sixty percent, most of whom actually professed a belief in The Source, were constantly bombarded by propaganda from The Church and subjected to unwelcome visits by zealous, neighborhood missionaries. They began to complain about this, first to local authorities, then to their elected representatives. They complained that their president wore his religion on his sleeve, and by his example gave The Church reason to expect all people to attend services, tithe, and pay the hundred sovereign tax the government imposed on all churchgoers. They complained that in a true democracy The Church and The State were distinct and separate, and one should have no influence on the other.

Khalil told them in a public speech he was sympathetic to their opinions, but did not agree with them. "To govern wisely requires a wisdom and spirituality based on principles set down by a higher power than humankind. We have that in The Source, and the teachings of His Church. I will follow those principles in every decision I make as long as I serve the people of Gan."

Shortly after that speech, the president sent a letter, each copy signed personally, to every priest on Gan, inviting them to a colloquium on the interaction between church and state. Four hundred people attended, discussed the laws of life as set down by The Source, and the applications to congressional lawmaking. With the urging and persuasion of Khalil, a study committee was formed, consisting of seven Bishops, one from each of the seven districts of The Church of Gan. The committee would study the issues, formulate a list of basic principles on which to base laws, and present their findings to the People's Congress to enter it as law. And in a press release after the colloquium, President Khalil first referred to that committee as 'The Council of Bishops'.

He gave the committee an opinion paper on what he felt should be first principles to be obeyed in the making of laws, principles requiring total unity of religious faith on any planet. There was one power beyond man, and it was The Source. There was only one Church, that of The Faithful. Unbelief in The Source was unbelief in His Principles, and thus tantamount to non-acceptance of the laws of The State. He knew they would incorporate most if not all of his paper into theirs, for they were all Bishops, the most conservative of the priests. In his last meeting with them he fondly said, "When I stand in your presence, and feel the warmth of your faith washing over me, it occurs to me I'm not just a president but a kind of bishop for the people, for I must lead in mind, body and spirit."

They were flattered by his remark, but did not understand the partial truth of what he'd just said.

To end the colloquium there was a lavish dinner with a speech by Khalil to flatter the priests for their attendance and hard work, and then a prayer for The Council of Bishops that moved all of them. This was truly a great man who led them, and he was one of The Faithful.

When the limousine returned him to the president's residence wing in the palace it was near midnight, later than he'd anticipated.

He hurried upstairs and sent the servants back to bed when they arrived to see to his needs. He ran his own bath scalding hot, disrobed and added a lavender-scented oil to the water before slipping into it. Instantly he was sweating, and the tension of the day was melting away. It had been a good day, and he was most gratified by it.

The call he was expecting came soon. It had come twice earlier, but he'd ignored it.

Finally.

Yes. I'm taking a nice bath, now. You know not to call me in the daytime.

Sorry. I felt it was urgent.

Your last news was good. I hope you don't spoil it now with something bad. Did the last of our associates survive, perhaps?

No, he died. I've been able to find out what he told them. They're looking for The Bishop, now. They suspect he's on Gan or Galena, think it could be industrial sabotage.

Ah, we can send them in a thousand directions with that one.

That's what I'm worried about. I tried to send you an update to the previous data, and it wouldn't go through. I tried four times, and the server said the address didn't exist, so I sent it to your office at Thisken.

Azar Khalil sat bolt upright in the tub. His face was red, and not just from the heat of the water.

I told you never to do that. Never!

I know. I'm sorry. The update showed some of the previous data was wrong. I panicked when I couldn't get it to you. Then today I tried to send it again to the usual address, and it went through. It could be a transient anomaly with the server, but it's never happened before.

That, or someone's playing a watching game with you, brother. Send nothing else electronically. Put it on cube and sent it by commercial mail. Updates can come slowly. I have an entire facility to build before we can test what you've sent us.

Okay. There's other news. We're being told the boy's body has been taken away by Zylak's people on an outbound vessel to follow his father to the core. Could this be?

Possible, even likely. The invasion could be underway. Zylak could be regrouping, if they haven't caught him yet. His son could be cloned and retrained in transit. The family empires of Zylak and his wife are all that can stand up to the power of The Bishops if they choose to do it. That's all out of our hands, brother. Things are going well here. Gan will greet the invasion with open arms when it comes.

That could be many years.

All the more time to prepare. Be careful, and call on the power of The Source within you.

Azar broke his connection with the field that bound them together, a connection they'd shared since one was playing with toy blocks while the other was still in the womb. He was angry with his brother, but understood. They were dealing with intelligent people. His brother might be found out. For one moment, Azar wondered if he should be eliminated. He was surprised by the pain the thought caused him. The decision could wait, anyway, since everything else was going so well.

Everything except communication. No signals could get through the brane, and ship-travel to the portal was nearly a lifetime. The invasion could be happening right now, and he wouldn't know about it for years. The new Zylak technology for smaller ships and longer jumps could shorten that time considerably, and give him the ability for blitzkrieg strategies with nearby planetary systems. This was in his hands. Let the invasion come when it could. When it arrived, he would hand over a dozen new worlds to them in the name of The Source, and the Council of Bishops at home would be most pleased they'd put their faith in him as the one true missionary of The Church of The Faithful.

The water in the tub had cooled. He dried himself off, dressed in silk, and slipped into bed in darkness. A silent prayer to The Source of his strength, and his mind drifted away to the sound, comforting sleep of the righteous, for that was what he truly thought himself to be.

CHAPTER 28

S o now we know who the enemy is," said Wallace.

"Thanks to you, yes. We just don't know why. It makes no sense to me. We're not competitors of his. His power and wealth aren't threatened, and he's an advocate of The Church. Why would he regard the Zylak family as a threat?"

"Could be our new technology, if it works. We could reach Gan with a fighting force in the blink of an eye. And now he has what we have, though somewhat modified and confusing, I hope." Wallace's fingers moved over his keyboard, and a new page came up on his screen.

"I've also been trying to understand why Marcellus Rosling is involved with assassinations and interplanetary political intrigue. He's not married, and regarded as a loner. No social life at all. He must be third lifetime; his records in business go back to the first century after settlement. The Rosling family tree to that point lists two generations. Marcellus had a sister and two brothers, two of them chemists like him, but one brother was a Bishop in The Church."

"A Bishop?"

"Yeah, I picked up on that, too, but it looks like Marcellus was the only Rosling to come through the brane. Maybe he and Khalil knew each other in a previous life on the other side. Still doesn't explain why they'd want to kill Zylak, unless they saw him as vital to the development of our new jump technology."

"Whatever. Keep a watch on him, and continue feeding him bad data."

"I will, but he's been quiet as a mouse for weeks. My game with the server scared him, I'm afraid. He's not a stupid man."

"Neither is Azar Khalil. I'm debating whether or not to go to our Intelligence Agency with what we have, but right now I don't even want our own government to know about the new tech we're working on until we're sure it works. Khalil is way behind us in manufacturing capability; let's get it done quickly, and fly it. You still have Myra, and Trae will be back in months. The rest is manufacturing."

"I saw her upstairs with him," said Wallace softly.

"What?" Thinking along another line, Meza was confused.

"Myra. She was upstairs in cloning when I went to check in the archives for any data on Rosling. She was there with the new Trae. He already looks ready to be born as an infant. Nice features. Myra had her hand on the window. She was talking to him. Boy, she was embarrassed when she saw me there. I told her it was all right, that I understood. Seemed to make her feel better."

"Sweet girl," said Meza, and put a hand on Wallace's shoulder. "Far too young for either of us. I just hope she isn't disappointed when Trae comes back as Anton. I encourage her, but I really don't know what to expect."

"Yeah," said Wallace.

CHAPTER 29

They came out of another forced sleep, and the ship droned on. At the rate they were going it would be thirty years to the known populated frontier. They'd only been traveling a year, and boredom had set in with a vengeance. Here they were again, backtracking a course to the portal after a break of only months for arrest and imprisonment to conclude a lifetime of travel. "There has to be a faster way to do this," said Leonid, and Tatjana agreed. Both hoped their only son had made progress in this direction, but as yet they'd been unable to contact him.

For Grandma Nat it was all a grand adventure. She'd read everything in Leonid's histories of Elderon, Galena and Gan, and was reading them again. She spent hours in the observation bubble, looking at the stars, and more time talking to the medical archivists who were on board another ship in the fleet. Already she was planning her new body, her new life. She wanted it completed and tested before they reached the frontier. She'd had minor medical problems in her current life: asthma, and a touch of arthritis. That would be corrected at the molecular level. There was also a lengthening of her face she desired, and a somewhat enhanced musculature. The doctors explained the difficulties in identifying and changing the combinations of base pairs and sequences responsible for these traits, but she assured them of her faith in their abilities, and ordered them to do what she wanted.

One did not say no to Grandma Nat. Strangely, one did not mind doing what she wanted, even when she was aggressively demanding about it, for the next moment she was totally charming and caring, and you were in love with her again.

Such were the ways of the family matriarch.

Much of their planning depended on contact with Trae, and indirectly the people he was working with. If the Bishops really intended to launch their invasion fleet the first line of defense was the Grand Portal, and that meant a minimum of ten thousand jumps from Elderon. Fifty total years of travel time, and that was pushing the limits of a modern ship. With the new technology potential, only forty jumps were needed, a mission of months to the portal. And if the ships themselves could produce minor branegates they would not just be defenders, but formidable aggressors in a fight with anyone.

They had to contact Trae, and he wasn't answering, and they worried, first because they needed to know what was going on, and second because he seemed to have disappeared.

The strange field binding them together was not understood. It was just there. It was as if all space were filled with a matrix of threads to be plucked by a thought, a vision, a contemplation within the mind, producing a musical note everywhere in space simultaneously and heard only by a select few connected by birth or life histories. The resonances were always there within close family members, but the rest seemed random, and were unexplained. Leonid and Tatjana had always had immediate contact with their son in both of his lives, and they agonized for many months when he didn't answer them. They went individually and together to that special place constructed from memories of their first days on Gan and along the coasts with the crashing seas, the cliffs, the rolling fields covered with wild flowers and gnarled, wind-beaten trees. The place where they'd made love and produced a child, and preached a doctrine of freedom to people who'd never known it.

Over a year out from the branegate guarding the other side, both of them began to despair. "He just isn't there. Something has happened to him. Our son no longer exists in this universe," said Tatjana.

"We'll keep trying. He has to be here," said Leonid, but he doubted it. Masking himself from his wife, he thought that Trae had somehow been found and destroyed forever by the Emperor of Gan.

And then suddenly, at the end of a ship's cycle, while they drowsed in each other's arms—they found him.

They'd gone to their cabin early, after a long session taking Grandma Nat through the details of their holdings on Elderon. Nat had already decided Elderon was the best place for her to settle, for it was the stronghold of her own kind and isolated from the political and religious squabbles of ordinary humans. She was determined to consolidate power on arrival. After her experience with The Council of Bishops, she would never again trust another government, even one appearing to be a democracy.

They were exhausted from the long discussions, and it was the tenth time they'd been over the same material and answered the same questions. By the time they were finished, the mess hall buffet had closed down and they ate sandwiches with the maintenance crew just going on red shift. The shift was named for red lights that went on in the ship during what passed for night in interstellar space.

Two jumps were scheduled for that night, and they wanted to be asleep for both of them. They undressed and zipped themselves into their bed. The bed fit them like the gentle squeeze of a gloved hand, but allowed them wiggle room. Indeed they wiggled playfully against each other before falling into a doze in each other's arms.

In the twilight of sleep, Leonid went to their flowery place on Gan, and Tatjana with him. Conditions varied with their moods. The sun was shining, and there was no breeze. The perfume of the flowers filled them. They lay next to each other, propped up on their elbows. They looked up the hill over the carpet of purple and red flowers towards a beautiful, old tree at the summit.

"If you're there, Trae, we'd sure like to have you with us," said Leonid. He knew it was all just a wonderful hope in their minds, but he wanted it to be real.

"He'll always be Anton to me. I want to hold him in my arms just one more time," said Tatjana. She had said it many times, but Leonid never reminded her of that. He would not allow himself to disturb the feeling behind it.

As she said it, there was movement at the top of the hill. A figure appeared, as if it had just stepped out from behind the tree. A man. He looked around, then right at them and began walking down the hill in their direction. Leonid's heart leapt; at first look he'd thought it was Trae, but Trae had dark hair and this man was blond. As he drew closer, they could see a strong resemblance, but he seemed a stranger.

The man was young, about the same age Trae would be now. He was beautiful: familiar, delicate features but deepest, blue eyes, and waves of golden hair draped across his forehead. His clothes were gray; pants and long-sleeved shirt, tailored to fit like a uniform. Something about the focus of the eyes struck Leonid as familiar, and Tatjana was giving the lad a huge smile.

He stopped a few feet away from them and shoved his hands deep into his pants' pockets. He looked embarrassed, seemed unwilling or afraid to meet their gaze. Finally his forehead wrinkled, and he asked rather forcefully, "Can you tell me how I got here?"

"We were calling for our son," said Tatjana.

"This isn't a real place, it's a memory," said Leonid. "Where do you come from?"

"I was asleep," said the young man. "I'm sure of it. I'm supposed to be released tomorrow."

He looked at Tatjana, now, his gaze fierce. "I know you -- I know both of you—you're—you're my Mother."

"Oh," said Tatjana, and choked back a cry.

"We don't recognize you," said Leonid, "but we were waiting to see our son. What's your name?"

"I want to say Anton, but it doesn't seem right," said the man.

Tatjana's image flickered, faded to near nothingness, and then came back again.

"The last time we saw our son he was called Trae. Do you know him?" asked Leonid.

"Oh, yes, he's here—I mean, I'm Trae—or I was—but now I'm Anton. I remember being here once before. You said I was conceived here, but—we were up there, nearer to the top, by those trees."

The man looked at Leonid, now. "You're my father. You gave me a list of things to do. I'm not finished, yet. Somebody killed me. They had to bring me back. They killed you, too -- my other father, I mean. It's so new; I'm trying to sort everything out."

"Petyr is dead?" asked Leonid.

"Yes, Petyr—that's his name. They shot him. I remember blood flying from his head. I—I don't know where he is, now. Dead, I guess."

"They'll restore him like they've restored you. They've followed my instructions; that's why you're called Anton, now."

"The way you'd be if you'd lived past childhood," said Tatjana, and she was still flickering in and out with surges of emotion. "Who <u>did</u> this awful thing?"

"I don't know," said Trae—now Anton. "Three men with guns—Petyr fired back—I was getting into a car. Going home. Is this place real? It feels so real. There's a breeze." Anton held out a hand to feel it.

"As real as we can imagine it," said Leonid.

Anton cocked his head, as if listening to someone else.

"Someone is with me. A woman. She's talking; a mumble, and I can't understand the words. I must still be asleep."

"You probably are," said Leonid, "but you heard us anyway. You said you were to be released tomorrow. Do you know what you'll do then?"

"I'll go back to work. The work you gave me to do. We were close to testing when I—when I went away. I'm sorry. I feel awake and asleep at the same time. At least I remember you." Now he smiled, and Tatjana was on her feet and hugging him, then Leonid, an arm around both of them with an imagined sense of touch and warmth not real but there.

"I can feel you," said Anton, surprised.

"Soon it'll be real, darling," said Tatjana. "We're headed towards you in a small fleet of ships right now."

"Well, maybe not so soon. Thirty or forty years," said Leonid. "I'm hoping you've made progress on that problem to make much longer jumps and more often in a small ship, maybe even open small branegates. You said you were ready to test."

They sat down in grass and flowers. Anton, or Trae, seemed more aware, now. His eyes sparkled with enthusiasm as he told them what he'd done: the new ideas, the simulations, fabrication of the new coils and the strange looking ship they were building, all of which Leonid was certain had been recently downloaded from memory cubes. The boy talked quickly, gesturing with his hands, the rapid-fire chatter of a brilliant mind just awakening. Tatjana smiled, and looked at him as if in worship.

Suddenly Anton sat up straight and alert, looked over their heads into the distance. "Myra," he said in wonderment. "Myra's with me. She touched me. She—"

He blinked hard, stared at nothing, then softly said, "She's crying. Don't cry, Myra."

"A friend?" asked Leonid.

"Yes—no—more than that. I didn't have the nerve to tell her how I feel before—before I was gone."

"Tell her when you wake up," said Tatjana.

"I will. We worked together. She's smart, pretty, and a little shy, like me. She can do geometrical modeling in her head. She was doing the sims for the testing models when I left. I wish you could see her; she's one of us, too."

Anton smiled at a memory. "She plays mind-games, pretending to be someone else, but I knew."

"Oh, my," said Tatjana. "You're smitten."

"We can see her another time," said Leonid. "Even if you're partially asleep it'll be difficult to channel her through to us, and we don't have the time. We've been trying to reach you for months, son. Some bad things have happened to us since we left Gan, and everything has changed. The work you've been doing isn't just business anymore, or a speed-up of travel between two universes. It could be our only defense against a force that will undo everything I worked for in this universe. It has to be done soon."

Anton sat back, and was focused again. "I don't understand. What's being threatened?"

Leonid told him everything: the Council of Bishops, their arrest and imprisonment, the invasion fleet hovering near the Grand Portal between the universes. "They could be in transit right now."

Anton sat still for a moment. His image seemed to blur.

"There are several ways to stop them, but we'll have to go to higher energies to get down to the pore-size of the brane. How do I communicate with you at such a large distance?"

"Just think of this place, and call us from here," said Leonid.

Anton smiled again, reached over to touch both of them on the hand. "I will. I remember everything, now, all the way back to the fire, and I remember you, both of you. I remember Petyr, my father always with me. I hope he'll come back, too. I know who I am. My name is new, but I'm still Trae. It's really good to be alive again."

His image blinked out, and he was gone.

Tatjana gasped, and took her husband's hand. The flowers and trees and rolling hills faded, and disappeared. They opened their eyes, faces close, their arms locked around each other. Their cabin walls shuddered with the drone of the ship. Leonid touched her face, felt wetness there. "Very soon, now," he said, "we'll all be back together again."

CHAPTER 30

She hadn't slept a wink, and it was all Meza's fault. He was the one who'd encouraged her to continue seeing Trae, clear up to the night before his official reincarnation. Three nights a week she'd watched him grow from fetus to man. At first it had only been a comfort to talk to him, knowing he couldn't hear her, but was there, alive, coming back however slowly as someone new. The first cubes were downloaded after only six weeks. The last six weeks it was a continuous process, the memories and experiences of two lifetimes building the neural net of a now developed brain, and in the last cube was Myra, the work she'd done with him, and any feelings he might have had for her.

The final four weeks, he'd been out of the tanks, unconscious on a hard bed, sprouting connective cables left and right to machines feeding him his past and scanning for accuracy. Others fed him nano-machines, and stimulated his muscles rhythmically with low voltage, high current pulses, a procedure she quickly learned to avoid observing. At those moments he was like a dancing doll, and she felt humiliated for him.

He was beautiful. Asleep, he looked so much like Trae, with high, prominent cheekbones, generous mouth, and a nicely arched nose. Slender, but well muscled. His hair was so light blond it seemed white at times. His eyes were always closed, but she knew they were blue; she'd been there when physicians had examined them. Trae's eyes had been brown, his hair dark. Sometimes she would just sit and watch him breathe, thinking he was another person. This was Anton, who had been Trae, now in his original form, she was told. How much more than memories would survive reincarnation? Would the personality, the sweet shyness and subtle sense of humor still be there?

She sat at his bedside and talked to him softly and watched his chest rise and fall. Mostly she talked to herself, bouncing ideas off his inanimate self the way she'd done when they'd worked together. She'd throw out an idea, and Trae would come back with one of his insightful questions, over and over again. The advantage he'd had was an enhanced neural net capable of access, analysis and recall of over three hundred years of research dating back to the other side. In frustration she'd asked him why she, or any of their kind, couldn't have such abilities. He'd said that she could have them, but the enhancements with nanomachines would take years before all that information could be downloaded to her. One person was enough, at least for now. That had satisfied her. If Trae had an ego, he'd never shown it, never given her any reason to think he felt superior in any way.

She'd gone to him the night before the day of his debriefing and release. She'd had dinner at the cafeteria, planned to stay only a few minutes. She hoped to see him walking the following day. It was later than usual when she got to his room. A physician was leaving as she arrived, and he smiled, knowing why she was there. She stood by Trae's bed and started talking, telling him about her day while reviewing it for herself, as was her habit. But when she looked down at him, something was different. His eyelids seemed to ripple, and she realized his eyes were moving beneath them. He was dreaming, following the course of some action in his sleep.

"Trae, it's Myra. Can you hear me? I'm right here beside you." She reached out and touched his shoulder softly.

His eyes stopped moving for just an instant, and then began again. Myra went back to a near whisper and talked about the strange new ship nearing completion in orbit, the ship that might carry them quickly to the center of the galaxy. And in the middle of her description she got the shock of her life.

Quite suddenly, Trae's eyes opened wide, and he said in a hoarse voice, "The work has to be done soon."

He closed his eyes and was deep asleep again, eyelids rippling.

Myra jumped back when he spoke, and her heart was thumping hard from the shock. The voice had been Trae's. For one horrible second she thought she might lose her dinner, but then the feeling passed.

She waited for Trae to say something else, but he didn't, and so she left the room shaken and went home to bed. She didn't sleep a wink that night.

In the morning she felt wasted and didn't eat anything. She got to work midmorning, went straight to her cubicle and closed the door behind her. Two cups of strong, black tea brought her closer to consciousness, but by noon she'd done nothing but stare at the screen, a slowly rotating galaxy and two globular clusters flickering there.

Midafternoon she dared lunch in the cafeteria, but the small soup and salad she ate only seemed to aggravate the jiggling in her stomach. All she could think about was Trae. What was he doing? What was it like to discover yourself in a new body different from the previous one? Myra could barely remember her own reincarnation. She'd lived to old age as a spinster, and come back an exact duplicate of that person to complete the work she'd begun, nothing more. But now there was something more, and it frightened her.

Late afternoon she actually called up the model she was working on, if for no other reason than to put some order into the chaos of her thinking. An hour passed, and she was warming to the task when there was a knocking on her door.

Her stomach jumped as she opened the door. Meza was standing there, a smile on his face. Wallace was behind him, standing in the doorway of his own office, arms folded, looking serious.

"Myra, I want you to meet your new assistant, just arrived. He'll be working on the testing models with you, and I'm sure you'll get along wonderfully."

He handed her a file. "Here's his dossier, and now meet Anton Denal."

Meza stepped aside, and Anton was there, and it was Trae, his hand outstretched. She shook it without thinking. His grip was firm and dry.

"Hello, Myra. Nice to meet you."

She somehow found her voice. "We've been expecting you." His hand engulfed hers, and lingered a moment before relaxing. Her breathing had become rapid, and shallow.

"I'll give you two an hour, and then dinner is on me. I need to go over the production timelines with you. Deadlines, deadlines," said Meza.

"Can you make it two hours?" asked Myra.

"Of course. I'll tell Wallace. He'll be joining us."

"Already heard," said Wallace from behind him, and now he smiled.

Trae stepped past her into the cubicle. She smelled mint. "Two hours, then," she said, closed the door before Meza could answer and heard his chuckle from the other side.

They sat down, knees almost touching, and there was a long, awkward silence. An invisible hand seemed to grip Myra by the throat, and her voice fled. Finally it was Trae who broke the silence.

"I'm back," he said, and the way one side of his mouth curved up in a smile made her heart ache.

He shook his head slowly. "This is all very weird. I'm a new person, but I feel the same. It's like I went to sleep. I remember the bullets hitting, and blacking out and -- and then dreams—recently— yesterday, maybe. I talked to my parents. I—tried to talk to you . . ."

"Sshhh," she said, reached over and touched his hand. The face, the hair, eyes, even the hand she touched was new, but it was still Trae: the speech pattern, the mannerisms, smile, all there. "I really missed you, Trae," she said softly.

"Oh, don't call me that," he said, and grasped her hand in both of his on his knees. "Whoever had me killed will expect reincarnation. They're supposed to think it'll happen someday on a ship very far from here. I'm Anton, now. It's who I really am, anyway. That's the weird part. Trae's body was slightly modified from the original clone for security. This is mine, the real me, from my first lifetime."

"I still missed you," she said, and was startled when he squeezed her hand and leaned close, and all she could see were his sky blue eyes.

"I missed you, too, Myra, as soon as I was conscious again. Everything came back in a rush, and I remembered you right away. You were with me before I woke up, I remember that too."

"I sat with you a while every week from the time you were inches long," she said, and smiled.

"Why?" He frowned.

"I wanted you back. It was a way to convince myself it was happening. Meza suggested it. I was having trouble concentrating on my work."

Trae looked down at her hand in his, and lightly ran a thumb across her palm. She shuddered, and he looked up at her and smiled his wry smile again. "How's the mysterious lady who used to talk to me in my mind?" he asked.

Myra grinned. "Okay, but she hasn't had anyone to talk to lately."

"When you see her again, tell her I like her. I like her a lot. Trae couldn't say it, but I can."

"Oh, Trae."

"Anton."

"Anton. I feel the same way. I was so afraid you wouldn't remember me."

He released her hand, and her heart was singing. "Not likely," he said. "A new life, a new chance. I promise to be more aware this time."

"Me, too." She put a hand on his knee, her eyes wide with sudden focus. "Trae—last night—it must have been as your incarnation was completed—you woke up for only seconds and said 'Our work must be done soon', and then you were asleep again. What was that about? It sounded so urgent."

"I think I know. I was talking to my parents, and it wasn't a dream. I was there with them in their minds."

"Attunement. I had it with my parents. I have it with you, but without images."

"They told me an incredible story. All our worlds will be in great danger if our work isn't finished quickly. An invasion force is coming, and all freedom will cease to exist here."

"How?"

He told her, speaking rapidly as she remembered when his mind was fully engaged and his genius was pouring forth unfettered. She listened silently, barely managing to keep up. Mixed in with the story of zealous Bishops and a fleet of warships poised on the other side were new ideas for resizing their own designs to manage the opening of ship-sized pores in the brane, a feat requiring power thirteen magnitudes higher than they'd considered. It went on for thirty minutes, but for Myra it seemed only seconds passed and at the end of it her head was throbbing.

"We're only weeks from testing. The ship is in orbit. We can't change it this late."

"Then build another. We're only resizing. I'll do the specs, you model, but in secret, on top of test data analysis. I don't want Meza or Wallace to know about it until we can build a new ship or refit an old one."

"The jump tests will be more than enough to occupy them," said Myra, now excited again for the first time in a year.

"We'll have to spend long hours together on this," said Trae.

"I don't intend to complain about it if you don't," she said coyly.

For one second, she thought he might kiss her, and knew the thought had entered his mind. Instead, he grabbed her hand again. "How much time do we have now?"

"The better part of two hours," she said.

"Then let's get to work."

They did, and less than two hours later, when Meza and Wallace came to get them, the design of a new class of ship having a rather unusual shape had already begun.

They called it the Guppy.

CHAPTER 31

I'm not a stupid person," said Grandma Nat. She perched on the throne of her chair and gave Leonid a haughty look that would have frozen lesser men.

"It's the only thing that makes sense. We're only a year out, so it's not likely the fleet has made a move. With one ship we can pose as a picket or a runabout between the portal keepers. As long as we stay in the right sectors nobody will even challenge us on this side. We have to know when and if that fleet moves."

"I'm not turning back," said Nat, and it was final.

"We're not asking you to. Give us one ship. Shuttle class will do. I'd like to have a few crewmembers for Tatjana and myself. The rest of you go on."

"Why does Tatjana have to go? This is your idea."

"It was a decision we made together, Grandma," said Tatjana. "We talked to Anton again yesterday, and this has to be done. His new ships won't be ready for another year or more. If the fleet comes through before he gets here he has to know its exact location at any time. He'll have to fight or somehow get them to turn back. If the fleet has not made transit by that time, Anton thinks he has a way to shut down the portal so they can never come through."

"What about the rest of us, the rest of your *family?*"

"Just stay on the same heading," said Leonid, "at the same speed. If Anton's ships can't turn the invasion back, we'll catch up to you fast, make our own exile. There are dozens of worlds we know of where The Church will never find us. We'll build our own civilization without them."

His plan was passionate, and thought out. It was a logical thing to do, but it would put Tatjana and Leonid in terrible danger. For a favorite grand daughter and a man who was like a son to her this was not easy to decide.

"I'll think about it," she said.

"Not for long," said Leonid. "Those ships could make transit any day."

Nat hated being forced, but understood the why. She slept on it overnight, and in the morning told them they could go.

They'd packed their things before she'd even chosen a ship and crew to assign to them. She gave them a B-class shuttle that had been ferrying the technical data stores of their empire, and assigned a crew of five. By the following morning cycle the stores had been transferred to her cruiser, the new crew was on board and the shuttle was running fifty yards off the starboard side of her ship's hull.

Leonid and Tatjana suited up, and said their goodbyes in an airlock. There were no tears; everyone was strangely calm. There were no thoughts of possible injury or death, just a mission to be accomplished.

Deep in her heart, Grandma Nat didn't care whether The Church won the battle for people's souls or not. She just wanted her family safe and intact, and it seemed to be ripping apart. She felt small, had to stand on tiptoes to hug and kiss Tatjana first, then Leonid. When he hugged her tightly, it was the closest she came to tears.

They closed their helmets, and she had to leave, watched through a window as the chamber was evacuated, saw the outer door open, the stars and a glowing patch of red beyond the black-hulled ship hovering some distance away. A ship-to-ship line had been rigged. Tatjana and Leonid floated to the door entrance and hooked up to the line. The little jets on their backpacks were like exhalations of air on a cold day. One by one, they scooted along the line and out to the ship awaiting them, human forms, then blobs of white, then gone, and the line were reeled in rapidly to her ship. The door closed, and two important people in her life had left her.

She wiped her eyes dry, went back to the bridge and distracted herself by issuing new orders to her crew.

On board Echo I, Leonid and Tatjana struggled out of their suits and met their new captain. His name was Ben Sparrow, a raw-boned, gaunt-faced man in his third lifetime of service to Grandma Nat. He'd known her as a child in first lifetime. "I was the driver's son, but it made no difference to her. When she asked for volunteers I was first in line. I'd do anything for that woman. You tell me what you want to do, and it's done."

They liked him immediately for the way he treated the crew as equal cogs in the wheels of the ship. There was a cook who doubled as electrician, a navigator, and two men with papers in hydraulics and mechanics. Nate, Jake, Ralph and Samuel. They never heard their last names, or anything else about them. Perhaps they all had pasts best forgotten.

Sparrow knew the plan; his crew knew their jobs. They were barely on board when they pulled away from Grandma Nat's cruiser, and watched the great ship shrink in the distance.

"This was hard for Grandma," said Tatjana.

Sparrow smiled. "Nat's beyond stoic. She can survive anything."

There was admiration in his voice, and something else: they'd never heard anyone else outside the family call Grandma by her pet name.

It was a small ship, and they were used to the luxurious expanse of a cruiser. The bridge had room for three men crammed in close. There was one lavatory for all of them, a small mess where they ate in pairs, an even smaller galley. The births were amidships, the crew stacked like cordwood, captain's cabin a bed with shelves on two sides and hooks in the ceiling for his clothes. Two bunks had been taken out of the cabin occupied by Leonid and Tatjana, giving them the luxury of twelve square feet of floor space outside of their bunks. The cabin neighbored mechanics, and it took them a week to get used to the murmurings and thumping from that area.

Over half the ship, separated from the working and sleeping area by a copper plug six feet thick, was the coil and plenum of the vacuum state energy drive that powered everything. Sucking in reaction mass by electromagnetic scoop, the engine provided thrust and an exhaust velocity nearing light speed. With the scoop off, all energy could be diverted to field mass-energy for small folds in space, a kind of pinching effect limited to only three light years by both coil energy and plenum size.

The design had been responsible for the family fortune, but for the task at hand it was not enough.

They wanted to get back to the vicinity of the Grand Portal as quickly as possible to monitor any movement of the invasion fleet. Their captain agreed with them. "We did two jumps a day on the way out. The best I can do is six. The plenum won't charge any faster than that."

That meant two months of travel, either being asleep all the time or suffering through bouts of vertigo and extreme nausea six times each day.

The chose the later, and it was the longest two months of their present lives. Captain Sparrow did what he could for them, gave them pills, alcohol, pills with alcohol, tried to teach them meditative techniques. Nothing worked, and the alcohol made things even worse. They did not keep down a solid meal completely for two months; except for the high protein meal they took just before collapsing into sleep at the end of ship's cycle. They managed to stay hydrated, and recovery was rapid between bouts of nausea. During the final two weeks they noticed a lessening of symptoms as their bodies somehow adapted finally to the pinching of spacetime around them.

The final jump brought them within light weeks of the massive branegate to the other side. On the view screen it was a greenish, elongated star. The scanners had been on continuously the entire trip, their range limited by the times spent in normal space, but they'd kept to the prescribed shipping lane for commercial transport. They'd spotted two freighters on the way, but no great fleet of ships had been seen.

They came in at a quarter light speed, and began deceleration a light week out. It was another month of days spent eating, sleeping and staring at the viewscreen until the gate keepers were visible, looking like planets at this distance.

The ship vibrated softly around them, in front of them the viewscreen showed the green oval of the portal, wisps of gases making a fog-like shroud around the black holes guarding it. Leonid took Tatjana's hand in his, and they closed their eyes, reaching out with their minds to pluck one string of the field binding them to their own kind.

Anton, it's father and mother here. We've reached the Grand Portal. No sighting of any invasion fleet yet. Do you hear us?

They'd thought they might have to wait for an answer, but his reply was immediate.

Yes—I'm here. Good news about our tests; I'll tell you later.

Glad you made it. Some things being discovered here; looks like there might be agents connected to the invasion, including some people in prominent positions. One of them probably had me killed. Very busy, now. I'll get back to you in a bit. Bye.

Anton was gone, but something was still there, a kind of awareness that held their focus, and then it disappeared.

"Did you feel that?" asked Leonid.

"Someone else was there," said Tatjana, "just listening."

"We'll ask him about it."

"Yes."

Knowing that communication with Anton was immediately available was comforting. It had been an unknown until now. They went back to their study of the viewscreen, and the scanner data as it came in. They were in the very center of the shipping lane, a mote among giants, passing huge freighters lining up for transit to the other side. Picket ships five times their size trundled from freighter to freighter, checking transit papers and cargo manifests. Their own tiny ship was ignored. They might be a taxi or personal craft, and nobody cared. On this side of the brane the only paranoia was in collecting transit taxes on cargos. The real paranoia began on the other side, and hopefully the great fleet poised for invasion was still there.

They would have to find out about it indirectly, for they had no intention of chancing a transit themselves.

Captain Sparrow had the answers to that. He'd spent a career working Grandma Nat's freighters, mostly on the other side, but had often made transits to transfer cargo to ships heading out of the core. He knew lots of people working either side of the brane, including keepers and the people who served them. Working the brane and manipulating the higher dimensional tunnel through it was a stressful job, and dreary when not stressful.

There were diversions.

One day out from Grand Portal there was a great wheel of a station more like a city than a port, and occasional visits kept the sanity of some forty thousand workers and merchantmen who frequented it. It had no real name, but was called The Palace, a warren of shops, theatres, bars, brothels and eateries crammed into a space shaped like two doughnuts skewered on a stick and powered by money. On any given off-cycle, The Palace had a population of ten thousand, people shoulder to shoulder in the single, winding street, or riding the long escalator from doughnut to doughnut in search of new pleasures. There was no red light district; the brothels were scattered everywhere. Shops were small, selling cheap to expensive trinkets, and art from both sides of the brane. Bars and nightclubs were large, plentiful and noisy, with barkers on the street to announce the pleasures inside. Prostitutes strolled the street in brief, exotic dress, handing out business cards to interested visitors, and filling their busy schedules in the brothels.

It was not a place frequented or graced by The Church of The Faithful.

Sparrow had contacts everywhere in The Palace, and so did his crew. Nate, the cook, knew every Madam on the station, and had done business with all of them. Merchantmen, keepers, the off-duty border cops who were bribed by them, all came together at The Palace for fun, frolic and easy conversation. And for the cost of a few drinks, a treasure trove of information could be found in any bar any off-cycle of the week.

It was not a place Leonid and Tatjana would ever have visited on their own. The first week they remained in the ship. Sparrow moved as close as he could to the Grand Portal, hovering at the edge of the shipping lane. At this distance the other side was only a hazy, black patch, but freighters could be seen moving back and forth in the chaos of reds, yellows and greens that marked the interaction of normal space and particles within the exotic composition of the brane.

No invasion fleet was there to be seen. Sparrow set up a kind of disguise for them, making darting runs between The Palace and the four, planet-sized keeper ships distorting space in gentle folds around masses of a dozen suns. The folds were there to aid the stability of a giant rip in the brane between two universes, a rip created by focused vacuum energy from a ring of eight moon-sized generators placed on each side of the brane. The generators were barely visible in the glow of the portal, each operated by remote control and sending beams of exotic particles to form the cusp of the transition space. A single station controlled the generators, with a crew of fifty men, and security was high. A police picket served as taxi to and from, and only for authorized personnel, but crews had downtime, and often spent it at The Palace. There, they talked freely, as did keeper and freighter crews, for nothing more than a drink, a woman, perhaps a coin or two. They knew about anything making transit, or scheduled to: origin, destination, cargo and crew. And they knew what was on the other side, all the way to the frontier.

After a week of darting around, and experiencing no response from the few picket ships on patrol outside the shipping lane, Sparrow docked at The Palace. He left Leonid and Tatjana on board and went off-ship with his crew. They waited anxiously, afraid police might arrive to check their papers, but their anxiety was wasted. This was The Palace, not a port. The only police here were off-duty, and focused on pleasures.

Sparrow returned with good news after only two hours. A freighter captain from the other side had seen the great fleet gathered there, had counted forty-three ships. The fleet had grown by eleven over the past few months. Still assembling. And the number of picket ships near the portal exit on the other side was also increasing, with more boarding and inspections of ships passing through. Complaints had been filed with port authorities, but there had been no response.

"At least they're still there," said Leonid, then, "The only way to stop them is to shut down the portal. They could move any day. We're in a race. I have to tell Anton."

But Anton didn't seem concerned, said there were other ways to stop the ships, ways he would test in the near future. "Hold tight," he said. "We should have all of this resolved in a year. Those ships aren't our only concern here, so be patient. I'll try hard to join you soon."

Again there was the feeling that someone else had been there with Anton, a strong presence less subtle each time they contacted him. Tatjana suggested they relax a bit, create that favorite place in their collective minds again and invite the new presence to join them there. But it seemed now that Anton was always in a rush; their contacts without visions, information transfer the only goal. There was no time to do what Tatjana wanted. She was patient, but determined to have her way.

They finally left the ship to hear firsthand what Sparrow and his crew were hearing. Leonid wore rough-woven clothing and sported a two-week-old beard. Tatjana was harder to dress for the occasion. Leonid courted retaliation by jokingly suggesting she wear something brief and sexy, and print up some business cards. She settled for trimming her hair short and wearing a heavy, oversized cap with loose clothing to make her look like a young apprentice merchantman.

The thing that bothered them the most was the noise, from the instant they came through the airlock. The rhythmic pounding of a drumbeat came all the way down the access tunnel to their entrance. An explosion of sound and bright lights, and they were in the street, and even here, along a long line of numbered access ports, people were jostling together. The Palace district started a hundred yards along the rim of the wheel, an archway of flashing lights welcoming them. After months of tenth-gee in their ships, three-tenths made them feel heavy, but within an hour their muscles had responded favorably for simple standing and walking. The sound was deafening, in waves, drumbeats and loud music coming from speakers over the entrances to clubs and bars, hawkers shouting through loudspeakers in front of shops and brothels. Flashing lights were everywhere, and there was the talking and shouts from the crowd itself, so thick that walking was more diffusion than travel, random progress as people banged into each other like particles of smoke in air.

Twenty minutes after arrival, Tatjana was propositioned by a prostitute for the first, but not last, time. The woman was attractive and tall, her makeup so thick it was a plastic mask. She bumped into Tatjana, put an arm around her, and handed her a card.

"I do women too, sweetie," she shouted into her ear.

Tatjana flushed beet red. "I beg your pardon?"

The woman leaned close again. "I can smell you, dear."

Seeing no interest there, the woman pushed herself away into the jostling crowd. And Leonid looked at Tatjana strangely, wondering why she was blushing so.

She never told him why.

There were several key bars frequented by the merchantmen. No dance floors, piped music, a few rooms on a balcony where the ladies did their work. Drinks were cheap, but watered thin. A man went there to catch up on news with his friends. There would be time for other pleasures later.

Sparrow had prearranged it. They went to 'Purple Rooster,' a place in the noisiest strip along the lower doughnut favored by working crew. They sat down at a table with Sparrow. An ancient waiter ready for reincarnation served them whisky-flavored water and a dish of salty nuts. They sipped slowly. Sparrow watched the crowd, stood up suddenly and beckoned to a man who'd just come into the bar. Gaunt and tall, he wore the form-fitting jacket of a merchant officer. He came to their table, sat down, and shook hands with Sparrow.

They were introduced as Leo and Tati, Sparrow's number one and a cabin steward. The man was Saul Briggs, second mate of Alterra, a Class A freighter registered in Port Angel, but running goods from Kratola to the frontier.

"Theo's an old friend," said Sparrow. "We shipped out together when we still had fuzz on our cheeks."

"Three lifetimes ago, it was," said Saul, and downed his drink in a gulp. Sparrow poured another for him. "Course I had one shortened a bit."

"Explosive decompression it was," said Sparrow. "Good thing the company had you archived."

"Bad days for the company. They'll do anything for freight, and I don't like it, Ben. That's what I wanted to tell you about."

"Have at it," said Ben Sparrow.

"Things ain't so good on the other side. A lot of industries left when the Bishops took over, abandoned stock, factories, everything. Nobody has taken over. Don't want to work for the Bishops, or don't know how to do anything. The economy is going down fast. People with money are trying to leave, but they're stopped at Port Angel. They have to give up everything they have to the Bishops to get over here, and then they can never go back."

"I have people on Kratola. They told me times were hard," said Leonid.

"Worse'n that. Pretty soon only poor people'll be there. Anyway, word is the Bishops want to take it all back, all the people who've left, the worlds they've settled, the fortunes they've made. The Bishops say the colonists have strayed from The Church. And they're gonna make transit soon to bring them back into the fold."

"That lie is so foul it smells," said Leonid. "The colonists voted in their own independence a long time ago, and owe no taxes or allegiance to Kratola. A lot of people there don't even know that planet exists, except in legend. This is all about power and money, and growing competition every time one of our ships crosses the brane."

"Coming through earlier last year, I saw a lot of ships on the other side. Looked like a military fleet," said Sparrow.

"That it is, but not like you think," said Saul. "They're all just freighters, all sizes up to mine, and unarmed. But inside they're loaded with military aircraft, armored vehicles and personnel. Must be forty or fifty thousand men."

Sparrow looked at Leonid. "Enough to take over any colony world, one at a time."

"I didn't include Alterra," said Saul. "Military vehicles out to the hull, and five hundred so-called 'civilian' passengers, all of them chisleheads if I ever saw one. We weren't boarded or checked on the other side or here. A lot of people are in on it. Word is the fleet is coming through within a month. Us and a couple of others have already come through, just to be sure the bribes are working. It all stinks. Don't the colonies have any defenses?"

"Not really," said Leonid. "They're too busy squabbling among themselves to get together on anything."

"Then The Church will do it for them. They're sure of themselves. None of this is a secret here. I doubt I'd be in any trouble for talking about it. And people here just don't care one way or the other. Bud here said y'all have family in the colonies, and are headed there. Maybe you can give'em some warning."

"One month wouldn't be much," said Leonid.

"Bud says you can make a few jumps a day. In Alterra and all the other class A's it's only two, with all that cargo. If you hammer it all the way back you could be years ahead of the big fleet."

"And do what?"

"Get them ready to fight, or run away," said Sparrow. "We should leave now."

"But the fleet might not even make transit."

"They're coming through. Believe me," said Saul. "I'd go with you if I could."

Sparrow glanced at Tatjana, who was biting her lip to remain quiet like a good little cabin boy. "All right, we'll wait until we see first signs of movement by the fleet, and then we're gone. Saul, what can I say but thanks. At least we know what's going on. You're a friend."

Saul took a piece of paper out of his pocket and handed it to Sparrow. "You can thank me by looking up these folks. They settled on a planet called Elderon."

Sparrow studied the paper. "Your parents?"

"No—wife, and two of my kids, a lifetime ago, it was. Couldn't stand me being shipped out all the time. If you find'em, tell'em I'm okay, that I think about them a lot, that I'm ready to settle down."

"Everyone is archived on Elderon. Should be easy to do," said Leonid.

"Yeah. I didn't think you were a merchantman," said Saul, "and that ain't no cabin boy. Too pretty for that." He smiled at Sparrow.

"I work for a very important, very powerful lady, Saul. She's headed to the colonies right now, with most of her family, and these are two of them."

"I don't need names," said Saul.

"If you ever get to Elderon, check in at the archives' center. We'll find you," said Leonid.

Saul nodded, picked up his glass, and lifted it in a toast.

"Here's to another lifetime," he said.

They drank.

After the meeting with Saul, they returned to The Palace once a week themselves, at least one of the crew on leave four days a week and keeping eyes and ears open for news. Leonid had expected to wait months for something to happen, but instead it was weeks, only a few days after Saul had shipped out on Alterra. His ship wasn't even up to cruising speed when they got the news.

Nate and Jake came back from an evening of physical fulfillment at one of the brothels. A fitter there had been complaining about the long delays at getting through the portal. Everything was being held up by the passage of a huge fleet of ships now lining up on the other side. No other traffic was being allowed until the fleet came through, and that would be at least two days of paperwork because there were fifty ships to process.

Captain Sparrow had them underway in four hours, and they had already made two jumps by the end of ship's cycle, leaving Saul's vessel far behind.

CHAPTER 32

It was an unusual looking ship, but not as strange as the one beyond it in a slightly higher orbit. That one was still under construction, and resembled a fish that had swallowed something huge. It would not be tested today.

The shuttle came in slowly, and their pilot took them over the top and around both sides to view the hull from all angles. Trae's first impression was of a military stealth vessel: black, vee-shaped, but with the characteristic ellipsoidal bulge aft for a superconducting torus of uncountable layers to power the jumps. Not a large ship by commercial standards, about a thousand feet long. Lots of angles on the hull for stealth, and a thick polymer coat, the test ship was designed for use only in space. Its partner, now in orbit on the other side of Elderon, sported a surface of ceramic tiles, and could be used surface to vacuum.

The shuttle docked forward. Trae and Myra crawled through the three-foot access tunnel and came out by the navigator's harness, just behind the cockpit. Pilot and co-pilot were already seated and going through pre-flight check. The navigator barely noticed them. All men were in a second lifetime of service to Zylak Industries, but none of them knew Trae's identity, only that he and Myra were test engineers on board for consultation and evaluation.

Aft of the cockpit was the engineer's compartment, lit up like a festival tree by the monitoring instruments there, everything from speed, outside and inside temperatures, plenum pressure and coil amperage, to a breakdown of the individual currents of exotic particles being drawn from the false vacuum of space. A single gauge showed the temperature of the superconducting coil only a few hundred feet from their position. Powered by weakly coupled electron pairs, the particles would decouple and move independently if the temperature went higher than a warm oven. The superconductor would then become a normal conductor, and with the billions of amps flowing through it they would be vaporized in an instant.

The engineer was seated at his console. Trae and Myra buckled into seats that would normally be occupied by maintenance astronauts, their suits hanging from a wall behind them. They put on their headsets and riffled through the list of tests they'd come to observe. Trae had added a new one only minutes before. The crew wouldn't like it, but they were at his command. He hoped to remain unobtrusive until that final test.

The shuttle de-coupled, and pulled away. There was a low whine as the first trickle of exotic matter flowed into the plenum vacuum. A trickle of normal matter, and they were moving, slowly at first, then going to a higher orbit with a burst of energy, then again. At a distance of two Elderon radii, they left orbit and soared into space on a tangent, heading outwards from their sun. Minutes later the vernier engines had all been cycled, and the main thruster had gone to four gee. Anton and Myra listened to the pilots. Nominal, nominal. Normal flight was a dream in this ship. All at low power.

The power went up at six radii from Elderon. There was a five-minute charge of the plenum, and the superconducting current was brought up in steps of a hundred thousand amps. At five million amps the exotic matter in the plenum followed normal matter compressed to near nuclear densities. One pulse of crossed electric and magnetic fields, and exotic matter was injected back into the false vacuum of space, the burst of mass-energy distorting space-time for an instant, and pinching it. Stars flickered in and out, and for a person there was an instant of fugue, a lapse of awareness.

Trae blinked, but Myra kept her eyes closed for a moment.

"Nominal," said the pilot calmly. "I read six-tenths of a light-year." They were on a pre-calibrated course, and the length of their jump was measured from the change in observed magnitude of nearby stars.

"Very smooth," said Trae. "Let's skip the test at one, and go to two light-years."

Again, as before. There was no change in sensation, and the coil temperature went up two degrees. They were already up to the maximum jump lengths for large ships, and just getting started.

"I think I'll enjoy flying this one," said the pilot, who knew Trae as Anton. "Good job, sir."

Myra made a little harrumph at being left out, but smiled at him. "Thanks, but now we get serious," said Trae. "Take it up to five, please."

The pilot was confident, for the moment. The plenum was charged two minutes longer this time, but not even close to capacity, and the instant before jump the coil current was hovering at two hundred twenty million amps, about one-third of the critical value for the nano-thick layers in the coil.

They jumped. Felt nothing new. The temperature of the coil went up seven degrees. "I read five-point-five," said the pilot. "There was a faint flash of green right at the start of the jump, along a cone ahead of us. Were you expecting that?"

"Yes," said Trae, but then lied, "an inductive effect."

Trae knew otherwise, and Myra's wide-eyed look and wiggling eyebrow told him she knew, too. At higher currents the greenish flash cone should shorten, but he didn't want to go above half critical. He could do more by increasing plenum pressure, and that was his next order.

They used the same current, and charged the plenum for five minutes this time. The high-pitched sound of it was like metal scouring metal.

"Coil T going up," said the engineer. "Another ten degrees, and rising." They were proceeding too fast for the radiant heat transfer vanes of the plenum.

"Go," said Trae, and the pilot didn't hesitate. Another lapse of awareness, and red lights flashed on the engineering console.

"Whoa! That was bright this time, right up to the nose of the ship and out from it. Looked like a shock wave." The pilot was excited, but there was an undertone of nervousness in his voice.

"We're near the end of the test course. How far do you want to push it? I think we've been lucky, so far."

They'd been in the ship for forty minutes, and were now eight and a half light years from their starting point. Myra was plotting performance curves, and shook her head at him. "More plenum," she mouthed.

"Turn the ship around to our outbound line, then go to twenty seven-point-four declination."

"That's hours out from Elderon at twenty-nine light years," said the engineer. "We did twelve-point-eight on the last one."

"But the line is clear," said Trae.

"Yes—nothing out to—maybe fifty light years." Charts riffled.

"We're going to jump along that line. I want a ten minute charge on the plenum, and the current at four hundred."

"That's pushing it, sir," said the pilot.

"I don't think so, but it'll give us one more data point and we can extrapolate a lot once we have it. We're well below critical here. Start the charge, now."

The hull screeched as if scraped by a steel claw. Loose metal objects, a paperclip, pen, rattled around on the console as the current increased in the monster coil behind them.

They went into the cockpit and squeezed themselves between the navigator and the pilots, getting down on their knees to look past shoulders to the outside. Only two bright stars were showing in the blackness, each window only a foot square, three inches of lutracine polymer and an interference film between them and vacuum.

They were no sooner settled in than the pilot announced, "Charged."

"Coil steady at four hundred. T up by twenty, and rising."

"We need bigger vanes on this ship," grumbled Trae. "I want no T increase up to five hundred meg in the production model. We should be able to cycle regularly at that current."

"Yes, sir. T still rising. I recommend we jump," said the engineer.

They craned their necks to look out the windows. "Do it," said Trae.

The same sensation, as if they'd made a long blink or drifted into a daydream. The stars outside disappeared, but as they did there was a tremendous flash of green, extending out in front of the ship in a cone. An ellipsoid flashed as if on fire in blues and reds, then flickered to blackness as the stars appeared again unchanged, at least to the naked eye.

The instruments said otherwise.

"By the Good Hand of The Source", murmured the engineer.

"What?" Trae blinked hard to clear away a residual image of green.

"The tables say forty-four-three, sir. We jumped over forty light years that time. T went up to three twenty K, but is already back down to two-eighty."

"We've overshot Elderon by sixteen light years," said the pilot.

Myra was scribbling notes. "Not quite exponential, but close."

"Good," said Trae. "On the way back we can fill in some more data points, keeping the coil current where we had it."

The pilot turned around to look at him. "Did you see all the fireworks out there? Did you?"

"Yes, we did. I'd sort of hoped to see something like that at half charge of the plenum."

"It was at forty percent," said the pilot. "What is it?"

"I think it was the very beginning of a branegate," said Trae.

"Like the Grand Portal," added Myra, "only a lot smaller. When we pinch space we create a singularity, as if an infinite mass is there. Additional energy opens up the pores of space, the pores of the brane connecting us to another universe at that point. A branegate was starting to form, but we didn't have enough energy left to form it, and certainly not enough to keep it stable."

"For this ship it's a bad thing, an energy loss that could have gone into a longer jump," said Trae.

"Oh, maybe ten percent loss," Myra quickly added. "It won't matter on a Guppy." She handed the pilot a slip of paper. "Could we return to Elderon in three jumps at those values? It'll really help me to fill out my curves."

Trae suppressed a chuckle, thinking that Myra didn't need any help in filling out her curves. "The Guppy is that pregnant fish-looking ship that was in orbit near us when we left port."

Myra gave him a mock-stern look. She'd heard his thought, but taken it as a compliment. "We expect that ship to open stable branegates and jump a hundred times farther than this one," she said. "Our thanks to you and your crew, sir. We're having a very good day here."

"Yes, ma'am," said the pilot, and read Myra's note, then, "If you don't have a test pilot yet for that new ship, I'd sure like to fly it. Wil Dietz is the name, and my crew comes with me."

"Got it," said Trae, "but let's get this ship into production while we're at it."

They went back to sit with the engineer again. Three jumps were made back to Elderon, Myra making predictions from her data each time. She was off twenty percent the first time, ten on the second and the third time, a jump of four light-years, was right on the money. The curves were simple power laws, she explained. Later she would find a special function that fit better.

When they came back into orbit around Elderon, they saw a swarm of workers on the Guppy. During active testing they had traveled one hundred and nine light years in something over three hours. "We should move right into production," said Myra. "Add the vanes you want. Without pushing too hard, at four hundred light years a day, it's only five months to the core."

Her enthusiasm was real, and justified. "Just wait til we fly Guppy," said Trae, and they were like two kids again, playing with fascinating, expensive and very dangerous toys, for the ships were also weapons of war, a thing they'd not looked at yet.

A butterfly-shaped shuttle kite met them in orbit, and they spent another two hours on a leisurely, helical-pathed float down through the atmosphere of Elderon to make a soft landing at the private port of Zylak Industries. Meza was there to greet them with Wallace and several of the engineers. All were overjoyed by the results of the tests. There were hugs, handshakes and backslaps all around. Wallace hugged Myra, and glowed red when she kissed him on the cheek.

There was a two-hour debriefing in a conference room, everyone taking notes. Myra did a quick calculation and suggested the vane areas be scaled up by two to three times. Another engineer said it was closer to two, and they later settled on that.

Lots of questions about the green glow and flashes observed, and surprise when Trae said it was the first flicker of a branegate. Myra backed him up with her calculations from supersymmetry models. Branegate formation energy for the Grand Portal was thousands of times greater than what either the test ship or the Guppy could generate, but that was for a stable gate. For a small gate the calculations gave a range of energies, and what they'd reached in the tests was just below the edge of it.

"Why was it so visible forward, and not all around the ship?" someone asked. "During jump, the whole ship was in the singularity."

"Remember this was excess energy being used beyond the requirements of the jump," said Myra. "The field follows the shape of the ship, and the energy density is highest at the nose. That's why the snout is on the Guppy. That ship will give us a branegate, I'm sure of it."

A young engineer raised his hand. "If it's a shaped field, it can be projected forward, so what happens if something is there?"

"If we make a branegate where the object is?"

"Yes."

"Well, I guess that something goes away to another universe. There's only gravity with the exotic matter; I suppose some photon showers from photinos. No, you'd just go away."

Everybody laughed. It seemed like an amusing idea at the time.

They went to more mundane matters. Myra insisted on more tests when the new vanes were installed. If all went well, they would move straight to production, were already tooled for it. As for the Guppy, current timeline gave six months for working tests and another six to production if everything worked perfectly the first time.

The meeting ended, and the engineers stood to leave. Meza and Wallace remained seated, motioned both Anton and Myra to sit down again. The door closed, and they were alone.

"Something else," said Meza. "It's personal, about you, Anton."

"Oh, I should go," said Myra, and moved her chair to stand up.

Trae grasped her forearm. "No, I want you to stay."

She sat down again, but looked embarrassed. Meza smiled, and so did Wallace, a bit unusual for him.

"Well, while you've been darting around in space, we've received results from some fine detective work our security people have been doing. One man in particular, he has good contacts on Galena and Gan and has apparently done a whiz of a job in the archives. He wants to see you at your apartment tonight, so be there.

"Anyway, we know for sure now who arranged for the murder of Trae, and probably why. We know who hired the assassins, and how they were paid. We know that same person is siphoning information and data on our jump craft and sending it to Gan."

"We've intercepted and altered most of it," said Wallace quickly, "but some good stuff got through. Gan will be working to build a duplicate of what you tested today."

"Who on Gan?" asked Anton.

"Gan, the government, the new president they freely elected. Also the richest man on the planet. Pretends to be a believer, goes to church, even set up a council of Bishops to provide guidelines for lawmaking. Calls himself a Bishop, but under all of it he's nothing more than a thief, liar, conspirator and now murderer. He ordered your murder. Probably wanted your father dead, too, but didn't get to him in time. A man on our own trustee's board arranged the assassination, and has been sending him information."

Little bells were going off in Trae's head. Council of Bishops. Something his father had said. He'd told both Meza and Wallace about the conversations with him. "If he thinks of himself as a Bishop, we're dealing with a zealot. I don't see how he could know about the invasion. It's too far away."

"Unless it was planned ahead. Azar Khalil goes back to the early years when your father was preaching freedom on Gan. He might even have arrived at the same time. I'll give you all I have on him, and on the man he's been working with. His family also goes back to the founding times, but here, not on Gan. Run this by your father. Maybe there's a connection with what's happening on the other side."

Meza pushed a file across the table to him. "It's all there. Get back to us soon with anything Leonid can add. This isn't going to stop, and there's no defense for it, only offense, and against a sovereign planetary government. We have to keep the new jump technology out of his hands."

"Or kill him," added Wallace, a man not known for liberal views on anything.

"We're not in that business, Wallace," said Meza.

"The new guy is. Let him handle it."

Meza shook his head. "The new guy, as he puts it, is John Haight, and he's the one coming to see you tonight. He wants to meet with you alone."

"I'll be there," said Trae, and glanced at Myra.

"I'll be at work. A lot of extrapolations to do for Guppy." She pushed back her chair, and stood up.

Call me when you're finished with him.

Okay.

"Well, we've had a great day, but if you think this was a breakthrough just wait until Guppy flies."

"Ugliest ship I've ever seen," said Meza, and laughed.

"Looks aren't everything," quipped Wallace. "Take me, for example."

Myra just shook her head at him.

He was exhausted, but still giddy from the events of the day. Trae's dinner in the cafeteria was a synthburger and protein bar, and he took a taxi home. His apartment complex was a two-story square of units around a central plaza with a pool and scalding sauna he used every evening before sleep. Twice he'd talked to his parents from there, and was eager to talk to them again. The fleet of The Bishops would have made transit by now, and be hurtling towards them at half light speed. Plenty of time, one might think, but no time for sloth.

His second floor apartment overlooked the pool. The sun was just setting when he let himself in. The air smelled of lavender and sandalwood, masking the old odors of overcooked, frozen dinners. A living room, dining room, bedroom and kitchen were spread over a thousand square feet, roomy and comfortable for just him. His computer was in the dining room, and with peripherals filled the area. A holoviewer in the front room was rarely used, and a table in front of a couch was heaped with technical journals. He ate at a small table in the kitchen.

He changed clothes, trading suit for swim trunks and a loose-fitting shirt, and settled himself in front of his computer. The model he and Myra had been working on several nights before was still there. Before his eyes the model was changing, a complex array of geometrical shapes rotating, shifting positions, their intersections representing solutions to families of equations. Myra was working on it at her station in the plant, and upgrading his file as she progressed. They often worked together at a distance; talking in geometries, visualizing, and letting the machines do the work. Trae prided himself in right-brain visualization, but was no match for Myra when it came to calculating. What the machines did exactly in minutes, Myra could do to a good approximation in her head in only seconds.

She'd been to his apartment once. They'd worked for a while, but drifted into talk about anything but work, and nothing got done. They were becoming quite close, and both knew it. The relation could grow at its own pace, but the work had to be done and was their focus, now.

A group of four toroids rotated suddenly on the screen, changing intersections with themselves, and a long cylinder pierced all of them. Myra was deep in supersymmetry, trying to model the very pores of the brane separating their universe from another. He watched, fascinated, and—

There was a sudden rapping on his door, slow but firm.

Trae opened the door quickly, having been warned about a visit.

At first sight, the man standing there evoked caution. Tall, slender, his dark eyes were deep-set above a hawkish nose. Thin lips, and a sharp chin, he had a dangerous look. His mouth curved into an attempt at a smile, and failed.

"I'm John Haight, Mister Zylak. Meza said you were expecting me."

"Yes, come in," said Trae, and closed the door behind them. Haight smelled like oil and burnt insulation, the odor of his clothing. He was dressed like a workman, with heavy shirt, pants and boots, and he carried a metal box that looked like a toolkit.

"I don't use Zylak. The last name is Denal. I'm Anton Denal."

"Just so you know that I know who you are," said Haight, and put down the toolbox.

"What's that for?" asked Trae, and pointed at the box.

"I'm a repairman, a plumber. You're having a problem with your sink."

"Oh."

"Actually I'm here to brief you on what I've found out about your recent demise. Welcome back, by the way. You're looking well."

Something about the man was vaguely familiar, but Trae couldn't place it. He was sure he'd never seen this man before. "Thank you," he said. "You're part of the security division?"

"I work with it as a consultant."

"Okay," said Trae, and smiled. He sat down by the computer, and motioned for the man to sit in the chair beside him. "So, what have you found?"

"You're an important person. The president of Gan, Azar Khalil, wanted you dead, and it was done. His accomplice is a trustee of our company, and I think the men are related, going back to the other side. Their families appear at exactly the same time in the archives, just after Leonid Zylak began his mission on Gan."

"I looked in the archives, and didn't see any of that," lied Trae. "You must have other sources."

"I do. Some on Gan, a few on Galena."

"Priests?"

"Only two. Few people go back as far as your father, and The Church of The Faithful wasn't even around then. It came a few years later, interestingly enough, not here, but on Gan, about the time I think a previous incarnation of Azar Khalil arrived."

The familiarity was growing stronger and stronger. "I missed a lot in the archives, or the people you know have prodigious memories."

"They do. Long ago the trustee involved in your murder had a brother on the other side. That brother was a Bishop of The Church, a prominent Bishop, but The Church was not so strong then. It preached love, and had no ambitions for power. A few disagreed with that."

"These people remember all that?" Trae's pulse rose. The piercing eyes, the cadence of speech, all so—

"*I* remember it. I was there on the other side, a novice in The Church. I remember Azar Khalil as the first Bishop of Kratola. I think The Church sent him after your father to gain a foothold in the colonies. And he's managed to make a substantial fortune while doing it. We even removed the Emperor of Gan for him, restoring democracy, or so we thought. Now he's taken power under the guise of democracy, but it's for The Church."

"Who's we?"

"You, the Zylak family. You're the enemy of The Church. It was seen that way on Kratola. It still is."

"You don't get any of this from the archives, or other people's memories. As much as I think it possible, it's conjecture without proof." Trae's pulse was racing, now, Haight's eyes locked onto his.

"Your father remembers all of it. And do you really think you're the only person who meets with him on a flower-covered hillside? Only Trae would believe that."

"You've talked to my father?"

"Why not? We've been responsible for you since the day you were first born. Only the bodies change."

Now John Haight really smiled, and the darkness in his eyes went away.

"Petyr?" said Trae, and his voice quavered.

"Hello again," said John Haight.

CHAPTER 33

In the first youth of Leonid Zylak, ten thousand souls left Kratola and its crowds to search for opportunities in another universe. Others had gone before them, and had never been heard from again. Even with ships cruising at half-light speed and capable of light-year jumps, the distances were too vast for communication.

This time was different. The new colonists vowed they would keep in touch with their home world by settling the first habitable worlds they found. This was not so easy a task as they thought, for it was one hundred and eighty years before they found a system with a suitable world. Many lived out their final lives on board ship, having lost hope of ever setting foot on land again.

Elderon was the first settlement, followed shortly by Galena, then Gan. Two thousand migrants took one ship and continued on towards the galactic rim. A lifetime later word came by wave that they'd settled a single world twenty light years away, but after that there was nothing. Perhaps they'd found other people living there, as they had on Galena, and especially Gan, people from earlier migrations before the age of nanomachines and multiple lifetimes. They settled in well with each other, still one people.

Elderon, Galena and Gan were considered by Kratola to be the colony worlds, still in touch with home.

And things were not going well for Kratola, or the colonies.

The exception was Elderon, with its figurehead president and government by an elected senate. A planet of industry and technology, mostly owned by a few families who'd been influential even on Kratola. Some of the more ambitious, especially those who wished riches without competition, had moved on to Galena and Gan. And that's where the problems began. Problems with dictators, and problems with The Church.

It was happening now on Gan, in particular, and getting worse by the day.

Azar Khalil succeeded in establishing The Council of Bishops by vote of The People's Congress, but the vote was extremely close. Many people demonstrated against it in the streets the day after the vote was taken, and several key congressmen were visibly shaken by that. There were calls for impeachment, and conciliatory remarks by representatives pointing out elections were only a year away.

Azar Khalil had other ideas, and had been preparing for them since his election.

In every respect he now owned the military, at least every senior officer in it. The gratuities he paid privately for their consultations more than doubled their salaries, and their lifestyles were now dependent on it.

The Church was his. He was The Church of Kratola, as manifested in the colonies. The Bishops who served his presidency just didn't know it yet. He would inform them soon. The colonies were but an extension of Kratola, The Church an arm of The Council of Bishops to rule them. Azar Khalil was Archbishop over them all.

There would be no elections. The Church would rule with Azar as its head, the Council of Bishops for guidance, and the military for enforcement. Selected members of congress would be kept on for a People's Advisory Council and taken seriously, for the needs and problems of the governed must always appear to be known and attended to for political stability.

One year from now.

Another problem was more immediate. Relations with Galena, once a large market for Azar's industrial empire, were deteriorating badly. He had only himself to blame for part of the problem; he'd moved too fast in trying to establish a proper church there, and now his priests had been rudely deported. He'd despised Emperor Sidique for being soft, but now despised him more for doing something decisive. For the moment, it was necessary for him to abandon his church ambitions for Galena, and focus on Gan. In a matter of years, still in this lifetime, the might of The Church would appear in the skies. Azar would make sure Galena fell quickly, and that Rasim Sidique would be the first to die.

*

Nicolus called late at night, and said the emergency was extreme. Rasim himself met the man at the west gate well before dawn, and they entered the service entrance to the palace. In a servants' lounge adjacent to the kitchen, they sat down for tea and day old rolls.

For several minutes, Rasim Sidique, Emperor of all Galena, listened in horror as his Bishop gave him the news transmitted by wave from Elderon.

Treachery, deceit, assassination, a government overthrown at home and now an invasion force on the way to expand power. Petyr had told them everything, and so must regard him as a friend. The man's faith was not misplaced, but what could Rasim do?

"My military is little more than a police force, and a small one at that. I couldn't make a move against Gan if I wanted to, even to overthrow Khalil. The assassinations he plotted were on Elderon. They should handle it."

"Their military is even smaller than yours," said Nicolus, "but Petyr said they have a new technology that's very powerful and can be used against a large force. He wouldn't give me details when I pressed him; perhaps his trust in you isn't total. Considering what has happened, I'm surprised he has any trust left in him."

"I understand, but he can't expect any military help from Galena. I cannot and will not attack Gan under any circumstances. Once was enough. I *can* and *will* do what I've done, and that's to remove any influence or troublemaking by Gan, or Azar's version of The Church, from our planet. But if an attack fleet comes, as he's described, I'll not be able to stand up to it, and I will not sacrifice lives for my reign. I'm a believer. Perhaps The Church will keep me on as a figurehead."

Nicolus shook his head sadly. "I'm the Bishop of your church, sire, a church practicing tolerance and love. You're beloved by our people as a person, but your rule has been so invisible they don't realize how fair and just it has been. They'll see it when it's gone. You and I will be the first to die if there's an invasion backed by Gan."

"We could flee to Elderon in exile, and regroup there."

"Possible, but Elderon might also be under attack. As I see it, they're our only hope, with their new technology."

"And we don't even know what it is," said Rassim.

He thought a moment then, "As long as our embassy is open on

Gan, we can watch what's happening and provide information for Elderon. We can also stop any shipments to Gan that might contribute to their military. Without being obvious, of course. We'll claim there are shortages. We'll subsidize the companies involved, to cover their losses, as I did earlier with munitions. The executives will understand the why when I explain the situation to them."

"Their prime interest is money, sire."

"If Azar Khalil and his supporters get control here, everything will belong to The Church. That should impress them."

"Unless promises have secretly been made," said Nicolus.

CHAPTER 34

've never seen you so happy. You really missed him," said Myra. She and Trae were sitting knee-to-knee in her cubicle, eating sandwiches. Toroids danced and melded on the computer screen beside them, a simulation of brane pores opening and closing.

"I guess I did," said Trae. "When I first came back he was just a memory, but then it grew. Even in a new body I still recognized him. Yes, I'm happy. I have two fathers again."

"I always thought his eyes were cold," she said. "He frightened me a little."

"He likes you," said Trae. "When we first arrived here he used to kid me about you, about the way I felt but couldn't express."

She put a hand on his knee. "Still have that problem?"

"I don't think so."

"Well, the door _is_ closed." Her hand moved along his thigh. She leaned forward, eyes open.

Trae leaned forward and kissed her gently, his lips together, but Myra leaned into the kiss and her lips parted, his following hers. Their tongues touched, and caressed softly. They exchanged sharp exhales of breath before parting.

Myra smiled, and patted his thigh. Trae swallowed hard. "Good for circulation. We'll get more work done," he said, and she laughed.

He licked his lips. "What is that taste?"

Myra took another bite of her sandwich. "Lambsynth and jelly," she said. Her face glowed.

I think I love you.

Me, too.

I'll call you Anton in public, but you'll always be Trae to me.

Okay, but only in private. Uh oh, I just thought of something.

What?

"The field is shaped, right? I mean Guppy's field. The forward edge moves in and out with energy."

"Yes."

"So how much more energy is needed to open the brane at the forward edge of the field?"

Myra laughed. "Your brain never stops, even when we're kissing."

"Neither does yours. Well?"

"Well yourself. At high asymmetry, with the new proboscis on Guppy, a fifty percent overload might open the brane a few ship lengths out, a few miles."

"And if we double the power overload?"

Myra rolled her eyes. "Double the distance. Should be roughly linear."

He knew that in her head she saw nothing but geometries, the intersections of shapes. Exact calculations would take a day to answer his questions, but he knew her answers would be close. They always were.

"I think we have a way to turn Guppy into a powerful weapon," he said, but Myra just stared at him until he explained it all to her.

CHAPTER 35

Grandma Nat was in a bad mood, and relished a moment of remorse and self-pity. She was perched on her special chair on the ship's bridge. Her captain was an arm's length from her, and looked bored. The viewscreen showed stars and faint nebulae in patterns totally unfamiliar to her. The vibrations of the ship hummed around her, and would do so for perhaps the next fifty years, even with two nauseating jumps per cycle. She had at best twenty years before rejuvenation, and could look forward to the first thirty years of her next life being cooped up in space in a too-small ship staring at a viewscreen showing foreign stars while the home of her first birth drifted even farther away. Her planet was crumbling under the tyranny of The Church, her family had split up in flight, and it was not likely she'd ever see two of her sons again. Other children were in other ships tagging along with her in black space towards a place only her grand daughter knew, a place soon to be under attack. The Bishops' ships were on their way, and it was only a matter of time.

Feel sorry for me, she thought. Feel sorry for my family. I miss my husband. I wish he were here. I wish I knew why he chose to end the cycles of his life.

She sniffed once, and then wiped her eyes dry with a tissue.

Well, enough of that. Now what?

"You'd think my grand daughter would call more often, just to let us know where they are," she said.

"Yes, ma'am," said her captain. "They're far out in front of us by now."

She pouted. "Distance has nothing to do with it."

There had been that one frantic call when she'd been trying to sleep through the buzz of the ship.

Gramma, it's Tatjana. Please answer!

What? I'm sleeping.

The invasion ships are making transit. We're making a run for it to meet our son. He thinks the invasion can be repelled, but isn't sure how. I'll be in touch later, when we have something new. Bye for now; we're making another jump. Oh, how I hate these things!

Weeks ago, and nothing since.

She drummed her fingers on the arm of her chair. "I don't know how you stand it, all this time in space. I don't belong out here. I feel like a spore trying to find a place to land so I can really live."

Her captain smiled. Nice smile. What was his name? Karl something. "I've spent a few lifetimes in ships like this," he said softly. "I love the peace and simplicity. No crowds, no politics. Just drift, and enjoy the view. It's not for everyone, but I like all of it, even the jumps."

"Ugh," she said, and he laughed.

She liked the man, and his attitude, and wished she could share it with him. There were others like him out there, guiding the ships containing the remnants of her family and all they needed to start again in some new place that would have them.

To pass the time, she and her captain began sharing stories about past lives, ten lives between the two of them. In the following seven cycles of the ship she tried twice to contact Tatjana, but received no reply. What was wrong now? And finally her captain came to her with disturbing news. The scanners had picked up a fleet of fifty ships, large and small, two days behind them, but coming from the galactic core.

"Fifty? That could be the invasion force," she said.

"We've been following the shipping lane, and so are they. Could be commercial," said her captain.

"I don't think so. Can we get farther away from them?"

"Certainly. We'll do a light-year jump right now if you like."

"I don't like, but do it," she said, and the moment was again both nauseating and disorienting. I'm too old for this, she thought.

When they came back into flat space the scanners showed nothing behind them. But only an hour later the fifty ships were there again, following them by only a day and a half.

And closing.

CHAPTER 36

There were seven ships in lower orbit, and one of them was *Nova*, the first ship Anton and Myra had tested. That ship had six companions, all tested at jumps up to forty light-years. Seven darts protruding from doughnuts spiked with radial vanes, and two oblong ports along the fuselage forward of the cockpit were the new features. The ships were engineered for war, armed with two railguns throwing thousand pound slugs of ferrite-doped uranium, and one-ton slugs of pure iron enclosing shaped charges of high explosives.

Seven ships were not many, but twenty more were in production, and more scheduled to follow. Anton and Myra surveyed the existing craft from the shuttle taking them to higher orbit for the first complete operational test of Guppy.

"We're actually going to war with these things?" murmured Myra.

"Yes."

"The whole concept of war seems wasteful to me."

"It bothers you."

"Of course. Doesn't it bother you?"

"It bothers me that some of our own people could be killed or badly injured. Otherwise, no. We're not the aggressors here. We're defending ourselves instead of giving up our way of life. Nobody wants to die a violent death, even with rejuvenation. I know from experience, it's not pleasant."

"Don't get me wrong," said Myra. "I'm not opposed to war when it's necessary. I've read enough history to know some aggressors can only be stopped by killing them. I just want to minimize the waste."

The shuttle pulled out in front of seven ships now in echelon formation. Fourteen, black apertures were the muzzles of missile tubes and railguns, there to spew death. Figures moved in the bridges of two ships, the first crews on board. In days, all the ships would be manned and ready to go. Timing depended on the results of the tests with Guppy today.

A two second burn, and they moved higher. Myra put a hand on his arm. "It was Azar Khalil who had Trae killed, not The Church," she said. "There are innocents involved."

"From what John tells me, Azar and The Church is the same thing. He's a Bishop from the other side, sent to establish political power over people's lives in the name of The Church and to dictate their beliefs."

"But many believers don't want that either, people who don't even attend services. They're not your enemy." She squeezed his arm for emphasis, and he looked down at her.

"I know," he said softly, and put his hand over hers. "My enemy, *our* enemy, is defined well enough. There's the invasion fleet and the Council of Bishops that sent it. We have Azar Khalil, and the church of extremists he's set up on Gan. These are the enemies, and I tell you this; they will stop what they're doing, or be destroyed."

Myra leaned her head against his arm. "I never heard Trae say such harsh words."

"That was another lifetime, Myra."

"I think talking with John Haight has hardened you."

"It has. He made me realize we have to go to war. I didn't want it, either."

"I know. I agree with you. I just hate the possibility of killing the wrong people."

"John wants to meet you, by the way. He remembers you from when you talked to me in my dreams."

Myra frowned. "He's still a security man, a hired killer, from what I hear. People at the plant are talking."

"They're wrong. He's my father, Myra, at least a part of him is. He knows how I feel about you. He wants to meet the woman I love."

Now she smiled. "Well—if you put it that way."

"After today's test?"

"If we survive it," she quipped.

"No reason we shouldn't."

"Oh, I can think of a thousand reasons. Can't you?"

He hugged her, and their eyes went back to the viewscreen. Three yellow specks in blackness, then blobs, then three strange ships coming in closer, each bulging at the front, and slender aft, like giant versions of some deep-sea predator with gaping jaws. The proboscis of each ship was now coiled up inside the hull for flat space travel and pinch topologies for spacetime jumps. Its purpose was singular, to open a pore in the brane, anywhere in space, expanding it to the size of the ship for transit.

They would test that today, the opening of a ship-sized brane-gate, but there was something else to do, something that would turn a peaceful ship into a weapon of war. That would be the final test of the day.

The three ships now in orbit with them had been tested several times for normal and jumped flight. The record was sixty light years for a jump, but Myra felt a hundred light-years was attainable with only two jumps per day. They'd not pushed too hard, yet, but intended to before taking the ships into battle. And far above them, in geosynch orbit, seven others like them were being assembled. They would be ready by the time the invasion fleet reached Elderon.

Trae had no intention of waiting so long.

They drifted in close to the lead ship in orbit, the first of its kind and the one they'd christened Guppy. Only close in could the size of the vessel be appreciated. Forward it was heart-shaped in cross-section, and over a mile across. Nova was small by comparison. The length was five miles, out of sight from where they came in to dock at a short, retractable port in the nose of the vessel.

They docked with a small bump and lurch, then went down stairs to the access tunnel and waited. A minute later the airlock coughed and opened, and Wil Dietz was there grinning at them. He motioned them forward.

"Thought I would have seen you again a lot sooner than this," he shouted.

"Slaves to the computer," said Trae, and they walked swaying down the flexible tunnel to meet him.

They shook hands. "You look like you're having a good time," said Trae.

Wil had been principle test pilot for both Nova and Guppy, and had oriented a dozen other pilots during testing. "Great time. Still not sure which I like best. Nova is a racecar. Guppy is more like a heavy truck, but it's sure more comfortable living in her. Come on in."

It was almost as if he were inviting them into his home. The hatch clanged shut behind them, and there was a shudder as the tunnel was disengaged, venting lock air into space. An open elevator lifted them up three levels to a passageway with pairs of empty seats on both sides, and they walked it to a roomy bridge seating seven crew. Two seats normally occupied by maintenance engineers were vacant for them. Co-pilot, navigator, and two flight engineers were already seated, and nodded greetings.

They sat down, buckled in, and put on headsets. Once in motion they would stand behind pilot and copilot so they could look outside through carbon-plas windows.

There was no lurch, no sensation as they lifted from orbit. "Ponderous, but stately," said Wil. "You can fly her with one hand. Here we go, then, ninety degrees above the ecliptic plane to two A.U. and mark."

Their weight was normal for several minutes, and then they coasted. Wil read the test list on his screen for comparison with the old-fashioned clipboard pages in their hands. Both of them still loved pen and paper for making notes and quick calculations.

"Mark. Setting DEC nine-thirty, RA twelve-thirty five-zero. We have a straight run of seventy light-years from here. Ready?"

"Proceed," said Anton.

"Deploying Sniffer," said Wil.

A low hum lasting seconds. "Deployed." The face of Guppy now had a forty-foot long protuberance that looked like a parrot's beak. From this would momentarily protrude 'Stinger', a tapered cone shaping the space-twisting field to pry open a single pore of the brane connecting all points in space.

"Plenum charging. Twenty seconds. Trickle rate twenty-five."

Anton and Myra made checks on their checklists. Sniffer would discharge the plenum, followed by a trickle of exotic particles interacting with the false vacuum of space. Ernst counted down from five. At zero the windows flashed green. Time to move. Anton and Myra stood up and leaned over Wil and his copilot to look outside. There was a bright green glow around Sniffer's beak, slightly oblong in shape.

"Good symmetry," mumbled Myra, and scribbled something.

"Deploying Stinger, five feet," said Wil.

Instinctively their hands grabbed the tops of the seats, but there was no lurch or other sudden motion. A tapered, solid cylinder slid out of the center of Sniffer's beak, and locked five feet out from it. The green glow intensified, and stretched out into an oblate spheroid three feet beyond the end of Stinger. A fuzzy, amoebic-shaped patch of green flickered just beyond the edge of that. Myra took one look, and actually giggled.

"Oh, it looks *just* like the fundamental geometry," she said, and scribbled again.

Trae saw only glowing shapes connecting, knowing that in her head Myra was performing rotations of what she saw, rotations giving the extra dimensions of the brane and its pores. She would have to show it all to him later.

Several tests later they knew the fuzzy patch near the end of Stinger detached when Stinger was deployed only seven feet. And by the time Stinger was out to its full extension of forty feet, the patch was nearly a mile away.

"Not as far as I'd like," grumbled Trae, "but it might have to do."

Wil looked back curiously at him, but only Myra knew what he'd meant by that.

They went back to a Stinger extension of only three feet, but charged the plenum for two minutes.

And watched in awe as a branegate opened up right in front of the ship.

All were silent, except Myra, who gave a little yelp and clapped her hands.

"We did it! We did it! There it is!"

An enormous cat's eye, then fatter, oriented vertically, with a maximum area twice that of Guppy's cross-section at the nose. Constant shape and size, flickering green on the edges, darker towards the center, an oblong there nearly black. A beautifully stabilized branegate right in their face, with no black holes or keeper planets to stabilize it.

"I really wondered if it was going to happen," Trae said, and grinned. Myra hugged him.

"Remember how the Grand Portal was first opened by accident? All the black holes there had already stressed space to the extreme, and gravity did most of the work. Big masses, big force, but large size. Takes a lot of work to keep that thing stable. Should have started small in the first place," said Myra.

She was excited, and giddy. She made him want to laugh.

"Do we go through it?" asked Wil, staring outside. Awed, he'd forgotten his checklist of tests.

"Not yet. Back to the list," said Trae, but he too could barely control his excitement.

It seemed that while plenum energy created the gate, trickler current sustained it, but the length of Stinger determined its position, and the effect was nonlinear. By the time Stinger was out to full extension the branegate was still there and stable, but it was over two miles away.

Myra was scribbling, and talking to air. "That's a real branegate, now. Two miles. I don't know what that other blob was, maybe like a crack in a doorway."

"What?" asked Trae, and then Myra's eyes focused again.

"You'll have a range of two miles with a full branegate."

"Oh."

They were down to the final two tests, one of which might end their lives. Everyone in the crew had spent years in spaceflight, but had never made transit through the Grand Portal or even seen it. Now, they were being asked to drive their ship through a miniature version of that thing, and return alive to tell about it.

This had taken some persuasion.

Myra had explained the basic concepts to them: the many extra dimensions folded up at any point in space, the extra-dimensional brane connecting two universes at each point, the unraveling and stretching of high dimensions to tunnel through the brane from one universe to another.

"When we go through the gate, we're just following the flow of exotic particles we use for power, and the trail is the same coming back. If we do it at rest we end up exactly at our starting point when we return. The brane is supposed to be continuous, the universes simply connected."

"And if it isn't?" asked an engineer.

"You don't want to think about that," said Myra.

They were not amused.

Stinger was drawn in to three feet. The window was filled with flickering green, the gate nearly touching them and showing a distinct black patch at its center.

"Setting coordinates," said an engineer, and loaded the pattern of stars giving them their exact position.

Wil's eyes were large when he looked up at them. "How do we know we won't come out in the middle of a star?"

"Hot gas would be blasting us from the gate right now, if that were true. Just pull Stinger in. If we have to leave fast, go back to three feet. We'll have to recharge the plenum with exotic matter coming from *this* side. I told you all this," said Myra.

A woman's frown was a signal for a man's action.

They'd shut down thrusters for testing, but still had a forward drift velocity of four hundred feet per second. "Coordinates?" asked Wil.

"Loaded. Clock on," said an engineer.

"Then here we go. Retrieving Stinger—slowly—slowly."

They were in the thing, flickering green all around them, the dark patch ahead growing rapidly. No sense of motion or turbulence, and a few anxious heartbeats later they were through. The glow around them flicked out, and ahead was only blackness.

It took a moment for their eyes to adjust after the bright green surroundings. A few blue stars glowed ahead of them, and there was a faint, hazy patch that might have been a galaxy.

"Recording," said the engineer. Four cameras on the hull of the ship were taking pictures in every direction. "The branegate is gone!" he said, too loudly.

"Of course it is. Recharge the plenum as before, two minutes."

"We're still moving, same velocity. Shouldn't I turn the ship around to return?" Wil then cleared his throat to calm his voice.

Myra rolled her eyes at Trae. She'd forgotten a small detail in orienting the crew.

"The two universes are connected at every point in space, both sides of the brane. If you keep your heading and open a gate right now we'll come back quite close to where we started. That's why the clock is running, so we can time our course."

"I have the star patterns, and there are two galaxies far out there in camera range. We're not in intergalactic space!" Now the engineer sounded excited. "Looks like we're in a space between two arms of a spiral galaxy."

"The home galaxy, but thousands of light years from its center," said Trae. "The Grand Portal is there, but now we have a shorter way back."

"We have pictures from the core area," said Myra. "What you have on camera should be enough to locate this position when we get home.

"Now?" asked Wil, with enthusiasm.

"Yes, now. Two minute plenum charge, Stinger to three feet, and open the door just like before." She was nonchalant about it, thinking about something else, but Trae noticed when she took his hand in hers and squeezed it.

In any experiment, there are always unknowns.

A two minute charge, and Wil moved with authority and no caution to open the gate, and it appeared before them as if by magic. With no hesitation, he pulled the gate to them as Stinger was reined in, and they were through it in an instant. The pattern of stars they'd left behind was there again. Pilot and crew laughed nervously, while out of their sight Trae and Myra breathed small sighs of relief.

"Still alive," quipped Anton. "And one more test before bragging rights are assigned. You know where to go."

"Yes, sir," said Wil, obviously relieved and happy. The most dangerous test was now behind them.

They went back into normal, powered flight with Stinger and Sniffer withdrawn, and returned to the ecliptic plane. A four-minute burn, followed by a drift of four hours brought them to a ring of icy debris between the two gas giants in their system. It was a thin ring, a few thousand miles across and several miles thick, populated by fragments of frozen water, methane, carbon dioxide and ammonia. Fragment diameters ran a spectrum of feet to several miles. They picked out an ellipsoidal piece over a mile in diameter, followed it a while, worked themselves in behind it in its travels.

"Let's start at two miles. I want the largest cross section we can get," said Trae.

The overall test was broken into several on their checklist, with plenum charges up to thirty minutes at constant trickle current limited only by the power of the superconducting coil. Still, trickle current seemed to serve mainly as a branegate stabilizer, especially as the gate was moved farther and farther from the ship. They set up a series of gates to a range of two miles, and then started all over again when thrusters were turned on to move them within two miles of their icy target.

The mountain of ice and frozen gases loomed in front of them, partially obscured by the bright glow of an established branegate only yards from their windows. Stinger was at three feet deployment.

"Take it to forty," said Anton softly.

Stinger went to forty feet out in seven seconds. The branegate moved with it, but faster, and growing in size as it was projected outwards.

The gate struck the mountain of ice dead center, its cross section barely larger than its target.

The mountain of ice disappeared. There was not even a flicker from the interior of the gate. And nothing came back out from it.

"End of test," said Trae, and Myra frowned again. "It's what we needed. Guppy isn't just a ship anymore. It's a weapon. Doesn't kill directly, just sends things away. Things like attacking ships."

"Doesn't kill if you're sealed in a ship, that is," said Myra.

"So we'll hope that's the only use necessary," said Anton, but both of them knew it might not be.

Myra was not satisfied with what he'd said. "We've done what we came to do, so let's go home."

They spoke only a few words to each other on the way back, while the crew chatted excitedly over their headsets. The day had been historic for them. For Myra and Anton it had also been exciting and fulfilling, but the success of the final test had turned it into a prelude to war.

The shuttle brought them down in a lazy, helical course to the sprawl of Zylak airbase. It was like sailing in a paper plane, and nearly lulled them to sleep after the stress of the day.

Meza and Wallace were there to greet them on the tarmac far out from the terminal. A limousine awaited them. There were embraces all around, and they got into the car. Wil and his crew were coming down in another shuttle two hours later, and already the techs and pilots were out on the tarmac to prepare a noisy welcome for them.

"An historic day," said Meza grandly. "We'll be making money from this a thousand years from now."

"I'm just glad the science turned out to be right," said Wallace, and smiled at Myra. The car went through a security gate, turned left, and sped towards town.

"And now we have a deterrent against invaders," added Trae.

"It's a good deterrent only if we don't have to kill someone with it," said Myra. "As far as I know, that chunk of ice didn't have a pulse."

"That chunk of ice wasn't attacking us, either. Look, if we use it against ships everyone is sealed in, and they have regenerating life support, the only impact is a long trip back home on the other side. I admit I'd use it against land targets if I could, but the range is only two miles, and Guppy can only operate in space. What's the problem?"

Myra frowned again, but had no argument. "There isn't any, as long as we don't kill innocent people."

"Too bad Khalil didn't share your opinion when he decided to get rid of me."

"You weren't an innocent to him, just like he isn't an innocent to me," Myra said coldly.

"Well, enough of that," said Meza. "Killing or not, we're going into production right away. By the time the invasion arrives, we should have plenty of ships to literally send them on their way."

"More than that. We can move against the Grand Portal itself. The keepers are too large, but we can take out a generator or two and destabilize the entire gate. We can police it," said Trae, and gestured with a fist in emphasis.

"We're in more of a rush than you think, not just with Guppy, but Nova as well. We'd be foolish to wait until the invasion gets here. We should meet them as far out as possible. Fifty ships are coming. I'd be comfortable if we had that many, or more, to meet them. We should also take control of Grand Portal. Two or three Guppies for that, plus a number of Nova gunships. And then there's the matter of Gan. I don't think Khalil will sit still while the invasion is coming. He should be removed from power right away."

"Trae!" said Myra in horror. "I can understand why you want him punished, but we have to focus on the invasion first."

"This is nothing to do directly with Khalil having me killed. If what John says is true, Khalil is an Archbishop from The Church on Kratola. He's a part of the scheme to invade us in the first place, and he'll soon do on Gan what has been done on Kratola. He has to go, one way or another."

"We can do all of that," said Wallace, "but only if we have enough ships."

"We can build new production lines for constituent parts, but the assembly has to be in space. We'll have to train an awful lot of new people for weightless vacuum work," said Meza.

"All I wanted to do was make a branegate," said Myra, "This thing just keeps getting more complicated." Her voice dripped ice.

They were still arguing about all of it when they reached the administration building of Zylak industries. Myra and Anton were continuing on to the research complex, so Meza and Wallace congratulated them again and reminded them of the evening debriefing before getting out of the car.

The door was about to close when another man fairly leapt into the car and sat himself down opposite them before pulling the door shut.

It was John Haight.

Myra made a little yelp and leaned against Trae as the car started to move again.

"Sorry. I guess you've had quite a day. Congratulations to both of you. Now we have something to work with."

"This is John Haight, Myra," said Trae.

John smiled, but it still didn't make him look friendly. "Nice to meet you. I remember you vaguely from another lifetime."

"Hello," said Myra, and nothing more. The silence was uncomfortable for a few seconds.

"Myra and I have been arguing about using Guppy as a weapon. She doesn't like it," said Trae.

"I wouldn't expect her to," said John. "Any war is terrible. It's a last resort, but often necessary. History has proven that. The best you can do is minimize casualties, and take out the people who need taking out. In our case it's the Council of Bishops on Kratola, but they're too far away to reach right now, except for one. That one is Azar Khalil."

"He's the elected president of Gan!" said Myra.

"Not anymore," said John. "We got news yesterday from Galena. Khalil has proclaimed himself Archbishop. There'll be no more elections, and he's established his own Council of Bishops to dictate policies. Just like on Kratola, and Galena will be next, then here. His military is enforcing his godship. Riots haven't started yet, but they will. Right now, people are stunned. They can't even be seen on the streets after dusk without being arrested. Want to live that way?" John stared right at Myra when he said it.

"*That* changes some things," muttered Myra.

"Can he mount an attack on us?" asked Trae.

"Our intelligence here is lousy," said John. "I could see that the first day I was back on the job. Bodyguarding you, I never even saw the problems. Now I can do something about it.

"Khalil has railguns and microwave, but no real gunships we know of. Plenty of transports with standard jump tech. His scientists are probably trying to figure out why the stuff he stole from us doesn't work. He can still be on us in a month, but I think the Novas can take out his ships in space, if we have enough of them."

"If the Guppies go after the invasion fleet, I'm going with them," said Trae.

"I figured that much," said John.

"Not without me, you aren't," added Myra, "and there won't be any argument about it."

Neither man answered that, figuring she could be talked out of it later on.

"We have three fronts, one more immediate than the others. As long as their embassy on Gan remains open, Galena can keep close watch on what's going on, but they're already under pressure to get off planet. Two of their people have been arrested as spies. Khalil is closing up, isolating Gan. He's preparing for war. Galena is helpless, and Elderon has no military. The Novas and Guppies are it, so we'd better build'em fast."

"Still the soldier," said Trae.

"Still a soldier of The Church, too," said John. "What's coming is an abomination of The Church, set up by power-hungry Bishops. It wasn't meant to be like this. I'm fighting for The Source and The Faithful, not the Bishops or even a planet. The Church was corrupt long ago, except for Elderon, maybe Galena."

"On Gan? When I was growing up?"

"Yes. Even in the caverns, the priests ruled. Dissenters who couldn't be silenced just disappeared. I had higher orders to get you out of there as soon as I could."

"Orders from my father?"

"Yes. He never trusted The Church."

"But *you* are his father," said Myra loudly, "and now <u>you</u> want him to fight your war."

John glared at both of them. "You two have become quite close, I see. Well, I approve, but outside your computers there's a real world, and you have to open your eyes to it. The freedom you enjoy was planted here by Leonid Zylak. He didn't come as a missionary for The Church. It seems that was left to Azar Khalil, and look what it's bringing us. It's going to stop—right now."

"I agree," said Trae.

Myra leaned against him, and said, "Maybe I agree, too. I'm not so naive as you think I am. The invasion fleet still doesn't seem real to me, but at the least I want Azar Khalil punished for murdering my Trae."

"I'm still here, hon," said Trae, and kissed the top of her head.

"But you died horribly."

"So did Petyr." Trae smiled at John, and the man actually smiled back, then looked at Myra.

"Let's start over. Hi. I'm John Haight, security agent, but a big part of me is Leonid Zylak, and that makes me Trae's father, and also Anton's. Confusing enough? I hear you two are in love, and I think that's great. I wish you a long and happy life together. How's that?"

"Better," said Myra, with a hint of a smile in her eyes. "I just don't like the idea of people dying in a war."

"I don't like it either," said John, his eyes narrowing, "but I've killed before, and I'll do it again for things I believe in."

Trae looked into the man's dark eyes, thinking, *and just who are you planning to kill next?*

CHAPTER 37

They're gaining on us, Madam. The smaller ships will be on us in hours unless we make a jump."

Grandma Nat sat rigid on the throne, her captain awaiting her orders when she really wanted to turn it all over to him. They'd played a kind of tag with the invasion fleet for weeks, had more or less remained on a constant heading to the frontier. The entire invasion fleet had followed their jumps, and a few ships had even reacted to the little test zigs and zags in their course. Nat wondered if the fleet commander thought they were commercial ships, or knew they were escapees from Kratola. In either case, it seemed they were now determined to confront them, and had closed to within a few light hours in the past two days. Small ships, perhaps fighters, were now racing ahead of the fleet to catch them.

This could not be allowed to happen.

"We'll have to separate," she said suddenly. "Get your captains on line and set up a later rendezvous. Each ship is on its own to jump different lengths in different directions. Pick one ship to follow and jump with mine, but not a ship that has any of my family on board. A ship with some technology we might offer up if we're boarded."

Her captain smiled. "Something minor?"

"Of course. I don't intend to be boarded anyway, if we can avoid it. I'll leave it to you to get us out of that."

"Yes, ma'am."

"Enough of the ma'am, Captain. Call me Nat. All the years you've worked for me, and I still can't remember your name."

"Ramon DiMarco, ma'am."

"That's Nat, or Natasha, when we're not in such a hurry."

"Nat," he said, and smiled broadly this time.

In minutes, Ramon had contacted the other captains, and they'd agreed on a plan. A rendezvous point a hundred light years ahead of them was set, but most of their little fleet would make several closely spaced jumps back towards the galactic core. A smaller ship loaded with basic office systems and records would remain on course with Nat's command vessel, and make several closely spaced jumps away from the core. Ramon reasoned the invasion fleet would not want to split forces in opposite directions, and would assume flight towards the frontier. A backup plan called for splitting up into many directions out of the shipping lane if anyone followed, but Nat's vessel would still plunge ahead.

"We'll do two jumps to start, and that'll be within the hour. Two more jumps the hour after, as fast as we can charge, so we'll be coasting," said Ramon.

"Oh, dear," said Nat. Every jump was still a nasty experience for her, though the nausea was much less severe than it had been. "I think I'd better lie down for this, and take a sedative."

"I'll give you half an hour," said Ramon. "Those ships they've sent after us are closing fast."

She went to her cramped cabin, took a double dose of sedative and laced herself into the wall hammock. In a few minutes her head was swimming. *Tatjana, you must answer me. We're being chased by elements of the invasion fleet, and we're trying to get away. We're splitting up, but intend to rendezvous a hundred light years from here, closer to the frontier. I'm sorry, I don't have the coordinates, but the invasion fleet is nearly on top of us right now. I've tried and tried to contact you. Why aren't you answering? Oh, I feel myself going to sleep, now. We're going to make a jump soon. Oh . . .*

Grandma Nat slipped into unconsciousness, and the answer from Tatjana came only a moment later.

Grandma, it's Tatjana. We'll contact my son and try to get help sent. We've been making one jump after the other, and I've been sick from it. We're getting close to the frontier. Keep in contact, and we'll get together there. I'll contact you again soon. Love you.

But Natasha slept a deep sleep, and heard none of it.

CHAPTER 38

*A*nton, *it's mother. I need you with me right now. My entire family is in danger, and you have to help us.*

It was like an explosion in his head, breaking the sweet reverie with the woman he loved. They'd cooked a light dinner for themselves in his apartment, and gone through a bottle of wine before settling themselves in a plush sofa to enjoy the sounds of a synth recording, the lights turned low. Myra's head rested on his shoulder when the mental explosion came, and it startled her.

Is it an emergency? I have someone with me.

Ah. We really must meet her, dear, but this is important. I finally got in touch with your great grandmother.

The family matriarch?

She's in flight from Kratola to here, and says the invasion ships are chasing her little fleet. My whole family could be captured, but I know her well. She'll suicide before allowing herself to be taken. Can you send ships to help her?

Myra was sitting rigid, and frowning at him. *You'll need exact coordinates.*

Ah, there you are.

This is Myra, mother. She's right, we'll need exact coordinates. It'll be a way to closely target the invasion ships, and we've waited long enough. We have several Guppies, now, but three are incompletely flight-tested. Maybe we can do it in transit. How far out is she?

Suddenly Leonid Zylak was there. *I estimate a couple of thousand light years out from Grand Portal, no more.*

That's several weeks away, even for the Guppies.

Then do the best you can. Grandma has played tag with that fleet for weeks. She can do it for a few more. She didn't answer just now, probably making a jump. We'll reach her and get the coordinates you need. Sorry to rush you.

With seven Guppies ready. We'd been talking about moving against both the invasion force and the portal itself. Four more big ships will be ready within the month. We have two fronts out there, and another here. Azar Khalil is taking Gan back to a dictatorship under The Church. We'll probably have to move against him. I'll have to keep one Guppy here for now, and the range is too far for our Nova class ships in such a short time. We'll send the big ships.

We'll tell her as soon as we can. Right now, I think it's time for us to quickly meet your lady, said Leonid.

Oh, yes, said mother.

Trae looked down at Myra. Her eyes were wide, and she shook her head.

She's a bit nervous about doing that.

We understand. Can you hear us, dear?

Myra nodded a yes.

She hears you, mother.

Our son loves you, and we want to love you, too. Just attune yourself to Anton, and we'll do the rest.

Trae squeezed her tightly to him, and she closed her eyes. He felt her warmth, her presence when they were together not just physically, but in the mind. He closed his eyes, and let himself slip away, then—

It was the same place, with the rolling hills covered with flowers in red and purple hues, and the huge, symmetrical tree silhouetted on a distant knoll. Mother and father were standing in front of him, knee deep in flowers. Mother held out her arms and embraced him closely. Father smiled, shook his hand, and then gave him a fierce hug. "Well, where is she?"

Myra wasn't there. "I can feel her. She's here. Come on, Myra, show yourself. This is important to me. Please."

She appeared, then, only a few steps away in a thick carpet of flowers. She wore a sleeveless, white dress with a pattern of flowers matching her surroundings. "I needed something appropriate to wear," she said shyly, and smiled.

"This is Myra," said Trae proudly. "My parents, Leonid and Tatjana Zylak."

Myra looked strangely at Leonid. "Petyr?" she said, and Trae put a finger to his lips in caution.

His parents didn't seem to notice Myra's momentary confusion. Mother rushed to embrace her, and father made an elegant show of kissing her hand. Myra came to Trae, and they held hands.

"Young people in love," said Mother. "I still remember."

"As do I," said Father. "It's good to see you two together. I hope we'll truly be together in person within a year or two, after this mess gets cleaned up. Not to be dramatic, but it looks like you and Zylak Industries are going to have to save the world."

"I'll be leaving soon with a small squad of Guppies. One flight of Novas will act as support, but nearly all of them will head for Grand Portal. We might need some firepower there with the picket ships. The Guppies have no standard weapons, and I'll be in the lead ship intercepting the invasion fleet."

"Not without me, you won't," said Myra, "and don't argue. You need me, and my math."

"I do need you," said Trae, and didn't argue with her.

"Wonderful," said Father, "but take care of yourselves. We don't think the ships of the invasion fleet have hull-mounted weapons, but some are large enough to carry attack spacecraft along with armored vehicles and soldiers. Your advantage should be the fact they won't be expecting an encounter in deep space."

"If we can turn them back and control Grand Portal, it would be best," said Trae.

"What about Azar Khalil?" said father Leonid.

"He'll have to wait until the invasion's been dealt with. He might even back down if he knows no help is coming from the other side."

"I doubt that," said Father. "He's power hungry, just like his fellow Bishops who've brought our home world to its knees."

"Hopefully the people will someday rise up and destroy them," said Mother, and it was the hardest thing Trae had ever heard her say.

"In the meantime, Grandma Nat and the rest of my family will be migrants," she said.

Leonid patted her shoulder. "Not on Elderon, dear. For us, we're coming home."

"You'll be very welcome there, all of you," said Myra.

"We can watch our grandchildren grow up," said Mother. Myra smiled, looked at Trae in a way that made him swallow hard.

"We'll send coordinates of your great-grandmother's fleet and the invasion force, as soon as we get them," said Father.

"Your mother and I are a few weeks from the frontier. We'll go straight to Elderon, and wait for you there."

"It might not be safe if Khalil decides to attack both Elderon and Galena, but Galena will be first. He tried infiltrating the Church there, but Galena's emperor threw them out. Khalil hates the man; he's sure to attack him. Gan is under military rule right now. Demonstrators have been shot."

"Kratola all over again," said Father, "and it'll all be done in the name of The Source."

"When do we meet again?" asked Trae.

"When we have something new."

"No. We have to meet regularly. Once each day, from now on, even if it's only for seconds. Things will change quickly now."

Father smiled. "Very well, every day, at this time." He looked at Myra. "We'll try not to disturb your work."

Myra looked up at Trae, raised an eyebrow seductively, and said, "Oh, we're not easily disturbed."

"A sense of humor, too," said Father, and embraced them both.

"Very soon, now," said Mother, and hugged them. "Love you both."

The dream-like vision fled, leaving them in darkness, for their eyes were still closed. The music was soft, and Myra's head warm against his shoulder.

"What a beautiful place," she said, "and such nice people."

"They like you," he said, "They told me once it was their favorite place on Elderon. I was conceived in all those flowers."

"Oh," she said, and smiled up at him. "What a lovely idea that is."

Trae made breakfast for her in his apartment the following morning.

CHAPTER 39

S *ome very large ships are being assembled in orbit around El-*
deron. There's been no mention of this to the Trustees, and the
project is totally hush-hush. My sources have provided photographs;
the ships don't look like any commercial vessels I've ever seen. Gun
ships are rolling off their assembly line, and we're being told they're
for use by our own military and police. I don't believe it. The ships
have railguns as well as conventional weapons. They can be used in
space.

Good work, brother. They must be getting information through
the Galenan embassy; I'm going to shut that place down. It won't be
long until we move against Galena, anyway. Keep me up-to-date on
those ships.

I will. Your day is coming, Khalil. The colonies will be united
under The Church and your leadership.

All power to The Source.

And to His Faithful.

Marcellus Rosling opened his eyes. The steam in the room smelled
like lavender, and the other men had left. It was well into evening, and
he was nicely cooked. Perhaps dinner at Ducci's, then some reading
before bed. The solitary life had its advantages, but it was always good
to reach his brother and contribute a little something for the man's
lifework. It was good to help the only piece of family he had left.

Marcellus went naked to the locker room, showered, air-dried
and dressed. He sat on a bench to tie his shoes, and thought he heard
a door close. Someone had come to the baths quite late. Or perhaps it
was the attendant.

He leaned forward to tie a shoe, heard a faint scuffling sound
behind him, but ignored it. He tied the other shoe, and then sat up,
stopped by something hard pressed against the back of his head.

"Not a sound," said a man behind him, and Marcellus' heart raced. Robbery was unheard of on Elderon, and here it was happening to him.

"What do you want? I carry little money with me," he said in a hoarse whisper.

"I don't want your money," said the man, and the hard thing on the back of Marcellus' head pressed even harder.

"I'm just a soldier of The Church, and I'm sending a message to your brother."

Something exploded in Marcellus' head, and his brain didn't have time to register the sound of it.

The silenced pistol in his hand coughed a second time. Blood splattered the floor and the locker against which Marcellus Rosling had slumped. John Haight turned the body over with his foot so that the man's staring eyes and ruined forehead were clearly visible. He holstered his pistol with the silencer still attached, in case someone was unfortunate enough to come in, then retrieved a small camera and took several shots of the body at different angles.

John rifled the man's pockets, took his keys and his cash with poly-gloved hands. He'd intended to exit through the kitchen, but when he got there an attendant was busily wiping down tables for the following day. He didn't see or hear John, and so his life was spared. John Haight walked out the front doors of the baths and into the night.

He drove to Marcellus' residence in a company car, and parked it in the curving driveway of the estate, a key opening the gate for him after three tries. The man had been a bookkeeper type, with rigid habits and schedules. John had watched him for weeks. It was a Thursday, and the estate was empty, the servants enjoying a day of their own freedom.

John made no efforts at silence, and tried five keys in the big front door before it opened. The foyer was empty and dark. There was a high ceiling, and two staircases ahead of him curving left and right. He exhaled softly with relief. He didn't want to kill an innocent servant, but would if one came. He reached up, seated the pistol more deeply into its holster, and climbed the stairs to the second floor of the residence.

He found what he was looking for in a small, cluttered office at the back of the house. The computer was linked by microwave to satellite, and then relay to both Galena and Gan. Wallace had provided him with all the access codes, and John Haight sat down to write a letter he hoped would provoke a war:

> *Thisken and Ost Hypergolics*
> *Executive Officer*
> *Link M, Route 36650, Gan 12*
> *Attn. Azar Khalil*
>
> *Dear Azar:*
>
> *Your brother is dead. I just killed him with two shots to the head, and I attach photos in evidence of same. My intention is to kill you next.*
> *I was just a young man when you were on the Council of Bishops of Kratola. That was before The Church took power, and became corrupted by it. I came here on a mission to create free societies in our colonies, and you were sent after me to corrupt all of it. This is reason enough to kill you, but I have more. You had my son murdered. He's back now, and so am I, but you will pay for that murder with your life.*
> *My son goes now to destroy the invasion fleet sent to aid you from the other side. Our new technology remains secret, but its power will be demonstrated soon, and I welcome any opportunity to engage with your military force. The best you can do is take what you can carry, and return to your fellow Bishops on Kratola before my hands are around your throat.*
>
> > *Respectfully yours,*
> > *Leonid Zylak*

John read the letter again, proofed it, and attached three photos. Blind carbons to the Emperor of Galena and the single Bishop there were instructed, and a single tap of a key sent all of it away into space.

He turned off the machine, left the house, and locked the door behind him. It was a ninety-minute walk to his apartment, but the night was clear and cool. He walked briskly, and thought about the ways Azar Khalil might react to his provocation.

By the time he reached the apartment, he felt he had plans for all eventualities.

*

When Nicolus called, Rasim Sidique had already read the message. The first thing he'd done was contact his embassy on Gan and order the staff off-planet within the hour, leaving behind a handful of carefully placed agents in the streets.

"He'll attack us for certain, now. He has to get past us to Elderon, and he needs our resources. We have no defense, sire," said Nicolus.

"I know that. I'm sure Leonid Zylak has thought of it, too. We'll just have to wait and see which direction Khalil jumps. He might even run away. I don't even know what new technology Zylak is talking about."

"You'll be safer on Elderon, sire. The people will understand."

"No they won't, and I don't intend to leave them," said the Emperor of Galena. "Everything is in the hands of The Source," he said, and then thought, *and in the hands of Leonid Zylak, wherever he is.*

CHAPTER 40

On the day Trae and Myra went off to war, John Haight went with them to the private shuttleport of Zylak Industries, and walked them to the shuttle. They shook hands.

"Take care of yourselves, and don't take anything for granted. Not having an alternative plan can kill you."

"Yes, sir," said Trae, and saluted him in mock seriousness.

"Not funny," said John. "None of us have experience with this sort of thing. You'll have to think fast."

"We *can* do that, you know. The crews heading to Grand Portal have the hardest job."

"I don't think so. The keepers, even the pickets, are on their own, with no connection to a particular government. *You'll* be dealing with military people dedicated to Kratola and The Church. They're ready to die, if necessary."

"What about Azar Khalil?"

"That's my concern. Don't worry about it. If he finds out the invasion fleet he's counting on has been destroyed or turned back, he probably won't be a problem. He's just biding his time, now. There's nothing new on him."

"See you in a few months, then," said Trae.

"That's the plan. I'll be right here to welcome you back."

Myra suddenly put her arms around John's neck, and gave him a hug.

John smiled. "What was that for?"

"You're Trae's father, and I felt like doing it."

"Anytime," said John, then, "Trust in The Source for wisdom and clarity of thought, but trust in yourselves to get the job done. Come back alive, please."

Trae shook his hand again, then turned abruptly and followed

Myra up the twelve steps into the shuttle. The door slid shut behind him, and there was a sudden unease in his stomach, a sudden thought that he might not ever see John Haight again.

They buckled in as liftoff fans began to whine. Myra grasped his arm. "You're worried about him? I bet he's more worried about us."

"Maybe. I don't think he told us everything about the situation on Gan. War could come here before we even get back."

The shuttle lifted off, rose to five thousand feet before thrusters cut in, and they enjoyed a few moments of two gee flight. There were no ports in the vessel, and no view. Seven minutes of flight, a slight bump when they locked onto their Guppy. They cycled through the lock, and climbed the ladder to the bridge, where Wil Dietz awaited them.

"Your seats are ready in engineering. Let the adventure begin," he said cheerfully.

"Only if we come out of it alive," said Trae, and Wil laughed.

"Glad to see you here as our pilot," said Myra. "We weren't certain it would happen."

"Thank you, ma'am, and also for recommending me." Wil smiled, and went back to his checklist for flight.

Engineering was an alcove off the bridge, and their seats were in the reclined position. They would be mildly sedated for much of the trip, making nearly fifty jumps a day and pushing the ship towards maximum capacity in their sprint towards the galactic core.

Through intelligence relayed by his parents, the location of the invasion fleet was known within a few light years, but its jumps were erratic as it chased his great-grandmother's fleet towards the frontier. Trae had to admire her stubborn courage. If she hadn't kept to her frontier-bound course she would long ago have lost her pursuers. The woman had a goal, and would not deviate from it.

Final version of Guppy had been modified to carry five Nova craft, and four internal missile pods had been added forward. For large targets, the branegate-generation capability remained their most formidable weapon. And they would be going up against fifty ships.

They strapped in, and put on their masks. The control of a nicely sedative gas was at their fingertips, as was a tube for water. For the next three weeks, they would live on protein and other synth bars, and have half an hour each ship's cycle for running and pulley exercises in a rotating cylinder aft of their compartment. Behind that, Nova pilots ate and slept in tiny cells near their spacecraft.

The ship was moving before they were completely strapped in. They'd eaten little that morning to minimize nausea, and now they were hungry.

"Commence jumps in twenty minutes," announced Wil, and they hastened to sip water and administer a trickle of sedative gas to themselves.

"Here comes the boring part," said Trae, trying to lighten the mood.

"Not for me," said Myra. "There are some interesting problems I can play with in my head, if I'm not too sick or hungry."

Acceleration went to one gee, and stayed there. They breathed their first whiffs of relaxing gas, and drifted off into a routine they expected to last three weeks at most: sleeping, eating, occasional exercise sandwiched in between nauseating, disorienting jumps at half-hour intervals.

In the quiet, boring hours of nothingness, Myra calculated in her head, and Trae reached out to his parents before and after passing them near the frontier. Mostly he received new coordinates of the invasion fleet relayed from his great-grandmother, who seemed to be enjoying her game of hide and seek. There were also serious moments when they discussed his future with Myra, hopefully on a planet free of Church tyranny.

Wil exercised with them once a day, running like a squirrel in a cage, pulling on elastic straps and going nowhere while they reviewed strategies once the invasion fleet was engaged. Three weeks came and went, and they still hadn't found it. Trae was now in touch hourly with his parents, for it was only his mother who had a direct link with great-grandmother Nat. With all the talk from and about the woman, Trae and Myra were becoming anxious to meet her. The elderly family matriarch was being a warrior in her own way. In her final message she said her little ship was now drifting, and she was allowing the invasion force to close in. She gave her coordinates, asked for them to please hurry, and broke contact.

Wil sent the message to the other three Guppies accompanying them, and a precise, final jump was calculated. Trae and Myra took no sedatives, and were quite awake when the jump was made. When the swirling in their heads began to subside, they unbuckled themselves and rushed to the bridge to look at the viewscreen.

Their Guppy had returned to real space a few hundred miles

ahead of the invasion fleet, and fifty ships larger than Guppy were rushing towards them at orbital speeds. The ships seemed to be slowing down. The scanners did a sweep, and sorted out ships according to size, finding nothing smaller than a B-class freighter.

There was no sign of great-grandmother Nat's ship.

CHAPTER 41

Of all the pilots on Elderon, only four had any history with Grand Portal or passage beyond it. One of these was Simon Ziel, now well into his seventh lifetime. And he had mostly spent all seven of them sailing into space.

Simon had originally been born on Kratola, had grown up there, watched his own father sail away in fusion powered ships to neighboring worlds before there had been a Grand Portal or a Council of Bishops. He'd apprenticed under his father for four years in hydraulics, then engineering. His performance was first rate, and he was sent to Marine Academy with tuition and living expenses paid. When he graduated with honors in Astronautical Engineering, he'd never seen his father so proud. The man had actually shed tears at the ceremony. But more reasons for pride were ahead. His father's company sponsored him for both pilot's training and an advanced engineering degree. And at the age of twenty-nine he sailed his own ship, a C-class freighter called 'Fate', into space.

Three lifetimes later he piloted an A-class freighter through Grand Portal and headed for the colonies, never to return, for Zylak Industries discovered him and made him an offer he couldn't refuse. And he piloted their ships for two-plus lifetimes back to Grand Portal, transferring goods to family industries on the other side.

Now in his early fifties, he hadn't flown for ten years, had assumed an executive position in Transportation, and was content with it. But then the Guppies were being assembled, and transportation to the galactic core in just weeks was suddenly possible, and an old friend, Wil Dietz, was badgering him to fly again.

It's in the blood, they say.

Simon had a wife and two grown children in this lifetime. He knew he had to fly again, and his wife agreed. He would only be away weeks at a time if he qualified. The ship was experimental, and far advanced technically. His age might work against him.

He qualified, flew seven test runs, making forty-six jumps and projecting twelve branegates up to distances of two miles. Only then did they tell him what his next assignment might be.

Telling him was left for Wil, for they were close friends. A war was coming, he said, an invasion fleet sent by Kratola to put the colonies under the thumb of The Church. Leonid Zylak's own son would lead a flight of Guppies to intercept the fleet, stop it, turn it around or destroy it, using the branegate as a weapon. Simon would lead a flight of four Guppies to Grand Portal and take control of it. He might be required to destabilize it or destroy the thing completely, depending on the outcome with the invasion fleet.

The idea was terrifying, but he was best qualified for the job. He talked it all out with his dear wife before making a decision.

Simon Ziel accepted the assignment, and had time for several practice runs, using the branegate against moonlets. After only three runs he was told his departure was at hand. An emergency had developed in handling the invasion fleet, and he had to leave earlier than anticipated.

He enjoyed a somewhat anxious but wonderful night with his wife. His children could only be told he was on a flight test. By noon of the following day he was on board *Guppy IV* and leading three other ships out of orbit.

Five weeks later he was seventy-five thousand light years away from his home and family. Grand Portal was a greenish, elongated star straight ahead, and one short jump away. Simon studied the scanner views on his screen. The portal was exactly as he remembered it from a lifetime ago, the same keepers, stabilizing power generators, nearby black holes only light days away. All unchanged. The generators were the vulnerable points, but he'd have to take out all of them to destroy the whole configuration. The keepers were too large to be handled by any branegate he could project.

They prepared for the final jump, and Nova pilots scrambled to their ships. Five-drop ports along the slender tail of *Guppy IV* could put them into space in seconds. Missiles were checked and armed, but ports kept closed during jump.

Charging time was exactly twelve seconds, not a millisecond more or less. "Initiating jump," said Simon softly, and pressed a button on his console to dump a mass of exotic particles from *Guppy IV's* plenum into the fabric of spacetime, pinching it.

After several lifetimes of space-time jumping, there was no lapse of awareness for Simon Ziel or his crew. They traveled four light-months in the blink of an eye, and Grand Portal filled the viewscreen at a distance of twenty thousand miles. Main thrusters were shut down, and they came in on vernier engines to one side of the broad transit lane. A few ships were moored there, held in place by their verniers in a gravitational field so complex the mooring could only be achieved by computer.

Within minutes they were hailed by Portal Authority on standard frequency.

"Unidentified vessel, please identify yourself and give origin and destination."

Simon pressed a button opening the four missile ports on the nose of his ship, and initiated a plenum charge. Behind him he could hear the faint whine of turbines in readying Nova craft.

"This is *Guppy IV*. We are a military vessel out of Elderon, a colony world, and have been sent here to defend ourselves against attack. We carry major weapons, and five attack spacecraft. Our adversary is Kratola, and the invasion fleet that planet has sent against us. That fleet passed through here several months ago."

There was a long pause, perhaps in astonishment, perhaps to alert picket ships. "Nova commanders, seal hatches, prepare for drop, target and destroy any attacking vessels," Simon said softly, but his heart was racing.

"*Guppy IV*, we do not berth military vessels, nor have any such vessels passed through Grand Portal. You are in error."

Simon sighed. "If you wish, I can give you an exact date fifty major vessels passed through here fully loaded with military personnel, armored vehicles and fighter craft bound for the frontier. These vessels were supposedly inspected, certified as merchant class, and passed through by Portal Authority. We have witnesses to the transit, and reason to believe you have indirectly participated in an eminent military attack on our planet and its neighboring worlds."

Again a long pause, then, "New blips, sir. Six small vessels coming at us from two o'clock. Going to optical." A picture from engineering came up on the screen. Six picket ships were headed towards them in vee formation at high speed.

"Drop," said Simon, and there was a thump as five Nova fighters dropped from the long belly of *Guppy IV.*

"Portal Authority, withdraw your pickets, or we will destroy them." Simon's heart was hammering hard, now.

The Nova fighters formed an arc beyond the nose of *Guppy IV* and hovered there. The picket ships slowed, and came to a standstill a mile off.

"Deploying your fighters can be considered an act of aggression, *Guppy IV.*"

"Not if we're defending ourselves against your pickets." Simon pressed a lever, and Sniffer was deployed in four seconds. "Charge plenum, two minutes," he said to his engineer.

Another long pause. Perhaps they'd noticed the strange beak appearing on *Guppy IV*'s face.

"We must board you for inspection and certification. Call back your attack spacecraft immediately."

"There's nothing to certify. We're not making transit. Our purpose is to be sure no other military vessels pass through here to attack our planets, and that the fleet you so carelessly let through goes home again or is destroyed. To that end we're prepared to destroy any ship that attacks us, and if necessary we'll destabilize Grand Portal or shut it down completely."

The man he was talking to actually laughed. "You must be mad."

"I can arrange a demonstration if you wish, but if you aren't Portal Captain, then I'm talking to the wrong person. He'll be responsible for any damage I cause here."

"Pickets targeted and locked," said the engineer. *Guppy IV*'s missiles would take them all out in a single salvo, but at considerable cost in human life.

"Wait a moment. I'll get him."

Simon settled in his chair to wait, but a new, gruff voice was on the speaker only seconds later.

"This is Janus Stark, senior officer of Portal Authority. This portal is non-political and independent, with no ties to any planet or league. What or who gives you the right to come here and disrupt the flow of commerce?"

Janus? It couldn't be, but it was the same rough voice.

"That's not our intention, sir. We only mean to—"

"I heard all of it. The military ships you're after weren't sent by us. Take it up with Kratola; the Bishops are no concern of ours."

"You admit those ships came through here?"

"Of course. There are no laws forbidding it. Any ship can make transit, once the correct portal tax is paid. Arrangements can always be made."

Simon smiled to himself. "You remind me of a midshipman I served with on *Lockspur* three lifetimes ago. He knew how to get all our money before we even reached port, but I heard he was killed later in a fire after I'd left for another ship."

A short, silent pause, then, "Who are you?"

"Simon Ziel, and I've never changed my name in seven lifetimes."

Another pause, even shorter, and, "One second. I'm going to another line."

It *was* Janus. He'd liked the man; though he was a rascal, he'd always been open about it. Simon had been saddened when he thought the man was dead.

Immediately, Janus was on the air again. "We're private, now. By The Source, Simon, what are you up to? I've a nice setup here, and I don't need anyone screwing around with it. You want something, let's negotiate a price, just like the old days."

"I thought you were dead in that fire on 'Larkspur.'"

"No. I had other business to attend to at the time. Came back late, after it was over. Lost friends in that fire. What do you want from me?"

"Well, what I said before is the truth. The Bishops have sent their ships to regain control of the colonies, but we have the technology to stop or destroy them. I work for Zylak Industries, and the vessels with me come from them."

"Ah, private industry," said Janus. "That makes you merchant class. I can offer you a good rate on the tax if you give me a semi-honest estimate of cargo value. We'll start with the five fighters you just deployed. What else?"

Simon suppressed a chuckle. "I've told you we're not making transit, and I told you the truth about the power of our ships. Here's what we can do."

Simon told him everything: armament, jump-rate and distance, and the powers of the branegate when deployed.

Jamus whistled at him. "Whoo, imagine that scaled up for heavy cargo. No company could compete with you. Zylak is public, I presume. I wouldn't mind having some stock in that company."

Simon blurted it out before he could control his tongue. "That can be arranged," he said.

"Really? Well, how does one earn such a valuable investment for his later years?"

"For starters, you can call off your pickets and allow us to berth here. Any military traffic will only be allowed towards the other side, and we'll enforce it as long as the colonies are threatened. I also want to send a message to The Bishops, to let them know we cannot only destroy their ships, but Grand Portal as well. A demonstration that won't harm anyone."

"I'm responsible for any damage here," said Janus, "and I worked nearly two lifetimes for this position."

"We're a military force with advanced technology; you were surprised and overwhelmed."

"My colleagues will know better."

"Not if they're sufficiently compensated. Zylak Industries is an eight hundred trillion gold sovereign conglomerate, Janus. How much do you want?"

The silence was not long. "A half billion in stock for myself, and one and a half billion in gold to divide among all the workers here. That's around a million per man, more than they'll see in a lifetime. It should be enough."

"Sounds more generous than I remember you being," said Simon.

"Oh, I'll get a chunk of the gold, too. I've a few businesses on The Wheel, and that's the only place for pleasures around here. I'll even take you there, if you stick around long enough. Do we have a deal?"

"Yes. I can have payment here in a few months, once our mission is accomplished. You'll have to trust me for it."

"And you'll have to trust me right now. I'm calling the pickets in, and you can have your berths, but I want no lives lost or any permanent damage to Grand Portal by this demonstration of yours."

"I was thinking of taking out a generator or two, and shutting down the portal for a day as a show of force. How easily can the generators be replaced?"

"Spares are parked days from here. We'd have to block all transits for a week. It would certainly get The Bishops' attention. Most of the ships through here are from Kratola."

"Make arrangements right now for a generator to be moved here.

Talk to your people about the compensation. Tell them we're a police force from the colonies, sent to keep military from coming through, and we're making a show of power. Nobody gets hurt."

"Better get the money here, Simon."

"You get the generator, I'll arrange for payment, right now."

"Okay, but recall your fighters. I'm leaving one picket to guide you to your berth. Maybe later we can have a drink for old times."

"Maybe," said Simon, "but not until I send my message to the Bishops on Kratola."

They were guided to their berths among a dozen other ships hovering near Grand Portal, most of them awaiting clearance for transit to the other side. Most were likely bound for Kratola. The Bishops would soon know their presence, even without a demonstration of power. Simon was certain of that. The word of huge sums offered to portal workers would be overnight headlines. Once on the other side, merchant ships would flash the news of a police force from the colonies blocking the passage of military vessels. The Bishops might disbelieve, or react with force. Simon had come prepared for all of it.

It took three days for tugs to bring in a replacement generator. A little over half a mile in diameter, it looked like an orange bristling with half protruding coins of gold.

Word went out about the demonstration. Traffic was halted, but for the crews it was free time on The Wheel, and a promise of pockets stuffed with gold.

Nobody grumbled.

Three thousand men and women watched viewscreens and looked out the windows of lounges and bars as a strange looking ship moved in close to a generator at the nine o'clock position around Grand Portal. A pimple appeared on the nose of the ship and began to glow bright green, and then a long protuberance could be seen, a long whisker glowing even brighter, and near its end a patch of flickering light in space itself. The patch grew brighter and began to move, growing larger and larger as it headed straight for the generator and struck it. There was a brilliant flash, and the generator was gone. The cats-eye of Grand Portal flickered and rippled, and the clear lane in the middle of it was filled with swirling colors. No sane man would have dared to pilot a craft through it, even the veterans of lifetimes. The turbulence in the transit lane grew for an hour before reaching a steady, boiling state. The effect was even greater than Simon had anticipated, and was explained later when word came back that the generator had reappeared exactly on the other side of Grand Portal. With one side missing a stabilizer, and the other side with excess, the effect had been more than double expectations.

Simon was more than pleased, and sent a message to Anton about the results and also the money arrangements to be made. The Guppies in his flight had brought enough gold for only a down payment on what he'd promised, for he'd not anticipated the magnitude of the bribe. He knew full well that a Guppy would reach Anton before the speed-of-light message did. He planned to dispatch one of them soon.

First, he had to see if the Bishops would react. Things had gone easier than he'd anticipated so far, mostly because Janus was in charge of Grand Portal. No force was ever necessary with that man, as long as there was money to be had.

Grand Portal was closed to traffic for over a week, though a new generator was in place in only four days. When it was turned on, some stability returned, but not all of it. There was a tiny lane only shuttles and pickets could get through. One picket dared it, and a day later total stability was restored when the excess generator on the other side was turned off and removed.

It was the last simple thing that happened for Simon Ziel.

Grand Portal had been stable again for only a day when the picket that had been sent through returned at high speed. And within minutes, Janus called Simon.

"Better move quick to defend yourself, or get out of here, friend. The picket I sent through just got back, and the pilot says there are ten B-class ships bristling with missile pods and railguns on the other side. A couple of them were nearing portal for transit when the picket came through. You only have a few minutes."

"I warned you about this, Janus."

"I'd better not lose a single worker," growled the man.

Simon broke contact, ordered his flight of Guppies into positions along the transit lane coming out of Grand Portal. Plenums were charged, Sniffers and Stingers deployed before they were even in position. There was a clear view down the transit lane, and the faint patch of black at its center. Transit itself took less than a minute, but anything coming through would be visible half that time.

He saw them coming far out, two large ships hurtling along in a line, several small escorts above and below them. The scenario had been discussed. Simon acted not by instinct, but by plan.

"Drop Novas! Target and destroy fighters! Project branegates to center on transit lane! Project!"

The transit lane coming out of Grand Portal exploded in bright green. Two large ships bristling with hull-mounted weapons burst out of Grand Portal and into green glow, from which they did not emerge. Several fighters avoided the branegates, veering out of the transit lane, firing missiles and railguns wildly as they maneuvered. Other fighters disappeared.

"Engage fighters! Wing one, send a Nova through Portal for reconnaissance and return!"

Guppy IV was rocked by impact or explosion. Fighters and Novas swarmed like insects outside. One missile heading straight for Simon's canopy was intercepted by another, and exploded, Debris rattled off the nose of the ship, and Stinger whipped wildly for a moment, like an antenna caught in strong wind.

A Nova fled back through Grand Portal, and in seconds a fighter chased after it. Fire flashed as missiles struck small craft, vaporizing them, but in only a few minutes the dogfights were over. Only three small craft remained. All of them were Novas.

"That's it. We're closing Grand Portal. Take out generators at one, four and eight o'clock!"

The remaining Novas hovered in the transit lane while the Guppies charged plenums and moved close in to three of the four stabilizing field generators around the edges of Grand Portal. A Nova rushed out of it shortly before they were in position. Simon gave the order to discharge, and there were four bright flashes of green.

Grand Portal boiled in chaos, and suddenly Janus was screaming into Simon's ear.

"Damn you, damn you, damn you!"

"Just think of the money, Janus," said Simon, and broke contact with him.

Two Nova craft and their pilots were gone. One Guppy had been damaged by railgun fire, its drop bay open to vacuum, but otherwise fully operational. Simon sent it to find Anton and tell him what had happened, including the financial settlement with Janus and his people. Three Novas went along for the ride in the vacuum of normal and folded space.

Grand Portal was now under Simon's control. When Janus was calm again he could arrange for three generators to be brought in, and traffic would eventually flow through the brane again. The invasion fleet would have a way to get home, if Simon allowed it, but privately he didn't want that to happen. Privately, he hoped that the military power of The Bishops would be destroyed by Anton, once and for all, in a place far from him, and the colonies would be left free of their influence forever.

CHAPTER 42

John Haight did not wait for Gan to attack Galena. He only needed justification for his own attack, and it came soon enough. It was a month after Trae and Myra had sailed off to fight a war near the galactic core.

Rasim still had his spies in place. His embassy had been closed, the staff fled only hours before Khalil's troops had moved in early morning hours to arrest them. Rasim had declared a formal break in diplomatic relations, and Khalil had retaliated with accusations of espionage and sabotage. Now he'd assembled a drop force of thousands for deployment in several ships to Galena. A highly placed source in the palace indicated an attack was eminent, would be explained publicly not as an occupation, but a return of democracy to Galena.

John intended to take out Khalil's ships before they could leave the ground, and settle an ancient debt with the man. He was not just a soldier of The Church, now, not just a bodyguard or surrogate father. He was, in every sense, Leonid Zylak, just as Petyr had also been in another life. He was accepted in the role of the man because Meza and the other powers in Zylak Industries knew it was truth. They'd explained his true identity to the pilots who would serve under him. John had met with them, explained their mission was not just to destroy the military of an aggressive, imperialistic planet. It would also wrest power from a zealot whose colleagues had usurped a peaceful government on the home world of all the colonies, and wanted to do the same to Elderon, Galena, Gan and all their neighbors. The pilots cheered, and cheered again when he said he'd be right there with them when they smashed Khalil's military to a bleeding pulp on the ground.

His force was a single Guppy, and twenty-five Novas. They flew together in normal space without jumps, a journey of two days. John flew in Guppy, a seat reserved for him in engineering, where he could watch and direct action on the ground. He had time to wonder about Trae and his encounter with the invasion fleet, whether or not they could be turned around with a show of force, or would have to be destroyed. The mission to Grand Portal was a holding action, and not likely to spark fighting; Simon only had to show the force he could bring against the portal to shut down commerce. But Trae and Myra could be in real danger.

In the quiet blackness of interplanetary space, John Haight thought of his early days on Kratola, before the time he and the missionary Leonid Zylak had become one person, a time when a young priest simply named John had rooted out and killed zealots of a fringe element seeking to transform The Church into a political force. They wanted to rule the planet in the name of The Source. And a man named Azar Khalil, a high Bishop, had been near the center of it even then.

Khalil was still alive, and now John would finally kill him, if all went according to plan.

With Khalil gone, peace would eventually come to Gan; the people had had a small taste of democracy, and would know how to win it again. But what of Kratola, truly his home world, and now under the thumbs of The Bishops? Even if the invasion fleet were destroyed, nothing would change for the people of Kratola. Their thoughts and lives would still be ruled by a handful of zealots who hid behind the teachings of The Source to keep power.

He was still thinking about this when the blue and green orb of Gan was large in his viewscreen. There was no time to pause, Gan's scanners were even now sweeping over them. John ordered the Nova fighters to go straight in from a thousand miles out, in two waves of ten and fifteen. With a time interval of only one minute between them, they would first target and destroy all fighter craft on or off the ground, then drop heavy ordinance on the transport ships there. Azar's palace was a secondary target. So close to the time of intended attack on Galena, the big ships might even now be loading drop troops.

The Nova formations streaked away towards Gan, and were soon glowing spots in its atmosphere. John ordered a test of Guppy's branegate projection as routine, in case any ships got off ground and managed to get above the atmosphere. Sniffer and Stinger were deployed, and the plenum charged for two minutes. The Nova squadrons were nearing ground when John's Guppy opened a branegate, and he was trying to watch two screens at once. One of the screens nearly blinded him.

In practice runs with Guppy's crew, John Haight had seen the projection of several branegates: spectacular, brilliant flashes of rich green, then the characteristic cat's-eye pattern of a tunnel to another universe. But this time, as the branegate was just forming, a terrible rush of yellow flame spewed out of it. The hull temperature went up so fast that within seconds John could feel heat radiating from the walls. His pilot reacted instinctively, and shut down the gate by cutting off trickle current to Stinger.

"By The Source, what was *that?*"

"Star on the other side, sir," said the pilot. "We were pulling flaming gas from its atmosphere. I can try again in another spot, but the result will likely be the same for thousands of miles around here.

"Can we use the branegate in that circumstance?"

"Sure can, sir. Just have to be quick about it. We've done it before, sir."

All so routine to the pilot, perhaps, but not to John Haight, and then a sudden thought occurred to him.

It was a sign, a sign from The Source of all wisdom and love, a sign to a soldier of His Church.

He watched the Nova fighters come in low over a large port with a few buildings and a hundred square miles of tarmac. Dozens of small fighter craft were in neat rows there, and tiny, insect specks were pilots scurrying to reach them. Before his eyes, three fighter craft lifted off, only three. Missiles streaked towards them, and they were orange clouds of burning vapor. The view on the screen shuddered from the vibration of railgun fire. Missiles were a criss-cross network of white vapor trails and sudden bursts of flame.

Beyond the fighter craft and far out on the tarmac sat a dozen B-class transports in the process of loading, long lines of troops spiraling out from them and scattering as the Nova attack came in. The view on the screen shuddered again. Flame and smoke belched from the ground below. John switched channels rapidly to follow the action from several aircraft cameras as the Novas swooped low over the field. The first wave had left the grounded fighters a smoking ruin, but four had managed to get off the ground. They chased the attacking Novas without even noticing the incoming second wave, and were shot out of the air before they could acquire targets.

Soldiers scattered, and ran for their lives towards buildings half a mile away. One transport blew, spreading a ring of flaming fuel that caught and incinerated many of them. The first wave moved on towards the palace only a minute away. The presidential banner in gold and blue was flying high on its mast as the front of the building erupted in smoke and flame under railgun fire. First wave nosed up and climbed for home, their ordinance exhausted.

Wave two left no grounded fighter untouched, and destroyed seven of the transports for certain. The tarmac was now covered with billowing clouds of black smoke, and kills could only be verified by fireballs bursting through it. When they reached the palace, the front of the building was blown away, and they emptied their railguns into the interior. Swerving away and preparing to climb, the camera on one Nova caught sight of a shuttle lifting off behind the palace and climbing rapidly upwards. Weapons empty, the pilot had presence of mind to move closer to the shuttle for a look. The shuttle was civilian, but emblazoned on its hull was the blue and gold starburst of Gan's president.

John Haight slammed both fists on his console, and the engineer looked at him strangely.

"All praise to The Source! You have given him to Your servant! Track that shuttle!"

"Satellite or large ship coming around in orbit," said the engineer. "The shuttle is heading for it."

"I want that shuttle intercepted!" screamed John.

A computer, a rattled engineer and alert pilot did the rest, and Guppy jumped like a Nova, slamming John back into his seat.

Now it comes. At last it comes, thought John Haight.

"Charge plenum, two minutes!" he shouted.

Azar Khalil was in his second floor office overlooking the front of the palace when his military was attacked. He heard several booms, like distant thunder, looked outside, saw nothing, not even a cloud in the sky. But as he watched, a column of black smoke rose above the horizon, then there were more booms, thuds, a cracking sound like railgun fire.

The office door burst open, and his secretary came in with two soldiers. "Hurry, sire. The assembly area is under attack by Nova-class fighters. They came straight down, so there must be attack vessels in orbit. Evac A, sire. We have to get you out of here!"

Azar obeyed without hesitation, for the plan had been his own. Even as he moved, his ego fought against it. He was giving up rule over a stupid and recalcitrant people, spiritually empty and without worth. On Kratola such people would all be imprisoned or shot. But Zylak had given him warning, and moved fast. Azar would not wait for the outcome. He would flee to the frontier and await arrival of the great force sent to aid him. And then he would return to Gan and eliminate all human life from it before beginning a new colony of selected, true believers, and loyal subjects of The Church.

They barely reached the lower hallway before the first projectiles struck. The entire front of the building exploded, raining boulders of cement and spears of wood down on them. His secretary went down pierced through the chest by a steel reinforcement bar, and they left him there staring at plaster rain from a ruined ceiling. The soldiers gripped his arms and propelled him towards the back of the building. Progress was slow as they clambered over debris and rubble from a collapsed upper floor.

The back door was stuck shut, and a soldier shot it away with his rifle. The shuttle was waiting for him, lift fans humming, in a court-yard surrounded by flowers, a place where he'd often meditated. *I'll miss it,* he thought, then the building behind him exploded again, the entire residence erupting in flame and black smoke.

The soldiers hustled him on board, and strapped him in along-side a pilot who looked terrified, then closed the door and were left to their own fate. The shuttle lifted off with a jerk as several Nova fighters passed directly overhead at low altitude. For a moment, Azar was certain he'd be shot down at liftoff, but nothing happened, the Novas now making a wide turn far out towards the horizon. Lift fans screamed as the pilot pushed them to the maximum, then lifted the nose up and cut in the thrusters. Azar gasped and sucked air. A Nova pulled right up alongside of them for only a second, then left them like they were standing still.

The Source is with me. All praise to Him, thought Azar.

Even at full thrust they climbed for several minutes while the pilot and his computer calculated a rendezvous with 'Spirit' in parking orbit three hundred miles above Gan. 'Spirit' would take him to a military freighter a thousand miles above that, and then it would be on to the frontier and rendezvous with Church forces in due time.

That was the plan.

But at an altitude of one-hundred-fifty miles they were intercepted by a strange looking ship that was not 'Spirit'. As long as a freighter, it had a slender hull and a bulbous nose with a strange protuberance, and was painted the yellow oxide color ordinarily used by the military. Large as it was, it followed them with ease on their ascent, and pulled slowly closer.

"Civilian shuttle, this is *Guppy VII* of Elderon. Good morning, Mister President."

"Who is this?" said Azar angrily.

"John Haight, Mister President, or Leonid Zylak, whichever you prefer. I warned you about this day. Maybe you didn't believe me."

"Elderon has committed an act of unprovoked war. There will be severe consequences for this, and not just from Gan."

"The consequences are yours to suffer, Mister President, for tyranny and murder. Initiating Stinger."

The huge ship outside dropped back behind them and slightly to one side. Azar turned halfway around in his seat to watch it. The entire nose of the vessel began to glow green, and then a bright spot was at its center. The spot grew in size and brightness as a protuberance like a huge needle was thrust towards him. The spot flickered, then boiled, becoming suddenly oblong. It approached rapidly, still growing. A yellow flame shot forth from it, then another. In the final second before it reached the shuttle, yellow fire burst forth from it with terrible intensity.

The brain and nervous system of Azar Khalil had just enough time to record a sensation of heat before being vaporized.

CHAPTER 43

Fifty ships plunged toward them in a wedge formation. Guppy pilots reacted instinctly to get out of the way, made a great loop out of the lane in a vee formation, came back to parallel their course, still slowing. It was then that Trae saw the one, tiny ship sandwiched between two juggernauts. "There she is," he said.

As he said it a new presence was in his mind with sudden force.

Well, it's about time. We were getting ready to set the detonator on our ship.

Who is this? I'm Anton Zylak, said Trae.

Well, well, my great-grandson will be my savior. These big ships have been chasing us for light-years. Now, what can you do to make them go away?

"We're being hailed," said his pilot, but Trae ignored him.

My great-grandma Nat, said Trae in wonder. *My mother has told me all about you. She says you're a fighter.*

That I am, but I can't fight these things. If you distract them, I can make another jump, and get out of here.

Do it, then, but only a light year towards the frontier, and stay in the shipping lane so we can find you. Get out, now, and be safe. It might get violent here. Charging for jump. I want to meet you safe at the frontier, or Elderon, or wherever I hope my family will come together again.

After I send these ships back to The Bishops. It might be a while.

I have time, lots of time, dear. My captain is ready, now. We're making the jump.

The little ship flickered, image rippling, and winked away. Trae's pilot flinched next to him. "Some general, sir. He's screaming in my ear. Better answer him."

"Okay. In the meantime, everyone charge plenums, two minutes, and deploy Sniffers. Nova pilots lock in."

"Charging. Rest is done, sir."

Myra entered their tiny bridge from the rear door. "Some excited pilots back there. They seem to think they're fighting a holy war."

"Maybe they are," said Trae.

Here we are, all alone for the moment. One light year out, and we'll hold our position. Eventually we'll have to find the rest of my little fleet, but they're likely ahead of us by now. Good hunting.

"Who's that?" asked Myra.

"My great-grandmother Nat. She jumped out of here just now."

"Oh."

"Sir, the general. He's threatening attack."

Trae grabbed the receiver harness offered to him and folded it around the back of his head. "This is Anton Zylak, commander of Guppy Wing One out of Elderon. Who am I talking to?"

"Finally!" shouted a man. "You've put yourself in a precarious position, commander. It's not wise to keep me waiting."

"To keep *who* waiting?"

"General Pizarro Asiz, commanding second and third drop battalions of Kratola, and on a mission for The Council of Bishops. We come in the name of The Source."

"Indeed. I suppose your mission is to restore the colony planets beyond the frontier back into the loving embrace of The Church."

"That is correct, sir."

"A noble task for brave soldiers of The Church to enforce such a thing in a universe that isn't theirs. The colonies are not connected to Kratola in any way, and owe no allegiance to it or The Church."

"The Council of Bishops feels otherwise, and we're here to enforce their opinion. Now get out of our way, or be destroyed."

"We're not in your way at the moment, we're paralleling your course."

"You're military vessels. I see railgun and missile ports. We have no hull-mounted weapons, but the two hundred Sprint fighters we carry can damage you beyond repair. I'll release them at the first shot you fire."

"I want no loss of life, general, but I will not allow you to continue on to the frontier. You'll turn back now, or I'll do it for you. Guppy commanders, form an echelon on my point, move!"

All had been planned and rehearsed. It was necessary they position themselves to view the fleet headlong. *Guppy I* accelerated, moved to the nose of the fleet formation and turned to face it from a distance of half a mile. The three other Guppies formed an echelon above it. Four ships of substantial size now faced fifty in the blackness of space.

"Do you really expect to attack my entire fleet with missiles and railguns, commander? My pilots have scrambled. A single shot from you, and they will be on you in an instant."

"That's not what I have in mind, general," said Trae. Myra stood behind his seat, leaning so close he could feel her hot breath on his neck. He clicked off his receiver, and looked up at her. "You might want to sit down for this."

"Not a chance," she said, and stared out through the window at the nearby bows of fifty invasion ships floating there.

"Have you located his ship?" Trae asked his pilot.

"Big one on the point of the spear, sir. He's leading his troops right out in front. We're a bit close, sir. I need to back off a mile or so with the verniers."

"Do it slowly."

"Aye, sir."

They backed slowly to a range of nearly two miles, and the rest of the Guppies followed them. At two miles the branegate size would be sufficient to cover the cross section of the largest ships in front of them.

"Having second thoughts, commander? Perhaps we can talk about it, come to some kind of understanding as fellow soldiers."

"Topping off plenum, one minute," said Trae's pilot softly. "Deploying Sniffer, initiating trickle current. All pilots, lock targets and confirm."

"Give me a moment to confer with my pilots," said Trae.

"Very well, but only a moment. Four against fifty, commander. It's a matter of common sense."

A soft, green glow now covered the windows of *Guppy I*. Myra made a little sound in her throat, but when he glanced up at her she looked excited, not scared. Just another experiment to her.

"Charged," said the pilot. "All targets acquired and locked."

"Your moment is up, commander. What do we do now?" said the general.

"I think we'll send you back home," Trae said, then, "Initiate gates."

The windows flashed bright green, walls vibrating with the deployment of Stinger. The expanding patch of glowing, exotic space expanded, materialized, formed its characteristic shape as it hurried away from them and struck the big ship at the point of the invading ships' formation. Three other gates simultaneously struck ships on both sides of it. There were four blinding flashes of light, and the ships were gone.

"Charging," said Trae's pilot.

The silence, the calm after that was long and terrible. Twenty Nova pilots sat tensely in their cockpits, ready for instant drop. There was no sign of reaction from the invasion ships, and no communication. The Guppies moved in closer, plenums recharged, noses glowing green. And as they settled into position, radio silence was finally broken.

"This is Colonel Caesar Olema, Kratola Expeditionary Force. I wish to speak with the person responsible for the attack on our ships before we take retaliatory action."

Trae clicked his headset on. "Anton Zylak, sir. Your general ignored our warning to turn back, so our action was necessary."

"Your action was unprovoked, and you've destroyed both ships and human lives. This is an act of war."

"Your ships haven't been destroyed; they've just been sent somewhere else, very likely to a position commensurate to our own but in your home universe. There should have been no loss of life, or even injuries. You've invaded our universe with the intent of conquering our worlds for rule under The Church. This will not be allowed. Now turn your ships around, and go home."

The colonel's voice was calm, and cold. "I understand your position, sir. Now understand mine. You've attacked our fleet without provocation, and destroyed ships with all personnel. We're on a mission for The Church, and it will not be turned aside so easily. You have one minute to prepare for battle, sir. My regards."

"Get it?" asked Trae, and his pilot nodded.

"Third ship up, just beyond the point."

"Target it, and send him home. Other Guppies hold fire. Those fighters will come straight at us. Spread the gates out in an arc covering our front. On my command."

"We'll only have one shot at them," said his pilot.

"Drop Novas if the gates don't take out the fighters. Ready, sir."

"Fire!" commanded Trae.

Green flash, the boiling mess of spacetime and beyond projected away from them and slamming into a distant ship, then another flash and that ship, too, was gone.

"Here they come!" cried his pilot.

Drop bays had opened on four of the invading ships, and fighters dropped out of them like a swarm of bees, coming together in a wedge-shape and heading straight for them. The front echelon had just released missiles when Trae shouted his command.

"Initiate branegates!"

A great arc of space glowed green in front of them. Three closely spaced gates covered an area a mile high and seven miles across. Most of the missiles simply disappeared. The rest exploded, first sent into tumbling trajectories, missing pieces. The fighters behind them were too close to react when the gates were formed, and flew straight into them.

The results were not satisfying to Myra, who hoped for a battle without bloodshed. Fighters striking gates directly simply disappeared, an effect Myra herself had experienced without harm. One would hope those fighters could rendezvous with the major transports already given forced transit to the other side. Otherwise, this far from Grand Portal, the fighters' environmental systems would give out before they could reach home.

The fighters, which didn't strike a branegate directly, suffered horrible fates. Wings, tail sections, entire cockpits were sucked away, the rest tumbled wildly by the chaotic and flickering dimensionality of the spaces between gates. There were several explosions, and debris formed a kind of bow shock that rained metal and human bone on the Guppies. Only the strong, ionizing fields induced by their Sniffers kept them from serious damage.

"Drop!" commanded Trae. The rear of the fighters' echelons had just had enough time to pull away. Some dozens of ships were now making great looping trajectories to come back down on them again. Trae had been saving missiles for use against the big ships, but suddenly changed his mind.

"Target missiles on the first pass of the fighters. Novas do the rest. Recharge plenums! We'll eat the fleet up from front to back!"

The missiles went out in seconds, seeking heat and finding it raining down on the Guppies. Fire flashed in space like exploding stars, just as Novas raced past Trae's window. The ensuing firefight lasted nearly half an hour, and their opponents weren't amateurs, but the first barrage of missiles from the Guppies had taken a horrible toll. A dozen surviving fighters limped back to a single transport near the front of the fleet.

Trae had it targeted, and sent it away through a branegate.

Three others followed its fate.

But seven Nova crews and their ships would never see home again.

Quiet descended on the fleet and four Guppies hovering in front of it, their noses glowing green again. Trae waited patiently for communication, but heard nothing at first.

And then, quite suddenly, one ship broke off from the invading fleet, then another. The rest followed them in a line, making a great sweeping turn out from the shipping lane, a turn of a hundred-eighty degrees.

They were heading home.

An understanding between them was necessary, so Trae called again, using the same frequency he'd used before.

"Kratola Expeditionary Force, this is Anton Zylak. We will accompany you back to Grand Portal. This is for your own safety, since we also have a squadron of our ships there. Please respond, so we can coordinate our jumps."

It was an hour before he received a reply. By necessity, command had been reshuffled again in the enemy fleet, and it was a Colonel Xavier Taller who replied. He was most cooperative, and set up a jump schedule back to Grand Portal with both dates and times. Trae pushed him to the maximum of a hundred thirty light years per day, something a Guppy could do in one jump. It would still be another month to follow the slow ships back to the core. Myra was determined not to sleep most of the way, since she had to anticipate an even longer trip home, and an additional wait for Trae's family to begin arriving at Elderon. She was now hardened to battle, but was bitter about the loss of lives. It was not something she ever wanted to see repeated again, and she said so to Trae.

"I don't want it, either, Myra, but this isn't the end of it. We still have Azar Khalil to contend with when we get home, and that could be a ground war," he said.

CHAPTER 44

The trip back to Grand Portal was broken up by the plethora of jumps they had to make, and the tension after each jump to make sure each ship of the invasion fleet had come through. In constant communication with the current commander, Trae got to know Colonel Taller better, and in the end decided he was just another soldier of The Church, sent on a mission he believed in. Petyr had been another such soldier, and now, perhaps, was John Haight, and there'd been others along the way, people Trae hadn't known in person, but people who'd influenced the course of his lives.

On their seventy-fifth jump, a damaged *Guppy VII* finally caught up with them, its drop bay half shot away. Trae heard the story of what had happened at Grand Portal, and the money promised to the crews there. He relayed this on to his father, along with the news of his own triumph over the invasion fleet. Father insisted on a meeting in the minds, and also invited Myra. At the end of ship's cycle, Trae and Myra went to their cell and snuggled together a while, had nearly fallen asleep when Mother called, and they were back on the rolling, flower-covered hillsides so familiar to them.

The four of them embraced. Father wore a white bodysuit, and Mother was in her flower-print dress without sleeves. *So nice to get away from low lighting and grease-smell,* she said. *Only a few months, now, and we'll be with you on Elderon. Myra, you look lovely.*

Myra had clothed herself in long pants and a yellow, short-sleeved blouse. Even in the group mind, she looked radiant. *I'm glad it's all over. I hope our history never has to record anything like it again.*

Agreed, said Father Leonid.

There's still Azar Khalil to deal with, said Trae.

Father and Mother were strangely silent when he said that, but

then, *John Haight will tell you about that. The money isn't a problem.
A Guppy can deliver the gold as soon as we arrive on Elderon, and
Janus will have his stock. We might even persuade him to invest more
with us. On the other hand, I might invest in some of his enterprises
on what he calls The Wheel.*

We don't invest in brothels, dear, said Mother.

Diversify, diversify, said Father, and grinned. *Now, you two, can
you wait until we reach Elderon so we can take part in your wedding?*

Of course, said Myra. *We'll only get there a few months ahead
of you.*

We want something small, with a few close friends and family,
said Trae.

*What a shame Grandma Nat can't be there. She's such a roman-
tic,* said Mother.

We can't wait twenty years, dear.

*Maybe fifteen, if she pushes it hard. At her age, the jumps aren't
so easy to take.*

Not easy to take at any age, quipped Myra, *especially when
you're pregnant.*

They were suddenly lying in each other's arms, and her face was
close. "Really?" he asked.

"Yes, really. I just found out."

What incredible news! Come back, come back!

They were standing in flowers again. Mother embraced them
both, while Father pounded Trae on the back. *Multiple lifetimes together, and finally we'll be grandparents. How wonderful!*

Mother and Father were still giddy when they left them. Back
in real space and time they were warm in each other's arms, and the
ship's hull vibrated softly around them, a second home. "I want this
to be the start of a dynasty," he murmured into Myra's ear, "one we
can watch grow over our lifetimes together."

She touched his face. The look in her eyes made his heart ache.
"I lived my previous lifetime to old age, and I was totally alone. It
wasn't exactly by choice, but I hadn't found you yet."

"I love you," he said, and kissed her. Their lips remained touching as they fell asleep. Dreams were not remembered, and the next
cycle was the same, herding the Bishops' ships back to them.

Great-grandma Nat didn't call. Trae hadn't expected her to, but
Mother did, and gradually became worried when she didn't hear from

her. They hoped some word would come when the family fleet finally reached the frontier.

The day finally came when they pinched spacetime and found Grand Portal in their viewscreens. They were immediately hailed by Simon, who'd impatiently awaited their arrival. He missed his family, and wanted to go home. A secondary invasion force had been turned away when he'd destabilized Grand Portal, but was still hovering on the other side in a kind of uneasy truce. Trae's hope was that when they heard about the colonial power used against the main invasion force the truce would not be so uneasy.

It was a grand show when the surviving military ships sent by The Bishops formed a long line and one by one made transit to the other side. Seven Guppies lined up on either side of the transit lane in a kind of salute. Four would be left behind to police Grand Portal, the crews to be cycled every six months. What happened on the other side was the concern of others, but the colony worlds would never again allow military ships to invade their universe, for either war or religious infection.

They said goodbye to a very drunk Janus after a grand party at one of his clubs. Myra bought some souvenir trinkets at a shop he had part interest in. He made her laugh, but privately she thought he was a crazy rogue.

Simon came on-board *Guppy I* with them for the trip home. Another three months of jump, jump, jump. Myra survived it surprisingly well, and her appetite for food became vast. They ate, read, talked, played interactive games on computer, and formulated possible strategies to use against Gan if war came. Father and Mother were now past the frontier, and had not heard a word from great-grandmother Nat. They talked about putting a small group of Guppies together to look for her.

Elderon's brown plains and dark green forests were on the viewscreens when they assembled for a final breakfast on *Guppy I*. A shuttle took them down to the surface, and they landed at the port of Zylak Industries without public fanfare. Meza and Wallace were there to greet them, and so was John Haight. And when the congratulations and back pounding were finished, it was John who stepped forward and told them what had happened to Azar Khalil and his government on Gan.

CHAPTER 45

For those who live multiple lifetimes there are few endings, but many beginnings. People come and go in their lives, and the absence of loved ones, while not permanent as in death, can last for hundreds of years.

Within a few months after returning from Grand Portal, and shortly before Misha was born, Trae gained a father and mother, and then lost a father again.

Leonid and Tatjana arrived to great public fanfare by the press, though the crowd present to applaud their arrival was mostly hand-picked political dignitaries and executives of Zylak Industries. Trae and Myra stood with John Haight at the bottom of the ramp leading up to the open maw of the shuttle when Leonid and Tatjana appeared and saw them. Tatjana fairly flew down the ramp and threw herself into Trae's open arms, and the crowd cheered behind them. In a blink, Tatjana also had Myra in her grasp.

"Finally! I don't care if I ever spend another minute in space. Look at you! You're ready to burst! Oh, we got here in time ..."

On and on, the two women in tears. Leonid walked down the ramp laughing, extended a hand. It was the first face of the father Trae had seen two lifetimes ago, with the chiseled features and neatly trimmed beard. He pumped Trae's hand vigorously, then a fierce hug that went on and on. "I thought the time would never come," he murmured.

It was then that Leonid saw John Haight standing there. He released Trae, reached out a hand, and John shook it.

"Petyr," said Leonid. "I see him in your eyes. Thank you so much for taking care of our son. If it hadn't been for your efforts, we wouldn't be together today."

"Thank you, sir," said John.

"I wish I could have been here to help you."

"I understand, sir. It was my pleasure."

"Not sir, John. You're not a servant. I said *our* son; I meant you and I. You've been a wonderful father. I hope to make up for the time I've been absent."

"I'm sure you will, sir," said John.

There was a formality there, a coldness they all felt at the moment. Perhaps it was some anger at a long absent father, or even some jealousy. In time it would likely go away, but at the moment there was no more conversation between Trae's two fathers.

Trae held a welcome party in his apartment that night. John Haight was invited, but didn't come, was out of sight for over a month. And then one day he called both Trae and Myra, and invited them for a light lunch and tea in the cafeteria below their offices.

John seemed distracted when he greeted them. His mood was gloomy. They filled their trays at the buffet, and a waiter served them tea at a secluded table in the corner of the room. Myra tried to make polite conversation for a while, but gave up when John only responded with faint smiles.

Finally, Trae said, "What's wrong? You invited us here, but haven't said a word."

John nodded, wiped his mouth with a napkin, and took a sip of tea.

"Well, it's not easy to say, but I guess I have to say it anyway. I'm going away."

"Away? Where's away?"

"Kratola. I'm going back."

Myra gasped. "Oh no, you can't, not now. At least wait until our baby's here!" Her eyes suddenly brimmed with tears.

"Why, John? There's nothing for you there," said Trae. "Your family is here."

"Leonid will be a fine grandfather."

"I *knew* that was it," said Myra. "What nonsense!"

"Our child will have two grandfathers. You can't run away from that. You, Petyr, whoever, were the only father I ever knew after the caverns and until I first met Leonid. I'm not going to throw that away."

"That's not the point. I have to go back to Kratola. The people there are slaves to The Church, and now is the time to stop it. Leonid has things to do here; I've talked to him about this, and he understands. I want you two to understand."

"Well, I *don't*," said Myra.

John reached over and put a hand on top of hers. "Look, Myra, what we are is more than genetics, it's experiences. I was someone else before being joined with Leonid Zylak. My first life was different from his. My life was The Church, before it was corrupted. The corruption is still there—on Kratola. I have to do what I'm compelled to do. My duties for Zylak are finished; it's time for the young priest in me to do his work again."

Trae smiled. "That young priest also did some things for me. Otherwise, I don't think I could ever have taken part in war, even for a noble cause."

"I'm glad you see that," said John.

"But why can't you wait at least a little bit, until our baby arrives?" said Myra, John's hand still on hers.

"Timing. The Bishops' military has been humiliated. The officers at least will know how lucky they are to be alive. There could be dissent in the ranks over being put into a hopeless situation by ignorant Bishops. If your theory is correct about where the branegates projected those ships they'll be straggling back to Kratola in a handful of years, but their fellows will be there in one, and as far as they know the ships are destroyed. I'd say it's a perfect time to stir things up, wouldn't you?"

"Just like you stirred up Azar Khalil," said Trae.

"Whatever it takes." John released Myra's hands after giving them a squeeze. He looked at her darkly.

"I do want to know my grandchild. I just can't wait for it. I'll come back when I can."

Myra sniffed, and looked down at her hands. "Whenever," she said.

But two weeks later she was with the family when they saw John off, driving far out on the tarmac with him to board a shuttle to *Guppy V*. Trae was the last to shake hands with him.

"I think you'll like Janus. He'll find a way to get you a new identity for transit. The guy knows everyone."

"Take care of your lovely wife and baby for me. I really will try to come back."

"I want that. I never said it, but I love both my fathers. I don't want to lose either of them."

John squeezed his hand hard. "The love is mutual—son."

Myra threw herself at him, and hugged him fiercely. "Come back to us," she sobbed. John held her at arms' length, and smiled, then turned and quickly walked up the ramp into the shuttle. The door closed up, and the family got back into two cars, driving halfway back to the terminal before the shuttle began liftoff.

And John Haight flew out of their lives.

For a while.

Mother was beside herself with excitement, and spent a day in the kitchen with Myra. In that one day, Myra heard the entire history of Grandma Nat and her loving yet firm rule over the family empire.

The contact had come suddenly in the middle of the day, when Mother was babysitting with the twins, and Misha was at school.

Hello my darlings, I'm back again! Sorry it's been so long, but I've been otherwise occupied. We should reach Elderon in two days. Please send us descent coordinates. So much news to catch up on, and I can't wait to see you all. Say hello to Anton for me; I can't seem to contact him. Love you all.

Chaos reigned in the house for two days, but at least it was his parents' place and not his. Mother didn't rest for over a day, with all the cleaning and cooking, for all had to be perfect for the family matriarch.

There was an old, gold-framed laser etch of the woman in the living room, a digital copy made when she was nearing sixty. She was small, portly, perched on thick cushions and with a somewhat haughty pose for the photograph, but there was a slight smile and sparkling eyes there. Mother had again reminded Myra that beneath the tyrannical facade beat a passionate and romantic heart that could steal yours in an instant.

The woman was now over ninety, had been chased by warships and endured a journey from the galactic core. Her family had lost much hope of ever seeing her again since her disappearance. It was not surprising that her grand daughter went to all lengths to ensure her comfort when she arrived. And Tatjana was still working at it when the time came for Nat's shuttle to arrive. Leonid arranged for a limousine, and the driver picked him up at the house and took him back to the private port of Zylak Industries to greet her.

Myra and Trae left work early that day. Misha, now twelve, came home from school and Myra helped him dress neatly in a black jumpsuit, his favorite. Thin and delicately boned, the boy favored his mother but had the broad shoulders and large hands of father Trae.

Grandma Tatjana dressed the twins herself. Natalie and Tina, now six, wore white lace dresses and had nets of tiny flowers in their hair. Porcelain skin contrasted attractively with their large, dark brown eyes, a feature bringing smiles to people meeting them for the first time. They were only vaguely aware of the day's importance to the family, but were caught up in the excitement of it, and ran everywhere.

Misha was helping his mother set the table when the door chimes sounded. Tatjana rushed out of the kitchen, but the door opened before she could reach it, and Leonid stepped inside smiling.

Behind him were two strangers.

The man was tall, had rugged but handsome features with a prominent nose, and he wore a blue, military-cut uniform with gold buttons. In contrast, the young woman was tiny, just over five feet in height, with a small nose and mouth and blazing, blue eyes. Tatjana gasped when the woman smiled and held out her arms to her.

"Tati! I'm here at last!"

"Grandma!" screamed Tatjana, and them came together in a fierce hug while the woman's companion laughed at them.

Tatjana held her at arm's length. "Just *look* at you! This is why you didn't answer us."

"She wouldn't let me say anything," said the man with her.

"Well, yes. I was in the tank, so to speak, and wasn't accepting calls. I wanted it to be a surprise, naughty me."

Trae came into the room, then, after chasing down the twins. Misha stepped up closer with his mother to be introduced. Tatjana could not do it fast enough; Grandma Nat was hugging everyone. The woman was beautiful, and looked to be in her early thirties. Misha blushed when she hugged him. She grabbed Trae fiercely, standing on her tiptoes to reach his ear.

"The family warrior. Thank you, thank you."

The twins were last. She knelt to hug them tight, and they were delighted by it. "Natalie and Tina. Oh, how sweet. My sweets, all of you."

She stood up, then, took the arm of the man who'd arrived with her. She leaned against his shoulder and said, "I want you to meet my man, my captain, my husband. We were married a month ago." She looked up lovingly at him. "I do like older men."

"Ramon DiMarco," said the man, and held out his hand, "and as you can see, I also like older women."

There were handshakes all around. Ramon's smile and sense of humor captured them all immediately.

Later they sat down at the dining table, and Tatjana served the meal she'd worked most of the day to prepare. Nine people were seated, the twins on risers, but there was one empty chair, one place setting that would not be used.

Grandma Nat pointed at it. "Is someone not here yet?"

Trae told her quickly about John Haight, about Petyr, a member of the family. Grandma got teary-eyed when she heard about his mission.

Leonid raised a glass in a toast. "To John, and freedom on Kratola!"

They drank to it, and enjoyed their first meal together as a family.

ABOUT THE AUTHOR

James won the Writers of the Future Grand
Prize in 1991. Since then he has published over
sixty stories in anthologies and magazines such
as *Aboriginal SF, Analog,* and *Talebones*. To
date he has published four story collections and
eight novels. He is a retired physics professor
and Dean and also paints landscapes in oils,
acrylics, watercolors and pastels. He and his
wife Gail divide their time between homes
in Spokane, Washington and Desert Hot
Springs, California. They are both active in
the convention scene and do many drumming
circles, playing drums, Native American flute
and didgeridoo. You can find out more about
Jim and his work at *www.sff.net/people/jglass/*

OTHER TITLES FROM FAIRWOOD/DARKWOOD PRESS

Brittle Innings
by Michael Bishop
trade paper: $19.99
ISBN: 978-1-933846-31-6

Permeable Borders
by Nina Kiriki Hoffman
trade paper: $16.99
ISBN: 978-1-933846-32-3

Unpossible
by Daryl Gregory
trade paper: $16.99
ISBN: 978-1-933846-30-9

End of an Aeon
Bridget & Marti McKenna, eds
trade paper: $16.99
ISBN: 978-1-933846-26-2

Dragon Virus
by Laura Anne Gilman
limited hardcover: $25
ISBN: 978-1-933846-25-5

The Best of Talebones
edited by Patrick Swenson
trade paper: $18.99
ISBN: 978-1-933846-24-8

A Cup of Normal
by Devon Monk
trade paper: $16.99
ISBN: 978-0-9820730-9-4

Boarding Instructions
by Ray Vukcevich
trade paper: $16.99
ISBN: 978-1-933846-3-1

www.fairwoodpress.com
21528 104th Street Court East
Bonney Lake, WA   98391

CPSIA information can be obtained at www.ICGtesting.com
Printed in the USA
BVOW081450270513

321731BV00002B/182/P